THE BALINTOL CYCLE I

The Dray Prescot Series

THE BALINTOL CYCLE I

Kenneth Bulmer

writing as
Alan Burt Akers

Published by
Bladud Books

Contents

Intrigue of Antares

Dray Prescot

With this volume, Intrigue of Antares, Dray Prescot begins an entirely new phase of his adventures on Kregen, that magnificent and terrible world four hundred light years from Earth. Since his meeting with the Star Lords, superhuman beings who brought him to Kregen to serve as a kregoinye in their schemes for the planet, he has told us nothing of what transpired. We do know that Delia, the glorious Delia of Delphond, Delia of the Blue Mountains, now also operates as a kregoinya for the Star Lords.

Dray Prescot has been described by someone who has seen him on this Earth as a man above middle height with brown hair and level brown eyes, brooding and dominating, with enormously broad shoulders and powerful physique. He moves like a savage hunting cat, sudden, silent and deadly. There is about him an abrasive honesty and an indomitable courage.

Reared in the harsh conditions of Nelson's Navy, he failed to find success on Earth but has succeeded in winning fortune on Kregen. He is called the Emperor of Emperors, the Emperor of Paz, but he himself regards these titles as meaningless. Paz, a vast grouping of continents and islands, is inhabited by innumerable races and nations—so why should they band together under Prescot? The Star Lords themselves have chosen him for this heavy task, for he has the yrium, that particular charisma that binds other mortals to his service.

Now the Star Lords have dispatched him to the town of Amintin in the continent of Balintol. Under the streaming mingled lights of the Suns of Scorpio, Dray Prescot must set forth on his new adventures.

Alan Burt Akers

One

The two fellows following me down the noxious alley in Amintin made a reasonable job of skulking in the shadows. When they crossed the open mouths of side alleys through the fuzzy pink moonlight they'd fail even the most elementary examination for any Assassin's Guild. They were most likely common footpads who'd picked me up as a likely victim the moment I'd entered the alley. They might not be. They might have other and altogether more sinister reasons for dogging my footsteps. Well, bad cess to 'em. There was a task I had to do here set to my hands by the Star Lords that overrode petty considerations like a couple of thugs or assassins.

"You will make contact with a man named Fweygo," the Star Lords had told me. "He will inform you of your duties."

In these latter days of my dealings with the Everoinye they still retained a flavor of their old arrogance even though my whole relationship with them had changed. This adventure was a whole new start, a completely fresh departure in my rackety life on Kregen. What the task was they had not deigned to tell me. Mind you, they had condescended to equip me with clothes and weapons and this unusual event still startled.

The hazy pink moonlight of The Maiden with the Many Smiles slanted into the unwholesome alley. The Star Lords had landed me just inside the dock wall of the river port. Some of the fortifications looked unusual to the eye of an old warrior; but this was a very foreign land. I'd chosen this dismal route to reach the tavern called The Net and Stikling as being less conspicuous than following the main street.

Amintin lay on the left bank of the river and was some ten miles from the coast. The stink of fish was not too pervasive. The two plug-uglies padding along in my footsteps probably smelled far worse.

I kept an intermittent observation on my back trail to make sure they didn't suddenly have a rush of blood to their tiny pointed heads and try to jump me.

A few massy clouds obscured the moon from time to time. Among the dingy buildings leaning over the alley no breath of wind disturbed the pools of muddy water between the cracked and ancient cobbles. Just up ahead a corner looked promising. There I could wait unseen and at precisely the right moment leap on my shadows. I had no interest in what their stories might be, not right now at any rate; I merely wished to get on with what the Star Lords had sent me to Amintin to accomplish.

The corner would conceal me admirably and I could stand without moving as the two men approached.

One of them was apim, Homo sapiens sapiens, like me. The other was a polsim with pointed ears and a narrow devil's face, with a deep vee-shaped mouth and the cunning lines of long and villainous experience engraved on his leathery skin. Still, like an apim, he had only two arms and two legs and did not have a flexible and deadly tail. Apim and polsim, they both wore raggedy garments that left their chests bare. The cudgels in their fists looked lethal enough and their knives would be sharp enough to pare skin from bone without drawing blood.

This alleyway led to the back entrance to The Net and Stikling. Dolorous though this little port of Amintin might be, one could sincerely hope that the parallel street would not be quite as narrow and sinister and the inn itself somewhat more salubrious. At the end of the next ramshackle building a blur of movement instantly stilled caught my eye.

Very well, I said to myself, that'll make three heads to knock together instead of two.

Going along silently and without any itchy feelings up my spine I saw a bulkier building thrusting a three storeyed wall against the alley. That must be the inn. A single amber light burned feebly over a closed doorway. All the windows had been pierced in the upper floors. That, to an old sea rover, was a significant factor.

This gray place was damned depressing and in my current mood I wanted none of that. By Vox! Wasn't I on Kregen, the most wonderful and terrible world where anything the heart desired might be found if you tried hard enough? Get these three rogues off my back, walk into The Net and Stikling, meet up with this character Fweygo whoever he might be, get the job done and then, by the Black Chunkrah, it was Esser Rarioch, home, and Delia!

Yes—just there where the moon-drenched cobbles faded into deepest shadows would be the spot. The smells of cooking wafted along the alley, mingled with the odors of saddle animals. Erratic clouds swathed the moon momentarily and I leaped for the shadows.

Turning to face back and stilling abruptly into motionlessness, I waited and watched and listened.

I saw only the briefest flicker of action. I heard a sharp succession of meaty thwacks. I did not see any bodies tumble onto the slimy cobbles. I did see a fellow come strolling lithely along towards me, whistling softly between his teeth.

"Hai, dom," he said in a strong musical baritone. "You must be Dray Prescot." His indistinct form emerged into full moonlight as the clouds passed and I saw he was a Kildoi. He shook his head. "A chicken right for the plucking. The Everoinye warned me you'd be difficult."

"Llahal, Fweygo."

"Llahal and Lahal, Dray Prescot."

"Lahal—I would prefer you to call me Drajak."

"So the Everoinye said."

He moved closer. He wore a simple buff colored tunic belted with weapons. His tail hand rested comfortably on his shoulder. I fancied he had not drawn a weapon to deal with the two footpads. "Let us go into the inn. You could probably down a stoup or three."

I did not sigh. I was perfectly used to this kind of attitude from other kregoinye, people who served the Everoinye, the Star Lords.

"Very well."

We went along beside the inn away from the alley. Fweygo whistled almost soundlessly between his teeth. He walked with a lithe spring that belied his solid bulk. Those two footpads must profoundly regret they'd bumped into this golden Kildoi. That thought made me say: "You did not kill them?"

"Sore heads only. This place doesn't have much law; but I do not wish to attract any attention I do not have to."

I did not reply. My good comrade and shield bearer Korero in all the many seasons I had known him had given only a limited insight into the psychology of Kildois. They held to themselves, private and contained. That they were fighters of extraordinary gifts I knew only too well.

The street in front of the inn was only a modicum wider than the alley, at that. A slightly brighter lamp burned above the double doors and the smells lessened from saddle animal pungency to fragrances of cooking and wines. At least, I considered as we stepped up onto the stoop and entered, whatever alcoholic beverages passed as wine hereabouts.

The place engulfed us with warmth, closeness, odors, laughter and the sense of haven. The clientele looked respectable, sitting at tables, eating and drinking, talking. The central space lay bare and I judged dancing would take place there at the appropriate times. Fweygo led me to one side and through a curtained opening leading to a stairway. He did not say a word until we reached one of the doors in the upstairs corridor. He lifted his tail hand to knock and then paused.

In the dim illumination of a single lamp his powerful face showed downdrawn brows, a thrust of chin, heavy golden eyebrows shadowing deep-set eyes. All Kildois in my experience were impressive; this Fweygo looked to be a man of parts.

"The Everoinye said you were difficult, Dray Prescot—Drajak. Those two footpads—you'll have to sharpen up. And be respectful to the princess—Princess Nandisha." He gave me a look as though bracing me up by the sheer power of his personality. "Do not address the princess as majestrix. She is incognito. Use my lady."

I just nodded. He bunched that sinewy tail hand into a fist and tapped discreetly, twice, on the door panel.

Almost instantly the door flew open and a massive numim scowled down, his golden fur glowing from shadowed illumination, his lion features dominating. The sword in his fist glittered.

Quickly, Fweygo rapped out: "This is Drajak, Ranaj, a friend."

The numim, Ranaj, visibly relaxed. He stepped silently aside and we entered the room.

Of the two people sitting down as we walked in, one stood up. She was a numim, as gloriously golden as Ranaj, beautiful in that special lion lady way that makes a numim man the envy of many other races of diffs.

The woman who remained seated must be Princess Nandisha. She was apim, with a face that I judged would normally be set in a serene look of self-possession. Now her dark eyes were clouded over and her low brow showed lines of concern. Her mouth was fixed into a closed line of determination. She wore a vast dark blue traveling cloak huddled about her, and one white hand, heavily jeweled, grasped the blue cloth tightly to her chin.

"We thought, Fweygo," she said, and stopped, and wet her lips. "We thought you had deserted us."

"Never, my lady. Just that I had to make sure Dray—Jak—reached here safely—"

"There was trouble?" Ranaj's numim voice grated in the room.

The numim lady, who must be his wife, put a hand to her bosom.

"No, no, my lady." Fweygo's strong voice carried reassurance. "And no need to worry, Ranaj. As soon as the animals are here we will leave."

The princess plucked fretting at the blue cloth. "I do wish they would hurry."

Now it appeared clear to me what the Star Lords wanted Fweygo and me to do. We had to escort Princess Nandisha and her people to safety out of Amintin. Just why the Everoinye wished this was not, of course, apparent to me. What they did stretched long results into the future. The people whom their kregoinye assisted might found dynasties, topple regimes, turn the whole world of Kregen on its ears. It was all one to me.

I said: "Where are we making for?"

"Be silent, Drajak, and speak when spoken to," said Ranaj. He spoke evenly, politely; but there was no mistaking the authority in his words.

Well, I said to myself, they'll get on well with the Kildoi, then.

The sense of tension, of fear barely suppressed, festered in the room. Something had either happened or was about to happen to these people that caused the presence of Fweygo and myself; something we had either to mend or prevent.

A thin high-pitched cry from beyond the far door brought the numim woman around instantly. She hurried to the door, saying: "That is little Nisha, the poor dear." She opened the door and went through.

Ranaj looked at me and said: "You are here to assist Fweygo and me. We have my lady's children, the princ— the little lady Nisha and lord Byrom to protect—"

"Also your children, Ranaj," interrupted Nandisha. "Your twins, Rofi and Rolan."

"Aye, my lady, I thank you."

H'mph! I said to myself, not well pleased. Four children to nursemaid through unknown perils—and however unknown the dangers might be, I knew as sure as Zim and Genodras rose each day over the eastern horizon to shine upon Kregen, there would be perils ahead, plenty of perils, by Krun.

Fweygo, with surprising confidence in view of his disparaging remarks about me, said firmly: "Drajak will play his part."

"We must reach the capital just as soon as we possibly can." The princess's voice sounded choked up. "The children... We are not safe."

"As soon as we reach Bharang, my lady, we will find fliers," said Ranaj.

The troubled noise of the child from the inner room stilled. The feeling of apprehension among these people bordering on incipient panic did not please me. They were frightened of something or someone. Well, then, if they expected me to lend a hand they ought to tell me just what or who, surely? But then, that was not the way of your typical lordling, your proud princess. Common folk like me were told what to do, to keep our mouths shut and to die in welterings of blood just so that the princess did not suffer.

I caught Fweygo's eye and jerked my head sideways. He frowned and shook his head, looked away. Whatever plans were afoot, he was too conscious of his obligations to the Star Lords to cause unnecessary trouble.

Because this world was Kregen where just about anything can happen, and in the words of the immortal song, probably will, the opposition menacing us could range from monsters to demons to regiments of demented archers. A soft tap on the outer door caused Nandisha to start up, trembling. Her face turned pale. Ranaj went swiftly to the door, the sword once more in his fist, and opened the panel a crack. A few words were spoken low-voiced and he turned back. "The animals are here."

Once action was upon them these people did not waste time. Ranaj's wife, whom he addressed as Serinka, brought the children out. They were all of an age, around seven or eight, and these unusual proceedings kept their eyes half-open despite their drowsiness. The four adults took a child each, leaving me the only childless person in the room. Ranaj led off out.

We went the opposite way along the corridor, through a low doorway and down an outside flight of steps. Moonlight tinged everything a mellow ruddy pink and I kept an eye on the shadows.

Two figures held the reins of five freymuls. No one spoke a word. The freymul, a useful saddle animal often called the poor man's zorca, comes normally in a chocolaty brown hide; these were more creamy. Assisted by the silent hostlers the party mounted. I felt the animal between my knees and although I guessed I'd have the worst animal, hoped he would prove not too bad. With a soft "tchk, tchk," Ranaj started off for the open gate of the yard. Smells of wine faded and the odors of the town strengthened.

Spots of rain started to fall. The children were swathed in the adults' riding cloaks. I had no cloak. My tunic began to get soaked.

Riding gently we went along the side alleyway towards that noxious alley where Fweygo had dealt with the two footpads.

I rode last.

Needless to say my head kept screwing around to survey the backtrail and every pink-tinged shadow was closely scrutinized.

Ahead a wider street with a few lamps guttering and splintering the falling rain into lances of multicolored fire offered better going. Fweygo gentled his freymul alongside mine and we rode stirrup to stirrup.

The child he carried had at last fallen asleep. He spoke so that only I could hear.

"We should get a voller at Bharang. After that the trip to the capital should not be difficult. Bharang's about eighty or so dwaburs off. Keep your eyes and ears open."

One useful thing about having four arms like a Kildoi is that you can grasp the reins, hold a child, and still have spare hands to grip weapons. In addition that cunning tail hand can give your mount a thwack or two to get him moving along smartly. Apims like me with only two arms and no tail are sometimes at a severe disadvantage on Kregen.

I said: "Who are these people afraid of? Who's chasing them?"

"Their flier broke down and they made an emergency landing here. Nandisha's uncle just died. There are dynastic problems. The Everoinye were vague on the point."

I refused to say anything like: "By Krun! How unusual!"

Mind you, the Star Lords probably confided a whole encyclopedia of information to this golden Kildoi Fweygo. They usually didn't even bother to let me look at the first page.

Even so, even so, they had acted in a vastly different way of late. Gently gently was the way ahead in my relations with the Star Lords.

"We'll have to cross one of the bridges to head west." Fweygo did not sound too concerned. "Unless Ranaj has organized a boat."

Looking rearwards along the street I could make out a few people moving about and a party of riders just appearing around a corner some hundred yards off. There were four of them and they were muffled in cloaks. That, I told myself, was because of the rain. They trotted gently along after us.

Our little party turned left down a street where the overhanging wooden houses cast deep serrated shadows. The center of the roadway ran with water. Ahead the river wall showed a humped tower block guarding the gateway.

That part of the problem of tonight's expedition was down to Ranaj in the lead. I fancied he'd carry enough authority and conviction for the task. A glance back confirmed the four riders had followed us around the corner. In the lead Ranaj turned left again at a slight angle away from the bridge. Here we passed between miserable buildings, little more than tumbledown huts, sagging in the rain. Mud squelched beneath the freymul's hooves. I hunched down in my soggy tunic and watched the backtrail.

The four riders did not appear. If they were following us, and given the usual desperate nature of these ventures of mine upon Kregen, they probably were, they could have cut down a parallel alleyway to reach the river.

"A boat, then," said Fweygo.

I said: "Four riders. They may be following."

Fweygo instantly switched around to look back. He shook his head. We went on through the rain towards the river.

The tangle of huts ended untidily against a shining expanse of mud where the town wall reared black by the river bank. Nets were hanging up on wooden racks. Small skiff-like boats lay pulled up onto the mud. Their exit onto the river lay through a small gate of iron bars beneath an arch under the wall. The whole set up would not be tolerated in Vallia. All the same, that was our way out.

The man who shambled across to meet us was a Gon with a cloak pulled up over his bald head. His eyes were red, his nose was red, and from time to time he sneezed like one of Congreve's rockets going off.

He indicated the boat we were to use. We never used it.

Even as Ranaj had one foot on the mud, the other still in the stirrup, a most ferocious bellowing uproar spouted up. Dark figures appeared over the wall directly to our front. In the glinting pink spears of the rain other and far more lethal spears glittered. A single glance, a simple deduction, were all that were required to assess the situation.

The Gon shrieked out: "Pirates!" and dashed madly back into the shadows past the nets.

Ranaj yelled: "Numi Hyrjiv! Back, back, now!"

He regained his saddle still cradling the infant. The princess stuttered out some incoherent cry. Ranaj seized her bridle and in an instant whisked the animal about, fairly dragging freymul and rider by main force.

Fweygo snatched at the other animal, leading Serinka as her husband led Nandisha. The whole party spurred back towards the huts.

The raiders swarmed over the wall, dropping down like ripe black flies. They made huge squelching sounds. Maybe they did not expect to find this expanse of mud within the walls; no doubt I would not have, it was not usual. Whatever—the obstacle gave us time to start off. The freymul is a willing animal if not as powerful as one might wish, and these five responded. We dashed back past the nets towards the low huts.

A few arrows went flick flick past; but the rain would interfere with serious shooting this night.

The raiders must have pulled up the river after dark and were now intent on butchery and pillage. Pirates were the reason Amintin was situated ten miles upriver from the coast and why no windows were pierced in the lower floors of larger buildings. No doubt the watch on the walls had been sheltering from the wet. What mattered now was that the pirates were in the town and we had not found a way out.

From squelchy sloshings to staccato raps the freymuls' hooves traversed mud and cobbles. Uproar surrounded us as the good folk of Amintin awoke to the ghastly realization of what was about to befall them.

Of one thing I felt sure as we racketed along towards the main street: this unholy lot ravening at our heels would not be the only pack of reivers to climb the walls this dark and stormy night.

As though Pixirr the god of mischief listened to my thoughts a mob of terrified Amintins stumbled up from the next side street and pursuing them with zest and venom a whole horde of reivers barred our way ahead.

Ranaj roared: "This way!"

He yanked his animal around and dragging Nandisha's freymul hurtled straight across the muddy street. Fweygo followed with Serinka. Knowing my place in their scheme of things I, as usual, brought up the rear.

Where the arrow came from that pierced Nandisha's freymul not even the most senior and devoted follower of Erthanfydd could have told. Quite possibly the shaft had been let fly by a frenzied townsman or woman. The result was Nandisha and the child toppling into the mud and Fweygo having the dickens of a job avoiding a catastrophic collision.

The poor freymul lay kicking his legs in spasm. Ranaj was rumbling incoherently and Serinka started to climb down to attend her mistress. I was there before her. The princess started up, still clutching the child.

"You are unharmed?"

"I—I think so—"

The bedlam at our backs increased. There was no time. I lifted her, and in Zair's good truth there was not much to her, and hoisted her onto my animal. Through it all she did not relinquish her grasp on the child.

Fweygo snarled something and I hurled back at him: "Ride, Fweygo!"

I gave the freymul a thumping great thwack over his rump and he started off with Nandisha holding on like a drunk holding onto a barstool.

"Drajak!" yelled Fweygo.

Ranaj dropped the wounded freymul's reins and sent his animal after Nandisha. Serinka said nothing. "Drajak!" shouted Fweygo again.

"Ride!" I roared up at him. "You know why!"

Even then I saw his Kildoi face twisted in indecision. Maybe he had never been disciplined by the Star Lords as I had; he certainly would not be banished four hundred light years across empty space in punishment. Running from a fight and abandoning a friend, of however recent an acquaintance, was not in his nature. But, as a good kregoinye, he understood what must be done when the Everoinye ordered.

"I'll see you later." As I spoke I dragged out the sword furnished me by the Star Lords.

"Yes, Drajak," he said, turning his animal and hauling Serinka along. "Yes. Make sure you do, make very sure." Then he galloped off.

So I turned to see what the devil I could make of this perilous situation.

Pirates were, it seemed in the erratic pink moonlight, running everywhere. Townsfolk screamed and fled and were cut down. One or two houses were already alight despite the rain and there would soon be illumination enough to see how to get oneself killed with no trouble.

The reivers had to be stopped from following Fweygo. That was my job. That task was down to me.

Objects became easier to see as the fires gained and the rain eased. The smell of wetness and of burning hung over the town. Directly opposite me the mouth of the alley down which Ranaj had led the rest of our party was where I had to make my stand. I had no bow, unfortunately. Well, if this was the way of it on Kregen, and this my doom and fate, then so be it. I'd do what I could before they cut me down.

Pulling back my shoulders I started off. I, Dray Prescot, Lord of Strombor and Krozair of Zy, strode off to make a valiant last stand.

My foot slipped on a patch of evilly glistening mud and over I went, twisting to regain my balance, to land smack on my back like an upended turtle.

So much for gallant exhibitionism!

Two

I stood up. I said nothing—absolutely nothing.

The tunic and breechclout given me by the Star Lords were soaking wet and clogged with mud. Glutinous mud squelched in the shoes. The scabbard, a cheap affair of thin leather, wood and green brass, was bent, shrunken and distorted. The sword, a reasonable weapon of the straight cut and thrust variety, had a wire-wrapped wooden handle, flimsy quillons, and a point that made it primarily a cutting weapon. I hefted it and looked around through a hedge of drenched and mud entangled hair.

With a gesture as much of resignation as irritation I shoved my hair back from my forehead, wiped a paw over my face, and glared about for anybody who wanted to pass by.

The situation was familiar and ugly enough. Pirates infested the coast and now the menace of the Shanks had been removed, even if only temporarily, the sea rovers ranged far and wide. People ran about crazily. The noise lifted and sank almost, it seemed, in rhythm to the drifts of smoke wafting over the roofs. Amintin was a poor enough place, Zair knew; it still had attractions for those damned renders. I knew about renders, having served with Viridia the Render, that most charming lady pirate, and my feelings were that this unhealthy lot were both the dregs and the scum of society.

Given my situation, standing like a loon in the mouth of an alley was a fine way of being chopped. Swiftly crossing into the shadows of the nearest house I checked the alley, which was now empty, and then faced the street again.

If any pirates had seen our party ride off none of them for the moment strutted along to investigate. I began to think I might pull back and scuttle along the alley and see about transport to catch up.

By this time during my life on Kregen I fought only when I had to and then reluctantly. But, like any seasoned warrior, once a fight was inevitable and joined then I'd go in with the ferocious determination to finish it as quickly as possible.

Most of the noise racketed from further back in the town. My guess was the renders had put in their surprise attack and had closed in past this spot. They'd be making for the fat and juicy targets. The people in the Net and Stikling, for instance, would be well barricaded in and ready to put up a stout resistance.

The decision made, I wasted no more time.

Padding along the alley with the sword in my fist I kept both eyes wide open, very wide open, by Krun.

The rain had appreciably lessened and the Maiden with the Many Smiles shone down her fuzzy pink light through gaps in the clouds. There were even one of two of Kregen's stars visible, twinkling away up there and vastly indifferent to what went on below.

Even then, sharply though I was keeping a lookout, they nearly had me. But I am an old leem hunter and am not easily ambushed.

Four of them leaped at me from a black-beamed doorway. They tried to degut me with spears and tridents and for a moment there was a swift and deadly series of passages, of cuts and slashes, of twists and evasions, before they all went down. The sword was a damned unhandy affair. I shook it in disgust.

From the next house along the sounds of combat spurted into the night. Your normal plunderer likes to help himself to loot with as little trouble as possible. No doubt these reivers had blood in their eye. It happens. Cautiously I padded along towards the fight.

The moon washed pink light across the house wall. Seven or eight renders were prancing about in the street trying to cut down the four men backed up against that rosy-glowing wall.

A number of bodies lay sprawled on the muddy cobbles.

There was no question of indecision here. I leaped forward.

Of course, they had their backs to me so I had no compunction in laying into the first of them to come to hand. One, two, three went down screeching before the others realized a new element had entered the equation.

A long spear with a bearded pirate at the other end of it thrust hard for my midriff. With a left hand that had hauled me up the rigging in hurricanes to daze the senses, I took the spear away. Economically I used it to clout its late owner over the head. He fell down.

Somewhere in the fracas over by the wall I heard a laugh. A light, peculiar, distinctly amused laugh, clear as a crystal chime through the hullabaloo, was not altogether unexpected. It told me someone was not taking this little scrap over-seriously. Without a moment's conscious reflection, engaged as I immediately was by a fresh customer, I formed an estimate of the laugher's character and personality and—well, that you must judge for yourself.

The renders mostly wore leather armor of sorts, bits and pieces. The fellow who challenged me now, a damned Chulik as ever was, wore metal. His yellow tusks were banded in silver. His chunky body strained against metal breast and back as we clashed weapons and then drew back so that I judged the armor he'd looted from somewhere was not a perfect fit.

Someone yelled: "Watch your back!"

The advice was not meant for me, so I reasoned; but you do not stay alive for very long if you ignore the slightest warnings. I leaped sideways and swung about, instantly reversing to slide the Chulik's venomous thrust. I sidestepped and he blundered past so that I gave him a thwack and the confounded sword broke in two.

He reared up, massively competent with weapons as all Chuliks are.

They do possess humanity, do the Yellow Tuskers, a modicum. This one showed obvious delight at my predicament. His round black eyes and oily yellow skin did not differentiate him from a thousand of his fellows. But he sneered at me and said: "Come sneaking up at my back, would you! By

Likshu the Treacherous, you have been rewarded!" He bored in with the sole intention of transfixing me upon his blade.

A movement to the right and a swaying reverse allowed me to use my forearm to force his sword arm away to the side. I put a fist into his snub nose and followed that by a crafty kick as taught very early on in the unarmed disciplines of the Krozairs of Zy. He yelled.

He yelled blue bloody murder.

He didn't have any metal armor there—he didn't have any armor there at all, just a dingy brown breechclout.

He doubled up so that my fist making contact with his chin received extra momentum from his own movement.

Then, as usual in these affairs, it was vitally necessary to keep low and spring away without thought.

The single-bladed axe swished down where my head had been and clanged into the cobbles. So fierce had the blow been the axe was twisted clean out of the grip of the Rapa who'd tried to cleave my skull in two.

In a matter of less than a second the Chulik's sword was in my grip and in the rest of the second was buried in the Rapa's side.

The sword possessed a strong curve to the blade, almost as much as a fancy sabre, and it slid in snugly enough doing the Rapa's business for him.

A swift glance around showed me the rest of the pirates sprawled in the mud. The Chulik lay doubled up and moaning. I confess I had kicked rather hard.

"My thanks, friend. Llahal." The voice was light and amused.

So I stared at him as he came forward from the wall, the bloodied rapier in his fist, the left-hand dagger its match. Dandified, oh yes, in the way a predatory bird's bright coat of feathers gives it a handsome appearance, he was all that and more. He was like the cold steel of his rapier with the charming colored jewels adorning the hilt.

"Llahal," I said.

His three friends were visibly relieved still to be alive.

He saw the Chulik groaning on the ground. One elegant dark eyebrow lifted. His lips although red were thin and firm. He stepped across and with delicate precision drove the blade through the Chulik's heart. As the Yellow Tusker was doubled up this fine amusing fellow thrust through from the back. I knew well enough the point of his rapier had struck straight past backbone and ribs and with unerring aim burst the heart asunder. That, I knew.

"Better to clean up any mess. I like to be neat and tidy."

His face was barely flushed after the combat. Over that thin mouth he affected a thin black moustache. Once he had cleaned his weapons the first thing he would do was run a forefinger along that elegant moustache.

Other sounds began to percolate into our attention as the immediate fury of the fight subsided. A devil of a lot of noise was erupting from the town. Orange glare reflected from the low clouds. The Maiden with the Many Smiles shone down to add her pink luster to the scene.

"What are we to do now, notor?" The fellow who spoke, short and wiry and with a shock of straw-colored hair dangling from under a round leather cap, clutched a hefty short sword with a smidgeon of blood upon the blade. His face showed all the marks of dependence on another, coupled with an animal cunning in twist of lip and slant of eye.

"Do, fambly, do? Why, we shake hands with this gentleman and thank him for his help."

The other two men who were already cleaning their weapons were clad in tough leather armor and their function in life as guards was patently apparent. They'd earned their hire, for they had killed well.

The lord eyed me calculatingly.

"Your name, my friend?"

"Drajak." I spoke pleasantly. "And yours?"

His servant sucked in his cheeks.

Notor is how one addresses a lord in many parts of Paz upon Kregen. I'd had my fill of kowtowing to lords of late and I had no intention of beginning again right now. I had urgent things to do—like following Fweygo and the rest and trusting to all the Beneficent Spirits of Uttar Soblime they had not been slaughtered.

His eyebrows drew down for an instant and then that light amused laugh eased the situation—at least, it eased the situation for him and his servant. I didn't give a damn who he was. I wanted to get on.

"I am Amak Dagert—Dagert of Paylen. Lahal."

"Lahal. Now, if you will excuse me I must—" He'd drawn a yellow cloth from under the short cape he wore over metal armor and was about to clean his sword. He wrapped the cloth again and stuffed it away with a gesture as elegant as a court dandy's. His voice chirred like oiled steel clearing scabbard.

"I think, Drajak, you must do something other than you intended."

Philosophically I turned around and followed his gaze. A whole bunch of renders crowded down the alley towards us. Now the rain had stopped they'd lit torches and the lurid lights glanced and danced off wet walls and cobbles, glinted redly from the black blood at our feet.

The two guards stood very still, staring at Dagert of Paylen. Their eyes looked like pebbles. The Amak's servant trembled. He licked his lips and kept flexing his grip on the short sword.

I looked around for another and possibly better weapon.

That amused low laugh, almost a self-satisfied chuckle, broke from Dagert. He looked back. The alley led off into a darkness relatively deeper than that in the opposite direction. It seemed to me as I picked up a sword of somewhat better construction than those I'd already used, that this Dagert of Paylen was deliberately tantalizing his servant. He was making the poor devil suffer. Well, that was between them.

"Notor—" The fellow's wet lips shone as he licked them again.

"Oh, you know me by now, Palfrey. When the odds are right—not otherwise. It has been pleasant meeting you, Drajak, and once more I offer you my thanks. Now it's time to depart."

With that and without more ado he turned abruptly and darted lithely away down the alley.

Mind you, he was right, assuredly, he was right, by Krun!

One thing you noticed about Dagert of Paylen that lingered in the mind was his eyes. Liquid and dark, they hid unfathomable depths. What he said was one thing, what he thought quite another.

There was no point my hanging about here any longer. My duty lay with the charges the Star Lords had placed in my care. Swiftly I followed Amak Dagert into the shadows of the alley.

The problem now was to get out of Amintin and that meant scaling the wall somewhere where that was practicable and preferably out of sight of townspeople and renders alike. The clouds were drifting away across the stars and if the sky cleared much more many of the comforting shadows would disappear.

The pirates had entered the town across more than the one wall over which we had seen them clambering and now they infested the whole place. The unholy noise racketed on. Flames twisted against the thinning clouds. There were people running about aimlessly, desperately seeking shelter. What the Amintin Watch might be doing, what the local lord in command might be ordering, appeared to me to be completely unimportant. This dreadful night the renders owned Amintin and did as they pleased.

The nearest wall now would be the one over to the east. More than once I had to skip smartly down an alleyway to avoid roistering mobs of pirates. Their domination had been swift and sudden and was now total.

Soon I entered an area of warehouses where no doubt the goods coming in and out along the caravan trails were stored. Other, more interesting odors competed with the stink of fish and mud.

Naturally, a quarter of the town holding goodies like this was not going to be overlooked by your conscientious looter. Oh, dear me, no!

Carefully sliding along by a painted wooden wall and looking everywhere about, I spotted parties already at work hauling out Amintin's wealth. Just past the end of this warehouse and past the opened double doors from which streamed yellow lantern light an open space fronted an inland gate. Undoubtedly the gate had a name. What it might be I neither knew nor cared. I did know that it did not represent my way out of the raped town. Further along would be the place, where steps led up to the ramparts.

I did not proceed without a plan. The chances of success rested firmly on the very speed with which the renders had entered and conquered.

Moving swiftly yet cautiously I skirted the open space where during a normal working day the pack animals and the carts would muster and cut across between the two end warehouses. The wall lay only a scant fifteen paces off.

The route I had followed, dictated both by my desire to avoid pirates and to reach the east wall, channeled other fugitives to the same point. Pink moonlight momentarily illuminated agile figures clambering up the steps onto the ramparts with the oddly-cut openings of the battlements beyond. I halted. There was no doubt I expected a shower of arrows or crossbow bolts to sleet into those refugees.

Nothing happened and they ran excitedly along the top of the wall and vanished into one of the small towers erected at intervals. I frowned. That did not look promising.

"Sink me!" I snarled to myself. "In for a ponsho in for a leem!"

I gathered myself up and started at a dead run for the dappled shadows at the foot of the steps. Before I reached the wall a group of people appeared from the side, racing along with bent heads. For all their apparent blind panic, weapons snouted in their fists.

We reached the wall together.

Dagert of Paylen called: "Up, up, you hulus. Bratch!"

In a bunch we panted up the steps. Moonlight filtered down and dimmed and shone. Dagert's lean handsome face with that trimmed moustache and dark eyes looked perfectly composed. He said: "We must be swift, Drajak." And, instantly: "Get on, get on, Palfrey, confound you!"

They started to run along in the shadow of the battlements towards the nearest small tower. I stopped and looked over the outside of the wall.

Praise be to Zair! My plan had come right! Dangling from the walls hung the rope ladders up which the pirates had swarmed to despoil Amintin. Dagert and his three followers were helter-skeltering along towards the tower. I called: "Dagert! This way is surer!"

He halted and swung about, a lithe, tense figure in that moon-dappled confusion.

I swung up into the gap and took the ropes into my fists. I wasn't prepared to hang about to be feathered waiting for anybody around here. Starting down, I called up: "Ladders, Dagert."

His voice cracked out like two flat boards striking together in one of those Shensi plays, all puppets and buffoonery. "This way!"

Before I'd reached halfway down I felt his weight above me on the ladder. Glancing up I saw the nimbleness with which he negotiated the rungs.

By the time I'd dropped into the dry moat—which was sticky with odiferous mud—he was halfway down and the rest of his party tumbled down after him.

Even then I had time to reflect on the illuminating fact that his followers had chosen the same ladder he had, the same one I'd chosen. There were other ladders dangling down. That told me a great deal.

He sprinted up to me as I hauled myself out on the other side of the moat.

"We'll have to reach the cover of those trees quickly."

A couple of hundred or so paces off the dark mass of trees did promise shelter.

"Aye," I said and started running over the muddy grass.

"My flier is parked to the north—" he was saying, and then stopped and saved his breath for running.

At that moment the first crossbow bolts began to whicker past our heads.

Three

Almost instantly Palfrey let out a scream—really the yelp he let out was more like a mouse squeak. The two guards ran on, heads high, chests outthrust, pacing Dagert of Paylen stride for stride. Well, that was their duty, what they were paid for. I glanced back.

Palfrey's shock of tow hair swung wildly as he danced and hobbled along, trying to clutch at his ankle and at the same time run after us.

Dagert did not turn his head.

"Come along, Palfrey, you hulu! Bratch!"

"I'm wounded, I'm wounded!" The words tumbled out all mixed up with squeaking and panting. "I'm skewered through!"

"No you're not!" Dagert hadn't even glanced back. "A scratch."

"Mama Thehico the Healer aid me! Help!"

Not sure to be amused or annoyed I swung back and seized the servant up under the armpits and carried him along like a bundle of cordwood. He did have a long graze down his left shin and blood shone greasily black. He was babbling something to himself under his breath; but he had the sense not to struggle. The need to run as fast as possible coupled with the equally important need of dodging about randomly caused me to carry poor old Palfrey with less gentleness than was seemly for a wounded fellow creature. He yelped a bit but remained still and limp.

Thankfully the shooting became highly erratic as we opened the range and by the time the leaves of the first trees closed over our heads we were in no danger from either arrow or quarrel.

Putting Palfrey down I carefully did not look at Dagert. Palfrey lay on his back with his leg in the air and he clutched his ankle as though it was about to fall off. "Oh, oh, oh," he moaned.

"Oh, do leave off, Palfrey, for the sweet sake of Harmonia!" Dagert's voice held a strong note of amusement, although his light laugh did not accompany his words. "Just say thank you nicely to Tyr Drajak."

"Thank you, master, thank you," gabbled Palfrey still clutching his leg which stuck up in the air like a half-masted flagpole. "I'm shot through!"

"No you're not, you fambly. Now get on your feet and run with us. D'you want me to leave you alone here—with all those pirates?"

The flagpole leg came down like a drawbridge and Palfrey shot to his feet. "Notor! You wouldn't—"

"Don't try me, is all." With that, Dagert of Paylen started off through the trees. Even on the uneven surface in the shadows he strode along with a lithe easy swagger, your bold adventurer, your dashing cavalier, to the life.

I bent and took Palfrey's foot in my hand and twisted it to get a look at his wound. He yelped. The gash was a mere graze with a little blood. He'd live.

I said: "As soon as we can safely stop we'll bind it up. Now come on." And I gave him a friendly push in the right direction.

"Oh, the persecution I have to put up with!" But he trotted along smartly enough and did not fall behind.

Well, now, I considered as we threaded our way between the tree trunks, my first objective of getting out of doomed Amintin had been achieved. Now it was necessary for me join up with Fweygo and our charges. My confidence in Fweygo was already very high even in the short time of our acquaintance and with the powerful numim Ranaj to assist, the party should have won clear with the head start I'd given them. They were making for Bharang which lay over to the west. Therefore, it was necessary to cross the river, preferably unobserved. That meant this same night as ever was.

If this bright spark Dagert had a flier parked somewhere to the north, he might give me a lift.

In the general confusion of the night, of my interrupted duty, of my feelings about getting this job done and haring off home to Delia, I was fully in the mood to make sure Dagert of Paylen offered me a lift.

Palfrey kept on glancing down the backtrail as he hobbled along.

"They won't bother to follow a few fugitives, dom," I told him. "They'll know that long before we can bring a rescue force they can be aboard their ships and vanished like ghosts."

"Oh, master, please don't mention ghosts!" He squeaked up the scale like a mouse caught in a trap. "Especially now, at night, in the forest! It's positively unhealthy!"

Each to his own. I made myself say in a grave voice as we went on: "All the same, you don't have to worry over the renders any longer."

Apart from his untidy shock of straw-colored hair, this Palfrey who was bodyservant to Dagert of Paylen possessed a round snub nose, a twist of native cunning to his lips, a feeling that he understood far more than he admitted. In the fight back there his short sword had been stained with blood, but only slightly, as though he'd stabbed at a reiver once and then considered his duty done. The half-cloak he drew about him from time to time with a nervous gesture was patched but of good quality. No doubt it was a reach me down from the Amak. I did not think you could easily pigeonhole friend Palfrey.

We spent the next couple of burs moving swiftly through the woods—they were scarcely the forest Palfrey had dubbed them—until we passed over a slanting hill tall with rough grass and descended the far slope towards the thin darkly-gleaming streak of the river. We did not speak.

At last Palfrey broke the silence.

"Notor! Can't we rest now—please? My leg burns like fire. I'm sure my foot is—"

"Your foot will do what feet are sent to Kregen to do. March!"

"Notor," wailed the unhappy Palfrey. But he kept on going.

We were circling wide around the town to reach the river north of Amintin. The thought occurred to me to wonder why Dagert of Paylen had considered it necessary to land his flier here, when there was bound to be a vollerdrome, however small, within the confines of the walls. That action smacked of secrecy. Bright spark though he was, there was a spirit of deviltry in this fellow, of that there could be no mistake.

Southwards to our left a dull orange reflection hung in the sky. What wind there was carried the sounds away from us. Pirates are, in general and with certain notable exceptions, unpleasant vermin. Their boldness this night of terror boded ill for the coastal towns, indicating a power that felt it economical to destroy a seaport. Killing geese that lay golden eggs is not an economical proposition for thieves.

Palfrey's injured foot hit a stone or other obstruction in the grass and he staggered and fell against me. I clapped an arm about his narrow waist and hoicked him up. A gasp of pain puffed between his lips.

"Hard," he half whispered, half stuttered. "H-Hard man!"

"The notor will rest in a moment."

"Only when we reach the ruins and the voller."

Judging by the fleeting glimpses of the Maiden with the Many Smiles as clouds passed overhead I fancied it would rain again before dawn. Used though I am to roughing it in all kinds of weather, like any normal person in any normal circumstances I generally prefer to be under cover and dry when it rains. These ruins would offer cover of a sort. If, that is, I could afford to waste time lollygagging about instead of being up and about my duty for the Everoinye.

Anyway, what in a Herrelldrin Hell was this fine fancy Dagert of Paylen doing hiding his flier in some ruins and then footslogging it into Amintin? Mind you, the Star Lords had flung me into the town in something like the same way. And—ruins. We were skirting the riverbank now, heading south towards the fireglow in the sky. The land looked unkempt. It has been said that when buildings grow old the English rebuild and add wings, the Americans knock them down and build new and bigger and the Irish just leave them and build new along the road. From the little I knew this was an ancient land shrouded in mystery with new peoples merely imposing a surface culture. A hardened adventurer feels many emotions at the prospect of ruins and, of these, two are pre-eminent. One: the excitement of financial gain. Two: the anticipation of danger and death.

Palfrey had called a few trees a forest. Dagert had chosen to conceal his voller in ruined buildings rather than in the woods. That presumably indicated they were both urbanites.

As Opaz in the guise of Whetti-Orbium ordained, the rain began as we reached the dark vegetation shrouded mass of the ruins. What they had been in their prime was hard to say; a monastery, a castle, a fortified villa, a series of structures at the least of considerable extent sloping down towards the riverbank. Rain pattered against ancient stone blocks. Mud slicked underfoot. One could hope that the deluge would extinguish the fiery agony of Amintin.

Dagert of Paylen did not hesitate. Between crumbled stone pillars he stalked into the half-darkness of a courtyard. Cracked paving stones surrounded what had once been a fountain. Low, jagged-edged walls surrounded the space. Here no roofs had survived. Everywhere in crack and crevice grew thistles, hardy, bright purple and lustrous green, and nettles of a richer lighter green, loaded with stingers. Ahead gaped blackness beneath an arch of desiccating brickwork. There must be some remnants of roof left over there, then.

Speaking in a soft voice, Dagert said: "Bring her out, Palfrey."

"Yes, notor."

Palfrey started across. The odd thing here was that he showed no apparent apprehension about wandering about sinister ruins at night yet he had expressed serious concern over ghosts in the woods. One would have thought that no matter how accustomed to city streets he might be, dark ruins would be another thing altogether.

Despite the smells of mud and damp vegetation the penetrating stink of incense irritated my nostrils before the monotonous sound of chanting reached my ears. Palfrey stopped as though poleaxed.

Dagert's fist reached down for the hilt of his rapier.

Palfrey half turned and his eyes were the whitest things in his face.

"Over here." Dagert's voice sounded like silk drawn over a sword blade. He pointed to the ruins of the courtyard to our right.

The two guards, silent, moving like clumsy dolls, vanished into the shadows as Dagert pulled Palfrey in. Here we were completely concealed and could look out without being observed. I glanced at Dagert's servant. Poor old Palfrey, his fears of the ghosts of the forests had transferred themselves across with sudden terror to these ruins.

Despite the rain that stench of incense wafted stronger. The chanting—low, monotonous, hypnotic—grew louder.

From the darkness emerged a procession. Now torchlight spilled around the edges of the ruined walls and scythed long streaks of red fire across the paving. Cloaked and hooded figures appeared, two by two, heads bowed and hands clasped. The torchlight illuminated their robes, all a dark red, smoky and sullen. The faces were shrouded in blackness.

Water hissed and sizzled against the orange flare of the torches.

The words of the chant were unintelligible to me. One word, often repeated, dominated. Oltomek. Or, it could have been Altamek. The rain spattered down, the torches hissed, the figures chanted and moved on two by two. At their head they carried a gilded pole on which was mounted a gilded figure of some beast from nightmare. Winged, taloned, fanged, the things ruby eyes glinted and sparkled in the torchlight. The sense of primeval evil reeked from the idol.

Immediately after this gilded blasphemy followed another staff, silvered, upon which a symbol swayed and nodded as the red-cloaked figure crossed the cracked paving. The symbol looked to be a stylized representation of a pair of upflung wings, joined at the bottom, almost touching at their tips, forming an oval round.

Chanting Ultumak or Oltomek, two by two, the figures passed across the courtyard and exited on the far side. Two by two they were swallowed up by darkness. The stench of incense cloyed sickeningly, then the wash of rain cleansed the air. The torchlights died.

Palfrey, shaking, said: "Notor—"

"Madmen," said Dagert of Paylen. His light laugh sounded more grim than usual. "Hanitcha the Harrower take them! By Krun! They're no business of mine!"

Four

"Brassud!" snapped Dagert of Paylen. "Or, as Malahak is my witness I shall burn your tail!"

Palfrey tried to brace himself up. "Notor," he quavered, "may Kaerlan the Merciful smile on us now! Let us get out of this terrible place before the evils of Kuerden the Merciless fall upon us."

One of the men at arms mumbled: "Amen to that, notor, by Havil the Green."

"Go on! Go on!" ordered Dagert. "Bratch!"

Palfrey bratched, jumping forward like a startled deer into the roofed darkness. Only moments later the nose of a small four-place flier eased out and she settled on the paving beside Dagert.

Palfrey's face, showing immediate signs of indigestion, peered down from the controls abaft the tiny windscreen. The guards waited.

"Up with you!" commanded Dagert. He turned to me and in that cloying dimness his teeth cut a curve of whiteness in the gloom. "Once again my thanks, Tyr Drajak. I shall not forget you. Now I must be off as fast as Wheesh-amakler, spirit of the winds, will allow."

I said: "If you are flying westwards, might—"

But he was up over the voller's polished coaming and staring down at me with his raffish smile. He prodded Palfrey in the back.

"Westwards? Ah—no, no. We fly north."

To this day I do not rightly know if there would have been time for me to leap up and board the craft. Palfrey was deuced quick. The little airboat lifted off soundlessly, scattering a few dead leaves, leaping straight up into the clouded sky. A faint: "Remberee, Drajak!" floated back. Then voller, Dagert, Palfrey and the two men at arms were gone.

"Remberee!" I said under my breath with great disgust. I added: "And by Makki Grodno's diseased liver and lights, you're getting slow, Dray Prescot, too damned slow!"

Oh, well, I had a sword of sorts that didn't fit the scabbard and had already split the shrunken leather and cracked wood. I had a red breech-clout and a decent tunic and a pair of reasonable shoes. Many times in the past, I, Dray Prescot, Lord of Strombor and Krozair of Zy, had started off on an adventure with much less. Much less, by Djan!

Without further ado I set off. The Maiden with the Many Smiles was dropping down to the western horizon. A couple of Kregen's lesser moons were whirling past low overhead but I couldn't see them through the clouds. The night would soon be gone and I wanted to be across the river before dawn.

Cutting across the slope I soon reached the river. If there were any nasties in there, then in the mood I then was I would have short shrift with them. Mind you, I'd said in a fine free way how I'd force Dagert to take me in his voller, and see where that stupid boast had got me.

He had not enquired for any additions to my name, although had he done so I'd have told him I was Drajak the Sudden. One of the men at arms had spoken to his comrade about Dagert's servant, calling him Palfrey the Pfiffer. Those two military guards had not spoken much, intent on protecting their lord and earning their hire. Truly, although conditions and customs vary widely over Kregen, as they do on this Earth, much remains almost the same wherever you go.

In the event I swam the river without problems. Wet yet heartened I crawled out on the opposite bank and started up the slope.

Zim and Genodras rose in the multicolored glory of a Kregen dawn. As I slogged along a trail between tall green crops a few birds were singing. My twin shadows loped ahead of me.

In the extraordinarily wide temperate regions of Kregen the Suns of Scorpio had little difficulty in drying up the overnight rain. The air freshened with that marvelous fragrance that is so very much Kregen's own. And I was ravenously hungry and thirsty and about ready to find a convenient spot to put my head down and catch up my missing sleep.

Better to go on for a bit yet, and look for somewhere promising, I decided. Even the Star Lords understood that mere humans, people like me, needed to sleep from time to time. The Everoinye had once been mortal human beings, so I believed. All the same, their ideas of the amount of sleep a fellow required fell far short of complete recuperation.

As I tramped on I cogitated about those red-robed figures. They probably belonged to some nutty religious cult or other. Zair knew, there were enough of them all over Kregen to fill the pages of a million encyclopedias. They'd scared Palfrey the Pfiffer all right. If I'd leaped for the flier and missed and merely got a fingernail clinging on, Palfrey would have lifted off regardless.

Not all the overnight clouds had dissipated and occasionally wide bands of shadows fleeted across the landscape. Red and green, an opaline mixture of colors, shadows and suns-light bathed the land in an ever-changing kaleidoscope of considerable charm.

The river here curved in a loop and the trail from the bank led into the concavity at almost right angles and after a bur or so brought me to what was evidently a highway. Paved, the road had been carved out in a series of straightish lines. Not quite a Roman road it bore the hallmarks of a technological level capable of transferring people, goods, and troops with celerity. Even those countries of Paz on Kregen who possess the benefit of airboats for rapid travel never have enough for everyone's needs. River and canal traffic is widespread. Here the rivers ran from north north west to south south east. The road ran west. That was my direction of travel, so I set off sturdily over the paving.

This route should lead me direct to Bharang and, considerably further on, to the capital.

Now my reading of Fweygo indicated to me he was a canny individual. He had been charged by the Star Lords with the safety of Princess Nandisha and her party. He had mounts who had to be handled carefully and nursed over long distances. He'd travel at night for safety's sake and lie up during the day. If I kept going with only short intervals for rest I anticipated catching him in the not too distant future.

Just who posed the threat to Nandisha I didn't know. It was quite likely Fweygo didn't know, either.

The news of the sacking of Amintin had already passed along the road. One might have expected farm carts on their way to the town with produce. I passed none. Twice I felt it prudent to slip off the highway and conceal myself in bushes as parties of troops marched past.

On the third occasion Five-handed Eos-Bakchi smiled on me. The Vallian spirit of good fortune arranged that I spotted a whole regiment of cavalry breaking camp and mounting up. When they had cantered off out of sight I inspected their campsite.

One item I noted mentally was that they appeared in no hurry to reach Amintin. The other was that they were a very high-powered lot for their camp was a treasure trove of abandoned items. What they'd left over would feed a poor family for a month of She of the Veils.

The regiment had been brilliantly attired and accoutred and they were riding zorcas. Their standards blazed in the lights of the suns. I found a discarded forage bag and was able to stuff it almost full of crusts, congealing porridge, a quarter-full pot of honey—real red slursh—and tumbled half under a bush a whole ham, a most splendid addition to my larder. I stuffed my inward parts before I stuffed the forage bag. Only a few ulms further on a small brook passed under a culvert and I was able to wash my breakfast down.

Feeling much more cheerful I looked about for a spot to rest. A few burs sleep would see me set up sufficiently to march all night.

This I duly did. This was the pattern of events for the next three days.

By eating just enough to keep me going I still had a splendid feast for a good few days ahead left in the forage bag.

The road passed through woods, over heathlands, and when it entered a town or village I felt it prudent to skirt around and bypass potential trouble.

Here and there the paving was cracked and a little overgrown although nowhere sufficiently so to impede progress. On the fourth day I avoided a road gang busily at work lifting and replacing paving stones.

The brilliance of the yellow sand they were tamping down as foundation indicated they knew what they were doing.

Each side of the road had trenches acting as gutters well kept and free of weeds. The cunning camber ensured rainwater would run off freely. All this told me a great deal about the societal level of these people.

On the fifth day more people were about and I felt it safe to stay on the road and offer a grave and polite salutation as we passed.

On this day, too, I saw a strange mountain configuration some way off to the north. In general aspect it reminded me strongly of Ayers Rock in Australia. The top was serrated but at that distance it was too difficult to determine if the protuberances were natural rock forms or buildings. The mingled streaming lights of Zim and Genodras struck from the face and drove deep shadowed fissures the whole sprawled length of the mountain.

Two days later I began to feel I ought to be catching up with Fweygo and the party.

In the early morning with the dew still on the grass I swung down a long slope. I felt fine. My only concern was the damned scabbard which was on the point of falling to pieces. My shoes were in perfect condition, my tunic was slung over my back and I could expand my lungs and breathe in that glorious Kregan air.

Nobody else traveled the road until I spied two figures walking slowly towards me. I kept on going, prepared for a polite: "Llahal, doms," and nothing more.

One of the people approaching was a man past the prime of life. On Kregen this meant he was over two hundred years old. He leaned heavily on a carved staff. He wore a brown robe with the hood thrown back to reveal a narrow head with wisps of hair hanging down. His face was puckered with pain and his mouth compressed into a thin slit. His eyes were strange, hidden beneath folds of flesh, swollen and reddish.

At his side and clearly guiding walked a lad, a young lad, in a brown tunic. His fresh face was twisted with concern. He went barefoot.

The old man had cloths wrapped about his feet. I saw among the rusty brown stains disfiguring the cloth new redder stains.

As they approached the old man stumbled. His staff slipped. All his weight came down on the lad.

Unable to sustain this, the lad was forced down and despite his desperate attempts the old man slid down and tumbled onto the paving.

I leaped forward.

The old man struggled to sit up on the dusty road. He licked those thin lips and said: "I am sorry, Nath. Truly sorry. My strength is gone out of me."

"Master!" Young Nath was close to tears. He made no attempt to try to get the old man to his feet. I stopped my foolish, useless leap, and just stopped in front of them.

Nath looked at me with glistening eyes.

I said: "Llahal." And then hesitated, quite uncertain what to say or do next.

Surprising me—and Nath, too, by his instinctive reaction of stretching out his hands to assist—the old man gripped his staff and hoisted himself up on his bleeding feet. I was not at all sure that, looking at me though he was, he was really seeing me.

"Llahal, my friend. You see me in parlous plight. Please overlook my weakness."

Feeling utterly helpless I just stared at them, master and lad.

Nath wiped a hand over his eyes and, sturdily, said: "This is San Padria na Fermintin. Lahal."

"Lahal. I am Drajak. What—?"

San Padria, in his hoarse but strong voice: "We are pilgrims on the road to Farinsee." I judged he used that voice to preach to vast congregations. "The way has been long and arduous; but we are nearly there."

"Yes, master," chipped in Nath. "Not far now. But your feet—"

"Are given by Cymbaro the Just to carry me about this world. Until they fail me utterly then they must carry me. Have I not taught you, young Nath, that pain is merely an extension of perception, to be treated no more and no less than any other perception?" He stood there in the dust, on those bleeding feet, leaning on his staff, and the dignity in him was a palpable force.

Young Nath's spindly legs sticking out under his brown tunic looked like sparrow's legs. His face was pinched. So was San Padria's. Struck by a thought, I said: "When did you last eat?"

"When the lord Cymbaro pleased. Sustenance is more than bread."

"Oh, aye," I said, and shifted the forage bag forward on its straps. I fished out two crusts, dovetailed together, and held them out in my hand whilst I lifted out the hambone. It was well-carved off by now; there was ample left to put more than metaphysical bread from Cymbaro into these two pilgrims stomachs. I looked up. They had not taken the crusts.

"Please," I said, and added, rather chancily, I suppose: "I trust that Cymbaro will approve."

Well, they hummed and hawed a bit but in the end they took the crusts and slices of ham and wolfed them down. Already San Padria looked healthier. It was just his damned feet.

They told me Bharang was six day's off; I judged that meant the distance would take me around a day and a bit. Farinsee turned out to be the mountain like Ayers Rock I'd passed. That meant they had at least twelve days to go at their speed. I did not hesitate further. "I own my own way of living." I tried to speak with a solemnity I wasn't really feeling. After all, the thing was so obvious. "You will cause me distress if you do not accept that." I took off my sturdy shoes and handed them to Nath and gave him a very hard, very domineering Dray Prescot look. "They will fit well enough, young Nath, because Cymbaro obviously has it in mind that San Padria should reach Farinsee. Help the san to put them on." Instantly he was on his knees and at work.

The shoes did fit, and extremely well, too.

They were stout of sole and soft of uppers. Young Nath sorted out strips of least bloodied cloth to bind the san's feet. There was no doubt whatsoever of the calm power both enshrouding and exuding from this man. Whatever religion owned his allegiance benefited greatly. I acknowledged that the religion must have formed and shaped him, so that in that case the partnership was a rounded and satisfying whole.

Nath, holding the san's arm, said to me: "I thank you, master."

Feeling the occasion called for it, I said: "No, Nath. It is for me to thank you and the san for accepting."

San Padria turned his face to me; but his eyes, just about hidden under those puffy folds of unhealthy-looking flesh, may not have seen me at all. "That is almost a quotation from the Fifth Book of Cymbaro's earliest teachings, before he ascended."

"Chapter ten, verse three," said Nath, as though prompted.

The san moved his feet experimentally on the paving stones. "Very nice. I feel their ibma welcomes me."

Prodding forward with his curiously carved staff he took the first steps on this last stage towards Farinsee. Young Nath walked determinedly by his side. I could not stand and watch and wait for them to trudge out of sight along the road. That would have taken an unconscionably long time at their crawl. I gave a sigh. I knew with absolute certainty that those shoes were far better employed right now than they had been when I, fully accustomed to walking barefoot, had worn them.

With a last look at that odd couple I swung about and resumed my march towards Bharang and the party with Fweygo.

Five

From my considerable experience of assassins I was aware they preferred to work to a timetable. The dying moments of the fracas ahead on the road, some couple of burs after I'd said remberee to San Padria and young Nath, told me the assassins were operating under the most urgent of orders. Here they were, openly attacking a little cavalcade in daylight on the highroad.

There was, it is true, a scraggle of woods either side of the road. The twin Suns of Scorpio shone down splendidly and lit up the unpleasant scene, when more often than not assassins like to work under the cloak of darkness—preferably in a night of Notor Zan.

There were already more than enough dead folk lying about by the time I reached the scene attracted by shouts and the slide and scrape of steel. Dragging the sword from that shrunken and twisted scabbard held me up fractionally.

There were zorcas standing in an uneasy group half in among the trees. They did not like the raw stink of blood and neither did I.

By the time I reached there the assassins had just about finished their ghastly work. I did give a whoop and a holler rushing in to startle them and perhaps save some last poor wight's life before they finished him off to turn to deal with me.

"You cowardly stikitches!" I bellowed. "Hai!"

Two of them, black capes flaring, swung about from a man sprawled on the paving with his back half-propped against a decorated carriage. Three black-clad men lay face down before him and blood oozed from them. From the side an assassin swinging a short axe charged at me. The two men checked their weapons, seeing me, and swung about to join their comrade. The three of them, working as a team of long experience, closed in.

Two swords and an axe against a sword of whose provenance and reliability I had the gravest of doubts—all right, then! In the normal fashion they tried to circle me. They were not prepared for the speed with which I hurtled into them.

The axeman's weapon faltered short as I chopped him down and in the next instant as I swung about to face the other two they were caught square on. Our blades clashed just the twice. A twisting slice saw the right hand one off and after a swift leap forward a thrust to the left dealt with the other.

It had all been very quick and deadly. Had it not been I would not be here to tell you the tale.

Mind you, as I'd mournfully guessed, the sword snapped in half. The stikitche reeled back, choking blood, and collapsed with half the blade stuck through his guts.

A single quick but extremely comprehensive glance about assured me no other assassins lived. Now I could bend to the dying man.

His first words were incomprehensible. Blood fouled his lips and ran down his chin.

"Easy, dom, easy." There was no use trying to move him to a more comfortable position. His internal injuries would only have been exacerbated and quite clearly he wanted to live long enough to tell me something.

The sword dropped from his blood-dabbled glove. He seized my arm in a weak grip. Blood oozed from under his gloved fingers.

"Strom Korden. Laha..." His voice garbled with the blood in his mouth. His breast under the bright robes and the banded armor barely moved. "Take the sword and..." A gobbet of blood gushed between his lips, to stain down with the rest. He tried again and only mumbles without meaning escaped him.

I saw him make a tremendous effort. He swallowed with a convulsive contortion of his mouth and face that trembled down along his limbs. His head rolled. He had been a strong man in the prime of life with a thick brown moustache and heavy shock of hair, exposed now that his helmet, badly dented, had fallen off and rolled under the carriage.

"To Hyr Kov Brannomar." His voice dropped in tone and volume. He was almost gone. "You must..." His eyes closed and his lips worked together. "By Cymbaro the Just I charge you!" That surged forth with the last remnant of his powers. He coughed and the blood poured down. His words were barely understandable and they trailed off into gibberish. "Take—take the sword—take the sword and..."

I bent and spoke gently into his ear.

"As Cymbaro is my witness, Strom Korden, I will take the sword to Hyr Kov Brannomar."

Only Opaz knew if he heard me. When I straightened up the life had gone from him and he was dead.

I sat back on my heels for a moment and mentally consigned him to the protection of Cymbaro the Just.

Then I stood up briskly and looked about.

Scenes like this, although repeated often enough upon Kregen, always have the power to disturb. What this nobleman's errand might be, to deliver the sword to Kov Brannomar, what the meaning was, I could not know. There was nothing else I could have done. Not a Krozair of Zy, not a Krovere of Iztar, not a koter of Vallia. Oh, no, I was bound by a sacred oath. I just hoped he had died with the comforting knowledge that he had done his duty as well as he could.

The sword must be the one he had gripped and used in his last fight. I bent and picked it up. There were plenty of black clothes to wipe the blade clean.

It was of that variety of sword more generally found in the easterly regions of Paz called a braxter. Nominally a straight cut and thruster it did have a slight and cunning curve to the blade. The steel rang with quality. The hilt was a plain affair of cross quillons and twisted silver wire grip. The only mark to distinguish it from a thousand other such braxters was the ruby set in the pommel. I judged the gem to be genuine although not of great value.

I took a deep breath and then expelled my breath in disgust. The sweet Kregish air lay flat and stinking on my tongue.

There was absolutely no use trying to force this sword into my shrunken and now useless scabbard. Strom Korden wore a plain leather belt about his waist, fastened by a bronze buckle. The lockets from which the simple scabbard swung were also of bronze. The whole rig was plain and work-manlike, a bladesman's harness. The sword belonged in that scabbard and no other. With due reverence I unbuckled the belt and slid it from around the strom's waist. I cleaned it up. I buckled it on and thrust the sword away. At that, by the Blade of Kurin, it felt right, far better than the rig I discarded.

Going around the dead bodies on the slight off chance one or two might still be alive, I found to my complete non-astonishment that all had been faithfully dealt with. These stikitches had known their trade and only the stout defense put up by Strom Korden had saved him for the short time left to discharge himself of his duty.

None of the armor available would fit me, that was obvious at a glance. Like any prudent warrior or paktun of Kregen who always tries to carry as much weaponry as is sensible and compatible with encumbrance and weight carried, I selected another braxter very like the sword I must carry to Kov Brannomar. I took its associated belt and scabbard and strapped on the rig. Also, I found a nice Bowie-type knife that could snug in the accus-tomed place I wore such a weapon, over my right hip. In addition, I availed myself of a quiver of arrows and a bow, one of the built and backed and heavily re-curved variety. No doubt my good blade comrade Seg Segutorio would have pulled a face; there were no great Lohvian longbows on offer.

As to transport, I rejected the carriage without hesitation. Still, I had a veritable remuda of zorcas at my disposal. Their spiral horns shone in the suns-light. Their wise spirited eyes regarded me warily; a clansman of the Great Plains of Segesthes knows well how to handle animals—voves, zor-cas, chunkrahs—and I had no trouble.

The carriage itself had a schturval painted on the door, and this device denoting name, family, house or clan looked to be a stylized representa-tion of a four-winged animal with a long tail and a double set of nasty looking teeth. Out of mythology, it was, and I had no idea of its name. Over its wicked head was painted a golden crown surmounting a helmet and two brailed scarves of red and blue trailed down tastefully.

There were also, I was extremely grateful to see, plenty of provisions, food and drink in good quantity and quality. There and then I tucked into a repast such as I had not tasted for far too long.

As I chewed and swallowed I reflected morosely on the injustice of the marvelous and terrible world of Kregen. Among the bodies lay six men each wearing a brown hooded robe like the one San Padria had worn.

All had been chopped down and only three of them had used weapons, as was readily apparent. Also, there were bodies that made my lips thin unpleasantly.

Five of them, five young girls at the beginning of their adult lives, each pretty in her own way, each now lying dead with no future ahead at all. They wore multicolored gowns short as to hem and their legs just looked pathetic. Some had bells fastened around their ankles, and as you know I still had not made up my mind if this custom was tasteful or merely vulgar.

My feelings made me want to leave this spot immediately, yet I had at least to think about giving these poor folk decent burials. My mind was made up on the instant by the sight of more travelers approaching along the way I had traveled. I did not want to get into the inevitable hassle that would follow if I stayed around. Anyway, I had to get on and the newcomers could perform the funeral rites far better than I.

The zorcas pricked up their ears as I approached and some pawed the ground under the trees. One animal looked likely, a gray with eyes that appeared to be saying: "Ride me! I am the best!" I walked up to him, soothing him, and put my hand on his bridle. A glint of light in the dapple of suns shine beneath the trees and a hefty thwunk as the flung dagger sank into the tree trunk by my head made me instinctively swirl about and hunker down and the bow was in my left fist and the arrow nocked and half-drawn ready before I caught up with my reactions.

A shrill cracked voice screamed: "Assassin!"

In a voice that smacked back like a thunderclap I yelled: "I'm not an assassin, you fambly!" I was wrought up. "As Cymbaro is my witness, I am no stikitche!" Then I managed to quieten down a bit and finished in a less belligerent but no less loud voice: "Do I look like one?"

The voice, hesitant, choked, said: "No! But—"

"I can see you, hiding behind the carriage. Come out and show yourself or I'll feather you between the spokes of the wheel."

"If I had another dagger you'd talk differently!"

"Here!" I fairly snarled out. I reached up and wrenched the pretty jeweled thing from the tree trunk. "Have it back!"

I hurled it so that it stuck into the side of the carriage.

"There you are!"

In a hesitating almost sobbing voice, she said: "You're stealing the strom's zorca!"

I breathed out thinly through my nose.

"I'm not stealing him! I'm borrowing him!"

"That's what they all say when they're caught."

"By the pendulous swag belly and monolithic veined thighs of Makki Grodno!" I bellowed out. I stood up and started across. "I've had enough of this. Come on out, miss, bratch!"

With the bow and shaft gripped in that cunning archer's hold and my right fist bunched and half-cocked I must have made a daunting sight as I marched across. I own my face must have glowered out a great deal of that demonic expression folk call the Dray Prescot Devil Look.

"Up!" I said, and I snapped it out sharply, like an order rapped out on the barrack square. "Come on out."

She wriggled her way out from under the carriage like a kitten squeezing through a narrow gap. Her pink dress was ripped all down the left side and flaps of it dangled. She made a half-hearted attempt to pull it up over her body. She stood up, breathing loudly. In her hands she cradled a bloody mess of hair. Tears stained down her cheeks and blood congealed all across the left side of her face and in her fair dusty hair. Whatever restraints had held that splendid hair were gone, smashed away in the blow that had done her damage, and despite the dust and blood her hair was truly a glory.

She saw me looking at the bloody mess she held so tightly against her, against her bare flesh where the pink dress flapped open. Some change of expression as I stared was reflected in the strange shift of color in her eyes, clear in the light of the suns, a swirl as of oil on water or silk drawn through the fingers. From green to gray her eyes mirrored my own change of expression.

"Bandi," she said, in a small voice. "My little Bandi." Tears trickled stickily down her dusty and bloodied cheeks.

The animal was a mili-milu, one of those small friendly monkey-like creatures women keep as pets, perched on their shoulders, quick and mischievous but delightful. This little fellow had done his duty by his mistress, for the savage blow that should have killed her outright had smashed the mili-milu and his death had softened the shock to the girl. She'd been lying unconscious and unnoticed under the vegetation-choked end of the carriage all the time.

In a voice I gentled as much as I could, I said: "Let me take Bandi and—"

"No!" she flared.

"People are coming along the road. I must leave before they arrive. They will see to the burials. Please."

She was young, like the other girls on the threshold of life. Of medium height, she was fully formed and I saw her legs were muscled in that particular way of a dancer's training. Despite all the horror she held herself well and her head struck defiantly erect.

I said: "Whatever—Strom Korden charged me with his last breath to do his duty. That I must do. So I shall say rembaree." I gave her a hard stare and turned to stalk off to the gray zorca. Over my shoulder I said: "Your dagger is stuck in the carriage door."

My reaction to her refusal to surrender the mangled remains of her pet clearly puzzled her. If she was a normal young girl, and I saw no reason to doubt otherwise, she'd be in shock. Normalcy in dealing with her now was vital.

My own rather overbearing first impression on her had been met and challenged by her own innate courage. She was a dancer well enough, and I was vaguely pleased to see she wore no bells around her ankles, and she was well-muscled, lithe and acrobatic without doubt. A tough little lady, then, whose toughness was all sliding muscle and rounded forms without a single unsightly bulge. I continued to stalk off as she spoke.

"At least, tell me your name."

"Drajak."

"You are very abrupt."

"Some people call me Drajak the Sudden. Now, if you—"

"I am called Tiri."

As I made no response but once more laid my hand on the zorca's bridle she flashed out with: "Tiri is short for Tirivenswatha."

I couldn't help saying, dryly: "I am glad to hear it. I have little truck with long names."

"I think the Lady Balsitha has deformed your ibma."

"As I do not know who the Lady Balsitha might be, nor yet what an ibma is, you must forgive me if I do not tremble in my shoes."

And she laughed.

"What shoes?"

I looked down, startled, and, by Krun! it was true.

As a hardened old adventurer and a sailor used to treading hard decks going about barefooted is no novelty to me. Still and all, a decent pair of shoes wouldn't come amiss. Somewhat disgruntled, I swung back.

Little time was spent in finding a good pair of shoes, tough of sole and soft of uppers as had been the others, and I hauled them on. The party walking and riding up the road were near by now. I straightened up and she surprised me again. Gravely, she handed me the red ruined remains of Bandi, her mili-milu.

Equally gravely I took the poor thing and then reverently placed it down beside the still form of Strom Korden. "They will give him a proper burial with the due observances." I turned back to her.

She had taken a belt and scabbard and was pulling the buckle tight. The tongue went into just about the last hole about her slender waist. She stuck a braxter into the scabbard with a snap.

I nodded, half in approval half in amusement.

"Very good, young Tiri. Now it is remberee. Farewell."

"No."

"No?"

For an insane instant I thought she might offer to challenge me.

She picked up an embroidered bag near the carriage and walked across to the zorcas under the trees.

"No. I am coming with you."

With that, she gave a strong athletic leap and was astride the gray zorca I had chosen and taking up his reins.

"Come on, Drajak the Sudden. What are you lollygagging about for?"

She swung the zorca's head and cantered out onto the road. Perforce I clambered aboard another likely-looking animal and chik-chikked him along. The other zorcas followed.

Resignedly, feeling something of the emotions of a fellow caught in a hurricane where he had been expecting a mild breeze. I trotted along in her wake.

Now what little she-madam was I embroiled with this time?

Six

Young Tiri did not say a word as we let our animals take us quietly along the road to Bharang. She rode with her head sunk down between her shoulders. Her slender body shook. Now and again she moaned. She was going through the agony of what had happened over and over again, reliving the nightmare. I could do nothing but let her get the shakes out of her system.

"Why," she would be saying to herself, the agony like live coals. "Why was I spared? Why do I live and all my friends are dead? And, why did it have to happen?"

As to the last, I fancied she knew far more about that than did I.

By the time we passed between agricultural fields and the outskirts of Bharang hove in sight she had largely recovered. She sat erect, her long slim dancer's legs very fine and bronzed in the light of the suns. That was one problem if not solved then shelved for the moment. Another problem was worrying me now. Was it because Tiri would have watched and perhaps formed a certain opinion that I had forgotten? I am a longtime mercenary, a zhanpaktun, and after a fracas like the fight around the carriage any paktun worth his salt will investigate the portable property of the slain.

I had not done so. That this was remiss of me I own. Except when it is clear the possessions of the slain in battle should be returned to next of kin, any fighting man expects both to give and to take. When my time comes then certain things should be returned to Delia. The balance becomes the spoils of the victor.

This meant I had no money to care for Tiri or myself in Bharang. Oh, well, I could always hope to sell a zorca. I admit to the sin of pride in that I had muchly looked forward to relishing the look on Fweygo's face when I turned up with a remuda of top class zorcas.

In the last hundred paces or so before we reached the town gates I looked up to see a magnificent scarlet and golden bird circling above my head. He swung in lazy effortless circles, pinions stretched wide. I knew him. This was the Gdoinye, the spy and messenger of the Star Lords. He watched me with his sharp beady eye, turning his head this way and that, circling.

Tiri took no notice for she would not see the Gdoinye.

I waited. Presently the raptor flew up and up, vanishing into the bright sky of Kregen. He had not uttered a single squawk of contempt or admonition. From this I took comfort. I must still be about my business for the Everoinye. Had I not been, by the maggot-infested nostrils of the Divine Lady of Belschutz! I'd have been snatched up into the eerie blue radiance of the Scorpion and whistled off to where I ought to be, and no mistake about that, by Krun!

The walls of the city looked to be in good repair and the spears and helmets of guards were only too obvious along the battlements. Onion shaped domes rose in profusion within the city, with tall towers and a multicolored variety of walls and roofs visible through the open gateway. A caravan of calsanys was just emerging, each pack animal laden down with a fat yellow plaited-straw pannier slung each side. The escort was sizeable in number and impressive in appearance. I pulled the zorcas out of the way to let the caravan pass.

The guards on the gate gave Tiri, the zorcas and me a cursory glance and said and did nothing as we trotted into the city.

The time was just past mid-afternoon and there were certain matters to be attended to in order and with some urgency before nightfall.

The smells of Bharang were not such as to offend, rather the mingled odors of animals and dust and sweat reflected off the closely-packed walls gave one a vague feeling of safety being within the stout walls of a city. The doings of the next few burs are simply told. I found a one-eared Rapa with straggly green feathers who bought a zorca without question. Any brandings would be skillfully removed, judging by the Rapa's manner. Tiri, in a distracted way, did say: "I have some money, Drajak. One silver Bhin and seven copper obs."

I nodded and smiled and said: "The next thing is to buy you some decent clothes. That pink dress, apart from the color, is not fit to be seen." We found her a nice dress of a deeper rose pink, a color she said she preferred, and some solid and sensible undergarments. Then it was time to find a respectable hostelry for the night. Neither of us mentioned what had happened on the road or of the circumstances of our strange meeting and unlikely partnership.

The Fluted Hen looked promising, in a street off the main drag. Its walls were of a yellow brick and its windows shone in the last of the suns. I halted Tiri and for a moment or two we watched the clientele entering and leaving. They looked respectable burghers of the place. So, in we went and obtained two separate rooms for the night. I had made no enquiries regarding Fweygo and the party. That would come when we were settled in comfortably.

The zorcas were stabled and seen to. We sat down in the general room for an evening meal. A group of mail-clad men entered, looking important, although their weapons were sheathed. At their head strutted a youngster wearing a uniform rather too grand for him. He was apim, yet most of the men following him were Hytaks. They are warriors to reckon with, good solid fighters. I began to give my order for the meal, taking no notice of the newcomers.

Now, as you know it is not my habit to sit in a strange place with my back towards the door. Although I say I took no notice of the newcomers, that would appear to be the case to any outward observer. When a shuffling movement attracted my closer attention I realized I had to act rapidly. From the plaited-straw purse the Rapa had put the gold in I shook out half a dozen of the rhoks, still shiny although well-worn, and passed them under the table to Tiri. Moving with deceptive slowness I unbuckled Strom Korden's sword and handed belt and sword to her.

"You say nothing, you know nothing. Keep this sword safely, and do not lose it!" Then I stood up, still slowly, and looking down finished: "If you run across a golden kildoi called Fweygo—tell him." Tankard in my fist I walked casually between the tables as though too impatient to wait for the Fristle serving girl and going for a refill myself. The proprietor, a little Och whose two middle limbs clasped together and whose right upper mopped his shiny forehead with a blue cloth, hurried forward towards the smart youngster in charge of the guard.

"Hikdar Ortyg! What a pleasure to see you here."

"I am on duty, master Olabal."

The Och didn't look worried; we had chosen a respectable establishment all right. The shuffling movement among the guards was repeated and the Rapa to whom I'd sold the zorca stumbled forward. His feathers were decidedly more bedraggled now. Two of the Hytaks held him firmly.

The youngster, this Hikdar Ortyg, said in his squeaky voice: "This is the man, you blintz?"

"Yes, master, yes, master—"

Ortyg put his hand on the hilt of his sword. "You will please come with me." He was perfectly polite about it.

I still wore the second braxter. He didn't know but he could have guessed that I could stick him through and then deal with the rest of the guard before he even cleared leather. His face was shiny and officious. I said: "You have business with me, hikdar?"

Give him credit. He stuck to his task manfully.

"You will please come with me." Then he motioned with his head and the four remaining Hytaks moved forward and surrounded me. I let them. A fracas here would serve no one's purpose. I said: "Of course."

So we marched off out of the hostelry and down the street and along the main road and still he hadn't thought to ask me for my sword. Either he was too cocky for words, or he was a coy, a greenhorn. The Hytaks looked useful and he was not stupid to rely on them. We reached a gray stone building after a number of twists and turns and the sound of the iron bars clanging on my rear was at once a doleful and familiar sound.

The rest of the night sizzled by rapidly. I was accused of selling a stolen zorca; other zorcas had been discovered in the stables of The Fluted Hen. All bore the marks of Strom Korden.

I told them my story, omitting the sword and Tiri.

Now, again to give them their due, they didn't chuck me into the cells straightaway. They considered my case. A magistrate came in, late as it was, a rotund, grave fellow, a numim, and he sized me up.

Stroking his darkly-golden whiskers, he gave his verdict.

"You will be held here until we can verify your unlikely story. Such dreadful news, if true, cannot be kept secret. Strom Nath will deal with you as soon as the case is proven. Take him away."

Off I went and at last they had their opportunity to chuck me into the cells.

By that time they'd taken sword and knife and the plaited-straw purse with the golden rhoks to prove my guilt.

Going to sleep in a prison cell is no new experience for me. As always, anywhere I am, my last thought was the same, then I went to sleep and dreamed, I do recall, of happy sunny days in Esser Rarioch.

Now if I sound utterly callous in this, the facts were different. I had thought of young Tiri before I slept; I hadn't really stopped worrying about the young temple dancer since I'd first bumped into her—or, rather, since she'd first flung a jeweled dagger at my head.

At first appraisal she looked to be a fresh bright-faced youngster, well-formed and beautifully graceful, full of life and spirits. That very bubbling aliveness had been dreadfully reduced by the horrific experience of seeing her friends butchered. Even her little Bandi piled horror upon horror. What experience of the wide world did she have? Temple dancers are trained rigidly and remorselessly; but there are differing varieties upon Kregen. She might simply be a dancer and nothing else until she became too old and her limbs too stiff to continue. She might graduate to higher offices within the temple. She might leave and marry and raise a family—there were some temples where married dancers were considered perfectly correct. Or, she might aspire to much greater ambitions.

Somehow or other I fancied young Tiri was destined to scale the rarefied heights of the inner mysteries, penetrate the hidden sanctuaries and participate in the most secret rites. Pure religion, fanciful cult, magical circle, whatever the doctrine of Cymbaro the Just might be, Tiri would, I could feel it in my bones, one day become the highest of the high—if she lived.

Right now, right here and now in Bharang as a young girl with limited experience still suffering from a mind-shattering horror—how could she be expected to react normally, as though life merely went on?

Oh, yes, by Zim-Zair, I suffered in that damned prison for young Tiri!

In addition to the young madam Tirivenswatha I had the problem of Princess Nandisha to concern me. Fweygo, I felt absolutely confident, was a perfectly competent kregoinye and he'd handle upsets and disasters with the same aplomb he'd handle successes and triumphs. There's an old saying on Kregen—'Don't dice with a four-armed fellow'—and I'd rolled the bones enough times with Korero to feel the truth of that, by Vox! Let alone that disgusting and yet ultimately pathetic cramph Mefto the Kazzur.

Most of the following day I spent in the cell being fed and watered and toileted with a strictness of regimen that told me Bharang did indeed belong to a civilization I could recognize. The city was the capital of the stromnate of the same name, and the strom was this Nath B'Bensarm. He was out of town and was not expected back for a few days.

The captain of the city guard turned out to be a seamed old veteran, an apim, named Mogper. He came in to see if I was all right.

"News came in," he told me severely. "They brought the bodies in for proper burial. Poor Strom Korden!" He kept his bright hooded gaze fixed on me. But he was at ease. "You're for the high jump."

"What about the stikitches?"

"Your accomplices, you mean?" He grimaced. "They deserved to be chucked into the ditch. Still, we don't foul our own drainage."

I opened my mouth to bawl at him, and then I closed it with a snap. That would be useless. The conversation made up my mind.

Later on I said to one of the Hytak guards: "Send for the captain."

"What for, apim? Are you going to confess?"

"That's between me and Mogper. Now—bratch!"

When Mogper came in still wiping gravy from his moustache with a yellow napkin, he wore lounging robes of watered blue silk, very chic, with a silver belt and fancy dagger. His slippers did have something of a curl to them. I hadn't shaved since my interview with the Star Lords and my own beard and moustaches were enough like Mogper's to pass. Dear old Deb-Lu-Quienyin, our comrade Wizard of Loh, had long ago taught me how to change the appearance of my face. Even better these days the trick did not fill my features with a thousand bee stings.

"What—?" began the captain of the city guard and then he went to sleep standing up and in a passable imitation of his gruff voice I finished: "—do you want interrupting my supper?"

I lowered him gently to the cell floor and quicker than it takes to tell I wore his blue robe, girded on the silver dagger belt, donned the slippers, and was ready to sally forth. I said a few choice words, with a couple of 'blintzes!' thrown in, a choice word of insult in these parts.

The Hytak outside snapped to attention as I passed and I strutted off in Mogper's heavy walk, saying: "He'll keep for the strom."

Up the steps and corridors down which I had been brought I went. My face was the face of Jiktar Mogper. No one challenged me. A Hytak guard opened the outer gate for me and I stepped through into the very last crimson rays of sunset, for Genodras had already set. I walked out and along and took a good hefty sniff of the evening air. By Zair! That tasted as sweet as wine of Jholaix!

The feeling of successfully pulling off the trick buoyed me up. It did not always succeed. That time when I'd assumed the face of a diff of the race of Quavens, folk with apim-looking faces but bodies of very strange configuration over in Sharver's End, still rankled. They'd taken a good look and then jumped me. Oh, well, that was back in my lurid past on Kregen.

Now—now I was out and running free.

Letting the contorted muscles of my face relax a trifle I set off with brisk determination for The Fluted Hen.

Seven

Up the back wall of the Fluted Hen I clambered with the aid of a trellised vine. The blue gown was wrapped up around my waist. I dug bare toes into crevices and heaved up and so tapped softly on Tiri's window.

Very quickly—remarkably quickly, considering the circumstances—the window opened outwards and I ducked my head to let it pass above me and then with a single muscular heave hauled myself over the sill into the bedroom. It was in darkness save for the tell-tale fan of light from a lamp with a metal hood shielding the flame. I heard heavy breathing. There was a loud rustling noise. Then a woman's voice, a rich, fruity, passionate voice, said: "Oh, my darling Ferdie! I knew you'd come to me after all my encouragement."

The metal shield was snatched away from the lamp by its wooden handle and light flooded the room.

The woman turned from the lamp table by the bed. Her nightgown hung in what she must fondly imagine to be enticing folds about her, parted from neck to hem. She was gross. Immense folds of fat rolled between deep creases horizontally about her non-existent waist, bulged her thighs and stomach where the white scars of stretch marks looked like a map of hell. Her face bulged with passionate longing and her moustache rivaled Mogper's. "Darling Ferdie! Your little Mimi longs for you so!"

In that heartbeat of time carved from apprehension, laughter and pity I slapped on a face of imbecilic incomprehension. She turned and saw me.

Whatever I expected I did not expect her to fling herself forward, fat arms outspread to engulf me, her nightdress draggling away over all that vast expanse of shining skin. "You're not Ferdie—I know, my darling, I know! But—you'll do!"

"Madam! You misunderstand—"

"You need not be coy, my little heart's-ease. You have seen me and Ferdie and you long for me! I know! Come to me!" Her lips were plum-colored in the light, spittle-flecked, her squashed nose a flower of passion. She lurched forward and I skipped away, looking desperately for the door.

She lumbered after me and tripped over the nightgown and toppled and almost fell. The sight was awe-inspiring. Demolition workers pulling down temples must experience that sensation of the mass of the world collapsing. I reached the door.

She made a convulsive effort to regain her balance, everything quivering like jelly. "Don't go! Don't go! Little Mimi needs you!"

"I assure you, madam, I am sensible of your most gracious offer. But I am otherwise engaged and must therefore with deep regret decline."

You couldn't say fairer than that, by Shansi, the Sprite of Love, who sends her loop of flowers down to entwine lovers.

"Please—" Spittle ran down her several chins like artificial waterfalls. I thought she'd start to cry in a minute and I didn't want that on my conscience. I wrenched the door open. "Madam Mimi, your devoted servant. Remberee." And I fairly scuttled off.

By the disgusting diseased liver and lights of Makki Grodno! What a turn up! Good luck to Ferdie, whoever he was.

If the whole hostelry awoke in an uproar I'd be done for. Where in a Herrelldrin Hell was Tiri's room?

I heard footsteps advancing along the passageway. A thin shaft of light from a lamp on the corner threw shadows into a door alcove and illuminated the rest. I ducked into the shadows.

A man walked along clad in a blue lounging robe not unlike Mogper's. He was tall and thin, although not a Ng'grogan. If Mimi could get her fat arms about anyone, she'd manage with skinny Ferdie. He saw her fat moonshining face around the edge of her door and he started to run, arms outstretched. "Mimi! My little turtle-dove!"

They went inside and the door slammed. I wiped the sweat off my forehead and Tiri put her head out of the next door along, puzzled, not so much alarmed as intrigued.

I stepped out and put a finger to my lips, remembering to lose the imbecilic face that had so enchanted Mimi.

In a trice we were in her room and the door shut silently at our backs. She wore a nice short nightdress and looked marvelous.

"Drajak!" she said in an accusing whisper. "Where have you been? What happened? The city guard—?"

"A matter of Strom Korden's zorca. I thought I could trust the rascality of that Rapa Rindle. Maybe he was careless. Anyway, I felt it prudent to get away, particularly after the news came in."

"It is all over the place. It has ousted the news of the death of the king's son. What have—?"

"I need to get out of this lounging robe and find some decent clobber. You have Strom Korden's sword safe?"

"Yes. Of course."

I studied her face carefully. She looked tired. There was no mistaking the jut of her rounded chin, the defiance with which she held her head erect. Her fair hair was brushed back and gleamed golden. She was a girl of parts, all right, struggling to come to terms with what had happened, facing head on the horror that had engulfed her world.

In that moment I felt I could rest more easily where young Tirivenswatha was concerned.

"Did the city guards question you?"

"No. I have kept very quiet. But—"

"But what?" We spoke in tense whispers.

"I should go to them and explain. That would soon—"

That had always been and possibly still was an obvious course of action. I had set my face against that from the start of the business.

"I want you kept out of it, Tiri."

"Oh, I know they worship Tolaar here in Bharang. Cymbaro is recognized as merely a cult. But, all the same, I am a dancer before Cymbaro and they will listen."

"I really do not think that a good idea. There'd be too many explanations."

I was thinking of Strom Korden's mysterious charge to me which I fully intended to honor.

"But you're a fugitive! A leemshead!"

"I've been that before and, no doubt, will be so again. Now, young lady, bed time for you. I'll kip down on the floor and in the morning we'll think better with clear heads."

She climbed up into the bed and hauled the covers up. Her gray-green eyes regarded me thoughtfully. "Don't think you will always be able to tell me what to do, Drajak. I can only return to Oxonium and seek comfort and advice at the shrine." She sounded positive. "San Paynor will make everything clear." And, with that, she snuggled down and in no time at all was fast asleep.

Oh, yes, I told myself, young Tiri was indeed a fine spirited girl of parts.

During the course of the following morning things fell out quite other than I had anticipated. Tiri ventured out with some gold rhoks and silver bhins and returned with clothes. I had specified a length of scarlet cloth for a breechclout and she brought with that a garment called shamlak, a tunic-like vestment which was worn with a gap of at least a hand's breadth down the front, from neck to hem. Shades of Mimi's nightgown! It fastened across the front with cords stretching from button to button, rather like a hussar's dolman. Both men and women wore the same fashion. Below it women wore skirts of a tiered style and men wore short kilts. The whole was designed for lightness, airiness and comfort in a climate mild and hospitable most of the time.

Also, a little breathlessly, she said: "And, Drajak! What do you think!"

Smiling, for smiling came easily where young Tiri was concerned when dark thoughts of the horror in both our minds could be pushed aside, I said: "Well, young lady. What do I think?"

"You can never guess. I saw Princess Nandisha!"

"Oh," I said, and remained dumb thereafter.

"I did! She was as close as you are. It was strange, though. Her golden numim was there, as they passed by, and the princess I am sure was trying to conceal her face. It was most odd. Everybody likes her."

"You didn't happen to see a big Kildoi?"

"No."

"Look, Tiri, you'll have to go out again and find Nandisha and then find Fweygo. Tell him what happened. All of it."

"But—?"

"It'll be all right. You'll see."

Although I was not at all sure that, indeed, it would be all right, I sincerely hoped so. Fweygo would fathom a way around the problem.

So, stuck in Tiri's bedroom, I waited. Some time elapsed. When at last she returned she waltzed in and, lo! in came Nandisha and Ranaj and

Fweygo. They were not looking particularly overjoyed and relieved at finding the lost member of their party. Ranaj had a scowl all across his features. Fweygo, alone, look undisturbed.

Before I'd even had a chance to get out a polite lahal, Ranaj started up: "Thanks to you, Drajak, and your onkerish behavior, the princess has had to reveal herself. Now—"

"It isn't all that bad." Nandisha sat in the only chair, looking far more relaxed than when we'd parted. "To obtain a lifter it would have been necessary, I suspect."

For my part, I suspected that now she was going to fly all the way to Oxonium, the capital, and safety, she felt the danger had passed.

Fweygo said: "You should have seen the guards jump when the princess spoke to them. They fell over themselves to please. You're in the clear now, Drajak. Stikitches did that foul deed."

"What about Strom Nath B'Bensarm na Bharang?" I used the full name because it intrigued me.

"He apologized for the over eagerness of his people." Nandisha spoke graciously.

Fweygo said: "I laughed."

I gave him a look. He sounded a likely partner.

Nandisha stood up. "If we are all ready, then we must fly." That was an unmistakable command.

As we went out the door, Ranaj said: "All the same. I do not like the thought of the princess being known to have been in Bharang."

Fweygo glanced at me meaningfully. Both of us knew probably for sure what Ranaj only suspected. The peril encompassing the princess and her children had not passed. We were still here. The Star Lords had not released us from this contract.

Just before we all walked out into the streaming mingled lights of the Suns of Scorpio, I said to the landlord, Olabal: "You'll find a blue silk lounging robe, a pair of curly slippers and a silver belt and dagger in the lady's bedroom. See they are returned to Jiktar Mogper at the city prison."

"Of course, master, of course. And thank you."

All his puffy chops lolling, all his four upper limbs working together, he kept on bowing to the princess. She nodded her head in that lofty regal way these grand folk of the world have. Oh, yes, every now and then even I, Dray Prescot, can relish the doors that influence can open!

On the streets a busy traffic went on. There passed and re-passed the astonishing variety of peoples of Kregen, races as distinct and diverse one from another as chickens are different from cats. We walked steadily towards the voller park where everything would be ready waiting for us.

A pastang of Undurkers marched past, their long borzoi faces high and most supercilious, their bows slung. Following, a pastang of Chuliks marched with their peculiar solidity of purpose, Yellow Tuskers, with long pigtails and shiny yellow skin, superb fighters and trained from birth for the mercenary trade.

The fellow in charge of the voller park was a Xuntalese whose handsome black face with its chiseled features reminded me of Balass the Hawk. All his assistants came from the same island of Xuntal. They produced a nice little eight-place airboat with a narrow-framed cabin of varnished wood and real glass windows. The craft reminded me muchly of those dainty steamers that ply the lakes, tall of funnel and gleaming of brasswork, going 'Toot-toot!' at every opportunity. We all climbed in and Fweygo took the controls.

There was little ceremony and absolutely no paperwork. Ranaj and his wife Serinka sat in the middle with the children occupying the central deck space and Nandisha and Tiri sat side-by-side in the stern. The princess and the dancing maiden had their heads inclined one to the other. It was perfectly clear they had struck up a new if unlikely friendship. I sat next to Fweygo.

"A trim craft," he said, and that was all.

Up we soared into the fragrance of a bright Kregan day. I quite relished the sensations of once more flying through thin air under the suns. Fweygo turned our heading to the west, pushed the speed lever full forward and when we had reached a comfortable cruising height leveled off. We settled down to the journey to Oxonium.

Presently Fweygo and I began a desultory conversation in tones low enough so that we could not be overheard. Anyway, the children were playing with one another in an unaffected way that indicated that for them, at any rate, the rank distinctions between princess and prince and retainers did not matter. Their noise effectively covered our talk.

As I had guessed, Fweygo had gone cautiously at night time and I'd passed him somewhere when he'd been off the road. He repeated his delight at Strom Nath's discomfiture when the princess had spoken to him with her eyebrows raised. My gear was all present and correct and I wore the sword kept safely by Tiri. Then Fweygo said: "I've been working for You Know Who for some time now and my judgment is we're on an inheritance mission. The old king's son and grandson died some time ago and the great grandson was therefore called the king's son. He's just died, him and all his family in a wretched accident."

"And you think this Nandisha is in line for the throne?"

Fweygo pursed up his lips. "Difficult to say. That's what all the fuss will be about. She's the daughter of a younger brother of the Prince Majister who's just died, Prince Nazrak, with all his family."

"So?"

"Her father was Prince Vanner. Their sister, Princess Shirree, sister to

Nazrak and Vanner, that is, is still alive and like them a direct descendant of the old king. Her son is in line."

I sensed an application of the Salic Law here. I said: "A woman cannot inherit the crown and throne?"

"Right. By law."

"But the line can descend through a female?"

Again Fweygo pursed his lips and started to whistle softly through his teeth before saying: "There's the rub. No one seems to know. There is argument."

"Well, if there's argument that must mean somewhere there is a descendant in the direct male line."

"Ha! Direct? That's what Hyr Kov Khonstanton would like everyone to believe. But, again, there is serious doubt about the legality of one of the unions in his ancestry. He comes down from a younger brother of the old king. That younger brother, Naghan, had a son and daughter. There was no chance of their inheriting whilst a direct male line existed from the old king. Now—"

Fweygo checked and gently steered the voller around a mass of white cloud, drenched with rose and viridian glory, before he resumed.

"The doubt is that whilst Khonstanton claims the son was his father, general opinion says that the daughter was."

"Um," I said. "An interesting knot."

"Oh, there's more. There are other siblings queuing up in the wings." He grimaced. "It is a knot, and you and me, Dray Prescot, are right in the middle of it!"

Eight

There was much to dwell on in what Fweygo told me. At first glance the presence of two kregoinyes assigned to protect this party must indicate the Star Lords wished one of Nandisha's children to succeed to the throne when the old king died. That was the way they operated.

Nandisha and her children were in danger, their lives at stake. Ergo, someone was out to kill them and thus put them out of the running for the crown. With the catalogue of deaths and accidents mentioned by Fweygo in the royal family tree that someone had already been busily at work.

Over the slipstream, for Fweygo had the flier cranked up to a fair old clip, and the racket of the children, Nandisha's voice cut clearly and sharply with that refined yet devastatingly puncturing regal voice. "Mabal and

Matol are nearing the horizon, Ranaj. We will go down and eat and rest."

"At once, princess." The numim growled at Fweygo: "Take the lifter down, Kildoi. Gently, now."

Fweygo didn't deign to respond. He put the voller's nose down and we started a long fast descent. He pulled back on the speed lever. We went on plummeting down. Fweygo gave the speed lever an impatient tug. Still, on we went in our headlong plunge.

"The thing's jammed," he said in a disgusted voice. "Take a look at the silver boxes."

"Right. Perhaps you had better—?"

"Naturally." He hauled back on the height lever.

There was no difference in our rate of descent. We were plunging towards the rapidly closing surface of the world, helpless to cut our speed or check our height.

Without wasting a second I ripped open the cover to the black box compartment housing the lifting mechanism. A vivid memory of the first time I had done this flooded into my mind. Delia and I, drifting over the Great Plains of Segesthes, and she, the mischievous minx, letting us drift and both of us sick with love one for the other and with no way to express our tumultuous emotions—oh, yes, I remembered!

In the intervening seasons refinements had taken place in airboat construction, for technology in Paz on Kregen is not stagnant. The controls were more elegant, more precise these days. The problem was immediately identifiable.

A sharp nail had been driven into the balass orbit so that when the sturmwood carrying frame passed over it, there was no obstruction. When the frame was brought back the bent over pointed-head of the nail stuck into the wood and prevented the silver boxes from being drawn apart. The second nail in the speed orbits stopped the boxes revolving each about its own axis. The arrangement in this voller, what these folk called a lifter, was somewhat different from that found in the vollers built in Hamal and Hyrklana. I understood the system. The boxes were positioned one abaft the other, fore and aft. Drawn close together the flier lifted, pulled apart she sank. Each box tilted around its own axis so that when they were horizontal the speed built up to rapid. When they revolved and assumed a ninety-degree position, upright, all forward motion ceased. The whole mechanism was encircled by the orbit that revolved laterally to change direction larboard or starboard.

"Hurry!" called Fweygo at the control levers above me. "The ground is coming up fast and it looks hard."

Somewhere in the background I heard high excited voices raised in alarm. I bent to the task, taking out the heavy knife I'd possessed at the scene of the massacre. There was no way I was going to lever the nails out.

"Ease forward," I shouted up. "Release the orbit, a nail is sticking in it."

He understood at once and the orbit inched forward, and with my help pushing, the sharpened nail-head came free. Now, using the point of a knife for this kind of work is a sure recipe for breaking off the knife's tip. That had no meaning now. I forced the blade under the bent over head of the nail stuck in the lifting orbit. That, first!

Levering with a desperation fuelled by the grim thought of the ground leaping up to smash us to firewood, I bent the nail up and then smashed it flat the other way. I didn't wait for Fweygo to pull the silver boxes apart. As I had done with Delia over the Great Plains of Segesthes, although then there had been no confounded treacherous nail in the way, I smashed the boxes apart. The wood checked and I felt the resistance, then I used my shoulders and strained and the sturmwood orbit slid over the balass, over the nail.

Whether or not our mad descent was checked enough I didn't know, nor did I stop to find out. The knife point was under the second nail and I heaved, the knife tip broke off and we hit the ground.

Everything flew to flinders.

Head over heels, with a cracking smack of shoulder against a control lever, up I flew. Up, over and over, and so down splat! flat on my back in damned stinging nettles and thorns tearing at my flesh.

I just lay there, winded, gasping for breath and if all the Bells of Beng Kishi were not ringing in my head, then, by Vox, most of them were donging away like a crazed collection of insane monks all tolling and clanging the end of the world.

Somebody sounding like Nandisha was screaming away and Ranaj was forcibly expressing himself on his opinion of clumsy, onkerish, useless Kildoi lifter pilots. I rolled out of the thorns and I did not say a word. The little numim girl, Rofi, was just sitting up close by. Her dainty lion maiden face expressed alarm and she pushed herself to her feet and ran off to the side. Thank Opaz at least one passenger was unharmed. I stood up to see Rofi helping the little princess, Nisha, to stagger up, gripping the numim girl. Ranaj stopped yelling and Nandisha stopped screaming. Serinka was cradling the princess to her bosom and making soothing noises. So that left the two lads, Fweygo, and Tiri.

As I might have expected, the numim lad, Rolan, was attending to the young prince Byrom and calming him down. I let out a breath. Where had Fweygo got to? Inspecting the interior of Cottmer's Caverns, perhaps? Or, the thought occurred darkly to me, on the long road down to the Ice Floes of Sicce? And the young madam? Was she smashed like the voller?

Looking about in a state of more alarm than I cared for, I saw we'd crashed into the side of a valley sloping down to a stream. No buildings were in sight and the ground was rough moorland. The last long rays of the suns spread ruby and emerald shadows among the trees by the river.

"Fweygo!" I bellowed in the old foretop hailing voice. "Tiri!"

No answer.

Bits and pieces of varnished wood lay about in confusion. Shards of glass lay like emerald and ruby daggers along the ground. I looked every which way, growing more and more apprehensive. The lightly-built lifter had blown to pieces like a child's toy under a careless adult foot.

We'd come to grief on the slope down to the river and that incline had saved us, appreciably lessening our angle of impact. Wreckage strewed itself downslope among the trees towards the river as though a giant had emptied his rubbish bin haphazardly. Once, twice, three times I screwed my head around in the fast-fading light looking away from the trees and along the moorland slopes and back again.

And I yelled.

Oh yes, I yelled. "Fweygo! Tiri!"

Ranaj looked across and snapped angrily: "Stop that noise, apim, you'll arouse Tolaar knows what."

I went on shouting and scouting downslope.

The thought crossed my mind with the speed a shiftik pounces on a flying insect and is gone that the splendid golden numim Ranaj could go shove his orders where they'd do the most good. My comrades could be lying dead or injured. A few lusty shouts were most definitely in order. The generous thought then occurred that the lionman was only doing his duty to the princess as he saw it. I went on bellowing.

A whole deck section had been hurled into the branches of a tree. Further on more deck and planking and broken glass in a fantail downslope looked pathetic in the gathering gloom. Three spots of fire popped into existence about fifty paces down. Lambent yellow, in a triangular form point uppermost, they suddenly appeared and hung man height in the dimness beneath the trees. I stopped and shut my mouth.

Ranaj, then, had been right, confound the numim.

Ahead between the spots of light and me the trees thinned out and as I stopped the lights advanced. They moved gently up and down and grew larger and brighter and then in the very first of the pink rays of The Maiden with the Many Smiles illuminating that small clearing, revealed themselves as three eyes set in a countenance from hell.

What the thing was I didn't know. It looked big and unhealthy. It walked on four clawed legs and it waved four clawed forelimbs about before that nightmarish head where the three eyes glowed. And, in that selfsame instant as the moon's beams brightened between the trees a slender figure rose up like a shadowy wisp and there was Tiri, standing over a formless lump on the ground.

My bow had been snapped in the crash and had vanished somewhere. I drew both swords. I ran down like a madman to hurl myself before Tiri.

She said in a simple small voice: "I didn't want to shout because of that. Fweygo is not dead."

"Can you drag him away?" I snarled it over my shoulder.

"I will try." The calmness in her had a steadying effect on me.

I set myself. There have been many times on Kregen when Dray Prescot has had to fight monsters and techniques have, as you know, been developed. I whirled the swords so that the moonlight flashed. The thing advanced remorselessly. It moved in silence. That was an unnerving experience, I can tell you, a great ugly monster with claws and fangs advancing soundlessly towards me in the moonlight.

Unpleasant to relate combats with animals, however ferocious they really are and however terminal their intentions. He had his way of life and things to do to eat and live. I had friends to protect, a mission to perform—and I had to stay alive for the sake of Delia. So, I fought the poor thing, and cut him up, and took my lumps—a long grazing slash of claws that left a red welt along my side ruining the new shamlak—until thankfully he turned away. By then he was missing two eyes and blood spattered over his hide and a forelimb dangled loosely. I lifted the strom's sword in salute as he lumbered off.

Tiri had dragged Fweygo a good distance off. Despite her attractive slimness she had muscles and was a tough young lady. She said—and I could not judge, could not judge at all, by Krun, what she was really saying, "I'd give you the jikai if I wasn't too busy dragging Fweygo off."

The blood fouling the sword blades could be wiped off on the ripped up shamlak. Not so easy, not so easy by a whole world of violence, by Krun, to wipe away the results of the taking of that blood. As if to ram home the somberness of my thoughts, Princess Nandisha called out.

"Why didn't you kill it, Drajak?"

"Yes," I said, wiping the swords and walking up the slope towards the others. "Yes, he had only one eye left and was sore wounded. Perhaps it would have been more merciful to have slain him than to have let him live."

"A stalking Obachnin," rumbled out Ranaj. "They terrorize the neighborhood. Better for them to die than live."

I bent to Tiri. "How is he?"

"Oh, he'll live. He must have a skull as thick as a lenken door."

Together we carried Fweygo back up and made him comfortable and before we'd had time to fuss his eyelids fluttered and his musical voice, roughened by dryness, said: "Wha' hoppon'd?"

"Just lie still." Tiri's youthful firmness was most impressive. The interesting fact here was that despite our predicament and all Fweygo's natural Kildoi assertiveness coupled with his race's aloof consciousness of self-value, he accepted the young madam's ministrations meekly, recognizing in this area her competence.

I kept my black-fanged wine spout fast clamped shut.

When at last we had settled our ruffled emotions down and rubbed some of Serinka's magic ointment on the children's bruises we took stock of our situation.

"We're in the middle of nowhere here," said Ranaj. Most of the countryside hereabouts tended to wildness between the centers of population. The highroads were kept in good condition. Other trails were merely tracks or non-existent. "Beasts like that Obachnin prowl where they can. We have a difficult march ahead." Ranaj sounded not so much defeated as resigned to an unpleasant experience.

Nandisha said: "Make a fire, will you, Ranaj."

At once the numim jumped up and then paused, as it were in mid-jump.

Before his hesitation could be translated into words, the princess went on in what was a highly pettish voice for so exalted a lady: "There is plenty of firewood from the lifter."

"Ah," said Fweygo as Ranaj said nothing. "Ah, princess, would that be wise? You might attract unwelcome visitors."

"The fire would frighten the stupid beasts away."

"I was not thinking of stupid beings."

"Oh!" she said, and put a hand to her breast. "Oh, I see."

At this latitude the night would not be cold. The Maiden with the Many Smiles would provide ample light. If it rained as it was likely to do we'd all get wet—well, Serinka would see the children were sheltered. We'd all had a busy day and were tired and so would sleep easily enough. Ranaj arranged watches. Fweygo and I wanted to talk to the lionman about those two deadly nails in the orbits of the flier.

Our voices rumbled low as the others stretched out on the ground beginning to fall asleep. Ranaj expressed himself as horrified and then ferociously angry. He had the grace to apologize to Fweygo for calling the Kildoi an incompetent lifter pilot.

"Who dunnit?" I said.

Ranaj lifted his hand helplessly in the pink moonlight. "It is all of a piece. I felt the lifter that failed and dumped us in Amintin should not have done so, even allowing for their fractious ways. The friends of Princess Nandisha are determined to see her son Byrom nominated as the legal heir to the throne; but—"

"But friends of other interested parties want their principals to be thus exalted."

Fweygo's words carried, at least to me, a strong note of cynical amusement, as though this were all a game. Well, in one very real sense it was. Fweygo's hint of sarcasm was perfectly justified in view of our task of keeping these folk alive. Beyond that, just who aspired to the throne was up to them and of no interest to Fweygo or me.

Ranaj grunted a sullen assent. "Aye. Other blintzes think they have a right. But they have no right to try to kill us."

Fweygo opened his mouth, shook his head and clamped his lips firmly. I could guess his reaction. Right is what you make it, even within the strict parameters of a stern religious creed. Ranaj, for example, would claim the right to stop anyone trying to stop him. So we stood our watches and slept as well as we could and with the rising of Mabal and Matol took stock of this new day upon fair Kregen.

Whilst Ranaj and Serinka busied themselves with their charges and pre-pared breakfast from provisions foraged from the scattered wreckage, I said to my companions: "We must find the silver boxes."

"Oh?" with two pairs of lifted eyebrows.

"Of course. I'll build a new lifter. If the boxes are intact."

"Oh!" this time with two pairs of wide-open eyes.

In the event Tiri found the vaol box and Fweygo the paol box. They were both unbroken. I heaved up a sigh of relief and a quick thankyou to Opaz, and set to work.

Construction of the hull was not difficult using the wreckage. All that was needed was a simple raft-like shape. The silver boxes would power the craft in lift and movement. The problem arose in their mounting. The balass, bronze and sturmwood orbits were a mere trash of splinters and distorted metal shapes. I could, of course, have held the boxes one in each hand and physically moved them up and down and around. The aura of effect operated in a kind of shroud about the boxes so that no one point had to sustain the weight of balance. Provided the boxes were fastened to the object they were lifting no heavy pressure bearings were required.

Eventually I decided to construct a simple sliding arrangement of wooden struts to provide lift and forward momentum. There was no fancy operation possible. We would go up and forward. Fweygo whistled near-soundlessly through his teeth and nodded.

"I can fly that."

The theory that there are areas of the human brain that lie as it were dark and unused has been challenged from time to time. Why did God provide them if they are of no use? Then, why did God provide an appen-dix? It has been suggested that once human beings could use telepathy, could teleport, use telekinetics, all the mysteries of psionics. Now we can-not and the dark areas of our brains are like the appendix. Again, it has been proposed that these dark areas are lying dormant waiting for the time when we have the knowledge to use them for such marvels as psionics. A further theory is that they are used and we simply do not have the knowl-edge or instruments to measure and discover what they do.

Looking at the Kildoi as he worked on the wreckage to build a voller gave me an inkling that on Kregen at least some of those dark areas of the brain are in active use. Fweygo picked up a length of wood with his tail hand and passed it across to his hand to position it exactly where I told him it needed to go, holding it against the upright held there by his hand. He picked up a nail that Tiri had straightened and knocked it in with the hammer in his fist. A tail hand and four hands hard at work and all beautifully coordinated. His brain could control his limbs in ways that folk with no tail hand and only two arms must envy.

How often has a poor girl with a brood of babies, the washing and ironing to do and the dinner to cook cried out: "Oh for another pair of hands!"

So the jury-rigged airboat was completed. We all piled in and Fweygo lifted us off for Oxonium the capital and Opaz-alone knew what fresh perils we must face.

Nine

"Well, I'm going," said Tiri, her chin defiantly up. "I'm going right away. And that's final."

We stood, the young temple dancer and the two kregoinyes, on a high terrace of Nandisha's palace overlooking Oxonium. The princess and the children were in the inner apartments resting and recuperating after their ordeal. Fweygo glanced sideways at me.

"One of us must stay with the princess."

"I'll go with—" I started to say.

Tiri cut in fiercely. "I am quite capable of going myself. I do not need to be nursemaided."

I looked out over the city bathed in the streaming mingled lights of the twin suns. Oxonium was an intriguing place, full of interest and contradictions. The inhabitants lived in some luxury and splendor on the flat tops of a number of steep-sided hills. In the runnels between the hills, some marshy, some drained and filled with the hovels of the poor and slaves, some allowing the rivers to flow to their conjunction by the grand central hill, the suns struck only around the hour of mid.

Perhaps the most striking facet of Oxonium had to be found in the interconnecting lines of cable cars running from hill to hill. The cables were supported at intervals across the valleys and at my softly-voiced query: "Why don't the poor or slaves who hate the rich burn the supports down?" the answer was a simple and brutal: "Because we would go down there and burn and destroy their hovels with them inside."

A balance was thus formed, as is often the case over Kregen.

A few lifters, not many, flew over the city. By far the larger number of airboats sailed past with their multicolored sails agleam in the suns light. Hooking keels of ethero-magnetic forces into that mysterious substratum of power furnished by five of the minerals in the silver boxes, these ovverers could lift up into the air. Lacking the remaining four minerals of the powered lifters they had no forward motion apart from that provided by the breeze. The ovverers sailed on their courses over the sinuous lengths of the cables from hill to hill and they came and went over the walls and rivers in a busy commerce. The whole panorama at once delighted and intrigued. There were many questions raised by the different systems of transport on display.

Fweygo said: "I think it wise for Drajak to accompany you, Tiri."

She pouted. "All I have to do is take a calimer." She referred to a cable car. "It will cost a few coppers, that is all. I do not even have to change cars, for the princess's palace is right next door to the grand central. I am not a child."

"Cymbaro forfend!" I said, and I own, humbly, that I did, in truth, half mock her. She flushed up.

Had she been my kregoinye comrade Mevancy, that flush would have rivaled the sunset glow of Zim and she'd have said: "Oh, you!"

Tiri did say: "If you insist on going with me, have the courtesy to remember I am a lady."

Fweygo whistled softly through his teeth and said nothing. I said, instantly: "Then as a lady accept a gentleman's honorable escort."

It was all petty and pretty and irrelevant—or so I thought.

She nodded. "Very well. Let us get started."

I took a great interest in the cable car system. The winding mechanism was situated in a small structure on the edge of the cliff. Where I had half-expected to see a gaggle of sorry-looking slaves being whipped to work, with the hateful cry of 'Grak!' in their ears, I found instead a neat brick-paved circle where calsanys moved endlessly around the windlass. A few people waited as the car climbed up the graceful curve of the cable towards us. The impression of height was conveyed vividly. The car clunked into its retaining slot as a car at the far end exactly balanced it. There were two other calimers spaced along the cables, both going and coming. Everything looked to be functional and efficient. We stepped aboard and the aerial trip began.

The experience was delightful. We soared out over the squalid collections of huts and hovels below, like favelas, and at that height the stinks down there did not reach us. The wheels ran smoothly and almost soundlessly and a little breeze swayed us just a trifle from side to side.

Grand central was indeed grand. This hill, the largest in Oxonium, contained the palace of the king, temples and courts, grandiose buildings serving a busy and important capital city. The cables themselves, so I was told, were fabricated from immensely long and tough vines strengthened by windings of treated reeds from the Lakes of Thrushness to the north of the country. In addition, strands of strung bronze further reinforced the cables. Breakages were rarer than snow in the Yellow Deserts of Caneldrin, the country to the north.

Like any gallant gentleman squiring a lady I carried Tiri's embroidered bag in my left hand. I could not help noticing that from time to time she would absently put up her hand to her shoulder and, just for an instant before she remembered, make gentle stroking movements. Oh, yes, young Tirivenswatha had undeniably lost more of her youth over the recent horrific occurrences than the death of her pet mili-milu, Bandi, yet that was the one horror that must have struck the keenest. That, despite all the other terrible deaths and the blood.

The young temple dancer shared with me the deep conviction that the death of innocence is just about the most dreadful of all deaths.

The terminus where we alighted was carved more elaborately than that on the hill where Nandisha's palace had been built. A paved open kyro extended before us, flanked by imposing buildings. People moved everywhere. The square buzzed with activity. The gorgeous array of Kregish diffs passed and repassed. Slaves slipped in and out of the crowds as slaves do on errands for those who own them. Many of them instead of wearing the almost universal—and hateful—gray, wore dingy brown.

Tiri marched on, head high, a pace or so in front of me. This pleased and amused me enormously.

Had she dragged along astern I'd have been worried about her state of mind. Of course, she could still just be putting up a brave front that would collapse the instant she was safely in the shrine.

Enquiries of Ranaj earlier had informed me that the laws relating to weapons were lax to the point of non-existence. Men and women wore all manner of racial and national weapons. With the constant frictions of the frontiers leading to open warfare at distressingly frequent intervals, folk tended to be well-equipped in the arsenal department.

As in Bharang, among the many and splendid varieties of diffs in Oxonium there were large numbers of Chuliks, Undurkers and Xuntalese.

Although most of the hills of Oxonium were flat-topped, either natural configurations or the patient handiwork of laborers over the seasons, some were more hilly. In the center of Grand Central reared the hill bearing the royal palace. This was the ancestral seat of the T'Tolin family. The name was hallowed. Nandisha's husband, Nath, now dead, when he'd married into the royal family had naturally taken the name T'Tolin and regarded that as the singular favor it was.

What Fweygo and I assumed was that we were here to assist Nandisha in her claim for her son Byrom to sit on the throne of the T'Tolin palace.

Yet, despite all this bustle and glitter of a busy day on Kregen, one great difference stood out starkly.

From flagstaffs protruding from every roof and balcony, from poles erected at intersections, flew somber drapes. The flags were white, with a white center surrounded by a black ring. This flag is the kaotresh, the flag of death. Around my arm I wore a white band containing that black ring encircling the white center, the symbol of death.

The whole city was in mourning. Had not the king's son just died?

The people we passed may not have been laughing and cheerful; all the same they were not weeping openly, devastated by this news. Life had to go on. The old king would choose a new successor and in the fullness of time, when the old king went on his long last journey down to the Ice Floes of Sicce, why, then a new king would wear the crown. For my own part I did not care who that was, Byrom or any other of the contenders. I have seen far too much bloodshed over royal successions. Still, even so, it did appear Fweygo and I were pitchforked into the middle of the controversy surrounding the rightful heir. Oh, well, I said to myself as we rounded a corner of the Kyro of the Fanciers, the old king would make that decision.

Nandisha's people had found fresh clothes for me, a smart dark blue shamlak with black broidery and loops. Tiri had a new dress, a pale shamlak of pale blue broidered in silver. She looked very nice.

A Rapa with canary yellow feathers had been hanging about the landing stage as our cable car docked, and as we turned the corner I caught a glimpse of him slipping along in our wake. He wore an arsenal of weapons girded around his olive green shamlak and his feet were cased in cracked sandals. I kept a weather-eye out for him.

Thinking about the moil in which we two kregoinyes found ourselves, I was just recalling a more somber saying of San Blarnoi, when Tiri spoke up. San Blarnoi's words are: "That the governance of a country should be left to blind heredity!" Tiri said: "Don't look back now. There's a villainous-looking Rapa following us."

The yellow-feathered beaky? Aye."

"You knew!"

"If you wish to stay alive you have to know these things."

"Yes, well."

Further along we passed the overly ornate facade of a temple whose massiveness could not make up for its overall lack of taste. Tiri's head went up even higher as we walked past and she hurried her steps. Her sweet young face was set in rigid lines of distaste. I said nothing and at last, when we had put some distance between us and the dominating pile she burst out with: "They worship the false idol Dokerty."

I glanced back in time to see a small procession of priests entering the portico up the wide shallow steps. They carried no flags or emblems. They walked two by two. They were clad all in deep somber red.

Soho! I said to myself. They have this grandiose temple on Grand Central of the capital city; why then do they need to skulk about secretly in ruins?

"I thought Tolaar was the religion—"

"There are many faiths. Tolaar is probably the largest." Tiri spoke in a tight, hard voice. "There is always trouble between them. Sometimes there are fights. It is ugly."

The shrine of Cymbaro turned out to be a very small and insignificant structure. Tiri explained that this shrine on Grand Central was merely there because of the necessity of maintaining a presence in Oxonium near the royal palace. "Sometimes the king listens to us."

We went into a cool courtyard where a fountain splashed. There was no doubt whatsoever that I felt a strong sense of peace, of a tranquility that rose above the petty problems of the city or the state. I guessed these folk were great metaphysicians. There was nobody about. Flowers gave off pleasant perfumes. I suppose it is possible that the custom of burning incense in temples began because the worshipers were an unwashed smelly lot. In these latter days the stink of incense is far worse than that of honest sweat.

Tiri led off between columns into another courtyard surrounded by cloisters. A youngish man wearing a brown robe advanced to meet us, smiling. "Tiri! We heard the dreadful news—you are well?"

"Perfectly, thank you, Logan. This is—ah—Drajak. He has been a power in the sight of Cymbaro. Now—I would like to see San Paynor."

"Of course." Logan spread white hands. "At the moment he is closeted with a visitor. I cannot disturb them. But I'm sure they won't be long. May I offer you refreshment?"

So down we sat on a bench and parclear and sazz and miscils were brought out and we waited. We waited some time.

Occasionally priests walked past, each one inclining his head to Tiri. A couple of excited girls danced up, all rosy faces and flowing drapes, to pester Tiri to tell them of her adventures. They became most subdued at the first mention of the deaths of their dancing friends. They started to cry. I, Dray Prescot, stood up and took a stroll around the courtyard, checking doorways, feeling in the way.

Presently Logan reappeared and beckoned, and Tiri and I followed him along the cloisters to a narrow doorway. We went through into a dimly lit passage and so into an anteroom. The door in the opposite wall was just opening and the sound of voices floated through. In the anteroom half a dozen sturdy looking fellows stood up at once. They wore armor, were well-armed and looked useful. All wore a badge of a leaping zhantil.

From the inner portal emerged two men, their heads together talking intently. The audience might be finished; what was being said was clearly not settled. One man must be San Paynor, not at all unlike San Padria, with that same selfless devotion to what he believed in. The other was a young fellow with a fine open face, smooth pale hair, with that habitual turn to his mobile lips indicating he laughed a lot. He wore a shamlak of a blue color very similar to that I wore but with gold loops. He had a rapier and main gauche belted to his waist. I noticed that both weapons were fastened to the same belt.

What they were saying was drowned in the smash of the door at our backs and the hullabaloo that began immediately.

I swung about.

This young fellow's guards jumped to protect him, as I immediately placed myself before Tiri.

Three brown clad priests staggered back, their robes slashed, blood spattering them. The wooden staves in their trembling hands were pitifully useless against the might that stormed in.

A swarm of men roared into the room, brandishing weapons, their faces dark with the lust for blood. Each wore olive green.

At once the anteroom echoed to the sound of combat.

Ten

I, Dray Prescot, of two worlds, tend to use anything that comes to hand as a weapon. In my left hand Tiri's embroidered bag whistled around in a vicious arc and smashed into the side of the first would-be killer's head. What the young madam kept in that bag I didn't know. It weighed enough, by Krun. Clunk! The fellow went over sideways, yowling. I kicked him as he went down and in a swooping motion snatched the sword as it toppled from his lax fingers.

Talk about the flailing handbags of little old ladies! The mop heads would have been proud of me then, not a doubt of it.

The two Rapas following on the heels of the first jumped forward with every intention of spitting me and Tiri. A twirling twinkle of blades followed by a stop thrust took care of the first. I was fully conscious of the uproar all about us in the anteroom; that was pushed aside as information only. The second Rapa swung savagely and a sliding deflection of my borrowed brand left him open. I hit him precisely where neck joined head in a ruffle of yellowish feathers. He went down all right; but the confounded Krasny-work blade snapped with a mocking ping.

Tiri yelped: "Your back!" but I was already ducking and swinging around. The Brokelsh quite clearly thought he had me at a disadvantage. His black-haired face showed pleasure. I threw the sword hilt into that plug-ugly countenance and, instantly drawing the braxter taken from the victim of the ambush, put the uncouth Brokelsh out of the fight.

A swift glance showed me Tiri with her sword clutched in her fist flashing away at the lumbering Brokelsh on her side. For a single heartbeat I watched, studying, before hurling forward. She could handle a blade, that was clear.

As is the way with a scrappy sort of combat of this nature one must concentrate on what immediately threatens. At the same time one is generally aware of the trend of the proceedings. I suspect most soldiers keep this cautious weather-eye open to show them whether they should bravely fight on or run. In this instance the young lord's guards although surprised were battling back and the attackers were not having it all their own way. The young lord himself was dragging San Paynor back and the priest was struggling to break free of his grip.

My forward movement caught Tiri's Brokelsh totally unprepared and between us the dancing girl and myself knocked him down.

"Get over to the san, Tiri."

She said tartly: "Yes, that is best. And if you've broken my Besoulon I'll have your hide."

Apart from not knowing what a Besoulon was although understanding it must be something fragile in her bag, I could not help seeing the difference between her now and the girl I'd found on the road.

In the space our attacks had provided we pushed up beside the lord and the san. Paynor stopped struggling and said: "Tiri!" He sounded as though he did not know if he should be glad or sorry to see her.

"San! This is dreadful!"

"Oh, aye," said the young lord. "And you will help me take this wonderful but stubborn san to safety—now!"

Some of his guards were down and one staggered towards us with a spear through him. The rush of attackers that followed was most ugly and we had a quick bout of duck, parry and lunge or slash before we cleared our front. One overlarge Fristle charged towards us yelling for others to support him. His olive green clothes were liberally bedecked with tatty gold lace, his whiskery cat's face blazed with fury, and he slished and sliced a monstrous sword like a falchion about ready to lop heads.

The young nobleman wielded his rapier with some dexterity; but I saw he possessed none of the higher arts of skill in the usage of that exacting weapon. At least, he was not exhibiting them now.

A flung spear hurtled towards Tiri's head and in that same instant my sword flashed angling upward to deflect the deadly weapon. The Fristle's blade sliced down at my body. Tiri thrust her braxter at the catman from the side as I drew myself away. I felt a stinging pain down across my left hip. "Get on! Get on!" screamed the Fristle, his armor breaking the force of Tiri's thrust. "Get the blintzes!"

For that instant of confusion everything became distorted, vague, as though these events were happening to other people. The Hytak in command of the lord's guard shouted: "Away, notor! Hurry!"

By this time San Paynor had had enough. He started for the inner door calling to Tiri. She refused to move and I gave her a shove so that for a moment the young lord and I faced the mob together. Only for a moment, though. As the attackers surged forward, he snapped out: "Go through the door. I will cover you. Bratch!"

Now it is not my custom to obey those who yell 'Bratch!' at me, even though this young spark's intentions were highly honorable. Also, as you must be aware by now, Dray Prescot runs away from foes sometimes; but, I venture to think, does not do so very often if comrades are left. Oh, yes, I know...

So, puffed with stupid pride, I said: "Do you go first, dom."

In the same instant it was necessary to deflect another spear. Everything had taken place at breakneck speed. I turned my face on the lord and realized he was not a youngster after all, but a man matured into the earliest portion of his Kregish adult life. I snarled out: "Go, fambly!"

We were interrupted in what might have turned into an acrimonious discussion by having to skip and jump and fight off another attack. His guard commander reached us, cutting down a polsim on the way. "Notor!"

The lord said: "This is no time to pursue this further. But I—"

From the open doorway through which Tiri and the priest had gone a scream knifed clear through all the hubbub.

I was through the doorway and running down the passage and to hell with the niceties of who scuttled off from the enemy first. Two men were trying to kill Tiri and the priest and the temple dancer was whirling her sword about splendidly. San Paynor had screamed. Sensible fellow. I simply roared into them, these two apims, and took no chances.

Tiri panted out, a lock of hair falling across her forehead: "They came through the inner court."

A yell from the lordling drew my instant attention. He and his guard commander were hurtling through the doorway and along the passageway towards us. His face was contorted. "Go!" he yelled.

The thought, instantly rejected, occurred to me that we might have attempted to barricade that door. Muscle, weight and axes would quickly have smashed a way through. San Paynor was already scuttling off and Tiri and I followed, the lord and his henchman tailing on.

The inner court showed the angled light of the suns among small trees whose leaves glowed like lambent green coins. Their perfume formed an incongruous backdrop to the reek of blood that must surely stench this pleasant court out shortly. More men—apims—wearing the olive green were dropping from the left hand wall.

"They have worked this well," said Tiri in her tight little voice.

"Useful to know your way around this place," I said with considerable sarcasm. I made my voice irascible. "Tiri! You and the san! I don't know what these rasts want but if it's you and the san they're going to be unlucky, by Krun. San Paynor! Take Tiri off to safety—now!"

"But, Drajak—"

"Now!"

This direct appeal to the priest of Cymbaro to do something positive worked like a treat. He seemed to grow in stature. He took Tiri by the hand, saying: "Your friend is right, my dear. Come."

They hurried off towards the right under a colonnade of lemon-colored marble where vines heavy with fruit hung down gracefully. I, your rough tough uncouth fighting man par example, faced the foe ready to fight to the death to secure the safety of my friends. Oh, well, that is often the way of it on Kregen.

The affray flickered into existence with a few dead bodies tumbling about and blood spouting. The lord's guard commander was a good fighter, as one would expect from a Hytak, and we performed well. But press of numbers forced us back.

"D'you know the layout of this place?" I said to the Hytak during one of these pauses that occur in combats of this nature as each side draws breath for a fresh round.

"No, dom." He was wiping the blood off the blade strapped to his tail. "You're a bonny fighter. I am Chulgar ti Daster. I earn my hire and fight to the death for my master and—"

"And you chatter too much, Chulgar, my friend," broke in his master. Chulgar fell silent and went on wiping his tail blade. But I knew what he was about to say. Now the reckoning of pay and service was due.

"I'm Drajak. We need to find a way out of this mess. And if that means we run off—" Here I turned towards the lordling and bent my brows on him, giving him a most devilish look, "then we run off."

"I am not in the habit—" he began, very stiffly.

"Nor am I, dom," I choked him off. "But—" I paused. I'd been about to say: 'Since I've been on Kregen.' That wouldn't do. I said: "But I've lived long enough to learn when to fight and when to—ah—disengage, fall back and reform." Then I added in a softer voice the word for 'D'you understand?' that, harshly spoken, does upset people. "Dernun?"

He gave me a hard look, trying to meet my glare. Then he turned his head away, looking into the courtyard. So he was quite able to cover any discomfiture he might have felt by snapping out: "Here they come again, Cymbaro rot 'em."

A bunch of Rapas and polsims mixed up with the apims advanced cautiously towards us. A sound at our backs brought my head around to see brown clad priests emerging into the light of the suns. They carried weapons and moved purposefully; but I could place no great reliance on them as fighting men. Naturally, the young madam was with them.

Amid a deal of shouting the two sides met and it was all hack and thrust and skip and jump and the fight sprawled across the courtyard. Mind you, by Krun, I was determined to grab Tiri and run off as soon as the opportunity afforded. Just what these olive green clad ruffians wanted I did not, as I had said, know. But the quicker Tiri and myself were off out of it the better.

Things did not turn out quite as I expected. Well, that is the way of Kregen, as I should have learned by now.

The ugly Fristle with his damned great falchion was there, knocking over priests and yeowling like a maniac. He had a nasty great hairy wart to the larboard of his nose. For a moment in the melee we faced off; then he rushed off to the side towards some priests who were doing remarkably well. I charged after him, a swirl of the fight engulfed us and I was surrounded by olive green-clad killers.

The pain along my hip where that confounded whiskery cat-man had hit me had been pushed away in the needs of getting on with the fight. As I battled against half a dozen of them, doing my best not to get spitted, I understood what else had happened when the Fristle sliced me with his falchion.

Knocking down a Brokelsh and clearing a space I pulled back to rejoin the priests. I heard, sharp and distinct over the hullabaloo, a pinging sound. Something like a lasso locked my knees together and over I went, sprawling helplessly along the tiles. My legs pulled free and twice I rolled over and over to come up spitting with fury. The warty-faced Fristle let out a scream of triumph and leaped.

He did not leap on me. He scooped up an abandoned scabbarded sword, gripping the hilt. I understood. I roared up to hurl myself at him. He ripped Strom Korden's sword from the scabbard to face off against me, falchion in right hand, braxter in left. That hit on my hip, besides nicking me, had sliced far enough through the strom's swordbelt to snap it after my frantic exertions. He yelled again and, turning, ran nimbly off.

Other attackers were in the way. The fury I felt was all mixed up with annoyance at my own stupidity. The courtyard rang and echoed with the clang of steel. The olive green-clad bodies were all retiring, were pulling back, and into the courtyard raced more men, men in armor and not an olive-green shamlak or tunic in sight.

The newcomers had swarmed over the same wall the attackers had used. The fight banged and caromed away and Amak Dagert of Paylen, very suave, strolled up to me, wiping his rapier.

"Hai!" he said. "I fancy my debt is paid, my friend."

I said: "Doubtless." I picked up the empty scabbard and slung it over my shoulder. The strom's sword was going back in there, or I'd know the reason why. Then I recognized the foolish pomposity of the boast. "I am glad to see you, amak. Those blintzes were becoming pests."

"All pests go down to the Ice Floes of Sicce in Hanitcha's good time. Now, what brings you here?"

Palfrey the Pfiffer walked up then. His shortsword was suspiciously clean for a loyal retainer in a fight with his lord. "They all ran off, notor."

"Palfrey," I said, acknowledging him. Then: "As to my presence here, it was a matter of temple business."

Paylen wasn't interested in me. In a sharp hectoring voice he demanded: "They were followed?"

"Oh, aye, my lord." Palfrey sounded injured. "Nath the Iarvin and his party."

Dagert nodded. He finished wiping his rapier and thrust it away. Then, characteristically, he ran a delicate forefinger over that black pencil moustache.

I started to say: "They took something of mine—" when the sound of running footsteps, a rushing swirl of skirts and a breathless voice all added up to Tiri gasping out: "Thank Cymbaro! I thought it certain sure you'd be dead!"

She still clasped her sword and there was dark blood upon the blade. Rather dryly, I said: "I am glad to see you are still in one piece. The san and the young lord?"

"Safe. Thanks to—" Her gaze dwelled on Dagert.

Making the pappattu to introduce them I wondered, idly, if it were possible for a temple dancer to marry an amak. What if? It was no business of mine. I said to Tiri: "It seems you are not safe even here in the shrine."

Dagert said: "This young lord is safe?"

Tiri nodded. "Yes, notor."

All I was conscious of rested on two items. One, Tiri had to be carted off back to Nandisha's for her own protection. Two: I had to get off after Strom Korden's sword sharpish. Its loss rankled.

With the loud trample of iron-shod boots the courtyard abruptly came to life with a new act in this drama. Men in the panoply of armor, brightly attired, girded with weapons, their faces bronzed and hard, surrounded us. A hikdar stepped forward, very formal. He addressed me.

"You are Drajak known as the Sudden?" At my nod he went on: "You will place yourself at my disposal." To his men: "Bring him!"

Eleven

"Well, Drajak known as the Sudden, where is it? Hand it across immediately!"

I stood in a hall of parquetry, surrounded by armed guards of a most particularly impressive appearance, facing a tall throne in which sat a noble who could have my head off by a mere gesture of his little finger.

I was, as they say in Clishdrin, well and truly paddleless up that famous creek. The armed men had turned out to be a mixture of the City Guard and a certain noble's retinue. You could tell the difference by their badges and insigne. I'd been marched past the sumptuous architecture of Oxonium where the kaotreshes flew in the breeze. There had been no need for us to leave Grand Central, for the palace of the noble lay hard by that of the king. Between two towers, one on each of their outer walls, king and noble had a private cable car system, spanning the branch of the artificial moat that surrounded the royal palace. Indeed, I was in powerful company here.

The hikdar of the detail, Tygnam ti Fralen, went to give me a poke with the chape of his scabbard. The noble held up a hand.

"Give him time to answer, Hikdar Tygnam."

"Quidang, notor!"

I relaxed. This anxious hikdar had treated me perfectly correctly and fully prepared though I was to give him a crafty kick where it would do the most good, I had no pleasure in it. As for the problem of the moment, I could see no way around it. No way, at least, in which I might come off with a whole skin. The habitual use of authority in this place was marked by humanity. That I had deduced from what I'd seen and heard. All the same, failure would not be tolerated.

Of course, I could lie and deny ever having had the blasted thing. But that wouldn't square with what I saw as a sacred promise to Strom Korden. In addition, the lie would be immediately punctured by the information these people had of me, my name and deeds on the road.

Could I claim the assassins had made off with it? Don't, Dray Prescot, I said to myself, be childish. Tirivenswatha knew.

So, I stared full on this puissant lord, this Hyr Kov Brannomar.

In the middle part of life, I judged him, although that is always a difficult assessment on Kregen. There is on that planet this rather rare condition—if it be a disease the savants and doctors have not yet discovered or decided—in which a person's hair, instead of retaining its full color over most of the span of years, turns gray or white relatively early on in life. Kov Brannomar's hair was a silvery cap. His beard and moustache were silvery in color. With his bronzed powerful face, hard etched with command, with bright dark eyes and thin but mobile mouth, that silver poll gave him the formidable appearance of your true lord of the ages. The scar slanting down his left cheek, brilliant against his skin, added rather than subtracted from that aura of omnipotence.

"Kov," I spoke up. "Notor. The sword was taken in the affray in the Shrine of Cymbaro."

A little ripple of a sigh escaped the lips of the man who stood on the steps of the dais immediately below the throne.

Him, I felt instinctively, it would benefit me to watch. He must be the kov's chief adviser, a pallan with powers almost as autocratic as those of Brannomar himself. He wore robes as ruby red as those of his master, although more ornate, for Brannomar's rig was as austere as the man himself. As to his face, this posed an enigma to which, at the moment, I did not have the answer. Like the kov, he was apim; but the darkness of his features, although not the true and velvet black of a Xuntalese, must indicate some of that island people's proud blood flowed in his veins.

"What, Hikdar Tygnam, did you see in the Shrine of Cymbaro?" The words were soft yet unmistakably they carried the stamp of authority this man held under the hand of the kov.

"There was great confusion, Lord Jazipur," responded the hikdar at once. "When I saw this man Drajak the fighting had ended and he was talking to his companions."

Kov Brannomar leaned a little forward. "Tell me, Drajak."

So I told him. I ended: "This Fristle who took the sword can easily be identified. With your leave I will—"

Lord Jazipur said: "He will be among the runnels by now."

Speaking up boldly, for, after all, I was well aware I was arguing for my liberty, if not my life, I snapped out: "Then I will follow him there!"

The kov leaned back. One firm brown hand, without rings or jewelry, touched his chin. "Enquiries will be made. Yes, Drajak, known as the Sudden, I think you will go down into the runnels between the hills and find this man. And I think you will bring me back the sword."

He didn't say what might happen if I didn't. He didn't have to.

This decision on the kov's part did not really ease the tension in the situation. The guard stood alertly. A number of people, all dressed according to their rank and position, waited each side of the chamber. Tall windows shed that mellow Kregish opaline radiance upon us.

Then the kov said: "Why, Drajak, when you arrived in Oxonium, did you not bring the sword to me immediately?"

This was the question I'd anticipated and had not relished. There were other pressing questions he could ask, and no doubt would, now. The very importance of actually getting his hands on the sword had been the big question, driving the others to wait their turn. I spoke harshly.

"It was necessary for me to see a lady to the shrine."

"And that was more important? Your paramour?"

I was curt. "No."

He gave absolutely no response to my rudeness. Hikdar Tygnam spoke up. "My lord, there was a temple dancer there."

Silence ensued for a moment in which, no doubt, one was supposed to imagine all manner of awful retributions. The next question, also, was obvious. "What did Strom Korden say to you?"

"He was dying, in pain and was almost incoherent. He simply said that I should take the sword and take it to Hyr Kov Brannomar."

"That is all?"

"It was difficult to understand. I took him for a gallant gentleman and was sorry to see him in that condition. That was all."

"Take the sword and take it to Hyr Kov Brannomar?"

"Exactly."

"Strom Korden was a gallant gentleman. I mourn his loss. I hope I shall not have to mourn the loss of his sword."

"If it can be found, then I—"

"Do not boast," cut in Lord Jazipur. "Or promise what you may not accomplish." His ice cold eyes looked at me as though I was a fish on a slab. "Your head is on it."

Kov Brannomar's hand half lifted, and then fell back. Was that a reflexive gesture in protest? Now that his chief pallan had made the threat, the kov, too, would be bound by it. At least, so I guessed.

"You will send someone with him, Lord Jazipur?"

"Assuredly, my lord. One of my best men."

In a soft voice, Brannomar said: "Make it your best man, Lord Jazipur."

Jazipur didn't say 'Quidang!' but he might as well have done by the way his back shot up. I did not smile.

With that the audience was over. They wheeled me out.

As though released by a spring, people moved in the chamber, going about their business for the kov. By the door as we passed under the archway a knot of people moved aside for the guard still surrounding me with military precision. Among the clerks and functionaries a man dressed in a shamlak so dark it was black looked across.

He saw me. He started to laugh, so that great shining tears rolled down his fat red cheeks.

We marched out through the halls and corridors to the main gates.

Now what, by the pustular armpits of the Divine Lady of Belschutz, was Naghan Raerdu, Naghan the Barrel, doing in Oxonium?

Naghan was just about the best of my personal spy apparat. Some of the network had been passed over to my lad Drak when he'd become Emperor of Vallia. Some, like Naghan, I'd kept on my personal and secret payroll.

Well, now! By Vox, what a turn up! We marched out and there was a fresh spring in my step. Things were looking up.

Things were, indeed, looking up.

Tygnam was going to take me off to meet the folk detailed by Jazipur to keep an eye on me in the runnels between the hills. A man, very sure of himself, stepped up to the hikdar, halting our progress.

"Hikdar!" His voice cut like sharpened steel, yet there was that lazy careless tone to it. "I'd like a word with that man."

"Only for a moment, notor—"

Ignoring that, Dagert of Paylen walked up to me, casual, raffish, one hand on the hilt of his rapier.

"I hear you're going after that Fristle."

"That's right."

How he knew so quickly was easily explained by gold and people listening and going out before me. Intrigue is a fecund plant.

"Palfrey thinks he knows the feller."

"Indeed."

If he could play this cool casual game then so could I.

He stroked his moustache, and his eyes for a moment gleamed white as he glanced up at my face.

"I owe you a favor, my friend."

"Which I thought you had reclaimed."

"A mere trifle." He twirled his right hand gracefully in the air. "Palfrey and I—we'll go with you. Bit of fun. Do a spot of rabble chasing down in the runnels. Show 'em who's master."

A whole new dimension opened up about Dagert of Paylen. Oh, I do not mean because of his distasteful references to poor folk. Anyway, even that could be pretense. He wanted to go after Strom Korden's sword. I felt that strongly.

"Thank you. Done."

He nodded, nodded to the hikdar, and stalked off. He made no remark about the way I addressed him. Any nonsense of notor this and notor that between us had been ditched, and he'd simply let that happen. Why?

Why? He wanted that damned sword, that's why!

Twelve

Give them their due, they did not stint on me.

They furnished a slap up meal of local produce with a great variety of vegetables and fruit, and to drink a light local beer—or, at least, a brown fluid they called beer—rather flattish and with a miniscule head as though it had been watered. There were palines to follow.

We sat in the guardroom annex for the meal and later on as the suns were thinking of declining beyond the western hills Lord Jazipur's man entered.

Hikdar Tygnam greeted him cautiously, standing up to do so. I remained seated, enjoying the palines' juiciness and freshness after the meal.

The fellow was of that breed that can insinuate itself into the crannies of society and sniff out gossip and tidbits of valuable information. He wore a drab tan tunic and a three-quarter length cape thrown back. He did not wear a shamlak. He did wear three swords and a plethora of daggers. As to his face, he was apim, clean-shaven, and narrow as to feature, with deep lines running from the corners of his mouth to the sides of his chin. His hat was perfectly in character, being wide and floppily down-drooping. It did not sport a feather.

He gave his name as Naghan—Naghan the Ordsetter.

"My men are waiting outside. Let us get on with it."

There was genuine relief visible in Hikdar Tygnam that he did not have to venture down into the warrens between the hills.

He bade me a courteous remberee and we stepped outside into the haze of jade and ruby dusk. It had rained earlier and up here on Grand Central the air tasted sweet.

"Amak Dagert and his men have offered to assist us." This Naghan the Ordsetter possessed a strange squeaky voice. "He will be useful if his man knows the whereabouts of the Fristle."

There was no answer called for. Dagert of Paylen and Palfrey joined us with a group of men at the cable car terminus. We were headed north, to the hill known as Rondjas's Hill. Apart from Palfrey saying in a quick excited voice that from there we must go to the Hill of Sturgies, we were a silent party as we boarded the car. The wheels whispered along the cable and the breeze blew in from the open cabin windows. The other cars passed us, swaying gracefully in their looping arcs from hill to hill.

Lights were springing up everywhere all over the city. Their sparkles were much like fairy lanterns. As we swayed through thin air suspended by slender cables the very trance-like air of this enterprise forced itself on me most strongly.

A lifter swooped down, passing us closely and flew on towards Rondjas's

Hill. It showed only riding lights. The car began to climb the last looping curve of cable towards the terminus.

Whilst this structure was nowhere near as ornate as that upon Grand Central, it had its architectural charm. A small knot of people waited to board our car. We alighted and, in a bunch of dark cloaked men, walked swiftly across the kyro and along a broad avenue towards the northern terminus. Here we would board the calimer for the Hill of Sturgies.

Palfrey started to chatter and Dagert of Paylen snapped: "Quiet!"

The clouds had mostly blown away and the stars glittered, high. The next leg of the journey was a replica of the first. The cable car swayed through the nighted air and the lights of the city passed away each side, scattered and dim along the runnels far below.

The next landing stage looked deserted under a single string of lamps. The car touched the guide ramps and bumped to a standstill. The door opened and we stepped out, keeping in that tightly bunched formation.

Something loud went Bang! The first noise was followed by others. Instantly we were enveloped in a cloud of stinging, choking black smoke. Just before all vision clamped down I saw a ceramic jar come flying through the air and go smash onto the stone slabs, letting out a searing spurt of evil black smoke. At once all was confusion as men shouted and fanned their hands against the smoke. A body collided with me and I braced myself and whoever it was bounced.

A hand gripped my upper arm. About to turn intemperately and bash my attacker, I heard a breathy voice, hoarse with urgency, whisper in my ear: "Majister!" At once this was followed by: "Jis—this way!"

I knew that voice. I relaxed. Whatever was to happen now, best to let it happen and then reckon up the consequences later. The hand guided me unerringly through the smoke. The noise of men swearing and shouting receded. That damned smoke was truly pungent, getting right up the hooter. It spread to encompass the whole landing area.

My eyes were streaming tears that felt hot, by Krun. I was pulled, staggering, along and presently, although I could barely see for the water in my eyes, realized we were out of the landing area and out of that pestiferous smoke.

"Jis—you are unharmed?"

"Aye, Naghan, apart from my eyes which burn fiercer than the Furnace Fires of Inshurfraz."

"Better that than being parted from your head. This way."

Other bodies surrounded me as we ran along a street I sensed led around the lip of the hill, a narrower street, judging by the echoes. Not that there were many of them. These fellows wore soft shoes. Naghan Raerdu had seen me as a prisoner. Ergo, he had put in hand a plot to rescue me. This was nothing less than I would have expected from such a master spy.

What he would say when I explained the situation I could only guess at. I did know, by Vox, that he would laugh!

In no time at all we halted and I was guided up a set of wooden steps, told to duck my head, and then seated in a padded chair. My vision remained blurred. Men were talking quietly some way off, in another room, I judged. Naghan said: "There is an ointment, jis; but the wizard said it is better to allow the eyes to recover naturally."

"How long?"

"A bur, maximum. We have masks with eyepieces that allow us to see and filters that allow us to breathe. Useless to put one over your face once the smoke was out of the pots. It would have merely trapped the smoke against your face." He let a low laugh rumble up from his belly. "Those cramphs coughed their lungs up! The gold was well spent on the mage."

I felt a familiar movement under me, a feeling of pressure and then of lightness. "This is the voller that passed the cable car?"

"Aye, jis. We've had an eye on you ever since I saw you in Kov Brannomar's hall."

"And who's the we?"

"Oh, a few of my Vallian fellows and some locals. I've set up a network in Oxonium. The locals are a strange lot. The wizards are not like the sorcerers at home. And the blood feuds and vendettas festering among the poor folk in the valleys are staggering. It is not easy to organize from one runnel to another between the hills."

"D'you know of a gang who wear olive green?"

"No, jis. I'll ask."

"That can wait for my eyes. There are other questions."

"Oh, yes. Tolindrin has been seeking an alliance with Vallia. They're in a peculiar position regarding the production of airboats, as are their neighbors to the north, Caneldrin and beyond them, Winlan and Enderlin. The other nations of the sub-continent are more client kingdoms than anything else. There is constant friction on all the frontiers—it's a way of life. But if all-out war erupts—who does Vallia consider? The Empress Delia considered it appropriate that Vallia should know more."

I admired his primness in thus talking of his mission. But how sweetly the sound of Delia's name fell on my ears! By Zair! Yes.

I said: "And the empress?"

"Blooming as the rose the last time I saw her, jis. Your eyes—?"

"Smarting like the devil. Is there a drink—?"

Almost before the words were out of my mouth a goblet was at my lips and a tartish wine sparked up my tongue. It was just the drink to clear my mouth of the stinking taste of that damned magical smoke.

Naghan the Barrel went on: "It is still necessary for us to buy airboats from one country or the other in Persinia and Balintol. If we judge wrongly in this, bang go our supplies. Now the old king's son is dead here in Tolindrin the choice of a successor becomes of vital importance." He let rip one of his tear-jerking wheezing laughs that made him shake all over. "May I ask, jis, what brings you here?"

So I told him about Strom Korden's charge to me. I added that I was bound to protect Princess Nandisha, although I did not tell him why. I finished: "That cramph of a Fristle has the sword. I now believe this fellow Dagert of Paylen is after it. I am determined to honor my pledge to Korden and take the confounded thing to Brannomar."

"Dagert of Paylen? A strange one, that. No one knows who he is working for; but it is certain sure someone pays him."

"Now you understand, Naghan, why I must somehow work my way back to the party with Naghan the Ordsetter and Dagert. That unhanged rogue Palfrey says he knows the Fristle."

"I can arrange that. Also, it seems sure that the sword contains something of value, if it is merely a common braxter."

"Aye. A hollow handle and a few lead weights to balance the feel."

"A paper, then?"

"More than likely. It could be a ring, any trifle of jewelry."

"Then it must be of great value, have significance of authority, be a religious symbol—or it is magical."

"Aye."

"H'm." I could imagine his scheming brain turning wheels. "Then it will be worthwhile taking a look first."

I moved uneasily in the chair. Slowly, I said: "Yes. But I feel that to be unethical after my promise to Korden."

"As you say, majister. Unethical."

There was no mistaking good, loyal Naghan the Barrel's feelings.

Items of the lifter's cabin were becoming clearer and the sting was ebbing from my abused eyes. Naghan wiped my face. He said: "I'll find out about this falchion-wielding Fristle in the olive green."

"He has an Opaz-forsaken hairy wart alongside his nose."

"He might as well shout who he is from the rooftops."

"The Hill of Sturgies. That's where Palfrey was headed."

"A moment only, jis. Here is more wine."

He was gone for the time I could take three leisurely sips. "One of the locals, Lingurd, a narrow-faced polsim, knows. We're headed there."

"I'll have to rejoin alone, Naghan."

"Oh, aye, jis. But we'll be around."

And, I own, by Krun, that was comforting!

On a thought, I asked: "Who's consul in Oxonium now?"

"A fine smart gentleman, by Vox! Elten Larghos Invordun na Thothsturboin. He's a high flyer, and no mistake."

Larghos Invordun, I remembered, had won his title of Elten at the Battle of Vendalume when we'd fought the perfidious Layco Jhansi. Since that fateful day he'd gone into the diplomatic service. One day he would become a fully-fledged ambassador. He was a career man now.

I nodded. "Well, no need to let him know I'm here."

"As you say, jis."

Out of the haze of darkness surrounding me the fat red friendly face of Naghan the Barrel swam, as it were, like a fish in a tank before my eyes. I blinked and felt the tears run and Naghan wiped them away.

"Now, jis, names. Are you Jak the Something? Chaadur?"

"Drajak the Sudden."

"Very good, Drajak."

With some feeling I said: "By Vox, Naghan, it was a damned lucky co-incidence you happened to be there in Brannomar's hall just then."

"Co-incidence, Drajak? Hardly. I haunt the places of power. Brannomar is the most powerful man in the kingdom after the old king. He holds the reins. He is utterly incorruptible. His wealth is fabulous."

"So if the old king were to die this Brannomar the Incorruptible might strike for the crown?"

Naghan's rubicund face, floating like a balloon before me, swayed from side to side as he shook his head. "No, Drajak, not in a million of the months of She of the Veils. He would abide by the old king's wishes as to the successor. It could be Brannomar would become regent. In that case there is no doubt whatsoever he would hold the authority in sacred trust and relinquish power when the new king came of age. No doubt at all."

"You confirm what I read in him. A trifle cold, though. Austere."

My spymaster's laugh bubbled up like the volcano of Muruaa. "I have enjoyed his companionship in a shbilliding that gave even me an echo of Beng Kishi's Bells between my ears."

"I am relieved to hear it. It makes him a whole man."

We talked more then as my eyes cleared, questions and answers and information exchanged. Naghan gave me one piece of news that saddened me.

Won Dimeholl, who was famous for his knowledge of illuminated scrolls and manuscripts, had a great interest in antiquities; his greatest fervor was for books of prophecy and prediction. He had been attacked many times but had always resisted stoutly. Now, at last, he had succumbed, and was gone from our lives. His loss distressed me grievously and I could only take what comfort there is in knowing he would have said get on with life. He was dead; we had to get on with life. Naghan's face showed in its down-drawn grimness a reflection of the sorrow at his passing that all who had known Won Dimeholl felt.

After a moment Naghan spoke up more forcefully than perhaps he intended. "Y'know—Drajak—you're running a pretty desperate risk."

He was accustomed to the odd idea that the man he had known as the Emperor of Vallia could be found turning up at different parts of Kregen engaged in skullduggery. He accepted the same behavior in the man supposed to be the Emperor of Emperors, the Emperor of Paz. Although, by Zair, that was a mere joke at the moment, despite its fulfillment being ordained by the Star Lords. As a masterspy, Naghan the Barrel was steeped in skullduggery, disguise and subterfuge. He knew I was, too.

"The Empress Delia asked you to come out here, Naghan. But what about the official spy network of Vallia run by Naghan Vanki? Has the Emperor Drak organized anything there?"

"Yes. Vanki sent the Voidal twins."

"Oh, well, I expect Drak and Vanki will sort something out."

"The Voidals have been concentrating on the old king. He is officially in mourning and no one has seen him for days. By the way, the Voidal twins, and Vanki for that matter, do not know I am here."

I found my lips moving in a smile. "They don't even know of your existence!"

"Pray Opaz that is the way it remains."

One other question I asked before, with Lingurd in the lead, we moved off into our night's adventure.

"This Dokerty religion, in opposition to Tolaar. Red robed priests two by two and damned great idols on poles. Is anything known? Why should they skulk about at night in ruins when they have tasteless and over-imposing temples to prance around in?"

He rolled his bulky shoulders. "The Dokerty cultists are an unwholesome lot. I do know that. As to the rest, no, nothing is known. I'll find out."

"Good."

I washed my face before we moved off and the bowl when I'd finished looked like black ink. Naghan had wiped my old beakhead once or twice during our conversation. During all that time he must have been busting a gut to laugh his incredible laugh at my appearance.

The lifter touched down on a darkened slope of rubble leading from the Hill of Sturgies. A short distance away dim lights tried to pierce the runnels with wan illumination. Clouds obscured the moons. We hitched up our weapons and descended into the darkness.

Thirteen

Torchlights flared smokily here and there along the narrow street between wooden and brick buildings which shared a common rundown appearance. What went on behind those ramshackle walls was best not dwelled on too long. People moved along the muddy way trying to steer a path between the filthy gutter in the center and the sides where any kind of evil fluids might be emptied upon their heads. As Lingurd the polsim and I moved deeper into the runnel between the hills, the torchlights grew in number and doors stood open, revealing mysterious interiors, filled with subdued lighting and shifting shadows.

"They call them taverns," said Lingurd, his thin polsim face twisted in contempt. "Traps for the gullible. Dopa dens. Head crunchers."

"Patronized, though," I observed, for dark-cloaked figures moved in and out constantly. More than one poor wretch was thrown out to land on his nose in the gutter this early in the evening's entertainment.

We moved on together. "Unwholesome, they are. Yet the young lords and the bloods venture down here for excitement." Lingurd's attitude conveyed exactly his feelings. "They find it, Tolaar knows."

This place down between the lofting hills pulsed with its own dark life. At almost every corner booths with ramshackle awnings offered all manner of commodities, tidbits of food, hot drinks, roasted nuts, trashy jewelry, fortune tellers with facile stories for the guileless, young lads importuning the passersby with delectable delights to be found in dubious dark alleys and hovels. Impoverished, desperate for the next bite, rogues all, yes, these folk were all that. But down in the runnels life pumped red and raw and uninhibited.

Our drab cloaks and floppy hats blended perfectly with the surroundings. We picked our way along, avoiding cutpurse and pickpocket and the attentions of those who wished to deprive us of money—and life, if necessary—in other less obvious ways.

Lingurd said: "I grew up not far from here. The gangs' territories have changed; but we're safe up to The Brass Lily."

One could imagine only too readily the gang fights over territory with its various incomes of devious and unlawful nature. The polsim went on: "The Lord Nath Shivenham has treated me well and I am glad to work for him." He referred, of course, to Naghan Raerdu. Naghan the Barrel, like me, was too canny to use his real name on desperate ventures like this.

Shortly thereafter we reached a building of somewhat greater pretensions than its neighbors where many torchlights threw their wavering orange light across the muddy street and stained walls. Over the door a glinting brass representation of a lily told the name of the establishment.

"Round the back," I said, brooking no argument.

We cut down the side alley, our shoes squelching in mud and pools of water from the recent rain. Refuse lay piled here and there. The smells had not yet resurfaced in force from the cleansing showers.

Give Lingurd the polsim his due. Of course, he had lived here and knew well what to expect. He caught my arm and drew me into the shadows of a projecting buttress. "Quiet, dom."

Instantly, I stilled. I heard the tramp of iron shod boots along the main street and had no need to be told to keep still. I watched.

With lamplights held high on metal-bound poles casting flickering illumination all about them, they passed the mouth of the alley. I knew their type. Rough, bearded, clad in a semblance of uniform and armor taken from their victims, they strutted along. Their weapons were bared and glittered ominously. They were representatives of many of the races of diffs of Kregen. In the lead marched a Kataki, bulky and ferocious, the dagger blade strapped to his tail flaunting high. Damned Katakis, I said, under my breath.

"Aye, dom," whispered Lingurd. We waited until the band had gone. Lingurd wiped a hand down his face. "They're bad news. And they have the authority, that's the pity of it."

"Authority? A Tolaar-forsaken bunch of slavers?"

"Oh, no, dom. Rather, yes, they deal in slaves. They're the Watch—"

"The Watch!" I was astounded. Katakis rarely take up any job other than slaving when they go abroad. "You mean the king has appointed that mob of masichieri—stinking bandits who call themselves mercenaries—as the Watch, to keep order down here?"

"That's right. He appointed Trako Ironbelly as Captain of the City Watch. A blintz of a Whiptail. Down here, in the runnels between the hills."

"And that indicates the regard the people on the hill have for the law and order they impose here. By Chozputz! It stinks!"

The contrast between the City Watch down here, composed of the lowest dregs of so-called military men and officered by Katakis, and the smart and resplendent City Guard on the hills was painful.

"In here, dom." Lingurd indicated a narrow doorway. "You wait." He was gone, silently, along the corridor and around the far corner. Perforce, I waited, hand on my sword hilt. When he came back his sharp-featured polsim face bore a smile. "I looked in the tavern's main room. They're all there, the ones we took you from in the sorcerer's smoke. They're waiting, pretending to be young bloods out for fun."

"And the Fristle?"

"Fonnell the Fractious is as cunning as a leem. He has a private snug at the back of the premises."

"I just hope he's still around. If he's parted with the item already I'm in more trouble than I am now." I could guess the way of it. After my disappearance Dagert of Paylen and the others, recovering, must have decided their best course was to come on to The Brass Lily. Palfrey knew the Fristle, Fonnell; none of them knew what the sword looked like. They were waiting for me to turn up, I suspected, as a forlorn hope. Failing that, Dagert would have Palfrey point out Fonnell and then they would question him. That would be a risky course of action, given the circumstances that the Fristle was on his home ground and surrounded by his olive-green clad cronies.

"If Fonnell's here, he'll be in his snug."

"Lead on."

We went cautiously along the passage and turned the other way from the main room of the tavern. Lamps burned low. Closed doors either side hinted at unlawful goings on inside. We padded on. At the end a door led onto a courtyard across which a brick building showed lights at narrow windows. "That's it." Lingurd wet his lips.

Silently we crept across the courtyard. A woman laughed shrilly in the night. Up against a window we cautiously peered within.

The room was well lit and comfortably furnished. The warty-faced Fristle sat at a table. On the table rested Strom Korden's sword. I let out a silent sigh of relief.

Whoever he was working for had not yet arrived to take the trophy. Then a voice spoke from inside the room beside the window and I realized I was wrong. "You have done well, Fonnell. Now it is time for payment."

A man moved into my view. His back was turned towards me and he stepped with sinuous grace towards the Fristle who reached across the table for a goblet. Fonnell lifted the goblet and the second man thrust him clean through. He used a rapier. He used it with a skill I recognized.

Swiftly, the man bent and snatched up Korden's naked sword.

Softly, I whispered to Lingurd: "That is the item."

Lingurd was no more moved by that sudden treacherous murder than was I. "He's almighty quick with that rapier of his."

"Yes." Well, he would be. I knew his type although, when he turned in the lamplight to leave the room by the door to the side, I did not know him. His like were to be found strutting the avenues and canal-side walks in Zenicce. He was your proper Bravo Fighter. A rapier and dagger man of exemplary skill, cunning and delicacy. He could spit you like a chicken, turn a fine phrase, and exquisitely wipe his blade clean on a shiningly white lace kerchief. Oh, yes, I sized him up. I did not know his House for on his pale gray clothes he wore no colors to distinguish him.

Whoever had employed Fonnell the Fractious to take the sword employed also, at a much higher level, this Bravo Fighter. There would be no traces left. Korden's sword had to be the key to a puzzle. Only—I didn't know what that puzzle could be.

The door made only the slightest of noise as the Bravo Fighter stepped out into the courtyard. In the next instant he took a single step forward and stopped, snatched upright before he fell by the dagger protruding from his eye. Lingurd said: "But not as quick as my dagger."

There was no use berating the polsim. He had seen the situation and reacted. The man from Zenicce would not now be able to tell me what I wanted to know. Swiftly I ran forward and scooped up Korden's sword.

About to consider the night's work just about over I turned away. Then I stopped. "Here," I snapped, handing the sword to Lingurd. "Hold this a moment and don't lose it." I bent to the dead man.

He wore his weapons, the Jiktar and the Hikdar, on separate belts as is proper for a rapier and main gauche man. Rapidly I unbuckled the belts and strapped them about my waist, hauling them up, for he had the beginnings of a bulge. Maybe he was growing too fat and slow for Zenicce and like many another before him had sought employment and wealth in foreign lands.

As I straightened up a tremendous racket burst out from the tavern. Yells and screams and the clash of weapons spoke eloquently of a rip-roaring fight going on in The Brass Lily. Women were screaming. A double-door a few paces along the wall from the door Lingurd and I had used broke open. A woman ran through, her hands clutched in the air, screaming and screaming. Her petticoats dragged around her waist. Following her two men ran, laughing and taunting, out for a spot of fun that had gone sour.

Lingurd called: "Dom — the Watch!"

I heard yet I didn't hear. Yes, I should not have done it. I freely admit I committed a grievous error. The woman had blood on her face, bright in the lamplight from the open door beside us. What else could I, Dray Prescot, onker of onkers, do?

I leaped forward.

The woman saw me and shrieked. Clearly in me she saw another attacker. She stumbled away, almost falling, staggering into the far side wall. The two men howled in triumph and I ran towards the woman.

She vanished. One moment she was there, the next she was gone, dropping into the ground.

And so I, Dray Prescot, like any zany coy, tumbled headlong and crashed down past the flapping trapdoors of the cellar, went head over heels into the hard stone floor beneath.

The only things in the world of Kregen were the black wings of Notor Zan enfolding me in his dark embrace.

Fourteen

Only four prisoners died of their injuries during the night and in the morning the gaolers dragged the bodies out with iron hooks.

Many of the rest of us were in bad case and all night the prison guards shouted at us miserable scum of the gutters to keep quiet. The place was much like an undercroft, low of arched roof, spacious and separated by massive hunched pillars. What little straw there was stank damply and verminously. I'd found a stone wall against which I propped my back and nursed my head where not only all the Bells of Beng Kishi persisted in ringing but Jen Jorah's ice drills pierced pitilessly from temple to temple.

Along with the other miscreants, drunks, petty thieves, and brawlers dredged from the gutters of the runnels of Oxonium I waited for my doom to be pronounced by whatever lord held my fate in his hands.

The last thing I remembered hearing was Lingurd yelling: "Dom—the Watch!"

Their acquaintance I had made. I still had a bruise or two to testify to that introduction. All my weapons and gear were gone. The dark blue shamlak I'd been given was, very very luckily, made from a cotton stuff and not silk. This part of Kregen is world famous for its silk. There were few silk garments in the prison, and those were hand-me-downs on the last frayed thread before being discarded. There was nothing, really, to mark me as being any different from any of the other fifty or so miserable wights arrested during the night. Tunics predominated over shamlaks; that was all, apart from short breeches-like nether garments in place of kilts.

Broken-down slaves brought us a meal that might laughingly be called the first breakfast. A cracked pottery bowl of water with half-a-dozen unidentifiable lumps floating in the greasy liquid, and a hunk of bread that demanded a hacksaw to address, comprised our repast. Still, always look on the bright side. Even under the Kataki-run City Watch we had been fed. There were no women in the prison. I'd kept myself to myself, nursing my bruises and my aching head, and pondering the best way of breaking out.

After the pottery bowls had been collected by the tame slaves the iron bars clashed open once more. A Kataki entered, whip coiling and curling and looking for targets. He was backed up by a formidable collection of so-called City Guards, unshaven, grimy, flamboyantly dressed with a deal of tatty embroidery and lace. The prisoners scrambled away, some on all fours, some gibbering in fear, all dreadfully aware of the doom that awaited them.

A most incongruous note was struck by the young, naive Relt stylor with them. He wore a clean white shamlak and kilt, with the belt of pouches containing the quills and ink and papers of his profession. His pointy-beaked face and his bright eyes were quite at variance with the horrors of this place. He kept putting a scented handkerchief to his beak.

"The Brass Lily?" growled the Kataki. "We'll soon sort them for you, stylor."

The guards moved in among us, ungently. They knew who their captives were and where they'd been picked up. I was hauled out with a dozen or so men and pushed and shoved into a double rank. The whip cracked.

"Grak!"

A visible shudder rippled through the prisoners at this hated word.

We grakked and stumbled along and as the whips whistled I took a couple of cuts. This was not the time or place to make a break. If we were being taken out of this dolorous dungeon then a time would come.

Among the men marched off along with me I saw not one wearing olive green. That would easily be explained in the gutter politics of the runnels; no doubt the City Watch had arrangements with certain gangs. I saw no one from the party with Dagert of Paylen or of Brannomar's men with Naghan the Ordsetter. These poor wights had been the patrons of The Brass Lily and had been swept up in the chaos of the fight when the City Guard swooped. And—I'd been scooped up with them.

Lingurd the polsim was not here. I just had to trust he'd had the sense to take Korden's sword straight to Naghan the Barrel.

Up we went along stone steps and corridors and archways and iron-barred gates. Prisons are like prisons. The stylor kept well ahead. Some of the stinks faded the higher we went and the air freshened.

In what was probably the charge room, formalities were concluded, the stylor signed for us, and we were placed under the charge of a guard of an altogether different description. These fellows of a variety of races of diffs wore half-armor with a deal of black and red trimmings. Their weapons were workmanlike and they marched like men who had once been soldiers before being taken on as some lord's personal guard. At their head a Deldar with a stomach and many feathers kept up the pace. We stumbled along between the ranks of guards. They took no chances with us.

The prison doorway in a long featureless gray wall led onto a kyro. Some of the passersby turned to stare at us; most ignored the unpleasant sight. We were crammed into a cable car a batch with guards at a time and transferred across two further hills. At least the sensation of swinging through the air and feeling the scented breeze came as a relief after the stenches of the dungeon. On the final hill we were gathered up and marched rapidly along broad avenues and under a low archway into a courtyard. This was the back entrance to a splendid palace. Through corridors of increasing splendor we stumbled and marched, checked by even more ornately dressed guards at various doors, ushered through until we entered a sizeable hall where the streaming mingled lights of the early morning suns fell athwart gilding and marble and tapestries. This, then, was where whatever was to happen would take place.

We were herded into the central space where we stood, shuffling our feet and gawping about. A dais in front supported the type of throne-like chair I'd seen occupied by Brannomar, backed by deep plum-colored drapes. Presently a party of servitors came in carrying sacks which they emptied onto a side table. A wonderful collection of wicked weaponry was displayed, an arsenal of muggery and mayhem. Among the coshes and daggers and swords I spotted the rapier and dagger I'd taken from the Bravo Fighter, alongside the braxter. They, then, were evidence.

As a matter of simple common sense I'd given my name as Nalgre the Unster. If Princess Nandisha wanted to repeat her trick of getting me out of gaol then Fweygo or Tiri would quickly ascertain the truth. So, among a miserable mob of miscreants, I, Nalgre the Unster, waited.

Next to me a shambling and untidy gauffrer looking rather like a pile of sweep's brooms trembled with uncontrolled fear. His eyes rolled whitely. "Khon the Mak," he mumbled. "He is death itself. Mak Khon."

Just how much religion there might be in this unholy crew I didn't know; but the next fellow, a Gon whose shaven head glistened in the lights, only slightly bristled from the night's growth, said: "Tolaar save us now."

He entered without a fanfare of trumpets although the instinctive reaction was that that would have been appropriate. He advanced after his retinue had positioned themselves about the dais and seated himself in the throne. So I looked at him. Well, now. If these whole proceedings resembled those in Hyr Kov Brannomar's palace, why, of course, they would. Great nobles live in palaces and sit in thrones and hire retainers to be at their beck and call. Also, with their own powers within the current laws, they are quite capable of lopping off the heads of rogues like my unfortunate companions and myself. In fact, many of them quite enjoy giving that grim order.

He was apim, with a face pale like death itself. His hair was very dark, blue-black like, as they say in Clishdrin, a raven's wing. His clothes were black with a little gold lace and red trimmings. He wore a deal of jewelry with fingers crusted with heavy rings. There was armor under the ornate if somber robes. His eyes pierced and he knew how to put an expression of implacable resolve on those pallid features. Oh, yes, he was impressive in that evil showy way, was Hyr Kov Khonstanton.

The Hyr Kovs of Kregen—the nearest terrestrial term is High Duke—are given the Hyr, as I have said, usually because they have that distinction of nobility or run a kovnate partitioned between different races. In Mak Khon's case the additional meaning applied, like the arch dukes of Austria-Hungary, betokening his blood relationship to the royal house.

This was one of the fellows Fweygo had warned me of, very possibly in contention for the inheritance to the throne of Tolindrin.

Had he, then, employed Fonnell's olive-green clad gang?

He brooded on us miserable wights, a beringed hand supporting his white chin. His lips were thin and almost bloodless. I must confess I was at once repelled by his appearance and manner. Mind you, that could have been because I found myself in the position I was in, by Krun, yes!

A fat black and red swathed major-domo banged his golden-banded staff on the carpeted stone flags. "Shastum! Silence!" His words came out all mealy-mouthed. Sweat glittered on his cheeks and forehead. "Which one of you is called Drajak known as the Sudden?"

The prisoners craned their heads about, looking at one another, silent, wondering who the condemned might be. I stood still.

"Speak up or it will go ill for you."

I, Dray Prescot, Lord of Strombor and Krozair of Zy, known as Drajak the Sudden and presently as Nalgre the Unster, said not a word.

Mind you, I could see all manner of unpleasant eventualities, and I was not at all impressed by this situation, not one slightest bit, by Zair!

It was perfectly clear they did not know what I or Korden's sword looked like and they were far too canny to dismantle the lot for fear of destroying what they were after. They'd find a way of discovering the truth. That way could be exceedingly painful and unpleasant.

A word from Khonstanton and a sharp command from the Hikdar saw half the guards unlimber their crossbows. They spanned them with the firm positive movements of men who knew what they were doing. The major-domo, sweating, organized the prisoners into a single file. One by one under the threat of the crossbows we approached the table to select our own weapons.

Among the coshes and blackjacks lay a number of swords of various descriptions—everyone had a dagger, of course. Two other pairs of rapiers and main gauches besides the pair I had filched indicated that I had a chance to get away with them alone. One pair was acknowledged by a tall gangling Rapa who looked ill at ease, and the other by an apim who had a dejected look about him, both attitudes I surmised being over and above everyone's normal apprehension of Mak Khon.

When it was my turn I picked up the Jiktar and the Hikdar and turned away from the table.

So, at the end, my braxter lay in lonely splendor.

The major-domo started to shout but Khonstanton waved him to silence. His parchment-like face cracked into a meaningful smile.

"It would seem," he said in his thin voice, "we have our sword."

Get on with it, sunshine, I thought to myself, and bad cess to you.

Of one thing there could be no doubt. Khonstanton had been quicker off the mark than Brannomar and had used his authority to have the prisoners transferred from the care of the City Watch to his own charge. There seemed no doubt, also, there would be bitter enmity between the two. That I sensed in the characters of the two men as I had observed the pair.

The major-domo was called up to the throne and a gaunt, gray-faced individual carrying a staff carved with runes and wearing flowing robes of rusty black garnished with red symbols joined them. The three put their heads together and spoke inaudibly. We all waited.

The gauffrer, who had taken a nasty-looking blackjack, shivered. Of course, we had not been allowed to keep the weapons we had chosen; they had been returned to the other end of the table far away from my lonely braxter. The crossbows did not waver, trained on us.

Presently the Hikdar received his orders and we were all marched off. The visible signs of terror were slow to part from the prisoners.

"Khon the Mak's as bad as a Kataki," said the gauffrer.

"Worse," growled the Gon.

The menace hanging over us had not passed. All my companions regarded us as lost men. Mak Khon or the Kataki run City Watch, either way we were doomed.

Carefully though I looked at the people gathered in Khonstanton's hall there was no sign of a fat friendly face with a blob of gristle for a nose and with tears squeezing from under closed eyelids as a gut-wrenching laugh erupted. Naghan the Barrel must be quietly going frantic at my disappearance. I could rely on him implicitly; could I rely on him to rescue me once again?

Along splendid corridors and down stairs and so into lesser passageways we were marched. Khonstanton's dungeons were dungeons; as you know I have had considerable experience of a variety of chundrogs on Kregen and no doubt the future holds further instruction, so I just slumped in a corner, and tried to think. The gauffrer, Nath the Solarkey, and the Gon, Nath the Nose, wanted to chatter on in their fear. I rolled over and let them get on with it and shortly thereafter the guards stamped in, brave and bold in their black and red, armed and armored. Lanterns threw long shards of light into the dungeon. The miserable wretches clawed up, white of eye and shaking of lip, staring in awful fascination at the guards. We all awaited our fate.

A man was dragged up between the guards and hauled upright. He looked ghastly. He'd been hauled along into the cell and now he was forced to stare at us prisoners in the light of the lanterns. He wore an open-necked white shirt and blue trousers. Both garments were liberally spattered with blood. Blood stained his face and was already seeping through the bandage around his head. His eyes were mere black smudges. He shook.

Even then, even then, with the guard's hands under his armpits, he tried to pass a trembling finger along his thin black moustache.

"Well, blintz?" growled out the Deldar. "Which one of the vermin is it?"

And so Dagert of Paylen pointed one shaking finger directly at me.

"Him."

Fifteen

The bully boy guards marched us off and they were not particularly gentle with us, not at all, by Krun. Dagert and I were dragged into a small square room with a single tiny window high up, and tied down with bristly ropes in chairs that were clamped to the floor. Neither of us spoke a word.

The room contained another chair, this one with a cushion, and a table along the side wall. Four lanterns burned. One of them needed to be trimmed and gave off a thin trail of black smoke. The guards waited.

He strutted in, this Khon the Mak, very brisk and businesslike. A couple of his retainers brought in two rapiers, two main gauches and the bits and pieces of a braxter. These exhibits were placed on the table. Khonstanton sat on the cushioned chair and regarded us balefully, one hand supporting that sharp, pale chin.

"I do not need," he said when he fancied his silence had cowed us enough, "to remind you that you are dead men. Unless, of course," he waved his other beringed hand negligently, "you tell me."

"I know only that this is the man." Dagert's voice sounded painful in the small room. "I own my shame that—"

"Yes, yes, amak. We share your regrets. You—" His eyes were not unlike two currants in a bun. "You tell me."

I looked at the table. They'd taken the braxter to pieces. They'd dismantled it, blade, quillons, hilt, bindings, the lot. I said: "I know nothing of the sword." There was little more I could say. I was not looking forward to my immediate future, I can tell you, no, by Krun!

Khonstanton stood up. "I am a busy man. I shall leave you two here to think about your situation. When I return I shall expect answers." With that he nodded to the guards. They all went out and left us alone.

"My dear feller. I'm sorry. How can I express it—?"

"Don't try. Pain loosens lips."

"Yes; but by Havil the Green! Oh, Hanitcha take the yetches!"

He winced as he spoke. Red dripped from under the bandage around his forehead and trickled down his cheeks and so fell, drop by drop, onto the wreck of his white shirt.

"I am an amak and so they hauled me out. But I was hit on the head, as you see. Where the devil that rogue Palfrey got himself to only Hito the Hunter knows."

There was no reply I cared to give to that.

Dagert licked his lips. "You'd think they'd give us something to drink. But, oh no! Kov Khonstanton is a hard man, my friend. We are in bad case here. If I knew about this Malahak-given sword I'd speak up. Hanitcha take it, I would!"

I wondered how long it would take him to get around to asking me how

I'd found my way to The Brass Lily. I'd have to invent some fancy tale. He did not ask that or any other of the questions he might have been expected to ask. Instead he kept blaspheming against Khonstanton and his pack of cronies, laying his tongue most roughly against them. A clicking, brittle snapping sounded from the locked door.

The door slowly opened. It did not crash back on its hinges. A round, snub-nosed face topped with a shock of untidy straw-yellow hair poked around the jamb.

"Notor!"

"Palfrey, you hulu! Get in fast and shut the door!"

Dagert's manservant sidled in, almost gliding. He held a lockpick in his fingers and his face, with that twisted mouth, expressed great fear. "The guard outside—I had to—I did not kill him, but—"

"Well, before that, you rogue, unfasten these ropes."

The lockpick vanished and a dagger appeared and slashed and the ropes fell away. Palfrey eyed me.

"Get on with it, you onker!" Dagert rubbed his wrists.

When I was free and swinging my arms about my first thought was to repossess the rapier and dagger. Dagert took up his. He gave me a shrewd stare. "Not your weapons, I think, my friend."

"No. They came to me by way of a flung dagger."

"Ah! Well, let us depart. Palfrey!"

"Yes, yes, notor."

Palfrey scuttled for the door. I picked up the dismantled parts of the braxter hilt. Dagert looked startled.

"That is—?"

"No," I told him. "But if that rast Khonstanton believes these bits and pieces contain whatever secret he is after—well, that may give him something to think on."

"Ha!" exclaimed Dagert of Paylen. "I like your style."

Outside a guard slumbered peacefully. I bent and took off his belt and sword. It was a munitions quality braxter.

"Yes." Dagert nodded knowingly. "That is more your weapon. The Jiktar and the Hikdar are hard taskmasters in learning the arts of rapier and dagger work. Years to grasp the higher points."

Without replying I set off along the corridor perfectly prepared to spit any guards who got in the way with braxter, rapier or dagger. I glanced back impatiently. Palfrey was already padding along but Dagert had stopped to pluck at his shirt. His face expressed the utmost distaste as he pulled the blood-stained fabric away from his skin. He looked at me.

"Ruined a perfectly good shirt. People here don't seem to know what a proper shirt is. All right, my dear feller, I'm with you." And Dagert of Paylen hitched up his rapier belt and followed along the corridor.

Palfrey the Pfiffer whispered: "I spent your gold, notor. A lesser chamberlain—squeaky little Och—good idea of the layout."

The relish in Dagert's reply could either amuse or repel a listener according to their sympathies. "I see, you rogue. If you contrive to extricate us from this Havil-forsaken palace safely I might think about not docking the gold from your wages."

I did hear Palfrey's reaction, mumbled under his breath. "When I do get paid, by Atchel the Usurer!"

Oh, yes, by Clichol the Covetous, master and man ever at loggerheads!

Our surroundings were those, I surmised, halfway between dungeon and the kov's quarters high above. Carpets clothed the floor, tapestries adorned the walls and the lamps burned with sufficient light for us to see all we needed. The scent of jasmine sweetened the air. We saw no guards. Palfrey hesitated occasionally at corners; but he led on with confidence.

"Where's the confounded door, you hulu?" demanded Dagert.

"Near, notor, near."

The atmosphere of this place had to be held at bay. It oppressed unpleasantly, and the knowledge that if we were recaptured we could look forward to torture of an extremely ferocious kind did nothing for our peace of mind. The rumble of voices from ahead made us jump swiftly into the shadows of a draped archway. We stood, still and silent, as people passed by.

A small knot of guards led, clad in the black and red with the addition of purple trimmings. They looked healthy and well fed and supremely assured of themselves. There followed a group of handmaidens, all pretty and adorned in feathers and pearls in the best traditions of the old stories and legends. The woman at the center of the party took my instant intrigued attention. Her face was bright and bold and like a hawk's, yet she was as apim as I. Her clothes were sumptuous with a wide cleavage down her shamlak. Everything about her bespoke eloquently of power and authority and yet, in the downdrawn set of her painted mouth, the wrinkles at the corners of her eyes, I detected dissatisfaction, a resentment of something that preyed on her mind.

When the rearguard passed out of sight and earshot Palfrey let out his breath. "The Lady Vita. Pray to Kaerlan the Merciful we do not fall under her hand for judgment." He licked his lips. "She leads her husband, the Lord Jazpur, a merry dance."

I was astonished. Was I, then, so outrageously wrong in my summation of the animosity between Brannomar and Khonstanton?

Dagert of Paylen, clearly, shared my own bewilderment. "Now what does she want here in Khon the Mak's palace? She was not a prisoner?"

"Didn't look like it," I agreed.

"Let us hurry, notor." Palfrey led off again. He did not exactly run; but we scuttled along to keep up.

Moving on side by side we followed Palfrey through a hall hung with brocades of the Hunt of the Nine Veiled Witches and into a narrow corridor where Dagert moved ahead. As he passed he turned his head to stare at me. "One thing puzzles me, Drajak. If the sword Khon the Mak took to pieces was not Strom Korden's sword—and you had it, everyone knows that—where is the real sword now?"

I said: "As Havil is my witness, I have not the slightest idea."

"Fonnell had it. We know that. And the Fristle is dead. So what did he do with the sword?" Now Dagert was ahead and he looked away, padding after his manservant. "D'you think those thieving Katakis of the City Watch filched it, the evil Whiptails that they are?"

"If they have, they will sell it to the highest bidder."

His low amused laugh sounded odd in these circumstances. "Yes, there are plenty of them, by Krun."

We reached a crossway and Palfrey hesitated. "Well, fambly?"

"Let me think, notor—"

"Ha! Think! As well let a calsany into a boudoir!"

"This way." Palfrey padded off.

"I've had him since he was a stable lad with straw as yellow as his hair stuck to him all over. I took him into my personal service and trained him and mollycoddled him and cared for him." Dagert breathed in and out. His nostrils pinched. "And this is the way he repays me."

"By Krun, Dagert!" I said, stung. "He rescued us and now he's leading us out of this infernal place. What more d'you want? Blood?"

"If necessary."

As I made no reply but forged on silently, Dagert went on: "And I notice you apostrophize the name of Krun."

"I've lived in Hamal for a time."

"Ah! D'you know Ruathytu?"

"The capital? I was there once." I did not elaborate.

Palfrey stopped and motioned us to join him. We peered over his shoulders. I was telling myself to keep my black-fanged winespout shut. I didn't particularly want Dagert of Paylen to know I'd roistered with the Bladesmen in the Sacred Quarter of Ruathytu. Information of that kind would do me no good here. We saw before us a wide stone-flagged hall lit by tall windows. A double-door stood at the far end. The place was deserted.

"That's it, notor." Palfrey sounded self-satisfied.

"The devil take it!" exclaimed Dagert. "There's no cover."

"The quicker the better then," I said, and started off at a run.

Their footsteps padded after me. I outdistanced them and reaching the doors flung them open. Oh, yes, it was reckless. But I was tired of this palace reeking of evil. Mingled sunlight streamed in and I stepped through.

There was time to glimpse a courtyard with baltrixes being led along by hostlers past stables at the far end. The blueness swooped in.

One moment I was ready to leap forward; the next I felt as though I'd been upended and was flying through the air, coldness chilling me through to the bone. All about me the gigantic form of the phantom blue Scorpion enveloped reason. Up I went, up and up to my confrontation with the Star Lords.

A final glimpse of the twin Suns of Scorpio dripping blood and verdigris down the sky flashed past my vision and I was hurtling headlong into that macabre mingling of ruby and sapphire, red and blue twining all about me. A soft springiness cushioned my body. I was sitting in a comfortable armchair, the scent of lavender sweetened the air and the world turned red in whorls of patterned color, falling away like the last leaves of autumn in whispering clouds of gold. I was sitting in a fashionable room with pictures of flowers and birds adorning the walls, with long purple-red drapes framing elegant windows, chandeliers shedding mellow radiance upon exquisite furniture, chairs and tables and chaise-longues of impeccable taste, and the last blue dregs of the phantom Scorpion's wings faded away and were gone. I drew a breath. Now my audience with the Star Lords would begin.

There was no delay.

"You have been brought here, Dray Prescot, to answer certain questions."

"Willingly." I spoke with measured deliberation. My relationship with the Everoinye had so far changed recently that I could speak to them normally—well, almost normally. They had once been human and I knew they still possessed a sense of humor. In truth, only a sense of humor could save their sanity, given their awesome powers that without the leaven of a good laugh must inevitably have driven them into the final darkness of ultimate madness. "And there is a question I would ask you."

"She is well and thrives." The hoarse remote voice brightened. "As a kregoinya, the Empress Delia is proving one of our finest. What she sets out to do, that she accomplishes in style."

"Of course," I said. "She is Delia."

"We had hopes that her husband might share that aptitude and mend his ways. Sadly, you remain a rebellious miscreant."

The voice from thin air did not threaten or bully; but there was no mistaking the old sharpness of condemnation so familiar from seasons of arguing with the Everoinye and of cautiously slanging them. I sat up.

"What have I done wrong now?"

"Once again, Dray Prescot, you presume."

"Oh, come on!" I said, baffled. "Princess Nandisha is safe. Fweygo and I have—"

"You have abandoned your charges to go about other pursuits."

I breathed in and then out. I did not want to get back to the old familiar relationship with the Star Lords, of the soul-shaking fear of being hurled back four hundred light years to Earth. I said: "All I did was honor a promise to a dying man. Anyway, it looks as though this confounded sword has a great deal to do with Nandisha's kids and their aspirations to be next in line for the throne. Is that right?"

If they'd gone on in the old hateful way of: "That is not for you to comprehend," I would not have been surprised. As it was, there followed a silence, and silences between us I was very used to, then the hoarse whispering voice said: "You misread the situation, Dray Prescot. We had thought your onkerish days over. It does seem you remain an onker of onkers, a get-onker and—" Here another voice took over the chant of condemnation. "Not a prince of onkers any longer. A veritable Emperor of Emperors of Onkers!"

"You dumped me down in Amintin and the princess is safe." I had wanted to chew another complaint over with them, so I went on forcefully: "You gave me a Krasny-work sword for the useless thing broke almost the first time I hit anybody. I do appreciate not being hurled naked and unarmed these days—"

"Perhaps you would prefer to return to that state of affairs?"

Before I answered I reflected that, indeed, over the seasons I had developed a technique for handling an argument with the Star Lords. I changed the subject of conversation and—more often than not—they followed up the new train of thought and left off avenues of enquiry I did not wish to pursue. So now with all the business of the onkers out—as I fondly hoped—of the way, I said: "No. On Kregen a weapon is vital, as well you know. I've had to skip and jump over the seasons to fend for myself—as again well you know."

"Yes. And because you have the yrium which gives you power over others you have always managed."

"That's as may be," I grumped. "But I don't like swords breaking in my fist when I hit a villain over the head."

"Dray Prescot, you are being tiresome. You know very well that Tolindrin has difficulty in forging steel of quality."

"They have money, do they not? Gold and silver? Let them buy swords from Zenicce where they know how to make them."

"You were sent to Tolindrin equipped as an ordinary fighting man. If you require superior weapons not easily come by you must provide them yourself. As you have always done."

"I will, I will. Fweygo and I will see Nandisha is safe so that her kids can have the inheritance of the crown—"

Was there a tinge of irritated tartness in the disembodied voice? Impatience at stupidity? "We told you you misread the situation." So they had; but I'd changed the subject of conversation.

"You do want Nandisha—?"

"Who succeeds to the throne of Tolindrin now is of no concern to us. You have been told that you, Dray Prescot, are to be the Emperor of Emperors, the Emperor of all Paz. That includes Tolindrin, does it not?"

Not for the first time talking to the Star Lords if I'd been wearing a hat I'd have torn it off and flung it down and jumped on it.

I managed to control myself enough to burst out: "And I've told you that the task is well-nigh impossible! By Zair! A whole parcel of continents and islands and all to be ruled over by one mortal man? It's insane!"

"Not so. You say only it is 'well-nigh' impossible. You have the yrium. It will be done."

There was no profit going on with this argument. My own views of maniacs who crave power and wish to rule over vast territories they'll never visit are well known. Still and all, I'd have to do what I could. Otherwise—I checked my thoughts. No, I would not think of that horror.

I growled out most ungraciously: "I'll try."

"Good."

Then what they had said sparked in my brain. "Not Nandisha? You do not care who? Then, who are Fweygo and I caring for?"

"The numim twins, Rofi and Rolan, of course. Who else?"

Sixteen

"Where have you been?" said Fweygo. "You look in a hell of a mess."

"I'll tell you." I slumped myself down in a chair in the room in Nandisha's palace given over to our use. The phantom blue Scorpion of the Star Lords, this time, had dumped me down in a quiet corner of a street on the same hill as the palace and I'd had only to walk along the Avenue of Musk and so cross the Kyro of Perfumers to reach here. "First of all, by Beng Dikkane, I need a wet."

Fweygo put down the sword he had been fiddling with and handed the jug across and I poured a healthy dose and took a huge swig. I wiped my hand across my mouth. "By Mother Zinzu the Blessed! I needed that!"

Fweygo didn't smile. He saw enough of my mood to allow me to explain in my own time. He took up the sword again and extended it. "Your opinion, Drajak?"

The blade was a drexer, that particular pattern of sword developed by Naghan the Gnat and myself. It had been made in Vallia. The hilt bore more ornamentation than I cared for. Weapons are made for a purpose.

Embellishment seems to be either redundant or in bad taste. Still, the auction rooms of Earth are filled with examples fetching inflated prices. Back in the seventeenth century they'd stopped using bone for inlay and began decorating weapons with mother of pearl. This sword I knew to be a fine fighting arm; all the mother of pearl in the world would not make it better. I gave the brand a few swishes and slashes. "Very fine."

"Picked it up in the aracloins. It cost gold; I believe it worth every last copper ob of the price."

The Star Lords had mentioned that in Tolindrin the forging of quality steel was difficult. Fweygo had a bargain here all right. He went on: "I see you are wearing a rapier and dagger for the left hand. I assume you know how to use them—they're called the Jiktar and the Hikdar."

"I've used them before." As I spoke I heard the ungraciousness of my tone. I had to rouse myself, get to grips with this new situation.

Fweygo eyed me and took a sip from his goblet. He put that down and said: "My father always took a walk through the forest, swishing at dead flowers with the cane he always carried. I felt that cane, too, from time to time. He was a good man, stern and upright. He never decapitated a flower in bloom. Never."

"I've been up to see the Everoinye. D'you know why we're here?"

The Kildoi whistled soundlessly through his teeth.

"I expect, my Sudden friend, you will inform me."

"Oh, aye." I handed him back the Vallian drexer. "It's not Nandisha. The numim twins, Rofi and Rolan."

He sucked breath through his teeth, did not whistle, and said: "The Everoinye charged me with the whole party. They have their ways of doing the great affairs on which they are engaged. I understand."

I glowered. As a good kregoinye he'd work for the Star Lords and never remotely think of questioning their motives. There was in him an undercurrent of feeling that differentiated his attitude from that of Pompino or Mevancy. They stood in awe of the Star Lords—and, by Krun, wasn't that a sensible thing to do!—and so did Fweygo; but he showed far less of the almost adulatory worship in other kregoinyes. I wondered how they'd recruited him. No doubt he'd tell me in his own good time.

"That being the case," he said, sliding the drexer away in its scabbard strapped among his arsenal, "protection of the princess makes very great sense. She extends her power over her retainers."

"I agree. It's just nice to know where we stand."

"All the same, I often ponder, as I am sure you must do also, on the ultimate reasons for the Everoinye's choices. Will the future be changed because of these numim twins? Will they affect the destiny of nations?"

As you will have realized I was in an odd mood. So I let my black-fanged winespout blabber on. "I once saved a young man and girl, at the command of the Everoinye, and they married and had a son. Seasons later that son, who was then a mighty king, murdered my own daughter."

His eyes widened and then his face remained expressionless. Kildois are not emotional folk as a rule. He said: "I am truly sorry."

I took another drink. My hand did not shake. Fweygo went on: "I trust you sent the blintz down to the Ice Floes of Sicce?"

"He went there all right. But not by my hand. My daughter's husband saw to that necessity."

"So be it. You, I think, my friend Drajak, are somewhat in need of different air."

"Somewhat." I suppose, truth to tell, the mention by the Star Lords of Delia was affecting me. She was headstrong, resourceful, utterly determined. If the Star Lords hurled her into situations similar to those they had so callously tossed me into then I had to believe she would be Delia, and would handle herself and the problems with her own vital spirit. She'd come out smiling and glorious and wonderful and—I felt my fingers gripping the goblet so that the knuckles gleamed like white skulls.

"As to your other activities, well, you'll tell me or not according to their relevance to our task here." His tail hand waved gracefully. "I own I am not too enamored of Oxonium."

There was no reason not to tell my comrade of Korden's sword and the misadventures attendant upon its loss. He pulled a whisker. "And you believe the sword to be important enough to neglect—"

"Oh, come on, Fweygo. You're here and you're worth a regiment."

He had the grace to smile at this. "Depends on the regiment."

So I smiled, too, and felt the better for it and one of Nandisha's servitors walked silently into the room to say: "Horters, your pardon. There is a man asking to see Horter Drajak the Sudden."

The use of the Havilfarese word for lord—notor—here in Tolindrin was paralleled by the use of the Havilfarese name for gentleman—horter. I nodded. "If he looks safe, Tafnu, send him in by all means."

Tafnu bowed and went out. Fweygo, idly, said: "Expecting anyone?"

"No. Hardly. Don't know anyone in Oxonium."

"It might be wise to keep your blade loose in its scabbard."

Thinking of my recent experiences I heartily agreed with Fweygo. At the same time I had every hope that this was Naghan the Barrel, or perhaps one of his men, bringing me back the sword that had caused me so much grief. I stood up and looked at the door.

Lightly, with enjoyment running behind his words, Fweygo said: "If it's an irate father with a loaded crossbow—count me out!"

The fellow who walked in with a peculiar gliding gait I recognized as one of Naghan's men from our escapade, Nalgre the Ron, for his hair was ginger and although it was not your true Lohvian red hair probably owed its color to a distant ancestor from Loh. "Horters," he said politely, and swallowed, and said no more. Fweygo drew himself up.

"No loaded crossbow, then. Right. I've a few errands." He went out and it was gracefully done. I eyed Nalgre the Ron.

He wore a brownish-yellow shamlak with black cords, one loop of which was broken. There was a nasty bruise on his left cheek. As Fweygo had well known when he made his jocular remark, there was no chance of a loaded crossbow, for Nalgre wore no weapons. Nandisha's guards had seen to that long before Nalgre even saw Tafnu. He spoke quietly.

"Horter. I am to take you where you wish to go."

"Was anyone hurt—killed?"

"Wounds only."

"I see. I am ready. Wenda!" I said. "Let's go!"

Outside I said to Tafnu: "I shall not be long, please tell the Kildoi. A matter of some urgency." As Tafnu bowed, Nalgre and I hurried along the corridor to the entrance hall. Here he was given his weapons back by the guard detail on duty. A dagger, of course, an essential item of wear upon Kregen, was slipped away followed by a chunky short-hafted axe. He had also one of those blades in length between braxter and shortsword called slikkers, much favored where steel is overly expensive. The day was warm so I took no cloak or cape. Nalgre did not speak until we had left the palace and were walking rapidly across the Kyro of Perfumers. Mabal and Matol, the twin Suns of Scorpio, shed their refulgent lights of jade and ruby across the flagstones and shot a glitter from dome and cornice above.

"Lingurd was cut up, and Roidon the Riscus lost a few feathers and had his beak knocked askew. That devil-spawned Kataki, Trako Ironbelly, should be sent down to the Ice Floes of Sicce with his tail lopped off."

We went along Ferndown Street and then turned again and came upon the cable car terminus from the opposite direction. A few people waited and when the next car docked there was no trouble. We paid our copper obs for the journey and swung and swayed across to the next hill. Eventually we crossed the Hill of Sturgies and Nalgre led me along unfamiliar streets to a small but respectable-looking house in a back alley. He knocked.

A bristle-haired Brokelsh, Tarbak the Sohan, answered. He, too, bore bruises. "By the Resplendent Bridzilkelsh! You took your time. Lingurd is nearly dead."

Naghan the Barrel rolled up from an inner room, his fat face grave. "This way."

In the darkened room poor old Lingurd the polsim lay on a bed and coughed blood down his chin. He had been stuck through and the bandages across his chest were soaked. A little Och lady was trying to change the dressings. She had dotted the various parts of his anatomy with her needles to ease the pain. Lingurd spoke through a bubble of blood.

"Do not worry, Mother Ivy. I'm done for, may Impolimar receive me at the end."

"Your sacred Impolimar will be vexed with you, Lingurd the Obstinate, if you do not let me attend you." As she spoke her left upper held a cold bandage to his forehead, her right upper held him down and her two middle limbs expertly re-dressed the wound. "There. Just lie still, you stryler."

Staring down on Lingurd I reflected he was in no real position to be obstinate, what in Kregish is called stryle, not with this brisk little Puncture Lady attending him. The wound looked bad; I judged he'd live.

"Speak up, Lingurd." Nalgre the Barrel's voice, fruity as ever, held just the edge of testiness.

"I waited for the notor," Lingurd said, with difficulty. "The trust—and the Watch—but I did not fail."

"I'm sure you didn't, Lingurd." I made my tones pleasant.

"They were on us. The item—I hid it." He tried to move restlessly and Mother Ivy soothed him. He went on in that weak voice: "In a barrel—you remember, notor, the barrels?"

I nodded. "Which one?"

"A chalk mark—yellow."

"I recall they all had a yellow mark."

"Yes. The sign for She of the Veils. And the figure ord."

The mark meant the eighth month of Kregan's fourth moon, She of the Veils.

Before I could answer Raerdu spluttered out: "You could have told us before this! I'll have some men go down there at once—"

"And," I cut in. "I shall go with them."

"But—"

"But, as they say in Clishdrin, me no buts, my friend. I am going."

Naghan Raerdu knew me of old. He ceased his protestations. Our venture would have to be carried out this night and so for the short time remaining I ate and drank and presently Nalgre the Ron started in humming a tune, some others joined in, and a spritely little sing-song was in progress. I felt these ruffians were not singing in an attempt to keep up their spirits for the night. Most, not all, Kregans love to sing and seize any opportunity to caterwaul the old favorite tunes. We had, I remember "The Maiden with the Single Veil" and "Zakryst's Great War Horse" among songs current over most of Paz. A comical song of Tolindrin, funny and at the same time, to a foreigner, pathetic in its wish-fulfillment is "Nath the Iarvin among the Clouds." This tells of how Nath the Iarvin, a simple candle-maker's son, sought his fortune in Caneldrin, the nation immediately to the north of Tolindrin. He found himself one day on one of the volgendrins that circle in the air in that country and by calling upon Tolaar the Mighty sailed the flying island all the way south to Tolindrin. The song finishes with Nath the Iarvin's joyous reception at home. As to why there are no volgendrins soaring in the air in Tolindrin—well that is another and altogether more painful truth of geography.

At last Naghan Raerdu stood up and the sing-song was over. A couple of his men went out to scout the neighborhood. If any spies had followed Nalgre the Ron and myself here they were far more expert than those two back in Amintin whom Fweygo had seen off. I had not been conscious of anybody tailing us and Nalgre confirmed that as his own feelings.

They found me another floppy hat and a short cloak and so, disguised as a right tearaway ruffian of the runnels, off I went with this band of cutthroats. The new rapier and left hand dagger were concealed by the cloak; the sword I'd taken from Palfrey's unconscious guard was buckled up in a handy position so that my fist could haul hilt fast.

We did not use the lifter but descended the rubble-strewn slope carefully. Occasionally the Maiden with the Many Smiles peeped out from the clouds but in general we had darkness to cloak our nefarious activities. This gang led by Naghan had followed me to The Brass Lily. We all knew the way along the dolorous runnels among the stews, avoiding the piles of refuse and the thickly clinging mud that never seemed to dry out. The smells choked up our nostrils once again and the weird cries that echoed among the buildings spoke eloquently—and hideously—of all manner of deviltry going on here.

At the penultimate block we halted. The tavern was visible through a thin mist that hung about dampl. A gyp lolloped across to a pile of rubbish and started to ferret about. Cautiously we skirted around to arrive at the rear of The Brass Lily. The sounds of revelry flowed muted from the front.

"This is the back entrance to the yard," grunted Naghan in my ear.

"And that's Fonnell's snug," I whispered, pointing to the building where the Fristle had met his death. "Not that he needs it now."

"So where are the damn barrels?"

"Right alongside the snug where poor Lingurd was standing. You can't see 'em from out here. Still," I nodded my head. "You can see that confounded trapdoor where I went down like offal down a mincer."

Naghan's laugh wheezed as he stifled his amusement. Here in Tolindrin the barrel of Northern countries was used as a container alongside the amphora of Southern lands. Both barrels and amphorae traveled the wide world of Kregen. The trade of coopering is demanding in its exactitude—but then, so is throwing a pot—and as a consequence barrels were cared for. This stack consisted of the empties, ready to be picked up and returned to the merchants.

Naghan moved forward, bulky and determined. He whispered over his shoulder. "Liftu, you and Nath the Nose keep watch out here." He passed me and said: "I'll just go in and—"

I took his arm. "Not so. It's down to me to go first." I added and even as I spoke, knew I shouldn't: "You should know me by now, my friend."

He grunted his wheezing snort. "Oh, aye, I know. I remember The Headless Zorcaman."

So, in I went, peering every which way in the erratic illumination.

As you know, although I was not absolutely sure, I had an inkling the Star Lords had given me the ability to see rather better in gloomy situations than a person with normal eyesight might expect. Certainly, the details of the yard were easy enough to make out. Noise from the front of The Brass Lily spurted through the night. I slunk in and turned towards Fonnell's snug and the stack of empty barrels. All bore yellow chalk markings.

The barrels were piled up differently from the way I pictured them in my mind. If the sword had been discovered... Rapidly I searched for the yellow chalk mark of the eighth month of She of the Veils.

There were many kinds of marks, many of them half obliterated and washed away by rain, some with new marks over old. What I sought was not visible in the first or second tier of barrels. The top two tiers leaned crazily out like projecting house fronts. There was nothing for it but to climb up.

At my elbow Naghan whispered: "I don't see it."

"Give me a leg up."

So, with Naghan's brawny fist under my shoe, up I went. I clawed at the lip of the top barrel and with a squirming wriggle like an eel hoisted myself onto the top. I lay there for a moment, hoping not enough noise had been made to attract attention through the racket from the tavern.

The yellow marks danced like abandoned sarabandas in a pagan temple. I blinked and cleared my eyes and looked and there the mark was, plain as a pikestaff, the eighth month of She of the Veils.

The empty barrel top came off easily and I reached in and the whole pile erupted like an avalanche and in an infernal thundering uproar the stack of barrels collapsed. Barrels bounced and rolled everywhere across the yard. Down I went like a skier whose somersault has come to grief. Smack flat down on my back I flopped like a landed fish, gasping. The barrels were rolling and booming and careening about all over the yard.

"Krug take it!" yelped Naghan as he went toppling over knocked flying by a maniacal barrel. I tried to sit up and was rolled flat again by a demonic booming monster plunging from the top rear tier. This was like being in the way of a vove cavalry charge. Gasping, I clawed up once more and stared in horror at the trundling devastation across the yard.

You couldn't have aroused more attention by beating a battalion's massed drums. The rear door of the tavern flew open, lamplight flowered across the tiles, and men bearing weapons tumbled out.

"By the leprous left ear and disgusting decayed right nostril of Makki

Grodno!" I fumed away as I leaped up. "What a way to conduct a silent secret nefarious operation!"

Seventeen

All the same—by Krun! you had to laugh!

One crazed barrel was spinning on its axis like a Whirling Dervish. A fellow from the tavern loosed at it and the bolt caromed from the revolving staves and steamed off into the night. The uproar bellowed splendidly in the back yard of The Brass Lily.

Uproariously amusing though this imbroglio was, time was dropping inexorably away, grain by grain, drop by drop. Where in a Herrelldrin Hell was that Djan-forsaken sword?

The men from the tavern were in no doubt that some rival gang had chosen this very night to stage a surprise attack on The Brass Lily. They stormed into the yard shooting at anything that moved. Bolts and arrows feathered into barrels or caromed away under the stars. Yells of order and counter-order spurted as they tried to discover what exactly was going on.

Then—and for the sweet sake of Opaz I let out a yelp of pure delight—a barrel swung on its last revolution and halted beside me and there, plain as the nose on your face, gleamed the yellow chalk mark I sought. I dived headlong.

The double-damned empty barrel was empty!

"Oh, my Divine Lady of Belschutz!" I ground out through my teeth. "You and Makki-Grodno were created one for the other!"

Now Naghan's men had been inordinately patient during all this furore. True, they were at the gate keeping watch. True, they were hired hands. But, equally truthfully, they had been paid good red gold for a task to their liking and so now when they were shot at it irked them. They shot back.

The result was instantaneous. In the flickering uncertain light as the moon shed her radiance down through the ever-shifting clouds the men from The Brass Lily let out yells of consternation. They turned and rushed back into the tavern. So much for their brave advance against the enemy!

Looking about this way and that, and I can tell you I was in a right old state by this time, I searched for that miserable sword. Try to do someone a good turn, try to fulfill a promise to a dying man, and look where it gets you... Caught up in a diabolical mess like this.

Kicking barrels out of the way and heaving them rolling in the general direction of the tavern, I peered about like a beggar searching for scraps in a refuse dump. A gleam from the end of a tub, a quick heave of my shoulders and—there it lay. The confounded sword caught a stray flash of light and winked, as it were, insolently at me, laughing at my concern.

I snatched it up and yelled: "All out! Wenda!"

In a tumbling mass we rollicked out of the yard and hared along up the alley. The Maiden with the Many Smiles took pity on us then and allowed drifting clouds to cover her roseate glory. In pungent gloom we hurried along.

Naghan the Barrel, wily as ever, called softly: "This way," and led off down a narrow-gutted alley even more dark and forbidding than the last.

That cross-way led into another. Naghan's sense of direction did not fail and I, a stranger here, sensed too the way we were heading. We pressed on. Naghan held up a hand and we all collided in a chain, bump, bump, bump, and so came to a halt. Ahead a wider street lay pooled with light from lanterns hitched thinly to corner buildings. The ominous tramp of iron-shod boots echoed into the night air.

There was no need for Naghan or anyone to say: "Shastum! Silence!" Like fearful mice we waited, suppressing our breathing, our eyes gleaming muddily like bad eggs, our weapons clutched in grimy fists. The Watch stalked past.

The Kataki Hikdar who led them was not, of course, Trako Ironbelly; no doubt he was a collateral relation and almost as bad. Itching though we might be to leap out and drub these licensed villains, we kept still and silent.

We gave the Watch ample time to march off—march! That was a laugh. They strolled along in no kind of step or order, masichieri, the lot of 'em.

"They're gone," whispered Nath the Nose.

"Aye," rumbled Naghan. "Gone to Cottmer's Caverns I hope."

After that we were able to negotiate the rest of the drab and festering warrens and so reach the rubble slope and climb back up to the fresher air of the hill. "Anybody could climb up here," I said to Naghan. "Don't the folk on the hills worry? Keep guards?"

"The rabble can climb up—to do what? The guards exist at points where they are needed. It would take half a dozen armies to guard every way up from the warrens to the hills."

"And," added Liftu, "they know if they do climb up a force will descend and wreak vengeance. Not a pretty sight, that."

"I can imagine," I said. And, by Krun, I could.

Nalgre the Ron, who despite his bruises had insisted on going with our expedition, brought up the rear of the party. He kept a wary eye out and, to our relief, was able to report that no one followed us.

We regrouped at the inconspicuous house and our immediate enquiries regarding Lingurd were answered by Mother Ivy saying he was in a deep sleep. No one questioned her further. Kregen, after all, is Kregen, and there the doctoring process very very often includes a magical element. We all went into the side room for a wet.

Although our adventures down at The Brass Lily seemed to have lasted an eternity, little time had elapsed and the night was still young. Time for me at last to rid myself of the sword and my obligation to Strom Korden. Taking my leave with due formality and an expression of thanks I advised Naghan Raerdu I could be reached at Princess Nandisha's palace. Then I set off for the palace of Hyr Kov Brannomar.

Naghan would not hear of my traversing the nighted streets of Oxonium alone, even though they were safe enough what with the Guard alert. A group accompanied me to Grand Central and I could hear them muttering questioningly among themselves at the downright foolish action on my part of boldly marching into the Hyr Kov's palace. I thanked them all again and promised to see them later. So, into the palace I went.

Brannomar ran a tight ship. The guards halted me under the first portico. They were polite about it; but the crossbows did not waver as they centered on my midriff. Their swords might be munitions quality, they'd be good and sharp within the quality of the steel.

"The lord is in a meeting," I was told by the Deldar, sharp, correct, his uniform immaculate, his Deldar's rank badges glittering in the lantern lights. He was a Pachak and his yellow hair showed a neat trim under the rim of his helmet.

"Please send a message to the Hyr Kov. Tell him Drajak the Sudden has that which—"

"You are Drajak known as the Sudden?"

"Aye."

Instantly a transformation occurred. The guard surrounded me, a Hikdar appeared, wiping his mouth with a yellow napkin, and off I was marched into the courtyard. Clearly, I was expected. A number of carriages stood about with grooms and coachmen in attendance. We went through the various passages until we reached those I recognized from my previous visit.

The inner guard, already alerted by a runner, took over here and in further I marched. I held my left hand on the hilt of Korden's sword nestling in the scabbard Naghan had provided. The brand had cost me a deal of sweat, toil and trouble—not to say pain—and the thought of losing it now at the last moment was not to be borne.

There was no hesitation about my introduction to the meeting. Double-doors were thrown open and the guard ushered me into a comfortable withdrawing room, furnished with couches and chairs and side tables. There were drinks on the tables together with light refreshments. From the faces of those in the meeting I judged this was no pleasant evening's entertainment.

Carefully, I looked at them all as Brannomar came forward, extending his hand. "You have it?"

"Aye, notor." I drew the blessed thing and, smartly reversing it and resting the blade on my arm, extended the hilt towards him. He took it into his fist with the grip of a devotee of Kurin and a little sigh escaped his lips. "Thank you." As I say, a polite noble, thank Zair!

Now the others in the room stood as though immersed in wax, absorbed in what was going on. Of them, Nandisha and Ranaj wore puzzled frowns. The spritely young fellow I'd met in the Shrine of Cymbaro with whom I'd had an argument about precedence through a door, and the faded woman sitting next to him, also looked puzzled by my entrance and the sword. Not so Khonstanton. His face drew down in a heavy frown. The young man standing in a pose of irritation near him almost started forward, and then halted, and so joined the rest in immobility.

Looking at Khonstanton I was minded to say something; but common sense held my lips sealed. Bad cess to him—he'd lost the precious sword!

The Lord Jazipur stared at Brannomar and the sword and his desire to leap forward and grasp the sword was written clearly on his face.

Brannomar turned away towards a table with the sword in his left hand. He drew a knife with his right. Now, I fancied, I'd find out what poor old Strom Korden's last dying words meant.

The atmosphere in the room breathed of tension. You could taste it. My entrance had interrupted a discussion that quite obviously was a full-blown argument. Passions boiled in these people's brains. You could almost see them bubbling and steaming ready to break out uncontrollably. Even Nandisha showed her puzzlement at my appearance and Brannomar's reaction tinged with a ladylike acerbity. 'What,' she was saying to herself in extreme annoyance, 'does this man Drajak want here?'

That, I thought to myself rather ungraciously, I want to find out too, my lady!

Apart from the numim Ranaj they were all apims in the room. The youthful looking man standing and fidgeting away wearing the hard black shamlak with double-looped gold cords wore his weasel face, it seemed to me, in an unpleasant frown that was a permanent disfigurement. Now, unable to control himself any longer, he started forward towards Brannomar. My own thought was that if this pipsqueak wanted to tangle with the Hyr Kov Brannomar he was as big a fool as he looked to be an unpleasant character. Still, you cannot always tell a zorca by the length of his horn and I could be dwaburs wide of the mark.

The very fact that these high-ranking nobles had gathered here during the night must indicate their business was of the utmost importance. As Brannomar went at the sword with his knife and everyone stared like a piranha in a blood-hungry shoal I stepped quietly away to stand with my back against a tapestried wall. Such was the intentness with which they all followed the Hyr Kov's every action they simply forgot all about me, a mere hireling paktun whose duty was now accomplished.

Anyway, who were the ones in here I didn't know?

The young man at whose shoulder I'd fought in the Shrine of Cymbaro had given me a single surprised look when I'd walked in, and then had concentrated on Brannomar and the sword. The faded woman must be his mother for the family resemblance was striking. And the other unhealthy-looking whippersnapper? My best guess was that they were the other princes I had heard of in line for the succession.

So that meant one was Ortyg and one was Tom. Which was which?

Weasel-face halted when he reached the table. Evidently the idea had belatedly occurred to him that Brannomar was no man to be hustled. Now the others crowded closer, the principals closer and their retainers or helpers craning over shoulders. My young friend from the temple assisted his mother to rise and allowed her plenty of space before him. Weasel-face positively exuded the sweat of anticipation. As I say, you cannot judge a sword by its decoration; all the same, the contrast here was painfully obvious.

Brannomar ran his knife point around the sword handle just below the pommel. As Naghan and I had surmised, a hollow handle would be the place to conceal whatever it was that so violently exercised these grandees. His knife slit around the bindings. He cut with precision and care and his hands had not the slightest quiver or shake. My impression of the kov as a tough customer, despite his white hair, were confirmed the more I saw of him.

The pommel came off and fell to roll away somewhere under the crowding feet. Brannomar upended the sword and shook. A chunk of lead plopped out.

"Ah!" exclaimed the Lord Jazipur. "Now we're getting somewhere."

The young fellow I had taken the instant and, to be honest, almost irrational dislike to shoved in further. He jostled Khonstanton.

Mak Khon twisted and looked down and his face showed a heavy flush of anger. "Have a care, Ortyg!"

"There is no chance for you, kov!" flared this fellow Prince Ortyg. "It is you who should have a care!"

"We shall see what the Red One brings, prince. You would do well to bear that in mind."

"As should you bear in mind the fate of all traitors!"

What might have occurred then Opaz alone knows. Brannomar shook the sword. Everyone expected something to pop out of the hilt, and my guess was Khonstanton and this Prince Ortyg had known what it was some time ago. Nandisha and the other young prince, who must be Tom, I equally judged had only recently found out—probably at this very night-time meeting.

Brannomar shook the sword. He shook it violently. Nothing slid out of the hollow handle. The scar slashed down the kov's left cheek blazed a white line down his bronzed skin.

"Well, kov?" ground out Khon the Mak. His heavy blue-black hair formed a striking contrast to the pallor of his face, intent, dominating, demanding.

Ordinary folk had always to remember that the principals in this room were high-born and high-flown nobles, choleric of temper, impatient if their every wish was not instantly fulfilled. They were used to having their own way. That, I knew from previous harsh experience on Kregen, applied to them all, every last one.

"Here, let me," rapped out Ortyg. He reached for the sword.

I did not let a little regretful sigh escape my lips, although I might well have done. This was like a vicious leem tangling with a zhantil.

"I am perfectly capable, thank you, Prince Ortyg." Brannomar's words came softly from those hard thin lips. Then: "Do not presume too far, boy."

Ortyg's face and shocked reaction spoke eloquently of the boiling passions, the vaunting ambitions devouring him. But he had the sense to remain silent.

"These Dokerty-contumed priests of Cymbaro," broke out Khonstanton. "They have played us false!"

"On the contrary," spoke up Prince Tom, firmly, his own passions well in hand. "They are to be trusted absolutely."

"The old king thought so," said Nandisha, "from what you have told us."

"The old king was in his two-hundred and fiftieth season dotage!" snarled Ortyg.

Brannomar did not deign to reply; but Khon the Mak took the opportunity to take another crack at Ortyg's presumptions. "The old king was half-dead when he arranged this stupid and pointless charade. But he could still take you and spit you out before breakfast!"

Young Ortyg's face resembled those little squirmy beasties that creep and crawl about through the eyesockets of the skulls piled in the Mausolea of Trannimora. Despite his appearance and manner to the contrary there must be in him some shreds of nobility through his inheritance, surely? Or was that just wishful thinking on my part? Here he was, a young and ambitious prince openly desirous of being selected as the legitimate successor to the old king and he was being put down left and right by his elders. Any youngster of spirit detests the know-it-all attitude of the senile oldsters who tell her or him just what to do and think. Oh, yes, despite the dislike for him I had to acknowledge as unworthy on my part, I could feel for him.

Just look at them, gathered at this secret nighttime conclave!

Four strands weaving a net of deception and treachery, they seemed to be to me. Nandisha, devoted to her children. Prince Tom, a little apart from the others in their naked greed for the crown. Prince Ortyg, craving for power and all that goes with it. And Hyr Kov Khonstanton so much more purposeful and deadly even than the others, the outsider, the dark rider, the one whose machinations would brook no interruptions whatsoever from anyone. As well for Dray Prescot if he remembered that that included him.

Brannomar shook Strom Korden's sword again. He upended it and tried to look into the handle. He prised in with his knife but the blade was too wide. On the instant a long thin poniard appeared in Ortyg's fingers. That slender lethal blade was not to be seen and then was there in a twinkling. "Here," he said, curtly. "Try this."

Brannomar took it, grunted something, and slid it into the sword hilt. He twisted about without success. Everyone stared in rapt fascination.

Ranaj looked on, stroking his golden whiskers, a part of all this because of his allegiance to Nandisha and yet further removed than the Lord Jazipur and Tom's mother. Nothing, it seemed, was to be discovered in the hollow handle of the sword.

If looks could kill the room would have been filled with dead bodies, by Krun!

The avarice and mutual hate driving these people filled the place with an almost palpable aura. The suffocating sense of violent passions barely suppressed choked the atmosphere. It made the spine tingle I can tell you! They might seem like small children squabbling over the exact division of a fruit cake; the powers each wielded made them antagonists to be feared. No mercy, none whatsoever in whatever pantheon any of them believed in, would be shown by them or to them. And may Opaz have mercy on the hindmost!

Brannomar looked up, the frustration on his bronzed face twisting the scar into an ivory serpent. "It has to be here, in Strom Korden's sword! It has to be!"

"Then let me," rapped out Khon the Mak. He reached out and to my surprise Brannomar handed the sword across.

"I suspect treachery here." Hyr Kov Brannomar took a breath. "If it is not to be found before the Feast of Beng T'Tolin then I shall sign the treaty with Vallia."

Khonstanton, who had been prodding and prying around in the hilt, jerked upright. "You! Only the king may sign a treaty of such significance to the well-being of Tolindrin!"

"I am well aware of that, kov. But if there is no king then I—"

"Not so fast!" Ortyg stepped forward, pent-up with baffled rage. "I have the best claim and therefore I should sign!"

"Nonsense, boy." Khonstanton simply snarled it out without any deference to rank. "It needs a man with experience, a man like me."

Nandisha put a finger to her mouth, eyes wide. Prince Tom said nothing at all but merely watched, a half smile on his lips.

If the bunch of them had drawn swords and gone at one another tooth and nail that would not have surprised me in the mood they were. I was fascinated by the reference to a treaty with Vallia. My lad Drak must have decided in Tolindrin's favor after all. As the Emperor of Vallia he could call on the advice of the various pallans and the Presidio of Vallia. In addition he had the inestimable advantage of having Silda, the daughter of my blade comrade Seg Segutorio, at his side as the Empress of Vallia. Vallia's need was for airboats, vollers that did not break down. The lifters of Tolindrin must have weighed in the balance, even against the airboats of the three other nations here who built lifters.

I had been learning a good deal of the entangled politics of this land. What had been said here had opened my eyes to a great deal of what had been going on since my arrival in Amintin. There were still pieces of the puzzle missing. Those, I felt sure in the martial benevolence of Djan, would come my way soon.

Again the sword that lay at the core of all this was shaken. Nothing fell from that hidden secret recess in the handle.

"Two days!" Khon the Mak snarled it out. "May the ibma of Slissur take it! Two days to the Feast of T'Tolin."

He would have said more; but Brannomar interrupted incisively.

"Two days in which to settle the inheritance." He glanced away from Khonstanton. "We shall settle it, never fear. Until then I remain in the position I hold and—"

"Oh, no!" Ortyg's narrow face was now distorted with the ambitions driving him. He was past the reckoning that had so far held him in check. Before he could go on Khonstanton's voice blattered him down.

"For once I agree with the whippersnapper. Nothing will be settled by this, Brannomar. You must recognize that now. I have reached the end of my patience. This means one thing. War!"

Brannomar snapped around to face Mak Khon. "If you are so foolish—"

Ortyg got out through his distorted mouth. "War!"

Brannomar lifted a hand. "And the very worst kind of war there is. Civil war."

"Aye!" Khon the Mak drew himself up. "A just war to gain the inheritance that is rightfully mine!"

"You prattle idly, kov." The fingers of Ortyg's left hand reached down for the hilt of his missing poniard in a gesture betrayingly automatic. "The people detest you, Khon the Mak. They look to me, to youth, to the future—"

"My twins," said Nandisha breathily, "have the direct line—"

"Not so!" and "Rubbish!" from Ortyg and Khonstanton.

Prince Tom half turned away, raising his shoulders in a helpless little gesture, at once amused and disgusted. "I want nothing of it."

"Then leave the business for those with the stomach for it!" Mak Khon shook the sword savagely. "All your schemes have come to grief, Brannomar. My troops are ready. We march on Oxonium—"

"As are mine!" flared Ortyg. "We shall see who can march faster—"

"You fools!" roared Brannomar. "You will destroy the nation."

In a display at once arrogant and repulsive, Khon the Mak turned to Nandisha. He looked down on her, and he tried to make that harsh face smile. "Your twins have always been near my heart, Nan. Join me and—"

Ortyg brayed a laugh as contemptuous as any calsany's.

What might have happened then Opaz alone knows. By sheer force of personality Brannomar brought them to silence, hand upraised. He ground his words out as the Mills of the Dahemin grind out the fates of mortal humanity. "If you must fight then Tolaar must have decreed it. But there is one thing you must see. Vallia! The treaty must not be jeopardized. Delay your criminal war until after the Feast of T'Tolin."

Through all the red-roaring passions of greed and anger and pride rattling away in these stiff-necked nobles' heads, the sheer commonsense of Brannomar's words struck through. Like fighting cocks stalking one another, although they stood in artificial poses of hauteur, they appeared to circle around, weapons ready, seeking the opening that would lead to the kill.

"Yes." Khonstanton spoke at last, nodding his head. "Yes. Ortyg—"

The ferret-face turned and a half-shadow fell across the thin features. "Yes. We may curse the name of Vallia; but the haughty shints are necessary. Yes, Khonstanton, to the Feast of T'Tolin."

Whether or not Mak Khon believed him I didn't know. I did know I wouldn't trust any of 'em as far as a baby in a cot could throw a longsword.

"No word must get out." Brannomar spoke with quiet emphasis that contrasted forcefully with the previous passionate upheavals. "If Vallia—"

"They will not find out from me!" snarled Mak Khon.

"Nor from me. But—" Here Ortyg swiveled so that the shadow turned his face into a mottled mask. He stared at me. "No one must know."

"That is no problem." Khonstanton drew his sword.

Nandisha's little gasp broke from her painfully. "No!"

"The shint means nothing." Ortyg's sword was in his fist.

Prince Tom swung back, clearly uncertain. Whatever he or Nandisha might feel, whatever regret might stir Brannomar, nothing was going to stop the other two from trying to chop me down and seal the lips of the only witness to their schemes.

Ortyg and Khonstanton, swords lifted, rushed straight for me.

Eighteen

I went through the flung-open double-doors faster than a hare avoiding a hound. The two guards outside were left gaping. Straight down the corridor I hurtled and the furious and baffled shouts of Khonstanton and Ortyg spurred me on. Oh, yes, surely, I could have stayed in that closed room of secrets and fought them and no doubt I'd have done for 'em into the bargain. But that would have been utterly foolish and stupidity of that kind formed no part of my plans.

Around the first corner I sprinted, skidding on a rug, regaining my balance and tearing on headlong.

Once I was fairly away from this high echelon area and among the maze of corridors and passageways and halls I could lose myself. These grandiose palaces of Kregen in general are honeycombed with secret passages and I'd used them before in my lurid goings on in that world four hundred light years from the planet of my birth. Now I had to use what skill I'd gained over the seasons to find a hidden entrance. And, by Krun, I had to find the damn thing quickly, very quickly indeed!

The state architect of the great deren in Vondium had taught me much and I'd developed the knack of looking out for the extra thickness of wall here or the oddly angled buttress there. Down half a dozen passages further on a door leading to a medium-sized chamber with dolphins as decoration was guarded by a Rapa leaning on his halberd. Before the feathered fellow had time to squawk he went to sleep standing up and as I eased him to the marble floor the thickness of the wall in which the door was set attracted my immediate attention.

Various protuberances in the carved and gilded foliage architrave merited further inspection. It was no use looking for a worn away knob. If you have a secret passage and wish to keep it secret then you do not advertise its presence. After a deal of pushing and pulling and pressing a nicely rounded dillope fruit, a juicy form of satsuma, yielded. There was no loud click; but a stem and branches revolved to disclose a narrow dark opening. Quick as a ferret down a rabbit hole I was in and the panel revolved shut at my back. Even without the Everoinye-bestowed lack-of-light vision, I could see by the aid of the pencil-thin shafts of radiance falling from various spyholes. Immediately I felt quite at home.

Although this was in the middle of the night the palace was astir like a disturbed ants' nest. That, by Vox, was my doing!

Well, bad cess to all of them. I knew what I had to do. The how of it was the problem. Hyr Kov Brannomar would be well guarded.

In addition, and on Kregen it is a weighty matter, by Krun! I was in need of sustenance, both food and drink. Particularly a wet. Off I set along the runnels between the walls, looking out, going silently, directing my cautious steps in the general downward direction of the kitchens.

When by the smells I knew I was close it was also borne in on me that whilst food was prepared day and night, for guards, servants, slaves, this level of activity meant the whole place was aroused—aye!—aroused and searching for me.

After a succession of store rooms I at last peered through a small hole into a kitchen. I say a kitchen, for undoubtedly there were more than one in such a large establishment. A rotund, buxom, sweating woman was unmercifully thrashing a scrawny knobbly-kneed lad who yelled blue murder.

Nonplussed I just stood for a moment, watching. Had that been a big man thrashing a young girl there would have been no problem. Oh, yes, I am well aware of all the contradictions in the contradictory nature of the fellow known as Dray Prescot. The girl or the lad could have done something so heinous that the punishment on the cruel world of Kregen was richly deserved. This strong woman with the bulging biceps was laying it on a bit thick, though. The lad was a mere bag of bones. The rolling pin being used on him would have laid out a zhanpaktun with a five-foot long pakai. So, being Dray Prescot and unable to stop putting my big nose into other people's affairs, I pushed the lever and jumped into the kitchen.

My foot landed on something greasy and off I went, skidding across the floor with my arms waving about like a manic orangutan. A desperate clutch at a table served only to overset the lot and a cascade of pots and pans clattered to the floor.

"Lawks 'a mussy!" screamed the woman. She used a round Kregish phrase; the meaning was the same and then I'd skidded all the way and was wrapping my arms about her massive frame to try to keep my balance.

She dropped the lad. She did not drop the rolling pin.

The boy let out a single bellow and was off like a greyhound.

The rolling pin went up and came down and bounced most tellingly off my ear. So, to be in the fashion, for the uproar was splendid, I let out a tremendous yell—the confounded rolling pin hurt!—and span the woman about. She collapsed and then we were tumbling to the floor.

"Murder!" she screamed. "Help! Guards! Help!"

The lad was well away by now. There was nothing left here for me to do except try to avoid the frenzied flailing of the rolling pin.

Somehow or other, all mixed up with greasy and smelly aprons and voluminous petticoats, I staggered to my feet.

"Get off! Get off! Murder! Help!"

I, Dray Prescot, emperor, king, prince, lord of this and that, just ran.

Now I may only be an apim, a Homo sapiens sapiens, with a mere two arms and hands. In like circumstances my kregoinye comrade Fweygo, a

Kildoi, would have done much better. As it was, I regained the shelter of the secret passage in the kitchen wall with a thick ham in one hand and a flagon in the other. The panel was closed by a smart doubling up so that my rear end clacked the door into place. I did not hang about.

These passageways were uniformly dusty, with spiders' webs festooning everywhere and flang skins littering every nook and cranny. Perhaps Brannomar had no use for hidden corridors. I had. When I was a goodly distance away from the debacle in the kitchen I slumped down with my back wedged comfortably into a corner and started on the provisions.

What a night this was turning into! First it was rolling barrels and then it was rolling pins. What next in the rolling menagerie awaited me?

The ham was good, the wine poor. After a time I stood up and started off again. This time my way led upwards.

There is no need to detail all the passageways and crevices I essayed in my search. Suffice it to say that towards morning I at last reached my goal.

Breathing silently, I stared through a chink in the wall into Kov Brannomar's retiring room. The place was furnished like a study, with well-filled bookshelves, desk, a comfortable chair, a lounging sofa, and a table at which sat Brannomar in person. I was unable to see the other end of the table from my point of observation and there were no other slits in the walls. I stood quietly watching and listening. Brannomar was speaking in a decisive, intolerant, almost menacing way.

"...you deserve to be calsany-whipped around the palace for your stupidity. Do you fully realize the damage you have caused?"

A woman's voice answered. As she spoke she advanced into my view.

"For my children, kov! Only for them—please, you must believe me!"

"But I do not believe you."

She wore a lounging robe of deep blue, gold trimmed with much lace. Her bright bold face, so much like a hawk's, was now set in lines of desperation. She was pleading for her life. Her hands clutched the lace at her breast and her hair fell to straggle across her shoulders.

"Please, notor, I meant no harm to you! I swear it!"

"You may swear on all the gods in creation, my lady Vita; all the same, what you have done has created much mischief. The kingdom is like to fall. By Beng T'Tolin, woman, your selfish meddling has brought war!"

"But I did not want—"

"I know what you wanted, Vita. The Lord Jazipur was good enough for you when you married him. He is a fine upright man—"

"Yes!" she flared at him. "So upright he has no ambitions left!"

"He serves me and my kovnate and through me the kingdom. He well understands his position. I value him as a friend. But you—"

"I did not know that they would do such dreadful things!"

"Had you taken counsel of your husband you would have understood more of the realities of politics. As it is, your ambitious meddling is past the point where anyone may intervene. The die is set. There will be war, woman, a war you have created!"

She shrank away, seemingly at last conscious of the enormity of her treachery. I'd seen her in Khonstanton's palace. It was not hard to guess what she'd been up to there. Any woman has the right to ambition and the right to want her husband to prosper. Destinies have been played out, empires risen and fallen on the desires of women. Men and women have no rights when they are born save those that lineage and civilization confer. Misuse brings tragedy. Poor Lady Vita had vaulted with her ambitions, and they had undone her.

They went on in much the same vein, arguing, recriminations and passionate defenses alternating, and the sense of much of it came clear.

Truth to tell, after a time I grew impatient with the pair of them. Brannomar was actually wrangling with the woman. This surprised me completely. Then, from what they said, I gathered the Lady Vita had once harbored ambitions to marry Hyr Kov Brannomar. He had refused her. She already had two children from an early marriage and this first husband had died. There was every reason to wonder if his death had not been accelerated by Vita. So she had married Brannomar's trusted right hand man. Jazipur had Brannomar's confidence and so far I judged that confidence not misplaced—save in this one instance of Jazipur's marriage.

At last the hyr kov stood up. He placed both hands flat on the table and so stood, glowering down on the Lady Vita.

"I shall not decide your fate yet. I must speak with the Lord Jazipur. You must add to your crimes of treachery the pain you have caused a good and honorable man. Guards!"

In they came in their bronze and iron and they took the Lady Vita away. To her credit, the last I saw of her then, she stopped her sobbing and wailing. She stuck her chin out and that bold hawk-like face up, and she stalked away surrounded by guards armed and in armor.

And then, confound it! Brannomar took himself off after them.

I was left fuming in my hidey-hole.

The trouble now was—would the Star Lords regard all this intrigue as a legitimate part of the task assigned Fweygo and me? If they did not, then I could face being hurled four hundred light years back to languish on Earth until either they relented or were in need of my services once more.

As they say in the jargon of Clishdrin, I reviewed my options. Eventually I came to the conclusion my best course of action was to hang on here until Brannomar returned to his study. He must work in private in this comfortable snug on his state papers, and the situation now with war looming meant he would carry a heavy work load. I stayed put.

Naturally enough, being fallibly human, I fretted over this decision debating with myself if I wasn't making a dreadful mistake. I shifted incautiously and a whole flood of dust and cobwebs fell about my head.

The clinging powdery dust got right up my hooter. I could feel the mother and father of a sneeze overtaking me. Scuttling like a demented crab I rushed off along the dark passage and then let rip with an almighty atishoo! Tears sprang to my eyes. I sneezed again. I sneezed half a dozen times, and then I swiped at my eyes and nose and felt better and so gingerly made my way back to my spyhole.

Brannomar was just turning around in my vision as I peered in. If he'd heard those gargantuan sneezes he gave no sign and in my agitated state I didn't pick up just what he was doing. I reached for the lever and pulled, the secret panel slid open, and I tumbled through.

He was quick. Oh, yes, Hyr Kov Brannomar was no slouch when it came to swordhandling. The braxter ripped free of the scabbard and the point snouted towards me.

I opened my mouth ready to say something like: "All right, kov. Stand easy." I opened my mouth all right and the sneeze roared up from the soles of my feet and through my shaking body and just erupted like a coruscating volcano. I sprayed everything in the vicinity. Water clouded my vision. Shaking my head and trying to get things in focus I was ready to try again when a gasp of utter astonishment burst from the side of the room I had not been able to see. Hands in the air I swung about.

The man who had just been ushered into the room, for the door was just closing at his back, wore sturdy buff clothes, the wide-shouldered jacket, the buff breeches and tall black boots I recognized immediately. His hand clasped the wide-brimmed hat with two slots cut in the forward brim and the jaunty feather was red and yellow. I knew him. He stared goggle-eyed at me. He knew enough not to go into the slavish full incline. That indignity had been done away with during my early days as Emperor of Vallia. He drew himself up to his full height.

"Majister!" said Elten Larghos Invordun na Thothsturboin. "By Vox! Majister!"

Nineteen

"Majister?" Brannomar's sword thrust forward. "What nonsense is this?"

"I have to tell you, kov," said Elten Larghos in a direct metallic voice, "if you try to harm this gentleman I shall kill you, immediately, without reck of the consequences."

Brannomar swung to face him and it was quite clear he'd never heard Larghos speak in that deadly tone of voice before.

"Now, now," I said. "Lahal, Larghos. There's no need of killing among friends."

"Majister!" spluttered Brannomar. "What the hell is going on?"

Elten Larghos in his usual diplomatic voice said: "Hyr Kov Brannomar, you have the honor to be in the presence of Dray Prescot."

Brannomar opened his mouth, shut it, and still carrying his sword he crossed to his chair and sat down. Rather, he collapsed into the seat. "Dray Prescot! Emperor of Vallia!" And then, of course, he realized the enormity of the disaster that he assumed had blighted his plans. "You heard everything!"

Ignoring the kov, Larghos said: "You are well, majister?" He eyed my dust-covered clothes with the cobwebs entangled in my hair. Now because of the many books and plays and puppet shows about Dray Prescot in Paz that portray him leaping about Kregen wearing the brave old scarlet breechclout and wielding the great Krozair longsword, no one is very much surprised when I turn up in unexpected places—like now. Larghos was not amazed at seeing me after the first moment; now he wanted to know if all went well with me in view of my deplorable condition.

"Perfectly well, thank you Larghos. Now I believe we have some explaining to do to the good kov here."

Looked at unemotionally—which could not, of course, be done—this whole situation was totally unreal. Here was a great and puissant noble in his own snug in his own palace suddenly confronted by a dust and cobwebbed figure leaping out of the wall at him. Then this lunatic turns out to be the ex-emperor of the very country with which the good kov so desperately needs to become allied. No wonder Brannomar with his white hair abruptly looked so haggard.

The Vallian ambassador to Tolindrin gave me a wry smile. "Aye, majister. I came in here to tie up a few loose ends in the treaty. Now I believe I need to know a great deal more before I sign on behalf of the Emperor Drak and Empress Silda and Vallia."

"Indeed, and so do I. There's skullduggery afoot in Oxonium. I know some of it and can guess more. Much of it is simple-minded. But there are one or two items of interest outstanding." I spoke directly to the hunched figure slumped at the table. "Brannomar! Perk up, man!"

"Dray Prescot." He spoke half to himself, whispering. Oh, surely, he'd read the books about that roaring desperado Dray Prescot!

Larghos fulfilling an ambassadorial function in a most diplomatic way poured a glass of parclear for the kov. Brannomar took it and drank and placed the glass down precisely before him. He looked up. He visibly took control of himself. Some of the old hard look of resolution returned.

"I believe you to be Dray Prescot. You now know how important the treaty is. I work for Tolindrin. I could summon guards and no more would be heard of you or the Vallian ambassador—"

Elten Larghos did not bother to draw his rapier or main gauche. He said, almost off-handedly: "But you would be dead first, kov."

"You boasted just now, Elten. Like you, do you think I reck the cost of service to my king and country?"

I sighed and said: "I could do with a wet right now, Brannomar. And, also, your old king is dead."

His head snapped up. Then his lips curled back. "You listened to us. It was not difficult to understand what was going on."

"True. By the Feast of Beng T'Tolin, when the old king was due to show himself to the people, you must have a new king."

"And you, of all people, had to be the one to bring the old king's will!" He shook that white poll. "Well, you know the will was not in Strom Korden's sword. The succession is not known. The old king trusted the priests of Cymbaro and they have played him false."

"Would the contestants have abided by the old king's will?"

"Yes."

"And, kov, you have no idea who it was he chose?"

"No."

"It is a moil. I gather the Lady Vita sold out—"

He was past being surprised at new revelations of what had been revealed of the intrigues festering away in Oxonium. "The Lady Vita is a lady of spirit, too much spirit, perhaps. I refused her, and am thankful for that. Poor Jazipur got a bad bargain there. She was discovered in her treachery by Naghan the Ordsetter. Ironic that Jazipur's spymaster should catch the wife of his employer. She planned well, one must say that."

It occurred to me to reinforce the impression he had of Dray Prescot by a piece of arrant boasting. This, I plead in my defense, was not pompous pride but calculated for effect.

"I saw the Lady Vita in Khonstanton's palace."

He just took that in with all the rest. "She has a granddaughter. She told Khonstanton about the will in the sword in return for a promise that Khon the Mak would marry the granddaughter to his son. Vita has absolute power over her children and grandchildren."

"So that's how that devil knew. From what I've seen of Khon Mak she was a fool to trust his word."

"She was blinded by ambition." He made a weary gesture. "Her grandson was to marry the infant daughter of Prince Ortyg—"

"By Krun!" I burst out. "So she played both ends against the middle! Whoever inherited, she thought she'd be running the show."

"Ortyg employed the Fristle, Fonnell the Fractious, and his olive green clad scum. He imagined they could not be traced back to him because—"

"He used a Bravo Fighter from Zenicce as a go between."

Oh, well, it was all adding up now. What Nandisha's chances in all this imbroglio were I couldn't tell. They looked slimmer by the moment. Then Brannomar added another piece to the puzzle.

"Prince Tomendishto has plans to do with the Shrine of Cymbaro. He has no interest in the throne. I believe him."

"And if the old king left the crown to Prince Tom?"

"I am not sure. It was through Tom that the old king took an interest in Cymbaro. For secrecy and safety they thought the priests could carry the new will after the king's son died and keep it in Farinsee."

Farinsee, from what I had seen from the distance, looked to be a stronghold of some importance, perched atop that strange mountain like Ayer's Rock. Even if the priests and their guards were only indifferent fighting men you'd need a good few regiments and engineers to take the place.

"Strom Korden was entrusted with the new will naming the heir, and then the old king died so the will became enforceable. It had to be returned to Oxonium at once." He spread his hands helplessly. "You, Dray Prescot, witnessed the first result of the Lady Vita's blind treachery."

"Yes." I spoke with an ugly voice. "Good men and young girls dead."

"And no will," said Larghos who had kept his silence throughout.

Brannomar said dully: "No will, no heir, and Civil War."

Silence fell in that comfortable study in the heart of a mighty palace. The inevitability of what the hyr kov prophesied weighed upon us all. Larghos cleared his throat and said: "The treaty, then, will not be made between Tolindrin and Vallia."

Brannomar looked up wearily, the scar almost invisible, his thin mouth curved downwards. "That would appear to be so. But I would implore you to reconsider—"

"It's not up to me," I said. "My son Drak and daughter-in-law Silda run Vallia now, thanks be to Opaz. But they are reasonable people."

Larghos nodded sagely. "If there is Civil War in Tolindrin then Vallia cannot look to receive, among other things, very much in the way of baltrixes, silk or lifters."

"We need good Vallian weapons, among many other trade items." The hyr kov spread his hands.

"And there's another ugly aspect to all this." I spoke harshly, for I felt warm upon the subject. "In addition to the theft of Korden's sword there have been attempts upon the lives of the Princess Nandisha and her children and upon Prince Tomendishto. Opaz alone knows how they've escaped death so far."

This information appeared to shake Brannomar. He stood up. "I assure you, majister, that this is not how affairs usually are in Tolindrin. Not in the days of the old king."

"That's how they are now." Larghos's diplomatic manner fell away to reveal the fighting man of Vallia. "Trust is forfeit."

I recalled the troubles through which poor old Nandisha and her kids had gone. They were not my immediate concern according to the Star Lords. All the same—I said: "I do not doubt Khon the Mak and Ortyg will try again. I would like to think they would fail through the efforts of loyal Tolindrese. As for the succession, it would be convenient if Nandisha's twins inherited—the boy, that is—and you, Brannomar, continued as Regent."

"The succession follows at the hands of the king."

"Yes, but—"

"That is how the matter lies, majister. If the will is not found then the inheritance will be decided by force of arms."

By the lice-infested hair and maggot-infested intestines of Makki Grodno! All I wanted to do was discharge my obligations to the numim twins placed in Fweygo's and my care and then head off home to Esser Rarioch. All this skullduggery gave a fellow a pain in the skull.

His mention of the old king's will festered away in Brannomar's thoughts. He thumped a fist down on the table. "If only we could find the will! Strom Korden must have hidden it safely. It is not in the sword. So where in the name of Tolaar is it?"

Elten Larghos stepped forward. He'd been a warrior for the Liberation Army of Vallia, a Freedom Fighter in the Times of Troubles. Now he was a diplomat. His mind was now attuned in different ways. He said softly: "Majister. You were there. What did Strom Korden say to you? Exactly."

My thoughts went back to that hideous scene on the road from Amintin. The dead men, the dead girls, the blood and stink. And young Tiri hiding behind the carriage. What had the dying man said?

"It was all indistinct. His mouth was filled with blood. He said: 'Strom Korden. Lahal. Take the sword and take it to Hyr Kov Brannomar. By Cymbaro the Just I charge you.'"

"That is all, majister?" demanded Larghos, sharply.

"Aye, Larghos. All. He repeated some of it in his desperate urgency to fulfill his mission."

"Take the sword and take it to Hyr Kov Brannomar."

"Just so. After a few scrapes I did that."

"And he was dying at the time? Able only to say a few words?"

"As I have said."

Then, of course, the understanding hit me. Oh, yes, it is very easy in hindsight. Hindsight confers a most remarkable access of understanding in all manner of arcane matters hidden before. No doubt you who listen to my narrative as the tape spins through the heads of the little recording machine must have been writhing at my blindness. Well, all I can say is that I'd had to hop, skip and jump to avoid sword points and keep my head—and others', by Krun!—on my shoulders. It was all so easy and clear now. Poor old Strom Korden, dying with the dreadful knowledge that he had failed in his charge to the old king, trying with the last few breaths left to him to make this uncouth fighting man bending over him grasp the supreme importance of what he must do for Tolindrin, would not waste precious words.

"Take the sword and take—" he'd managed to gasp out through the blood. "Take the sword and—"

There had been no second 'take' following that 'and'. I knew what he'd been trying to say. I understood now.

There was no doubt that if Khon the Mak or Ortyg laid hands on the will and discovered it did not name them that they'd destroy it. Better, perhaps, because they'd have clever people who had the skills, they'd have the will altered in their favor. Forgery for gold is not confined to Earth. Either way, if the will was not found and made public, the two antagonists would continue their intrigues right up to the moment war broke out. That must not be allowed to happen—for the good of Vallia if not for the benefit of Tolindrin.

My face felt stiff, as though stuck in hardened putty. Nothing of my turbulent thoughts registered in my expression. Larghos was looking at me with one eyebrow raised. As for Kov Brannomar, he was still caught up in his own mental turmoil, agonizing over the whereabouts of the old king's will, aghast at the prospects for his country. His concentration slipped past what Larghos and I had been saying to bring his thoughts to a point that he must consider central to the issue. I knew it was not; but when he spoke I did not contradict him.

"Majister. I see the will is vital to the interests of both Vallia and Tolindrin. Tolaar knows, it must be found. But you, you show yourself as Drajak the Sudden and I have read enough about Dray Prescot to understand that. Will you now step forth as the emperor and deny Tolindrin the treaty?"

"My son Drak is the Emperor of Vallia now. As you know I am called the Emperor of Emperors, the Emperor of Paz. Well, we will talk of that later. Right now I remain Drajak the Sudden. I would wish you to remember that, Brannomar." My tone hardened.

"Drajak the Sudden. Of course, majister."

Larghos, who had not stopped staring at me, said: "Very good, majister." He hitched up his sword belts. "Let us go and get the confounded will, and, by Vox! get this conundrum over with."

"Elten?" said Brannomar, suddenly all at sea.

"Oh," I said, and felt my lips curve into the semblance of a smile. "I've no wish to give Larghos a swelled head, but he wasn't picked to join the Vallian Diplomatic Service because he was slow on the uptake." I did not intend to elaborate on that blabber-mouth effusion; but further speech was chopped off by the abrupt slapping open of the door. A strange figure entered, bent over, seeming to be surrounded by a whirl of rags, shaking what looked like a morntarch.

Brannomar simply called out: "Sister. You find us at an awkward moment. Is this important?"

A female face stared from under the piled and drooping mass of hair. Brilliant eyes appeared inturned, the sharp nose, as it were, sniffing into corners, the mouth—so much like Brannomar's—firmly clamped. She took no notice of any of us. She prowled around the study, shaking the morntarch, its shaft wrapped in ribbons, only three small skulls rattling from silken cords to make that eerie, chilling sound that only the sorcerers who use morntarchs in their thaumaturgy may comprehend. She smelled all right; but she smelled sweetly of lavender water.

Around the study she circled. Larghos and I remained motionless. Most Kregans are mighty careful when it comes to dealing with the practitioners of the arcane arts. Brannomar's scar stood out pulsating against his bronzed skin. "Besti!" he said, an edge to his voice. "Sister!"

Completely ignoring the hyr kov the sorceress pried into every cranny. The atmosphere in the study suddenly choked in on me oppressively. Brannomar sucked in his cheeks; he said no more. When it was clear this strange female apparition was satisfied with whatever she'd been doing she gave Brannomar a sidelong, calculating look.

"You always were a credulous fambly, Bran." She shook her morntarch at him in a gesture at once annoyed and resigned. "Yet your credulity does not extend to what your dear twin sister can do—"

"The king's views prevail in Tolindrin, Besti. You and your ilk are tolerated if you behave. No wizards may—"

"Well, brother, I do! I know the old king is dead. And so do others. You prattled on here and that spineless, lily-livered, damned-to-Sicce wizard Wocut listened to you. His traces are plain here."

At once Larghos said: "Drajak—Wocut is a sorcerer who serves Khon the Mak. He is reputed to possess powers—"

"Ha!" spat this remarkable witch Besti. Her voice was not a cackle, as one might expect. It sounded like the chuckle of water over rapids. "Powers he stole from gullible San Nath the Farseeing."

This Wocut had to be the mage I'd seen in conference with Khonstanton and his fat major-domo. If he'd been listening—just how much damage could he cause? Larghos was saying: "They do not have the powers of Wizards of Loh—well, who has?—but best be wary of them, Drajak."

"Nice to have met you, Sana Besti," I rapped out. "Come on! To the guardhouse, Larghos. Brannomar—tell your guards we're on our way." The hyr kov jumped up from his chair and started for the door after us, calling: "Wait for me, confound you!"

That's better, I said to myself. He's remembering he's a hyr kov.

The first couple of guards who tried to stop our headlong rush were open-handed off. By then Brannomar was yelling at the top of his voice, a Hikdar fell in to run with us, and we had no further interruptions.

We reached the entrance to the palace guardhouse. Racing inside I headed at once for the corner where I'd sat down to eat the meal they'd provided. A jolly-faced apim who strained the banded iron of his armor and who was stuffing palines into his wide mouth spluttered in protest as I hauled him out. My hand dived down into the crevice of seat and back of the bench. This was where I'd left the damned thing. My fingers scrabbled around like a crab after morsels of food. Dust and breadcrumbs, a sliver of moldy green cheese, some disgusting gunk that stuck—but not that which I sought. Desperately I reached further in, pulling the wood. More and more frantically I hauled away, tearing the bench to pieces. Nothing!

It had been left here when I'd gone out to venture down into the runnels. By the hairy pendulous protuberances of the Divine Lady of Belschutz! Why did I get myself into these diabolical scrapes? I'd been called an onker enough times in my giddy career on Kregen, and in truth I was, an onker of onkers. I glared about, knowing the damn thing was not here. Hikdar Tygnam ti Fralen had walked into the guardroom and was speaking with Kov Brannomar. Brannomar nodded and called to me: "Drajak. All Strom Korden's possessions have been taken to his villa."

As I digested this information a new and horrible realization hit me.

"That pair of double-dyed villains! If we can work it out then so can they. And I've been too damn long about it." By this time I was wrapped up in this business and desperate to get it over with. If the Star Lords took it into their little pointy heads to decide I was neglecting my obligations to them I could find myself hurtling through the void back to Earth. "Where away is Korden's villa? I must get there at once, before they do."

Brannomar's sorceress sister, the Lady Besti, put her hand on his arm. "Yes, they know enough to go to the strom's villa. You will be too late—"

"I have to try!" I fairly snarled at her.

"There is a way. I can—"

Brannomar jumped. He reacted with a physical convulsion of his shoulders. His scar shone as though newly branded on his skin. "Besti! You know the king's ordinance. And it will drain you—"

"The old king is in no case to interfere, brother. The cost is worth the result. This—Drajak—is the man."

From my experiences with the arcane glamor of Deb-Lu-Quienyin and the college of mages I guessed what Besti meant. I stared at her, trying to put stern resolution into my features and knowing some of the old Dray Prescot Devil Look must have flashed across my face, for she lifted her morntarch involuntarily and gave it a tiny shake. The skulls rattled once.

"I understand, my Lady Besti. Please be quick."

"Yes. You are indeed the man. But do you apprehend the peril?"

"Yes. I have dealt with Wizards of Loh."

Her eyes widened at this. I wanted to scream at her in frustration.

She licked her lips. "You will be disoriented—"

"For the sake of your brother, for the sake of Tolindrin. Lady Besti—do it!"

Her eyes closed, her arms lifted, the skulls dangling from the morntarch rattled in frenzy—and I was off.

Twenty

Have you ever slipped on a banana skin? Have you ever tobogganed down an icy slope out of control? Have you ever been kicked up the back end by a fractious mule? Have you ever lost the path and fought your way back through thick snow-covered bushes? Have you ever walked in the dark slap bang into an unlighted lamp-post? Experiences of that order, multiplied by googol values, tried to tear me into little pieces.

By Zair! I tell you, that was a whole lifetime of diabolical experiences crammed into a few hectic moments I wouldn't like to have to do every morning before breakfast!

Completely disorientated, half-blind, the sound of Niagara in my ears, feeling pains as though my insides were being torn out and plastered all over my outsides, I arrived wherever it was the witch Lady Besti had flung me. And, yes, going over Niagara Falls in a barrel was in there somewhere, into the bargain.

These experiences were totally unlike those associated with going up to see the Star Lords, or being sent across the planes by Deb-Lu-Quienyin. Vastly different, by Krun!

A gray haziness hung before my eyes that was nothing like dusty spider-webs. Bright little sparks of spitting fire darted at me. I was firmly convinced I stood on my head at the same time as I stood on my heels. And all the time I was going up and down and around and around in that gut-wrenching roller-coaster that made Montezuma's Revenge—the best, or worst, ride in California according to the pundits—appear a ride in a chauffeured limousine along smooth blacktop.

This catalogue of dire impressions is mentioned in this way for two reasons. The actuality was far far worse than I care to recall. My arrival in Strom Korden's villa occurred in a fashion not at all in the Dray Prescot style.

The Yunivils, a race of diffs startlingly unlike apims but nice people, believe that they must be buried with their arms behind their backs and their hands grasping their heels. If they are not they will not be received into their heaven, instead they will be hurled down to their hell, Makchun, peculiarly theirs, which lies deep below the Ice Floes of Sicce. Executed criminals are buried with their hands on their heads. They stand no chance at all of entering the Yunivil paradise.

Now I knew what a poor condemned Yunivil felt like when he knew he was to be interred with his hands on his head.

I just didn't know what was going on. The Lady Besti must have transported me using her arcane arts. I must have arrived, for now I could feel hard floor under my feet. The miasma swirling about me writhed mockingly. I couldn't see a damn thing. A hand grasped my arm and a gruff voice blasted into my ear.

"You're done for, shint."

Another voice, hard, commanding, rattled out: "Stand fast, Larghos! I want that man! Drag him over here."

Another pair of hands helped by tugging my hair and away I went across the marble, dragged up towards the owner of that hard voice—Khon the Mak, as ever was.

If only I could get my hands off my head and grab my heels they might let me into heaven—no, no. I was an apim, Dray Prescot, Lord of Strombor and Krozair of Zy. Oh, no! I could not allow myself to be done for yet, oh, no, not by the pustular armpits and festering nostrils of Makki Grodno. Desperately I tried to peer into the mist.

Still badly disorientated I was slapped down on my knees and my head was forced up and back. The unmistakable kiss of cold steel touched my bared throat.

My eyes stung as though filled with freshly ground black pepper. Was that an indistinct outline forming before me, or only my fevered imagination presenting phantasms? The shape moved. It thickened and took on outlines. Ink-black hair, parchment-white face, oh, yes, there he stood, staring down on me in triumph.

With agonizing slowness my senses returned to near-enough normality. My surroundings, as it were, created themselves about me. I was in an atrium-like space of a comfortable villa, with columns and statuary and potted plants. Fish leaped in a small pool. The smells of jasmine cooled the air. And this confounded rast Khonstanton held all the aces as his bully boys held me down before him and a dagger was laid across my throat.

If I got out of this scrape I'd have a word or three with the good Lady Besti. Yes, by Krun! What a way to deliver a fellow!

The voice of Khonstanton's wizard sounded out of my sight as he said: "The man smells of sorcery, notor. He was dispatched through—that is—"

"Get on with it, San Wocut, if it is important. You are merely delaying this shint's death."

"I was going to say, notor, through thaumaturgical arts frowned upon by the late king. Power to bring him here has been used, there can be no doubt of that."

The Lady Besti's power might be kharrna I did not comprehend, I did know it put a fellow through torture worthy of the old Hanitchik in Ruathytu or of poor fat Queen Fahia in Huringa. My eyes unglued a little more. This fellow Larghos held his damned dagger close. In those first bemused moments I might well have imagined that the Vallian ambassador held the blade. Squinting up I saw he was a Chulik. His golden-banded tusks gleamed in the light; he enjoyed this kind of work.

"Slissur take the how of it." Mak Khon's voice grated. "The how of it is easy enough to guess. That dignified prig Brannomar! Before this scum dies he will tell us exactly."

Digesting that interesting item of information I came to the conclusion that I really could not hang about any longer. The dagger was cutting in unpleasantly. There were two of them holding me and although I couldn't see who it was dragging my head back by the hair he would be the first to go.

With an extremely sharp movement, a very sharp movement, by Vox! I laid the back of my heel into the space I knew he must be occupying. In the same instant an equally rapid jerk of the head took my throat away from that officiously sharp dagger. The fellow at my back yelped shrilly confirming the accuracy of my blind aim. In that tiny space that opened between dagger and throat I twisted. The Chulik doubled up, gobbling, and I span to finish off the other one.

Speed alone saved me. Two more savage blows followed by a charging run at Khonstanton saw me past. The kov staggered away from my shoulder, mouthing incoherently. I didn't stop to kick him as I took off, much though he deserved it, and the shadows of the columned arcades swallowed me up. No one even loosed or threw after me.

Running flat out under the arched roof I went with great speed through several archways and along more corridors. This place was not in the same architectural league as the great palaces of Oxonium, it still was a splendid villa with many rooms, passages and stairways. Reluctant though I might be to deal harshly with Strom Korden's folk, the desperate situation gave me no latitude. The first servant I grabbed just gibbered.

Pushing him away I hared off until a rotund Gon turned a corner to be gripped and held. My face glared into his. His shaven head shone with lavish ministrations of butter; his eyes goggled.

"Where are the strom's private apartments, oh Gon?"

He stuttered and shook and spittle ran down his chin.

"The strom is dead."

"As will you be," I said, unkindly, "if you do not show me the way."

He wore a decent yellow tunic and soft sandals so he was an indoor servant and would know his way about. I gave him a shove. The sight of my face convinced him. Sobbing and whining under his breath he led off.

Yes, I hate this kind of behavior; but so much depended on my getting to the strom's possessions first there was no time for niceties. That pack of killers would be hard on my heels by now.

The Gon did not play me false. Opaz alone knows what I would have done had he done so in the frame of mind I was in. We hurried along and I kept a sharp lookout.

The debilitating effects of the Lady Besti's sorcery wore off as we climbed higher in the villa to reach a series of tastefully furnished apartments over-looking the atrium where I'd landed. A few servants who saw us cowered away. I got the impression certain people had been here before me asking questions and not getting any answers.

Indeed, a Hytak guard stood at the door to the inner rooms; but he went to sleep peacefully before he had time to challenge us. I shoved the Gon through and in we went.

"All the strom's possessions that were brought here." I gave him a look. "Take me to them—now."

"Yes, yes, notor, yes. Please do not kill me."

"Your name, Gon?"

"Affleck the Wine, if it please you."

So I laughed as we bustled through. "A trifle of a wet would please me greatly, Affleck the Wine. Perhaps afterwards."

He gave me an odd look; but he stopped shaking. We entered the strom's bedchamber. Strom Korden lived the simple spartan life of the warrior and the practical furnishings of his bedroom confirmed that. Looking about it was easy to see his lifestyle before Khon the Mak or Prince Ortyg had him foully murdered. An iron-bound chest at the foot of the bed looked promising and I released the Gon with: "Stand still, Affleck!" He jumped and stood like a wooden hitching post. I threw the lid of the chest open.

Pitiful—pitiful—the garments, the harness, the boots, the brave helmet with the feathers—tumbled in here as Strom Korden would be placed in his tomb out in Kaodrin past the hills of Oxonium. Masons were already at work out there building the vast and awe-inspiring sepulchers to house the king's son and the old king when—in the eyes of the populace—he in his turn died. Strom Korden's tomb, although of far less magnificence, would hold the remains of a man of just as much, if not greater, worth.

I picked the thing up and buckled the belt around my waist.

A light, amused laugh came from the doorway followed by: "By Krun, my dear chap, you really are a fellow for getting into things."

The braxter was in my fist, for the moment the belt was buckled up I intended to transfer the blade. So, slowly, sword in hand, I turned to face him.

He took one pace into the strom's bedchamber and so stood, right leg a little advanced, gloved hands on hips, head thrown back and chin jutting. He was well aware of the dashing picture he made. He'd at last changed his shirt for a Tolindrinese shamlak, very suave in a rich silvery-gray material, and silvery-gray trousers were stuffed into black boots. He was what he was, what nature had intended him to be from the moment of his birth, no more and no less. Like him? Oh, yes, I had quite a fondness for him by this time. His light, peculiar, distinctive laugh bubbled through his words. He lifted one hand and stroked a forefinger along his thin black moustache.

"The game has been well worth it, Drajak, my friend. But, now—"

Like anything else in life he wasn't taking this seriously. He held out his hand. "I'll take it now, old feller, if you please."

There was absolutely no appreciation on his part of the incongruity of the request in these circumstances, no understanding of a viewpoint other than his own. He was self-centered to the point of sublimity.

Cautiously, I said: "I rather think—"

Before I could continue, a hullabaloo of shouting and smashing noises spurted up from outside. Moving swiftly sideways I looked out of the wide bedroom windows onto the atrium.

What looked like a whole damned army of fighting men poured into the space below, spreading out and prodding and prying. There was no mistaking the man intemperately directing their efforts. You couldn't miss that weasel face, the frenetic movements. I swung back to Dagert.

"Prince Ortyg. He'll cut out our livers and fry 'em—"

"Highly dramatic, don't you know—but all the same I think it best if you handed it across. I'll feel more reassured."

"There's no time for that now. We have to get away."

He gave an abrupt nod. He was handsome in his own dark and raffish way and now those clear-cut features set impassionately. "Of course."

"Affleck!" I called, swinging about. The Gon was gone. Affleck the Wine had taken the opportunity to scuttle back to his vats.

I glared at Dagert of Paylen. "D'you know your way around this confounded place?"

"Come on." Without hesitation he started for the door. I followed. I did not scabbard the braxter—just in case, by Djan!

Together we ran along corridors and through pleasant rooms. We reached double doors before which a wounded Hytak lay, blood seeping from his side. He lifted one hand painfully. Dagert went headlong through the open doorway and I almost trod on his heels.

The moment I saw the assemblage in the room and realized the tables were turned I skidded to a halt, frantically backpedaling. Dagert hauled up in front. Beyond him the chamber was filled with men wearing the badges of Hyr Kov Khonstanton, another whole damned army of 'em.

"Whoops!" I yelped. "Come on, Dagert. This is too unhealthy for us." Dagert swung back towards me. That handsome face showed pleasure. For an instant I imagined he was happy to take this bunch on single handed. He ripped out his rapier and main gauche in the practiced motions of a Bladesman. Then Khon the Mak walked forward from the ranks of his men.

"Well done, Amak. I was sure I could rely on you."

So we faced each other, Dagert of Paylen and Drajak the Sudden.

"You see how it is, my dear chap. Better hand it over right away."

"You," I said, foolishly. "You've damned well been working for Mak Khon all the time."

"As it happens, yes. It is to my advantage, as I'm sure you'd be the first to recognize."

The moment hung, poised. A number of incidents came clear.

"You drove those confounded nails into Nandisha's lifter controls."

"Not me, Palfrey. And he caused her to land in Amintin."

"And Strom Korden?"

His rapier made a graceful gesture. "Had that sorry affair been in my hands the resolution, I assure you, by Krun, would have been different."

"I believe you." And, by Vox, I did!

"Well now, don't delay any longer. I assure you—"

What all these assurances of his might have amounted to might well not have weighed against a feather. I shook my head like any onker and he flung himself forward, blades glittering.

Like a leem, he was, quick and lethal. The braxter switched across to block a lunge and a twist of the body avoided the dagger. I gave a sharp cut, his blade slammed across in immediate defense—and the blades met with a harsh and brittle crash. Good Ruathytu steel versus metal of munitions quality of Tolindrin—the braxter snapped across.

Furiously I hurled the hilted stump in his face, swiveled and ran.

He'd have no difficulty in avoiding the throw. He'd be after me instantly. So, I, Dray Prescot, Lord of Strombor and Krozair of Zy, ran.

Straight back down the passage I hurled, leaping over the poor devil of a wounded Hytak, haring on with Dagert of Paylen in full chase.

Room after room, chamber after chamber we kept up that mad race.

After a time I knew by the sounds that Dagert alone pursued for we outdistanced the pack. At last we reached a wide, low-ceiled upper room where benches and tables showed this to be a dining area. Man-high windows stood along one wall. At the far end a narrow door led—where? I didn't know and I was tired of running off. Once I had thrown Dagert of Paylen off my track I'd high tail it out of here. I hauled up and swung about to face him.

"Ah, at last, my dear chap." He didn't sound the least bit breathless. His blades snouted up. "Look here, why not hand it across and we'll say no more." His gloved left hand lifted the main gauche and a forefinger stroked along the pencil thin moustache. "The kov's folk will not be so understanding."

Without fuss I drew the rapier and left-hand dagger.

His face suddenly expressed comical surprise. "What! Surely—my dear fellow, I do assure you, I bear you no animosity whatsoever—surely you must understand. You have no chance with the Jiktar and the Hikdar."

"You tried to murder Nandisha and her children—"

"Hardly murder! I do draw the line somewhere, you know. Just a device to bring them down, that is all. Now, come along—"

"If you want the damn thing you must take it."

"Then, as they say in Clishdrin, on your own head be it." He leaped.

Our blades crossed in that soul-searing scrape and chingle of metal. Of two things I was firmly convinced. This fight had to be over quickly. And Dagert of Paylen would be a first-class Bladesman of Ruathytu. The fight was quite interesting. As you know I am always aware that one day on Kregen I may meet another Mefto the Kazzur who is my master with the sword. I do not now and never have claimed to be the best swordsman in two worlds. After a few passes I knew Dagert of Paylen was not another Mefto the Kazzur. His face, at first nonchalant with a tiresome chore to be done, slowly assumed a more sober expression. His attitude changed.

His first attacks were simple enough, designed, I truly believe, to disarm me. My responses brought a more determined onslaught. After a few more flourishes, when the blades met in cunning angles, he drew back.

"I see I misjudged you, my dear Drajak. It seems you have some skill, after all. Well, that is all one now, smoke blown with the wind. If you are pinked or stuck through—"

And on the words he was in with leem-like speed. A twist, the dagger angled just so, and I thrust. He skidded sideways, blades all askew. His face went white.

Pressing him, I forced him back. His skill was considerable and there was no taking chances. Around the room we went, leaping onto benches and tables, thrusting and riposting, the blades blurred slivers of deadly light.

As I say, this fight was an interesting one.

Eventually he realized he would not best me.

Eventually, too, I knew I would not thrust to kill. He was far too engaging a character.

He ran a few paces off and swiveled to face me. His bare chest beneath the shamlak moved more rapidly now.

"Yes," he said. "I see I have seriously misjudged you. The devil take it! Hyr Kov Khonstanton must do his dirty work himself."

With a sleight of hand I admired the rapier snicked up to tuck under his right armpit. The dagger appeared in his fingers, as it were, from nowhere. He flung full at me.

With the instinctive reaction of one versed in the Disciplines of the Krozairs of Zy I flicked the rapier up and the dagger chingled away to spin in a twinkling of light and embed itself in a table.

"Ha!" he exclaimed, whirling his blade back and scabbarding it and in the same motion sheathing the left-hand dagger. "A veritable prodigy!"

With that he turned suddenly, leaped for the man-high window nearest and plunged through in a welter of smashing glass and splintering frame. He vanished.

Running to the ruin of the window and looking out I glimpsed him leaping like a gazelle over the rooftops. He kept up that cheeky role to the end. At a chimney stack he paused and turned back. He gave me a wave of his gloved hand, almost an ironic salute. Then Dagert of Paylen, swordsman, killer, dandy—yet hardly a forsworn villain—disappeared.

After that the whole affair dwindled. Fresh uproar greeted me as I stared out and amidst the intermingled shouts I made out the cries of: "Khonstanton!" "Ortyg!" and, thankfully: "Brannomar!"

Cautiously making my way back to the atrium and wary of the slightest shadow, I found the place seething with armed and armored men. They were all there. With that charismatic presence at full blast, Brannomar sorted out the hubbub. People milled. Khonstanton, Ortyg and Brannomar stood together talking heatedly. Little would be required to set all these warriors at one another's throats. Prince Tom and Princess Nandisha appeared and walked towards the others. Abruptly, Fweygo and Tiri stood at my side, chattering away like magpies.

"I don't know what you've been up to—" began Fweygo.

"Drajak! You're safe, thanks be to Cymbaro!" Tiri grabbed my arm.

"Fweygo—the numims—?"

"Safe."

"I'll tell you all about it directly. First I have a duty to discharge." I pushed through the people towards the principals.

Brannomar saw me. I nodded. I made the nod significant and he understood at once. An expression of relief flickered across his bronzed face. I walked up to him and he spoke urgently.

"Not here. All of you, come. Let's have it done with."

In only a few moments the principals gathered in Strom Korden's best reception room. Nandisha looked agitated and I tried to give her a smile.

Tom, as ever, seemed distanced from all the excitement. As for Ortyg, his thin face wore the various expressions associated with greed and ambition and self-pride. Khonstanton stuck his hands on his hips.

"Well? Drajak the Sudden, you—"

"Don't worry, notor," I said. "Everything is under control." And let him chew the pips in that one, bad cess to him!

Brannomar extended his hand. "Drajak?"

I unbuckled the swordbelt I'd taken from Strom Korden's iron-bound chest and handed it across.

This was the article that had caused so much pain and bloodshed and pure bloody-minded grief. This, and not the sword, lay at the core of the intrigue.

Brannomar took it, his knife was out, and he went at the stitching with single-minded purpose. Layer by layer it unwrapped and its secret was revealed. Korden and the priests of Cymbaro had taken the old king's will, an imposing document—as well it must be—of solid parchment and had used the will itself to form the scabbard. Around it they'd stitched the outer cover and had lined it correctly. Now the stiff yellow pages unwrapped before our fascinated gazes.

"Forget the bequests," snarled Khonstanton. "The heir!" When a king died he left munificent bequests so there would be clause after clause. Ortyg shoved up to help hold the will flat. He was consumed. He was aflame with greed. If the old king had known anything about his descendants, as I guessed he would have, why then—I felt a pang of pity for this presumptuous prince.

Nandisha held her lower lip between her teeth. Well, yes, her son would do well to inherit, and Brannomar run the country as regent. That would suit Vallia and me nicely. As for Khonstanton, he'd be worse than Ortyg. Who, in a Herrelldrin Hell was it, then?

Brannomar read. He moved his head, and read again. He looked up.

"Come on, man!" ground out Khonstanton.

Ortyg tried to read the upside down will.

Hyr Kov Brannomar slowly turned. He looked directly at Prince Tom.

"Long live King Tomendishto!" he cried in a loud, firm voice. "Long live the king!"

Nandisha collapsed in a dead faint.

Ortyg swore and grabbed the parchment, feverishly reversing it and gobbling out his words as he read what he hated to see.

Khonstanton started to speak, said nothing, and stalked from the room.

The new king said, hesitatingly: "But—" and said no more.

What I said, to myself, was: "For the disgusting sake of the putrescent inward parts and festering outer parts of Makki Grodno! Thanks be that's over!"

I went over to give what assistance I could to Nandisha. As far as I was concerned, this affair was dead. Now the future must concern the fate of the numim twins, Rofi and Rolan. The Star Lords had shown much forbearance in allowing me to gad about in the regal affairs of Tolindrin. Now Fweygo and I must ensure that the numim twins were safe. And how long would that take? By the Black Chunkrah! All I wanted to do was go home to Esser Rarioch and live peacefully with Delia.

"There is a great deal to be done," declared Brannomar.

He was talking about Tom's accession and the coronation and boring formalities of that kind. I agreed with him for reasons he would never know, reasons to do with the Everoinye and four hundred light years of empty space. Carrying Nandisha I went out to find Fweygo and Tiri.

All the same, I wouldn't quickly forget the Amak Dagert, Dagert of Paylen. He was a bit of a card, more than a bit of a lad, by Krun!

Nandisha was beginning to stir as I went out into the atrium. Fweygo and Tiri saw me and hurried over. Overhead the twin Suns of Scorpio, Zim and Genodras, here known as Mabal and Matol, shone down their streaming mingled lights. I looked at my friends and tried to smile.

By Zair! I didn't know what my destiny might be on the beautiful and terrible world of Kregen. What I did know with great certitude was—I needed a wet! Delia forgive me.

By Mother Zinzu the Blessed—yes!

Gangs of Antares

Dray Prescot

Dray Prescot, as described by one who has seen him here on this Earth, is a man above middle height with brown hair and level brown eyes, brooding and dominating, with enormously broad shoulders and powerful physique. There is about him an abrasive honesty and an indomitable courage. He moves like a savage hunting cat, silent and lethal. Reared in the harsh conditions of Nelson's Navy he is a man who, relatively unsuccessful on Earth, is ideally suited to the new life to which he was called by the Star Lords.

Lit by the ruby and emerald fires of Antares, the planet Kregen, four hundred light years away, is a world harsh yet beautiful, terrible yet alluring. There any man or woman may achieve what the heart desires if they plan and struggle and keep faith with their innate purpose. Kregen has its share of weaklings and the faint of heart; but their names are not writ large in the footnotes to the sagas to be found under the Suns of Scorpio.

Prescot has adventured widely over Kregen both at the behest of the Star Lords and to further his own vision. Now he is in the subcontinent of Balintol where strangeness unlike any that he has previously encountered awaits him. These volumes are arranged to be read as individual books, and we are privileged to be afforded the opportunity of reading further of the adventures of Dray Prescot upon Kregen under the streaming mingled lights of the Suns of Scorpio.

Alan Burt Akers

One

They climbed up before dawn. Twelve of them, twelve young rascals clambering over the fallen boulders at the foot of the Hill of Dancing Ghosts. They slipped like wraiths into the hidden opening in the cliff face. Here torches were handed out. Young Dimpy grasped the rough wood of the handle, Big Balla lit the end from her torch half-blinding Dimpy, and he stumbled up the steps after the others feeling his heart thumping like a manic janzi pecker.

"Get on! Get on!" Sleed gave Dimpy a vicious push which sent him staggering up the steps. The stink of Sleed's greased hair cut acridly through the smells of damp earth and burning torches and sweat. Sleed was bigger than the others and unpleasant with it. He was known as Sleed the Slick and was in command of this section of novices in the Hellraisers. "You'll have to shape up if you wanna join us, you useless tanzy."

Dimpy struggled on up the slippery ascent. He didn't much mind being called a tanzy, for he knew he wasn't. He didn't care to be called Young Dimpy. Oh, sure, he was young all right, not as green as these scared novices, but younger than Sleed or Big Balla. Since the slide and the death of his father and brothers he'd matured in caring for his mother and sisters. The slide had knocked the heart out of his old gang, the Roaring Fifties, so that the Hellraisers had moved into the territory without serious opposition. Now, like it or not, he had to prove himself as a gang member all over again.

Screams splintered up from ahead and a couple of novices tumbled down the steps almost knocking Dimpy over. Confusion broke all along the line. Weird shadows fled across the stairway. Big Balla was already thrusting her way up and Sleed, with his customary vicious shove, pushed past Dimpy and started after her.

"If'n it's them stinking Screaming Leems I'll—" What Sleed intended to do to the rival gang was lost as his words drowned in the uproar. The Screaming Leems, considered Dimpy, had to be way out of their territory if they were mounting a raid here. He could feel the closeness of the walls, the slime underfoot, the dark stench of the place. The novices were caterwauling away, terrified out of their wits. Dimpy dragged in a gagging breath and started after Sleed. He was thinking of Big Balla.

Pushing novices out of his way Dimpy reached the top of the steps where the uncertain light revealed Big Balla and Sleed desperately using their torches to hold off a half-grown praxul whose three stalked eyes glinted red above the fanged slot between his jaws.

Dimpy knew about praxuls. Nasty beasts, squamous and scuttling, they inhabited the honeycombed interiors of the hills along with a whole horrendous slew of fellow monsters. Much of the hill's interior was illuminated by a fungus which gave light enough for the praxul's three eyes. He didn't much like the orange glare of the torches.

"Get his eyes!" shouted Dimpy. He darted in, thrust and skipped back. He missed. Luckily for him, the praxul's sweep of claw also missed.

"I know! I know!" snarled Sleed. "Get outta my way, tanzy." He jumped in, slashed his torch, missed and stumbled back.

The thing stood about waist high, warty of scaled hide, and its claws' reach made it difficult to get at. Like most denizens of the caverns the praxul could use other senses than sight to focus on its prey; but taking out his sight was the priority. The stink of its ooze sickened in Dimpy's nostrils, used as he was to the aromas of the warrens in the runnels between the lordly hills of Oxonium.

Big Balla lunged. Dimpy's reaction was instantaneous. In a single sweep his left fist gripped Big Balla's belt and a supple twisting turn span her away from the lethal slice of claw. A rip of cloth jagged off the girl's tunic caught in the claw. Big Balla yelped. In the same twisting motion Dimpy swirled his torch before them, blazing sparks in a fiery fountain. The praxul crouched back, weaving from side to side, hungrily seeking a way past the flame to his dinner.

"Let me at him!" Sleed tried to sidestep and slash his brand in at an angle. The beast weaved back and sliced and Sleed just managed to topple back, falling to a knee as the girl used her torch to cover him.

That tiny interruption in the flow of jump, thrust and retreat gave Dimpy the opportunity he needed. His actions were fast—very fast. His torch connected with one stalked eye. The eye sizzled. The praxul's claw flashed past his thigh. The thing screeched. The stench grew worse with the sour taste of frizzled eye.

The praxul was not unintelligent, with the instincts of his kind. He valued his sight, despite his other senses. He backed off further, hissing, weaving from side to side, claws waving. He was in pain. Despite all, Dimpy felt a stab of pity for the praxul. Then, clearly deciding his dinner was not to be found beyond the flare of the torches, he turned and scuttled off into the dimness.

Dimpy and Big Balla let out simultaneous whoops of relief. Sleed glared malevolently after the disappearing monster. He shook his torch. "I'd a done him good, by Ferzakl. Yeah—if he hadn't run off."

The girl touched Dimpy lightly on the shoulder. Her face became suddenly different, grave with the seriousness of sudden realization of just what had happened. "Thanks, Dimpy. He'd have had me, for sure." She tossed her hair back. "You were quick, by Ferzakl, mighty quick."

Dimpy felt it unnecessary to mention that he had acquired a reputation in the Roaring Fifties for the speed of his reflexes. He just let a small smile curve his lips. "Yes," he said.

Sleed swung about at the top of the steps. "Well, what are you tanzies waiting for? Come on! Come!"

The huddled novices with their torches quivering began to climb the last of the steps and venture along the uneven footing of the twisting, claustrophobic tunnel that lay ahead.

Noises echoed. The jagged roof lowered down over the scrambling party and splashes of torchlight glittered from condensation streaking the walls. Now Sleed the Slick had taken it upon his unlovely person to climb immediately abaft of Dimpy with Big Balla up front leading the way. She was no novice, being in training for the position of leader on a par with Sleed. At too frequent intervals Sleed prodded Dimpy on painfully. One of these days, said Dimpy to himself, controlling his anger with an almost physical shudder, one of these days I'll cut out this cramph's liver and lights and fricassee 'em in samphron oil and then feed 'em to the dogs — so help me!

The upward way turned into a level passage which opened out into a gallery. One side was slimed wall, the other was black emptiness. Noises seemed to be sucked out and down. Nobody spoke. The torches' orange hair shrank against the darkness.

The way eased when they left the galleried cavern and passed into an ordinary tunnel. A little further on they came to a blocked up side entrance with a Rapa skull gleaming ruddily yellow nailed into a crevice. Dimpy felt a pang. Somewhere through the maze of tunnels beyond that skull were the old ways of the Roaring Fifties. The slide had brought down tons of rubble and solid rock which besides squashing Fat Nath and Lora the Leemkin had sealed off the secret ways.

The next junction did not need to be marked off in so sinister a fashion. The distorted opening in the wall reeked of sulphur. The hell-spawned stink gushed out to be sucked up into a crevice in the roof.

"Bad jangles, that," remarked Big Balla, who stood passing the novices along.

"I'm in charge here, girl, and don't you forget it." Sleed the Slick was a Khibil and although as a race they considered themselves vastly superior to all other diffs, even Khibils might have checked at this specimen. "I'll tell these tanzies what's what."

Big Balla opened her mouth; then she closed it with a snap and jerked her jut of chin up. As a Hytak she knew her worth in the society of the gangs. But, also as a Hytak, she understood order and discipline even in so unruly a mob as the Hellraisers. And, as the second in command training to be a leader, she must, guessed Dimpy, feel ferocious distaste that she'd been stuck with this rast Sleed. The way up turned and twisted along treacherous tunnels. Dimpy had no difficulty in committing the tortuous passages to memory. Darkness partially pierced by the flare of the torches, dankness, the sense of pressure, of a closing in and suffocating weight, oppressed the party. They stumbled and hurried along, the novice gang members new to this experience, Sleed viciously impatient, Balla containing her emotions, and Dimpy clambering agilely along with them. Those first trepidations as he'd entered the hidden opening at the foot of the Hill of Dancing Ghosts that had so pumped up his heart rate he put down in his youthful arrogance to mere nostalgia—to the last time he'd gone up a Hill and all those painful memories.

That had been the day before the slide. He'd lost good friends then and more in the last futile resistance of the Roaring Fifties to the Hellraisers. The odd thing was, Dimpy wasn't at all sure that he did have a burning desire to prove himself to these Hellraisers. His desires had always been straightforward—to do everything for his family and comrades, and to the Red Hot Gullet of Karbonar the Inevitable with any and everyone else. And, said young Dimpy resolutely to himself, if you condemned him for that then to the Red Hot Gullet of Karbonar the Inevitable with you, too, dom.

Upwards the party climbed, following the ways marked with the secret signs of the Hellraisers. Dimpy committed all to his memory as Sleed and Big Balla counseled the novices. Dimpy did not know for sure if all the great Hills of Oxonium were honeycombed with passages; he'd admitted he'd be surprised if they were not. As for the Hills themselves where the lordly ones of the city lived, there lay the fat ponshos ripe for the plucking. His Uncle Petegland had once suffered an unpleasant experience with a Hill and from then on resolutely referred to them as Contours. A brown and black crawzer like a man size centipede had taken Uncle Petegland into its ashy jaws when for an instant he had been looking the other way.

Now Dimpy used a trick his father had taught him. His surroundings remained clear to him and he took note of all that went on; but he could think of other things, of what he intended to do with his life, of just how he would dispose of Sleed the Slick, of regrets that Big Balla was a Hytak, for although apim and Hytak could marry and produce beautiful children, he would—again in his youthful arrogance—have much preferred her to be apim like himself.

The boy in front turned his ankle on a loose stone and would have fallen had not Dimpy caught him in a supple grasp. He hauled the lad up with a quick: "You're all right, Staky. Just use your eyes—"

Sleed gave Dimpy an almighty shove in the small of the back. Dimpy staggered forward, still holding Staky, and the two collapsed.

"You useless tanzy! You stupid rast! Get on, get on!"

Even then—even then young Dimpy helped Staky to rise as he stood up himself. His fist closed around the handle of the short curved knife at his belt. Sleed saw that instinctive, betraying gesture.

The bigger lad's foxy face tightened. He was not yet old enough for his bristly whiskers to be more than stubble; but all a Khibil's pride in his race, all a Khibil's self-superiority, blazed out in an expression of utter hatred. Dimpy controlled himself in a way he found strange to him, swiveled, stony-faced, and went on up the rough passage. He found that look on the Khibil's face to be overdone, melodramatic. But young as he was he recognized that look's deadly intent.

Not quite as much in control of himself as he imagined, he banged his head against a low outcrop. Dimpy said something in reference to ibmas of the vilest kind and pushed on. His father had always said he had a skull like a vosk. The bang served merely to irritate him further with his surroundings, with his company, with the purpose of this raid.

Although the city of Oxonium existed on two general levels of altitude, there were many levels within the class structures of the higher and lower. From the warrens in the steep-sided canyons, calculating eyes studied the aristocratic inhabitants of the contours. From the summits, intolerant and suspicious eyes watched the human garbage festering in the runnels. The great lords employed guards and paid the infamous Kataki Watch to police the vermin below. The gangs trained their young people in all the arts of deception, theft and murder.

Here and there within the tortuous ascent the route had been cut by humans to link chambers. Some passageways were even paved and lined with masonry blocks. How long ago this work had been carried out no one really knew. Apocryphal stories abounded, of course, in the true Kregan way.

Sleed the Slick carried a broad dagger at his waist, and, like Dimpy and his curved knife, had had the sense not to use that against the praxul. If, said Dimpy to himself, if the cramph prods me with that I'll—well, and what would he do—here underground and surrounded by aspiring members of the Hellraisers? He clenched his teeth and went on and up in a most foul mood.

Water dropped from the roof to splash into a stream alongside the footway. Far up ahead a spark of light glittered.

"Quiet," snarled Sleed.

The spark turned into a lantern perched on a ledge. A youngster wearing a ponsho skin stood up as the party approached. His sallow face looked peaky under the hood and his eyes gleamed. Silently he motioned upwards.

Big Balla took the lead and began the climb. Rough-cut steps, ten to a flight, zigzagged back and forth from landing to landing. Dimpy counted six flights before he followed Staky through an open trapdoor to step onto a wooden floor.

A stale musty odor surrounded him; but the cellar was dry. A pile of long sausage-like sacks stood against one wall. Steps led up.

The formalities here were very similar to those Dimpy had been accustomed to with his old gang. They climbed into the back room of a store. Rolled carpets everywhere indicated the nature of the establishment. The tenseness in the recruits might have affected Dimpy had he not been so wound up and irritated by what he considered the totally unnecessary ritual test in his case. The novices, yes, let them prove their fitness to join the gang. He'd been a fully qualified gang member and chapter deldar, young as he was.

A fat Rapa with mangy feathers looked them over with his beak high. He sniffed. "You know what you have to do. Do not return until you are successful. On no account return here if you are followed." He touched the dagger at his waist. "Remember."

One by one the urchins left the shop to join up at a discreet distance. When it was Dimpy's turn he felt at once the strangeness of an alien place and the familiarity of crowded streets filled with people bustling about their daily lives. The clamor of people chaffering and laughing and shouting beat at him. The clatter of hooves and the grinding of bronze rimmed wheels added a touch of unreality to a lad brought up in the dens below. The air—ah, the sweet, sweet air of Kregen!

The breeze blew cleanly, scented with baking bread and cakes and the juices of fruits, sullied only slightly by the coarser smells of commerce. The air tasted good to young Dimpy.

The Hill of Dancing Ghosts was also known as Barter Hill and whilst the folk up here might not be the great and lordly ones they were well fed and clothed and walked with confident steps. Their slaves and servants, of course, did not share these attributes.

The aspirant gang members moved into their pre-arranged groups slinking as they had been taught to merge and become invisible among the slaves, eyes downcast. Dimpy owned to a genuine feeling of pleasure that Big Balla stood at his elbow.

Splitting one from the other as they trod ways they had never seen before save in the scratched markings in the dust of their den, the novices penetrated deeper into the clustered buildings of the Hill of Barter. Other young lads with respectable clothes, the Perfume Patrol of Oxonium, dashed past. Crowds jostled everywhere. Smells floated in the warm air, varying from one street and bazaar to the next. Dimpy rescinded his original decision to get this whole farce over with as quickly as possible. He was fully aware that Sleed would be keeping a very personal and hostile eye on him, so he decided to make the cramph wait. He kept to the shady sides of the streets, head bowed in the universal servitude of the slave, eyes picking up everything that went on.

From the corner of a plaza he saw one of the gang members over the way sneak up to the rear of a self-important-looking Fristle. Lolalee was quick. Her curved knife flashed once in the lights of the suns. Then she was running fleet as a hare with the sword she had slashed from its hangings already concealed under the rags clothing her thin body. The Fristle swung about, his cat-face mean, and began yelling. By the time that happened and the crowd started to think of pursuit, Lolalee had vanished.

"Well done," said Big Balla, softly.

"I like her style."

"There's Staky over there looking—looking unhappy. The idiot's dithering. You be careful, Dimpy." With that, she was off.

From his knowledge of the city and this Contour, Dimpy knew the next square was the Kyro of Nath the Haggler. The platz was busy, its stalls well patronized. Dimpy rounded the corner to see Sleed running towards him holding out a sword hilt-first. Instinctively Dimpy took the weapon into his fist and Sleed, without a word, hared off.

Dimpy did not, just did not, believe what happened next.

The big, ugly and altogether unpleasant Kataki to whom Sleed spoke reacted at once. From the crowds a shrill cry shocked up.

"My sword! Thief! Thief!"

The Kataki ran lumberingly for Dimpy.

Without thinking, Dimpy threw down the sword and ran.

Two

If you think my short sojourn in the mysterious continent of Balintol gave me an understanding of that exotic land then you are completely misinformed. The world of Kregen abounds with remarkable tales of Balintol. In the bazaars and at the corners of public buildings you can always find storytellers with their clusters of gawpers bending close. The fables of Balintol are among the perennial favorites of Kregen.

Just at the moment I was cautiously following a Rapa thief along the crowded Avenue of Lochrivarn trying not to lose him and at the same time prevent his cunning dark eyes from spotting what I was up to. Where you have classes so very far apart in wealth you have thieves, or so it seems on Kregen as on Earth. The Rapa's accomplice, a mangy-appearing Fristle, had snatched Tiri's purse as she'd been about to pay for a trifle in the Souk of Laces. The Rapa had received the purse with such calm aplomb that no one could possibly imagine him involved in anything remotely illegal. As for the catman, he'd used a slender blade to cut the purse strings and flicked his tail to snatch it. That tail possessed a cunning little bronze hook attachment strapped to it in place of the fashionable dagger. Oh, yes, an accomplished pair of cutpurses, these two. Also, the ancient racial animosity between Rapa and Fristle, so common when I'd first arrived on Kregen, was dying down as this double-act so eloquently proved.

The thief slipped across the avenue with a sudden dart that took him beyond a passing string of calsanys. Not wishing to upset these patient animals and suffer the noisome results I scuttled across abaft the last one's tail, narrowly avoiding an imperious fellow astride a much-decorated zorca, and reached the far side. The dratted Rapa thief was not visible among the passing throngs.

Useless to curse, the fellow was a master of his craft. All the same, I did not feel inclined to abandon my pursuit.

Anyway, I said to myself, I needed some exercise after the last few weeks of inaction. All hell was due to break out in the country of Tolindrin, and the city of Oxonium, as the capital, was like to receive more than its share, that seemed obvious, by Vox. Carrying on at a brisk pace and looking as far ahead through the crowds as possible I could still see no sign of the thief. Barter Hill tended to be more crowded and confused than many of the Hills of Oxonium by reason of the multitude of markets traditionally setting up shop here. The noises were not unpleasantly clamorous and the smells were kept down by the Perfume Patrol. These lads went around spraying scents and disinfectants, their services paid for by a city levy on the stallholders and shopkeepers.

Among all this hullabaloo, where had the dratted fellow got himself to?

The avenue debouched onto a sizeable square, the Kyro of Nath the Haggler. The twin Suns of Scorpio slanted their emerald and ruby fires down onto the mass of humanity busy bargaining, peddling, swindling and making livings varying from fairly honest to downright villainous.

Perhaps because my senses had been heightened by detecting a couple of professional thieves at work, I noticed at once what was going on at the corner of the adjacent street.

A young lad, an apim like me, sidled with exquisite casualness alongside a portly and gesticulating fellow haggling over the purchase of a length of azure silk. The vendor, narrow of eye and hooked of nose, kept one of those eyes constantly swiveling. Both vendor and purchaser must have been well aware of the provenance of the merchandise, by Krun. All the same, hook-nose's roving eye failed to detect the ragged lad's activities.

With a movement fluid and fast the rascal cut the leathers of the purchaser's sword. So engrossed in the enjoyable business, the portly one failed to notice at once. The short sword vanished into the ragged robes swathing the boy and he turned to run.

He must have seen the Kataki at the same time I did.

Katakis are bad news at the best of times. For this sword snatcher, now was a very bad time, a very very bad time. The Whiptail did not wear uniform but a simple dark shamlak and I surmised if he was not a member of the City Watch up here to buy he could be a hired thug employed to protect a local business. He'd just love to grip his fist into the lad's frayed collar and flick him a few times—hard—with the flat of the dagger strapped to his tail.

A second young lad, slightly smaller but just as ragged as the first, rounded the corner. The youngster with the stolen sword moved swiftly. Crossing to the newcomer he whipped out the sword and thrust it forward, hilt first. The sword was taken in that instinctive way anyone will grab at an unsharpened object poked at them. As I watched, by now fascinated at these goings on, the lads parted. The boy with the sword stood there looking at the blade in what I could clearly see was stupefaction, surprising though that seemed to me in the circumstances. The thief ran across to the Kataki guard.

At that juncture the rotund purchaser of dubious azure silk woke up to the fact that his sword no longer weighed down his belt. Immediately he set up a-braying.

"My sword! Thief! Thief!"

I shook my head. This was just life as it was lived in Oxonium in Tolindrin in the continent of Balintol on the planet Kregen four hundred light years from the world of my birth and no business of mine.

The sword thief jabbered briefly and excitedly to the Kataki.

He pointed.

The lad holding the sword stood there for two heartbeats with that accusing finger pointing at him. Then he threw down the sword and started running as the Whiptail lumbered for him.

The real sword snatcher stood still and even at this distance the look of satisfaction on his swarthy face repelled me. After the theft he could have dodged off with absolute security with no one the wiser until the shout of "Thief!" went up. Instead, he had deliberately framed the second youth and dropped him right in it up to the ears.

As the boy raced swiftly in my direction finding clear spaces among the crowds with eel like grace, sometimes hidden from view by bartering figures, the look on his face was quite different from what one would expect. By Vox, yes! There was no fear there, no hunted look of terror. His expression was one of such fury as to scare off a leem. He raged with anger as he leaped along pursued by the Kataki guard.

The cry of 'Stop Thief!' rang as loudly and as many times in the souks and markets of Oxonium as of any other bustling commercial city of Kregen. Chaffering people looked around smartly, hands flying to purses. Fists gripped sword and dagger hilts.

The athleticism of the victim of this obscure plot to have him arrested proved instructive. He hurdled stalls, ducked under awnings, swerved like a veritable racing zorca around knots of folk all staring whichways. Those fables of Balintol recurred to me in the famous story which opens with just such a young lad flying through a crowded marketplace clutching a chicken by the legs, his warning colors flaming before his inward eye. I admired this young rapscallion's dash and still that dark expression of fury drew his face into a compressed knot.

A man wearing a green shamlak whisked out his rapier. The fellow's spiky ears stuck up almost to the crown of his head. An Ift, he regarded himself as sharp and knowing enough to strike shrewd bargains in this bustling city market as of living comfortably in the forests of his home, that was perfectly clear. His rapier slashed.

The tip sliced down the lad's thigh as he swerved a fraction too late.

He did not cry out.

"You blintz!" yelled the Ift. He waved the rapier with its point bloodied. But he did not run in pursuit.

Dark redness stained down the boy's thigh. The scratch, light though it was, tumbled him off balance and he staggered helplessly into a wheeled stall. This immediately upended and sprayed everything with ripe vegetables. A little Och woman threw up her apron in dismay.

When I next caught sight of the fugitive he had a patch of blood on his forehead and he limped. Yet, still he eluded them all.

The Ift's act had been a trifle over the top, I fancied. Some of these highbrow forest folk can be a mite spiteful. The youngster's tribulations were not yet over. Trying to maintain his pace he skidded askew a wet patch and where normally he would have recovered with natural grace and gone haring on, now the two wounds troubled him enough to make him lose his balance. He skidded and toppled full length into a calsany mess strewing the ground. The effort he made to spring up instantly told on him. He disappeared from my view past a line of stalls. I let out a little sigh.

This was no business of mine.

No business whatsoever. The best thing to do was simply to step back around the corner and then walk off. The Rapa cutpurse had long since vanished and among the throngs there was now no chance of finding him.

Tiri's purse must be consigned along with many another votive offering to the greater glory of Diproo the Nimble Fingered.

So I stepped back around the corner into the slanting shadows where Zim and Genodras, all flushed crimson and deep emerald light upon the opposite buildings, pooled darkness in doorways and windows. The ferociously angry lad rounded the corner and hurled headlong down on me.

Beyond the jut of the building and for the moment out of sight the hue and cry howled on making an unholy racket. The boy staggered. The rapier slash must be paining him now and his head must be ringing where he'd clouted his skull against the hard wood of the barrow. The muck coating his legs plastered the blood into a paste so that he did not leave a betraying trail of blood drops.

Sink me! I said to myself in vast annoyance. By the Black Chunkrah! No business of mine or not, this despicable frame up and the ugly pursuit smelled to the highest heaven or the lowest hell of Kregen.

Like a wrestler catching his opponent bouncing from the ropes, I stuck out my arm and clothes lined him in.

He came reeling in like a shining sliptinger hooked from the torrent. I swiveled with his momentum like a weathervane and bundled him into the slot of darkness and turned about and pressed my back against him in the cleft of shadow.

"Stand still, lad!" I snarled. "Make not a sound if you value your life."

They were lines from a famous play he'd probably never heard of let alone seen, and melodramatically colored though they were, they fitted this tempestuous situation. He made a single effort to wriggle out and run off and I shoved back hard and growled: "Stay still, you fambly. The damned Kataki's on his evil way." His slight form lurched against me and then he stilled, panting softly.

The shouting pack led by the Kataki guard stormed into view.

Their blood was up. There was a thief to be caught. This was a hunt, they had the scent and they were out for the kill.

Innocence before guilt had absolutely no part in their thought processes. The Kataki stared hotly down the street where people were turning to look enquiringly for the source of all this hubbub. To my great satisfaction the Whiptail saw no sight of his quarry. He hauled up opposite me and the crowd piled on abaft. He saw me, leaning negligently against the wall. His eyes squinted.

"Where did he go?" he rapped out in that ugly Kataki way.

"Who?" I said, quite pleasantly, considering the circumstances. "Oh, you mean the lad running." I gave a casual gesture with a languid hand. "He dodged down the next alley I think."

"By Chezra-Gon-Kranak! I'll jikaider the blintz!" He gave me a hard stare. Then: "What d'ye mean, you think?"

I returned that hard stare with interest. Some spark of that evil expression folk call the Dray Prescot Devil Look must have flashed into my face for his dark brows drew down and he sucked in a sudden quick breath between his snaggly teeth. I spoke levelly.

"What I said." My voice hardened. "Why?"

He got the message all right. If he hadn't been in hot pursuit he'd have loved to have taken up the challenge. As it was he simply swung away and started running off towards the next alley with the mob following him all a-yelling and a-waving of fists and daggers. The rout caterwauled down the next alleyway.

A voice in my ear said: "What in the sweet name of the Lady Balsitha is going on, Drajak?" The voice was light and mellifluous and tart, oh, yes, by Zair, very tart.

"Your purse is stowed away in the bronze-bound chest of Diproo the Nimble Fingered, Tiri," I said, without turning around. "I lost the Rapa. I found a lad who needs our assistance." Then I turned to face her.

At that moment an Aephar woman walked past with her daughter, both of them incredibly beautiful as Aephar women are. They saw the filthy and blood-smeared boy as he emerged from the shadows. The beauty of their faces changed only in a subtle fashion to express pity. Their smoothly undulating walk did not falter. The Aephar women went on around the corner into the bedlam of the market.

Tiri and I exchanged glances. Beauty of outward form is not the only beauty possessed by Aephar ladies.

With an eel like squirm and a sudden dart the lad tried to run off. That, by Krun, was a perfectly natural reaction. A fist in his collar hauled him up.

"Whoa, lad. You're safe now. And the muck you have in that wound must be attended to."

"Lemme go!" He spat it out, wriggling and squirming. His injured leg jarred up as he tried to break free and scamper off. His face, already twisted in the anger suffusing him, contorted with the sudden stab of pain. This sobered him. Panting only a little he ripped out: "I know why you saved me. Slaver!"

"Oh, no!" broke in Tiri. "You do us an injustice."

He sagged in my grip. "Not slavers? You really saved me? Then may Mother Saphira of the Gutters bless you with my thanks. But I must go back—"

"You're going nowhere my feller me lad until that leg is seen to."

At least he had spoken his thanks with a courtesy not often found in the stews. He relaxed even more in my grasp so that I was forewarned. With an abrupt and defiant leap he tried suddenly to break away as my attention and hold on him, as he supposed, slackened.

Even as I halted that last desperate surge, Tiri took his arm.

"Best come along with us. We'll soon have that leg fixed."

Do not ask why I thus persisted in the attempt to aid this young lad. Perhaps it was the cut of his jib, perhaps the injustice he had suffered. Opaz knew, hadn't I been just such a youngster harshly treated by an insensitive world? Even though that world was four hundred light years away from Kregen. He wore sandal-like shoes, it is true, where I had gone barefooted. The lad himself settled the argument. Like a sack of flour dumped down into the bakery he slumped and would have fallen but for our supporting holds. After that it was a mere matter of swathing my shamlak as a cloak over him and assisting him along. We went the other way avoiding any further meetings with the unpleasant Whiptail and the mob.

Having said that I realize the tautology. Who ever knew a pleasant Kataki? Well, perhaps I had, once, far away in the Eye of the World in Turismond.

I looked at my two companions. They were of an age. Tiri had reacted in the way I had come to expect of her in our relatively short acquaintance after she had first flung a jeweled dagger at my head. Her fair hair was neatly combed back and gleamed golden. As a temple dancer she walked with the grace of an Aephar girl, her lithe whipcord tough body rounded and beautifully graceful. Her bright face with that determined little jut of chin would do the business for many and many a poor love-besotted oaf under the Suns of Scorpio. Oh, yes, a most wonderful young madam full of high spirits and a bubbling aliveness that enchanted and a tongue as sharp as a rapier. She danced to the greater glory of Cymbaro the Just and of that religion I had formed a higher opinion than many upon the face of Kregen.

Then a thought occurred to me that made my old beakhead of a face scowl and then crease into a grimace that could have been mistaken for a smile.

"Your guts paining you, Drajak?" Oh, how sweet the words!

"I was just thinking what our comrade Fweygo will say when we report we lost your purse to a—"

She tossed that imperious little head. "As a Kildoi, Fweygo will surmise—aloud—how we could be so easily gulled and where was the Watch. They believe in law and order."

"Sometimes." I thought of Mefto the Kazzur...

What Tiri didn't know was that Fweygo and I were kregoinyes sent to Tolindrin to protect the numim twins. She thought we worked for Princess Nandisha who employed the numim twins' parents to care for her and for her twins, lady Nisha and lord Byrom. The intrigues fomented by the death of the king and the appointment of his successor had not been resolved. Rather, they had grown worse and would become diabolically more troublesome in the immediate future.

Right in the middle of it all, for our sins, stood Fweygo and I.

We paid the few coppers for our fare in the cable car from Barter Hill. I had heard the place referred to as the Hill of Dancing Ghosts but I had not pursued the question as to why. We reached Nandisha's palace without incident and the moment we were inside, here came Fweygo, clad in armor and wearing swords, a most sullen annoyed Kildoi expression on his handsome Kildoi face.

His tail hand, I saw, grasped a dagger of which he was particularly fond. A great deal of shouting and screaming echoed from further inside the palace.

"What—?" began Tiri.

"The young prince, lord Byrom. He is missing. It is certain sure he has been kidnapped."

Instantly I saw why my comrade was so annoyed. Our task, given to us by the Star Lords, was to protect the numim twins. Now, though, we would have to divert all our efforts into rescuing the little lord for whose mother, nominally, we worked.

"The princess?" Tiri showed her concern.

"Badly shaken and upset; but her people are with her. She is resting." A lion roar battered around our ears. Ranaj, the powerful father of the numim twins was girt for battle like Fweygo, and his energy blazed. "You are ready? Don't stand gawping, Drajak. What a hulu! Come on, and you, Fweygo. They've taken the prince to the Clipped Rhok. A den of ancient evil. Come on! Come on!"

Perforce, willy-nilly, Star Lords or no, we were hustled out to do the duty we owed Princess Nandisha and her son.

Three

"Tiri!" I yelled back over my shoulder. "Look out for our smelly young friend."

"Yes. You—I hope the young prince is—all right."

There was no point in recovering my shamlak—that had already pinched in the nostrils of my friends. There was just time to grab a replacement and then we all hurried out and down the steps from Nandisha's palace. People in the normal course of the day do not walk about clad in full plate armor and carrying an arsenal of weapons; when they do so other folk know they are engaged on urgent business of a lethal kind. All I had was the new shamlak—a tasteful mid-blue in color—and my rapier and main gauche, with the heavy knife over my right hip. Fweygo, Ranaj and the bunch of fighting men from Princess Nandisha's guard were armored and armed—I assure you—up to the eyebrows rather than merely to the teeth.

The Clipped Rhok, a most unsavory hostelry, was situated on the Hill of Lurking Shadows and we drew only cursory glances of enquiry as we took the necessary cable cars to reach our destination.

Fweygo filled me in on the details of what had happened and, as is often the case in these disasters, simple human error was to blame.

One guard late, another feeling unwell, the prince with just a single guardian, the sudden rush of black-clad forms, one dead guard and the result—here we were hot on the rescue trail.

Fweygo nodded towards one youthful guard running with us.

"At least Sammle the Erkanstater kept his head. He was too late to intervene. He followed the kidnappers, saw where they went, and rushed back to report to Ranaj."

"Good for him."

Lurking Shadows turned out to be an apt description of the hill. The slanting rays of Zim and Genodras, here in Balintol called Mabal and Matol, seemed only to draw deep crimson and emerald shadows into the narrow and winding streets. Buildings leaned over us. No-one offered to stop us, an armed and purposeful body of men; had that happened I would not have been surprised.

The impression of these mean streets drove out the mood of farce that had been strong with me since the episode with the young lad despite the underlying seriousness of it all. The kidnap of the prince had merely served to add to that unreal feeling of comicality. Now, the chase was serious, the stakes high—and both Fweygo and I expected that at any moment the Everoinye would reach down and pluck us aloft and so hurl us down to where we should be—guarding the numim twins.

Ranaj didn't intend to go roaring like a blustering lionman into the tavern. He sent a small party ahead, some pressed on to seal the rear exits, and we stalked on, wary for every shadow.

Although the buildings of the Hill of Lurking Shadows were oppressive enough and the narrow streets winding and treacherous, this place was in no real way comparable with the runnels of the warrens between the hills. Up here might not be heaven; down there was well on the way to hell.

Ranaj with his golden fur and his superb lionman physique performed many functions within Nandisha's household; butler, major-domo, footman, quartermaster. As her cadade, the captain of the guard, a position of the utmost responsibility in every noble household, he perhaps took this task as his most important. He'd hired on Fweygo and me as temporary reinforcements during a time of particular difficulty, and now, having seen us operate, was evidently reluctant to part with our services. Certainly, he did not treat us like two ordinary swods of the palace guard.

It seemed to me that Ranaj would be as unlikely to accept the human error explanation for the kidnap as I would be in his position. One guard late, one unwell, and the poor devil left on duty murdered? Oh no, by the disgusting diseased liver and lights of Makki Grodno! Those two dubious characters would be up and facing an enquiry instanter. Sammle the Erkanstater, a numim, had been late because he'd been sent along to replace the sick dutyman; no, it was the other latecomer and the fellow with the gut ache who'd be questioned.

From the advance party, Naghan the Twist, a Gon, reported back. He told Ranaj the tavern was only lightly patronized at this time of day, and the best chances were that prince Byrom was being held in one of the upstairs rooms. He gave a rapid rundown on the layout of The Clipped Rhok.

Speed, quite obviously, was essential and Ranaj went for the direct solution. Some of us would keep the patrons entertained whilst others stormed up the stairs. Any escape would be blocked off front and back and all windows would be covered.

Ranaj said very curtly: "Fweygo, Drajak. You stay with me."

We nodded our assent. Mind you, I did wonder if we would be able to obey if the Everoinye decided differently, yes, by Krun.

The Clipped Rhok turned out to be an impressive structure in these surroundings, although on other hills it would look a wreck.

At the front hung a white flag with a black circle surrounding a white center. This was the kaotresh, the flag of death, and even the semi-criminal fraternity inhabiting this place had the sense to fly the kaotresh to mourn the passing of the king. Only when the new king, King Tomendishto, was crowned would his bright flags be unfurled.

The advance party under Naghan the Twist's orders from the cadade went inside as we approached and when we entered we had a clear run to the stairs. Any possibility of someone running up to warn those aloft was instantly checked. No one made the attempt.

The lionman went up the blackwood stairs three at a time. Fweygo and I followed, with Sammle and the rest at our backs.

A pot-bellied fellow with a huge beard appeared at the top of the steps and Ranaj simply hit him over the head and Fweygo caught him as he fell. I passed the limp body on down. All this was done in silence, apart from the soft thwunk of the blow.

A corridor dimly lit by a dirty window at the far end revealed closed doors each side. Ranaj motioned with his drawn sword. We all took up our positions outside the doors and looked at the cadade. He nodded his head with a look of the utmost determination on his golden-whiskered face and we smashed the doors in and sprang inside.

My room contained an apim and a Sylvie closely entwined on the grimy bed. To anyone with fastidious tastes there was nothing in the sordid room to interest in the slightest. I shot back into the corridor and now shouts and screams broke out. Fweygo catapulted out of the next door and shook his head. Others of our party were re-entering the corridor, Ranaj among them. Noises blurted from the end.

We all ran along in a jumbled mass, picking up other men as they found empty or innocuous rooms. Directly in front of us Neap the Traiky came flying out of the end room to land on his ear in the corridor. He yelled. A flung dagger went 'zip!' past his head as he tried to sit up. Traiky means Lucky, and surely Neap was most fortunate in that the dagger missed his polsim head and even more lucky, immeasurably so, when we burst into the room and saw just who had thrown him out.

Two of our men lay unconscious where they had been thrown into a corner, and a third was shaking like a leaf, hands in front of him empty and his sword tossed down at his feet.

The four Chuliks had evidently been playing one of their obscure Chulik games, for dice and cards strewed a small table, wine and snacks stood ready to hand and they'd been enjoying themselves in ways strange to those who were not Chuliks.

The four Yellow-tuskers glared at us with their round black eyes showing annoyance. They had not drawn weapons. Their smooth oily yellow faces glistened in the lamplight. Apart from them and our unfortunate fellows there was no one else in the gaming room.

Ranaj bellowed a curse and then: "We apologize for intruding. We have no quarrel with you—unless you know the whereabouts of the young prince." He sounded wrought up and dangerous.

Before the Chuliks could answer, a burst of light slashed into the room from the window, half-blinding us. An enormous thunder clap followed so rapidly that the storm must be directly above us.

I felt a force seize me up. The window was as black as a Herrelldrin Hell. That force lifted me and hurled me straight at the window. Glass and wood smashed away as I hurtled through. A crazy glimpse of Fweygo flying at my side and a blurred impression of darkness beneath sped away. Surrounded by a roaring maelstrom I went flying through thin air.

No rain spattered me. I could see nothing apart from blackness. Over and over I flew, suspended, deafened, exasperated.

My feet hit hard marble. I staggered forward and my sight cleared. Fweygo spluttered at my side. We stood in a corridor of Nandisha's palace. Directly before us the princess struggled in the grip of two hefty Brokelsh, all hairy and armored. A Rapa swished his sword about facing—facing the cause of our supernatural flight through some other plane of existence.

Serinka, Ranaj's numim wife, lay on the floor with a dribble of blood from the corner of her mouth. She stared up with horrified eyes, staring at her twins. Young Rofi and Rolan, slender daggers in their fists, were poised to hurl themselves upon the despoilers of their mother.

"So that's it!" grated Fweygo.

In the next instant the numim twins who were the charges given into our protection by the Star Lords would rush in to protect their mother and Princess Nandisha, and these fine bully boys would cut them down without mercy.

Four

Fweygo just went bull-headed for the Rapa. The fellow was one of those vulture-headed Rapas, blackly-feathered. His beaked face shocked in startlement, and no wonder. Suddenly, apparently from nowhere, two fighting men blocked him from carrying out this easy assignment. Fweygo roared in, his sword a bar of reflected light in the corridor lamps' glow.

That left the two Brokelsh to me. There was absolutely no doubt in my mind that Fweygo, a glorious golden Kildoi, would deal with the Rapa in extremely short order, and that was the more important of the two fights here.

Nandisha kept up her shrieking. "Help me! Help!"

There was just time to hear Fweygo bellow: "Rofi! Rolan! Stand out of the way—now!" Then I gave the nearest Brokelsh a clout over the head with the steel guarded hilt of the left hand dagger. He reeled away but did not fall. The other Brokelsh let go of the princess who incontinently collapsed. Her screaming died away to a low moaning as she cowered on the patterned marble.

The Brokelsh used a straight sword, the braxter of Balintol, and he was still surprised enough at our sudden arrival to be slow in his reactions. I should have spitted him there and then; but Nandisha, still moaning: "Help! Oh, help me!" twined her arms about my legs as I stepped forward. She nearly had me over. The Brokelsh regained the initiative. He came at me with the sword snouting and cut at my head. I ducked and swayed back like a tree gripped fast by its roots blown savagely by a howling gale.

"Leggo, princess!"

"Help me!"

"I will if you'll leggo!"

The Brokelsh laughed nastily and I saw the way his eyes darted a glance past my shoulder, so I ducked again. I couldn't kick back but I swung the main gauche back in a flailing arc as far as I could. I felt it connect with a reasonably satisfying thump and heard the first Brokelsh let out another yelp. The rapier in my right fist switched the sneering Brokelsh's blade away; but I couldn't take the necessary step forward to run him through.

These two nasty pieces of work were wearing brass-studded leather armor. Just above the rim of the leather, right through the throat; that was the target.

Nandisha screamed some more and hugged me tight. Nearly toppling over I wriggled my body to keep some sort of balance. What a carry on! What a way for a tough old ruffianly warrior to fight!

A bubbling scream burst up at my back and was followed by a soggy sound of a body falling.

That was the fellow at my back attended to. Good old Fweygo!

A silver dazzlement of light streaked over my shoulder. The dagger embedded itself in the eye of the Brokelsh who was just about to leap forward and settle my hash once and for all.

He looked quite surprised—again. He folded up in the middle and then sank to his knees. He toppled forward quite slowly until the dagger hilt touched the marble. The blade went in a little further. He rolled over sideways and emitted a ghoulish grunt, as air was expelled from his lungs.

"I thought, Drajak," said Fweygo in a most kindly fashion, "I really was beginning to think that you were getting the hang of fighting." His tone of voice was soft and regretful—and cut like the sharpest sword that ever came out of the armories of Zenicce, cut to the quick, by Krun!

He stepped around the ludicrous statue-like pair of us, me fast gripped in the octopus-like wrapping of Nandisha's arms. He shook his head sorrowfully as he careful pulled his dagger free, using his considerable strength. He began to wipe the blade, still shaking that golden head of his thoughtfully.

"Y'know, Drajak, I can't understand why you don't use a proper sword. That rapier and dagger work, it's complicated, as I know only too well from my youth."

I swallowed down hard. I said: "Would you kindly ask the princess to release her prisoner?"

He let out a low amused laugh. "This sword. It is a most splendid weapon, as I suspected when I first saw it in the market."

That blade was a drexer, and it had been designed by Naghan the Gnat and me in my home in Esser Rarioch. The quality of the steel was so superior to the Krasny-work weaponry of Tolindrin as to allow of no comparison. Fweygo had been most fortunate to find the drexer so far from its place of origin. There was a story in that, I knew; and most probably a damned sad story too, by Vox.

My unblooded weapons could be placed carefully on the marble. I bent down. "Princess." I began to prise her fingers away from my legs. "If you will release me, please—"

Her tear-streaked face turned up and she looked at me in deep puzzlement. "What? Oh, it's you, Drajak." She came to her senses, more or less. She looked around. The numim twins were helping their mother to rise. She shook herself and started towards the princess. Nandisha let out a tiny scream, quickly stifled.

"Serinka! You—what—you are all right?"

"Thank you, princess. Here, let me attend you." With that Serinka, a most gracious numim lady, started to untwine Nandisha's octopus grip. I let out a breath. Fweygo gave me a most comical look, one golden eyebrow raised. There was no blood on the dagger he gripped in his tail hand. Of course, being a Kildoi, he had been able to draw the dagger from the eye of the Brokelsh and wipe the blade of his drexer at the same time. Apims like me, with only a miserable pair of arms and no tail hand, could not do those simple things any Kildoi did without thinking.

The numim lady assisted the apim princess to an overstuffed couch against the corridor wall. They talked quickly together, and both turned to ask at the same time what our news of the prince was. Fweygo said simply that he had not yet been found at The Clipped Rhok. Nandisha sank back, looking pale and weak, and Serinka chafed her hands. The two women did not enquire how it was we had so fortunately turned up to save them. For all they knew we could have left the tavern ages ago and walked quietly back. No doubt they expected to see Ranaj and his guardsmen soon.

What they didn't know was that we two kregoinyes had been summarily hurled through some outlandish and eerie other dimension. The Star Lords wanted us to guard the numim twins. We had no right to go gallivanting off in pursuit of other objectives.

Also, and this sent a shiver of alarm up through my spine, I knew I'd been lucky. The Star Lords could always hurl me back through four hundred light years to Earth as punishment if I disobeyed them. That thought brought the image of Delia smack bang into the forefront of my mind. There really is no time when the thought of Delia is absent from my brain; but brutal incidents similar to what had transpired here shocked me with the disaster I had so narrowly courted. No. Oh, no, by Zair! There was nothing I would not do to stay on Kregen with Delia, Delia of the Blue Mountains, Delia of Delphond.

Fweygo thrust his cleaned drexer back into the scabbard and the door opened again and he instantly drew the brand again and hurled himself forward.

Nandisha let out a little moan and Serinka said: "Tolaar rot them."

Princess Nisha in a short white dress was casually slung over the shoulder of the second fellow through the doorway. She made no sound or movement so she'd probably fainted. The three other men, all apims, following on, carried their blades naked in their fists.

The first kidnapper striding on ahead past the door he'd kicked open was a Chulik. His greasy yellow face shone in the lamp light. His pigtail—an anonymous black—was pulled forward over his left shoulder. His pakai was long, there were many rings forming the string of the pakai, each ring taken from the body of each of his past fights. He saw the golden Kildoi charging upon him and his sword snouted up into the en guarde. Highly professional fighters are Chuliks, trained up from birth to become mercenaries and to fight for gold. They had more humanity than at first I had believed; all the same, that humanity was not high and was seldom overtly exhibited.

Before I went hurtling in to assist my comrade I called across to the numim twins. "Rofi! Rolan! Please help your mother to take the princess away. Make sure you are safe. Hurry!"

Rolan hesitated. He still held that slender dagger. As a numim he could feel all his ancestral blood rebelling at the idea of thus tamely running off. I scowled at him and then, as I started off, snapped at his sister. "Rofi!

Make Rolan see sense—find a safe place to hide. He can always go looking for our guards if he wants. Now—bratch!"

They jumped and moved towards the couch and passed out of my vision. Kildoi and Chulik exchanged blows and circled and I skipped past them. Noise built up in the corridor, the chirr of steel on steel, the grunts of effort, yells from the men following—and, no doubt, Nandisha was in there screaming away, too.

For a tiny instant of time speaking to the children I'd wondered if I was telling them to do the right thing. It might not be clever to have them wandering off. Perhaps they'd be safer nearer Fweygo and me. One of the men towards whom I charged settled that uneasy question.

He yelled savagely and the twinkle of steel in his fingers changed abruptly into a streaking line. Automatically I flicked up my blade to deflect the throwing dagger. I needn't have bothered. He wasn't hurling at me. The wicked thing whistled past my head. I did a stupid thing, then, with these cut throats ready to chop me.

I turned my head to watch in horror as the flung dagger sliced towards the women and children. If Rolan or Rofi were hit and died...

The throwing dagger chingled into the wall, rang like a gong, and rebounded to ricochet across to the other side and so tumble uselessly to the floor. There was no time to let out a breath of relief.

Instantly I flung about again and the rapier was just in time to flick away the first blade slashing towards me. I jumped away to the side and gave the fellow holding Nisha a smack with the hilt of the main gauche. I didn't care to use the blade for fear of Nisha; as it was the blow did not connect cleanly and narrowly missed the limp form of the girl.

Two swords thrust for me and I circled them with my blade. I thrust in turn, nicking the first man's forearm as he attempted to cut back, and then instantly slicing around the other way to make the second fellow jump back. He let out an explosive oath and his stubbly face went even meaner.

The third apim bore in. They all wore brass-studded leather armor and good though the steel of the rapier was, I was not prepared to chance it trying to thrust through armor, leather or not. He foined as I sprang away from the first two, his blade going around and around quite prettily. There was no time for niceties of that nature. I started him one way, snapped back and stuck him through the throat. Then it was an immediate leap back and swivel to front the attack from the others.

The man carrying Nisha did not want to get into the fight and that was eminently sensible of him. He had a sword in his right fist and his left held onto the girl over his shoulder. He hovered. He didn't get into the fight; he didn't run off.

I flung a quick glance towards the other combat. The Chulik was not enjoying himself. Blood spattered down his armor and he was parrying the Kildoi's attack with growing desperation. Fweygo was up against a top-class swordsman, no doubt of that; there was also absolutely no doubt in my mind that like other Golden Wonders I knew he would very soon overcome this top class opposition.

I swung back to the business in hand.

Steel grated on steel. They tried to come at me from two sides simultaneously. I wasn't having any nonsense like that. With a fresh turn of speed I sprang at the left hand one, flurried my blade at him, forced him back, swiveled and was on the other fellow like a leem taking a ponsho. He swashed his sword at me—he had no buckler—and clearly was unaccustomed to dealing with rapiers. His own braxter could cut me up into little pieces, unarmored as I was, and he was patently baffled by his inability to do so. There was no time even with the breathing space I had created to finish him off. His comrade roared in from the back, trying to spit me through, so I stepped briskly to the side and turned and so had them nicely together again.

The noise in the corridor had died to a rhythmic stamp of feet, of indrawn breaths, gasps of effort, and the chingle of steel. No one in that fight was an amateur. This heartened me. They most probably would not care to hang around and fight to the death.

Still the kidnapper with Nisha did not try to escape.

These two villains had to be disposed of quickly before he made up his mind to run off.

Either that or appeal to their professionalism to admit they had failed in their kidnap attempt. They would not see it that way at the moment; I would make the appeal with cold steel.

Side by side they fronted me. The rapier swirled. One, two, three and back, not to one again but to two. This flummoxed them. Their braxters even in combination could not prevent the rapier point from snicking through left-hand's throat and right-hand's eye. They both fell—quite slowly—and the one with only one eye made a considerable noise about it. I swung for the fellow grasping Nisha.

"Put the princess down gently, dom."

Fweygo used his tail hand dagger to finish off the Chulik right at that moment. That added tremendous impetus to my words.

"I'm only—I meant her no harm—"

"Oh, I quite believe you. Just put her down gently."

He did exactly as I expected him to do. Fweygo also guessed aright. He said: "You catch. I'll—" He didn't finish for what we both anticipated occurred then.

The kidnapper heaved up the little princess and hurled her at us and then started to run off.

Obeying Fweygo I dropped my blades and caught Nisha, cradling her.

The Kildoi had just started to hare off after the fleeing man when he hauled up. He laughed delightedly.

The fellow leaped abruptly a foot into the air, span about, eyes goggling, mouth open trying to scream. That was rather too much for him to achieve, what with the dagger transfixing his throat. The throwing dagger had knifed from the shadows of a doorway, a single thin streak of light. From that doorway Tiri stepped into view.

She said: "Rolan told me—Nisha—?"

"Has fainted." I looked reproachfully at Fweygo. "You were damned unfair! You should have caught Nisha. I've only got two arms!"

Tiri moved swiftly in her graceful walk. She held out her arms. "I'll take her, poor little thing."

The more I saw of this talented temple dancer the more I became impressed. Her gray-green eyes looked down in sympathy on the girl, who began to stir. "Where are the others?" Tiri wanted to know.

I bent down to retrieve my weapons, leaving it to the Kildoi to answer. "Oh—they'll be here soon I expect. We'd better find Princess Nandisha and the numims."

"Yes, by Zair! And sharply, too."

Five

Princess Nandisha's cadade would have carried out a ruthless enquiry. Ranaj was spared that chore. The two men of his guard he suspected of treachery—the one who was late and the other who was unwell—had been among our unfortunate fellows slain by the kidnappers.

"They have no feelings for those they buy," he commented.

The general opinion was that this two-pronged onslaught was not the work of the Hyr Kov Khonstanton, Khon the Mak, but rather that of Prince Ortyg.

"It's that slimy little creature's style," said Nandisha. She panted and her hair was ruffled and wild. She had not fully recovered, half out of her wits with fear for her missing son. No trace of him had been found at The Clipped Rhok. The City Watch had been informed but no one expected a result from them. We would have to wait for the kidnappers to contact us—if Prince Byrom still lived. As for the City Guard who patrolled in the upper city, they just might have an informer somewhere with knowledge of what went forward in this plot against Nandisha and who would talk in return for gold.

Serinka insisted that her mistress must rest and we all trooped out leaving a strong guard at every entrance to her quarters. Tiri told me our new young acquaintance was called Dimpy and that the Puncture Lady had stuck him with soothing needles, bound up his wounds and given him a sleeping draught. He would be out for burs yet.

I reflected as we went along to the refectory for much needed inner sustenance that Tiri, Fweygo and I were forming a nice little team.

There appeared little chance that nice state of affairs would continue much longer. Tiri had tasks to perform in the Temple of Cymbaro to which we were not privy and we had tasks for the Star Lords. Again I realized how fortunate I'd been that my gross dereliction of duty had not been punished by a trip back to Earth. All the same, whilst Tiri remained with us I would take pleasure from her company. Fweygo and I discussed our predicament. Prince Tom, a nice lad who was more interested in the religion of Cymbaro than being king, was now the king of Tolindrin. Weasel-faced Prince Ortyg and menacing Khon the Mak both craved the crown and were prepared to go to extreme lengths to obtain that bauble. This despite the old king's will that named Tom the successor and to which this pair of rogues had agreed.

Also, Princess Nandisha craved the crown for her son.

I said to Fweygo: "The numim twins are going to be under threat as long as their parents work for Nandisha."

"Agreed."

"Well, for the sweet sake of Madam Moly Mushtaq! How long do the Star Lords expect us to hang about? The numims aren't going to abandon Nandisha in the near future, are they?"

"I do not believe so."

I swigged down my drink and banged the mug on the table. It was absolutely no use to become heated and start raving. Fweygo's cool manner must not be allowed to irritate me. But I felt that little imp of the perverse grab hold of me, and to prod him a trifle I said: "Well, if we can't get rid of those rasts Ortyg and Khon the Mak, perhaps we could dispose of Nandisha's claim to the throne. Then—"

"Apart from the fact her claim has been kidnapped, that would be a despicable and dishonorable act, Dray Prescot. You surprise me."

I grunted and went over to the serving counter for a fresh wet. The mood I was in I hardly cared if he believed me or not. At least, my words had elicited a reaction from him.

He stood in awe of the Everoinye—well, that was clearly the only sensible attitude—and was perfectly content to do their bidding for as long as they wished. At least, the Star Lords intervened in a more positive fashion in my affairs after the latest understanding we had reached. Quite possibly Fweygo's presence also materially helped there. Our abrupt departure from The Clipped Rhok was put down to our astute realization that the kidnapping of Byrom was a plot to draw off the guards from Nandisha and Nisha. The Star Lords would have had no trouble covering our disappearance and of convincing Ranaj and his guards. No trouble at all, by Krun!

Carrying the mug I went back to Fweygo. He gave me an upward slanting look from under his golden eyebrows.

"The best thing Nandisha can do is go and see Prince—I mean King Tomendishto. And it wouldn't hurt to see Hyr Kov Brannomar. He's one honest broker around here, I believe, even if he is a nob."

Fweygo favored me with an odd look. He started to say something, stopped, changed his mind, and said: "Well, aren't you?"

"Whatever the Everoinye told you about me—"

"Some."

"I'm supposed to be some damnfool Emperor of Emperors."

"The Emperor of Paz. Yes, I know."

I told him I was heartily glad to see that the crazy idea impressed him as little as it did me.

So, of course, what did he reply? It shook me, I can tell you, shook me to my roots, by Vox!

"The Everoinye charged me with assisting you in any way I can."

I moved the mug on the table in circles. In a most subdued tone of voice I started to explain. We were alone; I still kept my voice low. I asked him how much of Paz he knew, had visited, and he was able to convince me that he had traveled and knew a lot of the continents and islands. So I expounded on the craziness of any one person attempting to be the ruler of this vast mass of lands and peoples. The scheme smacked of the insane ambitions of others I had known who had aspired to rule vast domains quite beyond their grasp.

"And they're nearly all dead and gone, now," I finished.

"Nevertheless, Dray Prescot, that which the Everoinye command will be done."

If I'd had a hat on I'd have torn it off, chucked it down on the floor and jumped on it! By Zair! No, by Vox. This idiocy, I said to myself most put out, was worthy of a 'By Zim-Zair!'

By the leprous lips and pendulous posterior of Makki Grodno! The Star Lords had the infernal nerve to embroil poor old Fweygo, a willing and loyal kregoinye, in their maniacal schemes for me and for Paz. Well, at least he had the sense not to bow and scrape before this so puissant emperor. Perhaps the Star Lords had told him I disapproved of the full incline and slavish behavior of that kind. He treated me in ways not too dissimilar from the superior ways of my good comrade Pompino the Iarvin. Then the thought hit me. Djan have mercy! Suppose the Star Lords sent Pompino to me to help! Opaz forfend!

Fweygo said: "The Everoinye told me this today, when you and Tiri were fussing over that new young scruffy friend of yours. I am not sure—not quite sure—just how I should react, treat you, seeing how incompetent you are and in need of my constant care and attention."

I favored him with a look that was more quizzical than hard. Extraordinarily difficult to tell what these confounded Kildois were thinking in their cool and crafty skulls behind those handsome faces. Yes, he could be speaking what he believed to be the truth. Or, he could be teasing me in that dry Kildoi fashion.

So, I made no direct reply.

Instead, I said, casually: "Oh, we are kregoinyes and we work well together. I hope we will become even better comrades. Let's leave it at that."

"Quidang!"

When he said that, the formal acceptance of an order, I knew he wasn't altogether serious.

He changed the subject of conversation easily enough by taking out his new sword and examining it again. He shook his head.

"This blade is a marvel. It serves amazingly well—the balance is perfect. As for the edge, it is sharp, satisfyingly sharp."

"I know Tolindrin steel is poor quality. Is there no decent steel in all of Balintol, then?"

"We have a small supply of good iron ore in Kildrin; as you can imagine that is reserved for those with money."

Kildrin lay on the west coast north of Tolindrin and south of Winlan with the mountains barring off the east. Most, but not by any means all, Kildois hailed from there. That's where that rast Mefto the Kazzur was born on an evil day.

Later on that day after Tiri and I had taken a quick look in the bedroom Nandisha had generously put at our disposal for Dimpy, we started to think it time for a proper slap-up Kregen meal. Ranaj was out with the City Guard trying to discover some clue to Byrom's whereabouts. Nisha and her mother were still resting. I'd made up my mind to have a colored salad in preference to a green salad, the weather being on the hot side of warm, when one of the stewards bustled in. He said that a woman wanted to see me and that the guards had searched her and found no weapons beyond a little dagger which they had temporarily confiscated. She waited in one of the anterooms.

Excusing myself to the others, off I went, slightly intrigued.

The most probable explanation was that my private spy, Naghan the Barrel, wanted to see me. He'd been a tower of strength so far in Oxonium. The woman stood up as I entered. The guard looked blank-faced at me. I nodded. "It's all right, Ranto. You may leave us." He saluted and went out, closing the door softly. I motioned to the chair and the woman resumed her seat. She was perfectly composed.

She wore a shamlak in the best fashion, not a tunic, and the cleavage down the front was wider than narrower, revealing glistening black skin. Her face was handsome, almost haughty, with dark eyes that must have slain many a poor fellow. Her hair was most tastefully done up into a pile upon that imperious little head. Her jewelry spoke eloquently of good taste. She was a Xuntalese, from the island off the southern tip of Balintol.

"You are Drajak known as the Sudden?"

"Yes."

"I have a message. I will whisper it." She stood up again.

Her breath was warm and sweetly scented in my ear.

"The Crystal Griffon. When the suns set. A man wearing a red eyepatch over his left eye." She stepped back. She did not sit.

"I know the place. I will be there. Thank you."

Those fine eyes widened at that. Then she smiled, a most charming smile that radiated personality. "I see why you are called what you are called."

"And you will not tell me what you are called."

She shook her head, still smiling.

"Then I bid you remberee."

"Remberee, Drajak the Sudden."

She walked with a seductive swaying movement towards the door and I opened it for her as was her due. Trust old Naghan the Barrel to find top class agents to employ in his schemes!

Tiri wanted to know who the mystery woman was and I told her the truth, adding that I had to meet a man later this evening. So, of course, I then had to convince her that she couldn't come along.

She became most hoity-toity at that so I mentioned Dimpy and she reluctantly acknowledged that, yes, well, she supposed she'd better stay. Her bottom lip stuck out. Fweygo said not a word.

So, just before the twin suns set, off I sallied. I wore my decent dark blue shamlak with a narrow cleavage well belted up. The rapier, the left-hand dagger and my heavy knife—I habitually refer to that lethal weapon as my sailor knife—over my right hip for my companions.

Just the once I glanced back crossing an avenue to see if Tiri was imp-ishly following me. I didn't see her. I did see a fellow with golden hair just turning to look into a jewelry shop. Now Kildois can hold their lower pair of arms inside their clothes and wrap their tails around their waists under trousers or kilt and pass as apims. The golden color they share with numims would betray them so if they wish to pass completely that hair has to be dyed. Fweygo obviously hadn't had time to dye his hair. All the same, he looked apim enough, something like those golden-haired folk from Vil-lodrin over in the continent of Loh.

Had I been in the habit of smirking I'd have felt a good smirk right now fully justified. Good old Fweygo! He wasn't following me out of idle curiosity. Oh, no, by Krun! He was on my tail because of what the Star Lords had told him; that I firmly believed. And my smirk would be because I'd spotted him.

Now the superior Xuntalese lady had not said those usual conspiratorial words so uniformly used in these situations. She had not in a dark and mysterious voice said: "Come alone!"

From that and my feelings that this was an effective way for Naghan to contact me I did not think I was walking into a trap.

Of course, on Kregen, that wonderful and terrifying world under Antares, all kinds of skullduggery—including traps—must routinely be expected. At the least, it made life interesting and kept the old blood pumping.

The last streamers of deep emerald and lustrous rose were fading and the first stars were pricking out when I entered The Crystal Griffon.

My hope clearly was that Naghan had turned up some information on the whereabouts of the young lord Byrom. Poor old Princess Nandisha and her daughter lady Nisha were in a dreadful state and I felt for them, by Zair. The unpleasant thought that Byrom was already dead had to be kept in perspective. Kidnappers are unpleasant people; until we knew to the contrary we had to assume they wanted something for the return of Byrom. Had they just wanted the young prince dead then they could have cut him down, there and then, finish.

The Crystal Griffon, as its name implied, was an upmarket establishment. They did quality meals here and the wines were of the first vintages, although, unfortunately, their cellars had no Jholaix. The red eye patch was easily identifiable. The man was a Gon, from whose head every vestige of white hair had been shaved and whose scalp gleamed with butter. He'd use the saponifying effects of the butter to shave religiously each day. Well, his race of diffs suffered from the mistaken belief that their white hair was unbecoming if not downright ugly. Thankfully, most of their women did not shave their hair and it glowed silvery white and splendid in the lights of the suns. He wore dark clothes and carried weapons. I sat down opposite him and the serving girl, a dainty Fristle fifi with impertinent eyes and roving tail, brought me a yellow Charwis, not too sweet and with a decent taste.

The Gon said: "Lahal, majister. I am—"

The look I shot him brought his backbone up. He was tall, as many Gons are, with smooth even features. A little flush seeped in over his cheekbones.

"Your pardon, Drajak." He spoke in a soft voice and no one could overhear us in the noise of the tavern. All the same...!

I nodded my head and drank some Charwis.

He went on: "I am Nalgre ti Poventer. I was at the Battle of the Ruined Abbey. Third Phalanx. Bratchlin. I saw you there."

"Lahal, Nalgre. Go on."

He had recovered his composure and now drank a little wine and wiped his lips with a yellow kerchief. Very fussy, are Gons.

"The ambassador wishes to see you. By using me as an intermediary he hopes to avoid throwing suspicion upon you, maj—Drajak."

That explained his elementary mistake. He didn't work for Naghan at all. He was employed by the Vallian embassy here in Oxonium. Elten Larghos Invordun, the Vallian ambassador here, had helped me already and I knew him for a loyal and clever man.

"When?" I said.

"I have a room here. There is a disguise. Tonight."

I finished off the Charwis and stood up. Instantly Nalgre ti Poventer slapped his unfinished drink onto the table and rose. I sighed to myself. He was no conspirator, that was for sure. So I sat down again and called for more wine. He sat down too, slowly, and gave me a most puzzled glance. I leaned forward.

"For the sweet sake of Opaz, Nalgre! Relax. You're supposed not to attract any attention."

He licked his lips. "I'm a brumbyte, a soldier more used to hefting my pike in the files. I'm used to showing respect."

"If it hadn't been for people like you, Nalgre, we'd never have won Vallia's liberty. Now you have a new job that is different. We'll just saunter up, casually."

"Quida—" He checked himself, and said: "A good idea."

I allowed a gargoylish old Dray Prescot smile to plaster itself all over the inside of my head. To Nalgre I just looked what I must have looked like to him back during the Battle of the Ruined Abbey. The Third Phalanx, I recalled, had suffered casualties that day of blood. To him, I was the Emperor, the Majister, to be shown the utmost respect and to be faithfully obeyed in all things. If only he knew how I spurned all these titles and ranks! I loved giving away titles and estates to those who deserved them, and I valued the way in which things could be done simply because I was who I was. But through all that I remained Dray Prescot, a simple sailorman.

Fweygo was sitting inconspicuously in a corner where he could keep an eye on me. I didn't want him taking Nalgre to pieces. Nalgre had been a Bratchlin, a closer of the file, and was therefore well-used to issuing orders and keeping people up to the mark. But he'd be no match for the Kildoi—a redundant remark, that; very few fighting tricks were unknown to them.

As we were going up the stairs, Fweygo stood up and went out the front door. If I knew him he'd be looking for another way in. Nalgre's room lay at the far end of the second floor corridor, and, indeed, in that far end wall was a door which must lead to stairs going down outside. Just how long would it take my kregoinye comrade to make his way in there?

In Nalgre's room, furnished to a good state of inn comfort, he unwrapped a parcel. I did not feel surprise. I shrugged off my blue shamlak and donned the buff jacket with the wide wings, the buff breeches and tall boots and clapped on the wide-brimmed hat with the red and yellow feather. Then my weapons went about me again.

Nalgre also put on his Vallian clothes. He said: "I feel more comfortable in civilized clothes—Drajak."

"Oh, they're more or less decently civilized here in Tolindrin, Nalgre. Except for some cramphs I've met. As to the other countries to the north, that has to be tested."

"I was up in Enderli recently." He hitched his rapier forward. "I can't say I cared overmuch for 'em. Nice zorcas, though."

Ready, we moved out. He opened the door onto the stairs and held the key in his hand ready to lock up after us and there stood Fweygo on the top step, a dagger in one of his fists, just about to force the lock.

Instantly the dagger disappeared. Only a couple of Kregen's smaller moons went scampering past so it was pretty dark. I kept the wide brim of the Vallian hat down over my face.

The Kildoi in his most pleasant voice said: "Your pardon, doms. I have a rendezvous and have lost my key—"

Whether or not he expected a couple of Vallians in a foreign country to believe him I couldn't guess. Sensible people like to stay out of trouble. Nalgre simply said: "I will lock up after you, dom."

From the light in the corridor at our backs which threw us into silhouette I could see Fweygo's face clearly. His trick had rebounded on him. I was confident he did not suspect it was Dray Prescot who stood before him. Our Vallian attire was unmistakable even in silhouette with those wide shoulder wings and breeches and the broad-brimmed hats. He kept his composure remarkably.

"Thank you, dom. But—how do I get out afterward?"

"Why, dom, you must go with Cymbaro's grace."

Fweygo had been hoist, as they say in Clishdrin, by his own varter. His handsome face, smooth and polite in the lamplight, smiled. Oh, yes, by Krun! I was getting to know my new comrade better at each stroke of adventure. "Why, thank you again, dom. I am sure I shall find a way out."

Well, and of course he would! If he didn't knock the door out he'd knock over anyone who got in his way trompling down the inner staircase. That, of course, would be after he'd sorted me out, no doubt considering he'd once again rescued me from peril.

So, wishing not to attract attention to anyone of our party, I had to say something. What? Would it matter if Nalgre ti Poventer knew that Fweygo and I were acquainted? Perhaps I had become obsessed with secrecy, always plotting subterfuges, wearing disguises. But that must be in my scorpion nature. And, anyway, by Krun, it had saved my hide on innumerable occasions.

I said: "The lady became tired of waiting. She left."

Nalgre half-turned to give me a quick puzzled glance, so he missed Fweygo's reaction. The Kildoi shuffled his feet around on the top step, said: "Women! Thank you, dom," and started off down.

Nalgre's low laugh was only half amused. "He's right, by Vox!"

By the time Nalgre had locked up and we reached the alley running past the foot of the stairs, Fweygo had vanished into the shadows. The Maiden with the Many Smiles would be up tonight, and the Twins would add their lustrous pink radiance later on. Nalgre led. He hadn't sounded overly bitter in his remark about the ladies of Kregen so perhaps that was just a lover's tiff. Well, and by Mother Diocaster, there are plenty of them on two worlds.

A couple of streets along in the pinkish moonlight we heard a hullaba-loo and a rout of people came storming along, all tangled up and bashing away with cudgels and blatterers and dwablatters. Nalgre and I jumped into a conveniently shadowed doorway as the rout hacked and hewed past.

The light showed up the favors, the schturvals plain.

"Khon the Mak's roughs fighting with Prince Ortyg's toughs," commented Nalgre. "For the benefit of Vallia they can break one another's heads in and to the Ice Floes of Sicce with 'em."

"Aye. King Tom or Hyr Kov Brannomar are the folk Vallia must deal with."

The City Guard took its time about sorting out the riot and this made me uneasy. It could be that they'd been bribed. It could simply be that law and order were breaking down in Oxonium under the pressures of the strains between the nobles. When the street lay deserted under The Maiden with the Many Smiles we set off again.

Fweygo would be somewhere near keeping an obbo on us.

We reached the Vallian embassy and Nalgre led around the back to a wicket gate to which he had the key. Inside the archway four extremely efficient guards shone lights upon us and demanded credentials as their weapons glittered. The Deldar recognized Nalgre and stood his men at ease and marched us off. At sight of the brave old Vallian uniform I felt all the nostalgia of a fellow cast adrift in the world dwaburs from his home. So many and many a time have I said why can't a simple sailorman like me be left on the beach in his home in Esser Rarioch with Delia? The Star Lords dictate otherwise, that's why.

The fuming sense of injustice boiled up again. The Everoinye and their insane idea that I, a single man, could become the Emperor of Emperors, the Emperor of Paz! Even if I did have the yrium, the special even stronger power than mere charisma, to assist? Ludicrous!

The Elten of Thothsturboin stepped forward eagerly when we were ushered into his study. He was as I remembered him, efficient, now a skilled diplomat instead of a tough warrior of Vallia.

"Lahal—Drajak?"

I nodded. Even here I saw no need to have the majister this and majister that bandied about. We sat down, refreshments were served and the occasion for this nocturnal meeting was revealed.

"You remember when you discovered the secret of the old king's sword, and your identity was discovered to Hyr Kov Brannomar, who Drajak the Sudden really is, we were overheard by Wocut."

San Wocut was Khon the Mak's personal wizard, that gaunt, gray-faced individual I'd seen next to Khonstanton. He was not a Wizard of Loh; he had powers. Elten Larghos said he had a remarkable approach from the sorcerer Wocut. "He has not revealed your secret to Khon the Mak and—"

"Blackmail?"

"Of course. In return for his silence he requests asylum in Vallia, a pension, a villa, immunity from Khon the Mak's vengeance."

"He will trust us to keep our word—once he's home?"

"He knows the stories of Dray Prescot."

"Um."

This, as you may well imagine, had been a great worry to me. Kov Brannomar, who knew, could be trusted to keep his mouth shut. Khon the Mak would seize the opportunity for deviltry. With all the tensions in the city one more strain in connection with Vallia could tip everything into chaos. That was a very real possibility. Not everyone wanted the treaty between Tolindrin and Vallia that Kov Brannomar had so set his heart on. Khonstanton might realistically want the treaty; if he could use me and the treaty to foment disorder to his own advantage he would do so, do so at a run, by Vox!

The signing of the treaty had been postponed until after Tom's coronation. He had made the necessary appearance as king at the Feast of Beng T'Tolin and preparations for the festivities of the coronation were well in hand. Khonstanton—and Prince Ortyg—would make use of anything to seize the crown. Tom wasn't really interested but Brannomar had persuaded him that he was the old king's choice and must therefore do his duty. Oh, yes, a secret regarding Dray Prescot would act like a fuse in this situation.

Nalgre ti Poventer coughed and said: "If I may?" At our assent he wanted to know if, in our turn, we could trust Wocut. "He is able, is he not, to spy on us from a distance?"

Elten Larghos smiled. "The famous Wizards of Loh from Vallia have inspected the embassy and removed certain objects."

Well, by Vox, I knew what that was about. Deb-Lu or Khe-Hi or Ling-Li made it their business to clean all our overseas buildings of signomants, the magical discs through which wizards may more easily observe at a distance. Also they placed detectors to warn if any wizard had gone into lupu to spy on us.

I told them it looked as though the chances were on our side. Once Wocut had committed himself he knew he would be in our power. I left the details of the transaction to the ambassador and scribbled a quick note to Drak, Emperor of Vallia, suggesting Khe-Hi check it out.

After another drink it was time to get back to the problems facing me here in Oxonium—the numim twins, and, interestingly, a rapscallion of an imp of Sicce called Dimpy.

Six

On the way back to The Crystal Griffon we witnessed another street brawl. This time the skull beating erupted between the adherents of Tolaar, the major religion of these parts, and that other, darker and more mysterious cult of Dokerty. Being practical, cautious fellows, we stood aside and let them get on with it.

As I doffed the buff Vallian costume and resumed the blue shamlak of Tolindrin I reflected that I had omitted to congratulate Elten Larghos Invordun na Thothsturboin on his promotion from consul to full flown ambassador. That must have come as a result of his work respecting the succession and the treaty. My lad Drak, like me, was overfond of rewarding people. In that he showed a trait at variance with the generality of his personality, which was stern and upright. Yet, as Delia knew, he was a loving and loyal son. So the fact that the Emperor of Vallia had chosen to elevate his representative in Tolindrin to the heights of full ambassador must strike Kov Brannomar as a positive omen of good relations between the two countries. Alliance, he must assume, was just over the horizon.

I asked Nalgre to congratulate Larghos for me, and added: "I think I'll keep the Vallian clothes—if that's all right."

"Of course. They may serve again."

Having given Nalgre my thanks and bid him remberee I trotted off back to Nandisha's palace. The cable cars still ran at night, at less frequent intervals. There were quite a lot of people about and everyone looked keyed up, tense. Trouble seemed to smoke on the air. The quicker the coronation took place and the treaty with Vallia signed, the quicker Oxonium could settle down.

Only a few lights burned in the palace as I answered the guard's challenge and went in. I gave an almighty yawn. A left-over scrap of vosk pie and a swingeing draught of red wine tucked away, and into bed I crawled and thought my last thought of every day, closed my eyes and awoke to see Fweygo bending over me, saying: "Up, you lazy gyp! Up!"

Blinking and stretching I tumbled out. I'd missed the first breakfast. On the way down Fweygo said: "Tiri's made up her mind. She's off today."

I grunted. Fweygo and I were employed by Ranaj on behalf of Nandisha. The lady Tirivenswatha was a guest, staying on here in the circumstances of our acquaintance with the princess. The dancing girl had responsibilities at the Temple of Cymbaro and San Paynor, the chief priest before Cymbaro at his shrine in Oxonium, required her return. She was already eating at the second breakfast when we went in, the youngster Dimpy, looking resentful, sitting at her side. She pouted just a trifle and her lower lip stuck out. She said: "I love my work in the shrine and San Paynor. But I do like living here. In the dormitory with the other girls... Well, it's not like here."

"We'll come and visit you," Fweygo told her.

"All these religions are fakes." Dimpy spoke around a mouthful of breakfast. "All they want is your money."

"Oh, Dimpy, you are dreadful!"

"Well, it's true, by Dromang!"

They glared at each other, eyeball to eyeball, high of color and breathing too rapidly. Fweygo's sly glance in my direction and my own reading of the situation curved my hard old lips a fraction. If Dimpy's business had not been done for him by this curvaceous and lively lass then I hadn't much idea of true romance. They were both of them quite clearly oblivious of anyone else in the refectory. Fweygo's tail hand swept across the table and knocked over a jug. The clatter brought them out of that locked glance of future passion. I heaved up a sigh inside myself—Delia! Delia!

I wanted to know what Dimpy intended to do about the frame-up and as we finished breakfast he told us his story. He was worried over his mother and sisters. If Sleed the Slick harmed them, Dimpy did not wish to face the consequences of that horrific thought.

"And it's not safe for you to return to the Hellraisers?" Tiri's question was just too artless to pass muster.

All the same, Dimpy bit. "I know how much I owe you for your help. Believe me, I am very grateful. But I'll hafta go back."

"We'll speak to Ranaj," said Fweygo in a casual way. "He'll find you a job in the palace. That'll be better than thieving for a living."

Dimpy flared up. "I'm not a thief! I told you, that was a stupid Hellraiser test. Anyway, anything we take up here's been taken from us down there before!"

Tiri started up then and Fweygo and I realized when we weren't wanted.

Dimpy was in an awkward position. He had a splendid chance to get out of the warrens, one not easily come by in the normal course of events, yet the problem of his family remained. I fancied young Tirivenswatha would have a hand in sorting out what eventuated. They made a fine couple, at that. The idea was not too ridiculous. We joined a group where Fat Lardo, one of the cooks, was retailing the latest gossip from the streets.

Yet another beautiful young girl had been found dead. Her naked and bloody body had been discovered early this morning dumped in the gutter of Penitence Alley which ran alongside the Temple of Tolaar. She had been murdered in a most brutal fashion, badly cut up, and her heart had not been found.

"Who was she?" Fweygo wanted to know.

"Paline Lanto. She was a respectable shop girl."

"A lover's tiff?"

Oily Nath, the fry-up artist, burst out: "Blood and guts everywhere? Some lover! Some tiff!"

That appeared an appropriate comment and everyone solemnly nodded heads. Poor little Paline Lanto was only the last in a horrific line of murder victims. All had been nauseatingly mutilated. Affairs of this nature are best left to the proper authorities. The City Guard ought to be investigating. So far they had told us nothing regarding Byrom's kidnapping and I doubted if they'd have any greater success over these murders.

A waft of cold air breezed over us and Fweygo looked around sharply, one of his fists going to the hilt of his sword.

Directly opposite me a blue mist irradiated by an inner glow formed. I did not change expression; but I felt my heart give an almighty thump.

Slowly the blue mist thickened and took on the form of a man in a long robe. The familiar kindly features of San Deb-Lu beamed out at me. No one took any notice. Our comrade Wizard of Loh had powers, by Zair, powers! He beckoned. I stood up, excusing myself, and followed the apparition out and along the passage to a storeroom.

"Lahal, Jak."

"Lahal, San."

"This fellow Wocut—calls himself a sorcerer. Odd Type." By the inflexion in his voice I could tell Deb-Lu was using capital letters to express deeper meanings to his words. "I've already checked him out. In his desire to emigrate to Vallia I Believe Him To Be Sincere." Deb-Lu went on to say that Drak had given his assent and that in Vondium Wocut would have a very close eye kept on him by Khe-Hi and Ling-Li. So, naturally, I wanted to know all the news from home, and the sorcerer retailed many fascinating details.

He finished by saying in his doubtful voice: "I cannot pretend to understand why you remain here in Balintol, Dray. I do know there is a reason.

Vallia muchly wants this treaty for the airboats and riding animals Tolindrin can provide. If I—"

I dared to interrupt the Wizard of Loh.

"The old king here did not approve of most sorcery. It is mostly religion and its mysteries. And I believe there are many."

He sniffed. "Well, I must go. It is good to see you again, Dray. Leave your friend Wocut to us. Now I bid you remberee."

"Remberee, Deb-Lu."

Without a plop of displaced air, phut, he was gone.

Because of that meeting, so eerie to someone who does not do much business with wizards, I went to tell Fweygo I would go with Tiri to the shrine of Cymbaro. He nodded emphatically. "Yes. The greater danger lies with the lion children, and so I should be here."

Well, by Krun, and what else would you expect?

My words to Deb-Lu about religion here barely scratched the surface. There were temples to many goddesses and gods and minor godlings on all the hills and a motley bunch to form any sort of pantheon they were, too. Unlike our Ancient Greeks they didn't have a temple to the unknown god. Any cult could run up a shrine, always provided they paid their taxes to the king, promptly and in full. The thought occurred to me to wonder if wriggling out of paying taxes was the reason why the red-robed priests of Dokerty met secretly, at night and in remote ruins.

Tiri had more luggage now than when we'd arrived and Ranaj appointed a porter to carry it for her to the temple. Standing by the doorway with her baggage at her feet, she looked a little forlorn. The porter, a powerful Brukaj, hovered, waiting.

As I approached, Dimpy appeared from the opposite direction and walked sturdily towards us, head up, color high. I could guess what he intended to do.

At that moment the blue wavering radiance formed before me and the phantom shape of Deb-Lu appeared, still smiling. He raised a hand. Striding on, Dimpy marched clean through that ghostly apparition. He shivered, suddenly, and looked about with wary eyes, as though expecting an ambush.

"By Dromang! What was that?" He lost some of his color.

Tiri's imperious little head twitched up and she frowned. In her clear acid voice, she said: "Unbelievers believe many foolish things, fambly."

Dimpy bristled at that. Deb-Lu said: "What you suspected is perfectly correct, Dray. The young prince is being held prisoner by this charming fellow Prince Ortyg at one of his hideouts down below."

"Thank you, Deb-Lu. Directions?"

Since the death of the Fristle, Fonnell the Fractious, his gang had split up. Some of the olive-green clad rogues had formed a smaller gang, some had joined up with other groupings of the ruffians down in the warrens and Ranaj—and King Tom—had made it their business to keep tabs on them. I had an idea of some of the spies they used; not all. Ortyg, who had employed Fonnell, must be continuing to use some members of the old olive-green gang.

The Wizard of Loh told me the way to the particular warren. He finished: "By the Seven Arcades, Drak! They're a mighty unhealthy bunch there."

"Oh, aye."

"You Watch Out. This whippersnapper Prince Ortyg is what people in these parts, I believe, call a right blintz."

"They do. All the same, as ever, I wonder if he really—"

"Like your doubts about Phu-Si-Yantong?"

"I suppose so, yes."

Tiri and Dimpy were eyeing each other, not hearing a word we said. The porter stared vacantly about, rubbing his head. Oh, yes, by Vox. Wizards of Loh have powers!

By those same powers my sorcerous comrade cloaked my own words. I asked him if Byrom stood in immediate danger and was reassured by the reply. What the kidnappers' plans were we did not know. The fact that there was no ransom demand was certainly worrying; Deb-Lu considered they wanted something more than merely money, or putting Nandisha's son out of the running for the crown. When the princess was distracted past her wits' end, Deb-Lu suggested, then the weasel-faced Prince Ortyg would strike.

Deb-Lu-Quienyin just put up his hand in time to prevent his bulbous turban from toppling over an ear. I enjoyed the sight, by Krun! After a few more words we said the remberees and Deb-Lu vanished.

With Fweygo to guard the numims I had two options. Tiri or Byrom. Ranaj was happy to provide an escort for the temple dancer and Dimpy stoutly declared his intention of going along. I excused myself, without explanation, and made the necessary preparations.

Within the bur I was kitted up and off into the devil's kitchens of the stews between the hills.

Seven

An arrow chinked off the wall a handbreadth from my head. I slid into the shadow of an ale barrel like a ferret down a rabbit hole.

Across the intersection of roads running at right angles through two valleys a crude barricade had been thrown up. Tables, wardrobes, barrels, upended carts, all jumbled together to make an obstacle to Nagzalla's Nasty Neemus. They shot at the defenders of the dismal street at my back and tried a charge which carried some of the barricade. The Raging Volcanoes fell back, slashing axes about in desperation.

These two gangs at each other's throats were damned inconvenient, by Krun. A girl staggered into my ale barrel and collapsed, an arrow through her throat. She gargled blood. Her grimy face carried a look of profound shock and her ripped-open tunic revealed a pallid body smothered in blood. She toppled and fell close by my side.

More arrows skimmed in, to chingle against the wall and tumble uselessly to the muddy ground. The girl twitched, dark blood pulsing with the last force of her heartbeats past the shaft. Her eyes glazed. The noise and confusion hammered on unheedingly.

What waste! What nonsense! Destruction, horror and death, and all for a measly hundred paces or so of tumbledown houses, filthy dopa dens and a muddle of ramshackle shacks. A spotted strowger with a broken arrow in his flank yip-yip-yipped across the road. I felt sorry for the little fellow; but—what could aid him now?

Mind you, I'd known a fat queen whose pet spotted strowgers loved nothing better than to chew on the bodies of her victims. The opposite cliff face glowed high up with the opaline radiance of the Suns; down here in the slot the shadows crawled as torches flared. The battle continued in mayhem and carnage. The Raging Volcanoes mustered a reserve and smashed back at Nagzalla's Nasty Neemus. Weapons clashed all along the barricade. Men and women screamed. Bodies tumbled to fall in red ruin and be trampled on by the blood lusting combatants.

Well, by Vox! The sharper I got out of this mess the sooner I'd be on my way to finding young Byrom.

Crouching behind an ale barrel as a fight erupted in front of me seemed to me, Dray Prescot, Vovedeer, Lord of Strombor and Krozair of Zy, to be the most sensible course of action in two worlds, too right, by the diseased and pendulous nether parts of Makki-Grodno!

The sides of the hills here were capable of being climbed with great difficulty so this is where I'd been led down, for where I wanted to go was hemmed in by practically vertical cliffs. There'd been no difficulty in contacting Naghan Raerdu through one of his men, for we'd arranged to have a reliable person on watch. Milsi the Slinky had given me no recognition; but at my jerk of the head she'd led off to where Naghan the Barrel could be found at this time. He moved around the city, logically enough. After that he simply detailed a party to escort me down, grumbling at the danger I insisted on placing myself in, and I sent them off long before reaching the bottom. Now I found myself embroiled in this infuriating fracas. By the hairy and infested nostrils of the Divine Lady of Belschutz! It was enough to make a fellow mad clean through!

A move had to be made soon if I was to succeed.

Nagzalla's Nasty Neemus held three arms of the crossroads and they wanted the fourth arm, currently in the possession of the Raging Volcanoes. Whatever treaty had been agreed in the past had fallen through, as was the way down in the warrens of Oxonium as up on the hills. I was on the Nasty's side of the barricade and my target lay somewhere down at the far end of the Volcanoes' street.

Among the frantic figures fighting to defend the makeshift wall a dozen or so wore the olive green of Fonnell's old gang. So that explained why Byrom had been spirited away there. Prince Ortyg had maintained his connection with the olive green gang members.

This poor dead urchin girl at my side represented so much of what was wrong with two worlds. This profound if obvious thought was abruptly shattered. Something exceedingly hard and sharp pushed into my back. A voice like a bottle emptying growled: "Skulking, hey! I'll soon sort you out, by Reder, yes!"

That damned uncomfortable object prodding my back was a sword. Slowly I turned my head. He was hairy, broad, flat of nose and coarse of lip. In the nature of the fellow a glisten of scar ran down his left cheek and the eye above was puckered up. He was a Brokelsh. "Up, skulker!" He jabbed. "Up and at that barricade!"

In all the noise the door at my back had opened silently. I didn't sweat; the ugly thought crossed my mind that perhaps I was getting slow. One thing an old leem-hunter and a fighting man must never is is slow. I stood up and pointed to the dead girl.

"Easy, dom. Came back to see—"

"Save your whining excuses. I don't know you. I'll know you again, skulker, by Reder, I'll know you."

Nagzalla's Nasty Neemus must be a sizeable gang, then. Fair enough that anyone wouldn't know personally all the members. I'd get by all right. When no one recognized me, as must inevitably follow, then, by Krun, would be the time to worry.

He took the sword away. He pushed me out from the barrel into the street. Mud slicked underfoot. There were more torches now and shadows lay uncertainly across the furious scene. A fresh onslaught developed as the Nasty's hurled once more at the defenders.

Caught up in the attack I found myself trying to clamber up an overturned hand barrow. A Rapa made determined efforts to degut me with his spear. My left fist wrapped around the shaft and I pulled.

He yowled and flew over the barrow to land on his beak. My new acquaintance stuck his sword through the Rapa who twisted and shrieked and tried to wriggle away.

"Stinking Beaky!"

A crossbow bolt flicked over my shoulder. The Fristle ahead threw down the weapon and dragged out a scimitar and slashed. My own return blocked the blow and sent the braxter darting at his chest. Startled, he backed off. The Brokelsh jumped up beside me. More Volcanoes were running up to guard this sudden breach. It was a matter of skip and jump, of cut and thrust, as we tried to hold the hand barrow for Nagzalla. An advang whose porcine features were convulsed with fury leaped alongside us to help hold the barrow. He swung a broad-bladed polearm and swept the head from the shoulders of a poor devil who failed to dodge in time. Blood spouted everywhere.

"To me!" roared the Brokelsh, hair flying all over the place. "Neemus! Neemus! To Brory the Bold! Neemus!"

A couple more Nagzallas ran up and for a space we held the barrow, trying to force our way on and being pressed back. In the erratic torchlight every move was dangerous. Keeping a balance and picking a target, hitting and trying not to be hit, the whole crazy combat proved difficult. A loud crack splintered up followed by two more splitting bangs. The barrow's bottom just caved in. Down we all tumbled, inextricably mixed up, arms and legs and heads all jumbled together like crabs in a basket.

Something clunked against my nose and water started into my eyes. I gave an almighty heave. Smelly hair thrust against my lips. I bit. I bit damned hard, I can tell you, not caring whose hide it was. In all the uproar any yell was lost. I got a good purchase and shoved the hairy one aside and rose up out of the shambles. The stink of blood roughened on my tongue. The Fristle clawed up beside me. He tried to give me a thwack but his scimitar had no room to swing and I just belted him on the nose with a clenched fist. He flopped back into the pile of bodies.

A bellowed roar: "Back! Set back, fanshos!" and we Nagzallas tumbled back out of the wreckage.

They were all panting, blood-smeared, evil of eye. We pulled back to rejoin the rest of the gang in their positions. For a space now it would be shooting until another charge could be mounted.

"By Reder, Brory!" The advang's snout was all aquiver. "We nearly did it! Another push and—"

"And we'd be cut off and chopped!"

That was true, by Krun. More Volcanoes had been closing on the barrow in the moments before it collapsed.

Brory the Bold eyed me. He were standing in the shadows of a doorway and every now and then an arrow fleeted in. "You fought well, skulker. Your name?"

"Kadar the Hammer." The name popped into my head. I'd used it before and it was serviceable.

He grunted. "Stick close by me when we attack again."

When I'd kitted myself out for this jaunt I'd selected a simple tan leather jack with a few greenish brass studs here and there. I'd taken off the shamlak and under the jack wore a common brown tunic. The braxter was munitions quality from Nandisha's armory and I was surprised and pleased the thing hadn't snapped across yet. In view of that almost inevitable happening I carried another scabbarded alongside the rapier. Brory the Bold gave the rapier a leery look.

"Fancy yourself with the toothpick, do you, dom?"

I summoned up a casual shrug. "When necessary."

He grunted again in that coarse Brokelsh way.

He did not comment on the short-hafted single-bladed axe I had slung over my shoulder. Axes are useful in some fights. This specimen was not unlike one of the axes wielded by my Clansmen on the Great Plains of Segesthes. That, of course, was not surprising as those fair grazing and hunting grounds lay to the north over the mountains.

High above our heads a cluster of lights traveled slowly from one hill to the next. Up there, riding in the calimer on the invisible cables, haughty folk wouldn't even bother to look down at the chasms beneath. The lights of the cable car, high against the dark sky, did look romantic and mysterious. Down here it was all blood, dirt and death.

Most of the gangs organized themselves into sub-divisions called chapters and with conscious ostentation named their leaders with military ranks. This Brokelsh, Brory the Bold, turned out to be a chapter Jiktar, meaning he ran the chapter. Dimpy had told us he'd been a chapter deldar in his broken-up gang. Now the Jiktar busied himself putting together a fresh force for the next attack.

In my not un-extensive experience of street fighting I'd found that charging maniacally up an open street was usually a sure recipe for disaster. We generally burrowed our way through the buildings flanking the street. It seemed to me that Brory considered the barricade no real obstacle. Well, by Djan, it was a ramshackle enough structure; it had already proved too tough a nut for these bully boys to crack.

A pang shot through me. By Vox, yes! I could envisage my swods of the Emperor's Sword Watch or the Emperor's Yellow Jackets cleaning up this street like a giant broom. And the brumbytes of the Phalanx—they'd just swarm over the chairs and tables and carts like a tidal wave. Oh, well, they were far away and no doubt busy.

So that the next whooping charge met with the same fate as the previous efforts.

Although the valley was narrow the central roadway was flanked by buildings. I eyed them meanly. In my bones I could feel strongly that the Star Lords would not allow me to disport myself like this for much longer. They'd want me back on duty. They'd hoick me out in the very near future, that I darkly surmised. It behooved me to get that move on I'd promised myself some time ago when the Suns were flooding the opposite crest with opaline radiance. Now the slot lay in total darkness, and The Maiden with the Many Smiles would drift down a fuzzy pinkish light soon that would do something to relieve this infernal imitation of a night of Notor Zan.

Brory had taken a slight cut over an ear and his head was bound up in a red-stained yellow bandage. He grunted when I spoke to him; but he listened. He told me, curtly, that to go through the houses would destroy what they were fighting to gain. I said that they'd gain nothing but more dead and wounded if they didn't, whereat he grunted again. "You may crave violent action," I said. "But action has to be directed. If you weren't the chapter Jiktar I'd say you were acting like a tanzy."

He didn't grunt at that. Oh, no, by Djan! He bristled up in his uncouth hairy Brokelsh way. "Who the hell do you think you are? I run the chapter—not you! I don't even know where you come from. Nobody seems to know you."

"Did I or did I not fight on the barricade?"

"You did."

There were no torches near us so I could stand out in the street and point—dramatically!—at the barricade.

"Send your people to their deaths, Brory! Have them shot down and cut up! I'll find a way through the buildings."

The blessed or cursed power I have, the yrium, blazed forth. The Star Lords had chosen me to be this impossible Emperor of Emperors. Wishing it were otherwise, still, I knew they had chosen well. Brory wilted. He caught the blast of the yrium in full flight. He obeyed.

Not sullenly, as might be expected, but in a sprightly way he organized afresh. He ran the chapter responsible for this end of the street. Other streets had their own chapters. He called in his hikdars and told them and they told the deldars and they shouted at the—I hesitate to call these ragamuffin rapscallions swods—at the bedraggled gang members who'd been beaten back so many times.

I did discover that Nagzalla's Nasty Neemus were in fact attempting to retake this section of streets they'd lost a season or so ago. They'd been weaker then. They'd been called Nagzalla's Neemus then. As they rebuilt their strength they'd put in the word Nasty to remind them that they had a debt to pay and territory to take from the Raging Volcanoes.

Brory might obey authority when he could see the sense of it. That did not mean he would forget his own position. He said: "You are not a member of the Neemus."

"No. I'm tazll at the moment."

By that he knew I was an unemployed mercenary.

He nodded emphatically. "When this shindig is all over and we've taken Nath Market Street and if you're still alive, I feel we will accept you as a full member." He brushed hair away from the bandage. "As a paktun you understand these things."

"Aye."

Most of the runnels of Oxonium crossed a trifle askew of right angles so we chose the diagonal point with the least houses on the corner. Pickaxes were brought up. Unlit torches were handed out. There was a tenseness among these Neemus, a way of holding the breath, of speaking in clipped syllables. They'd taken a beating in their attempts to take back what they considered rightfully theirs. Now they were about to embark on what could be a crazy adventure. They could die more certainly this way than on the barricade.

And—at whose say so?

Some unknown plug-ugly who had suddenly appeared among them, telling their leaders what to do, handing out orders, cutting them down to size—merciless in his criticism.

Oh, yes, by the ruptured entrails and dangling eyeballs of Makki Grodno! This fellow Kadar the Hammer drove 'em, drove 'em good.

As for me, plain Dray Prescot, alias Kadar the Hammer, I looked around on this rabble, their eyes like coals, their grimy fists clutched about weapons, their mouths open and panting like wolves.

"For the sake of Reder! Wenda! Let's go!"

Eight

The last chunk of rock eased away and shuttered lanternlight struck across the room beyond. A storehouse, the place smelled acridly of vegetables in store too long. Brory shouldered through the gap we had made, wasting no time, sword in fist.

Other Neemus at our back pressed on, wraithlike in the encompassing dimness. We made as little noise as possible. All the same we were well aware that the Volcanoes must soon detect our activities and take immediate action in retaliation. The buildings at the end of the row were constructed of rocks fallen from the cliffs cemented together. Further on there were wattle and daub shacks and lath and plaster houses.

Brory gestured for men to start on the opposite wall.

"Quiet, you hulus!" he snarled and the picks chinked more delicately.

Outside in the cross street, noise flowered up into the starlit sky. The Neemus were putting in another doomed frontal attack to cover our activities. If this stratagem failed—I refused even to contemplate such an eventuality. On a purely personal basis I had to succeed. As San Blarnoi says: 'A single man may succeed where an army will fail.'

Well, by Krun, all well and good, that might be true. I was that single man. On Kregen an army at your back is a mighty comfort. An opening was made, the rocks carefully prised loose and placed gently on the floor. This next building was a house from which the family had long since fled back into the warrens owned by the Volcanoes. A few simple furnishings stood forlornly abandoned. When—and not if, Brory had declared—the Neemus regained this street the people of theirs who had been dispossessed would return to what were their own homes. The noise outside increased. We were penetrating through the houses to the point where the barricade had been set up and we were under no illusions that the house would be undefended.

I said: "Make larger holes. We want to get reinforcements through as quickly as possible."

Brory nodded and whispered the orders. All Nagzalla's gang wore a representation of a black neemu somewhere about their persons. The Volcanoes wore some fantastic spouting triangle. Up front, I peered into a room where slanting lanternlight revealed a window in the far wall. I frowned.

Whilst most of the houses were built in rows, not all were terraced, and here we had a cross alleyway leading from the main street to the trackway at the foot of the cliffs. A few strides took me to the window.

The alley was not wide and the structure opposite, wreathed in shadow, would be the building abutting the barricade.

Brory wanted to know if we should make a hole in the wall and I told him yes. We needed to get men up front as fast as we could. What I didn't say was that we might have to run for it just as damn fast, by Krun.

The uproar along the barricade died down a trifle. The Neemus must be faltering in the forlorn attack. We must hurry.

Through the window I went and sprinted to crouch by the opposite wall beneath a window. Cautiously I stuck an eyeball around the side of the frame.

I froze. A small brown scorpion waddled easily across the window sill in front of my nose. He moved in the arrogant swing of your true scorpion. I held my breath. He scuttled off into the shadows of the cemented-together stones forming the window surround and architrave. I let my breath out silently. Yes, I said to myself, oh, yes, by Zair. I agree. I agree with you absolutely, Everoinye. What was I doing puddling about in alleyways with a gang of cutthroats when I was supposed to be about the business of becoming an emperor? What indeed! Circumstances distort actions, as the Star Lords well knew. I had to get on with this affair, muy pronto. This thought made me more reckless than I usually am, Opaz forgive me.

I'd no idea if this scorpion was truly from the Star Lords or was simply a fellow who lived in these parts. That didn't matter. What did was the effect he had on me and on the subsequent events.

To my right the alley ran into the shadows of the cliff face. To the left shards of torchlight threw up the grotesque contortions of men and women locked in battle. I realized I'd done this all wrong.

I'd hoped to be able to worm through the houses and come out at the back of the barricade. The Volcanoes were too canny for that simple stratagem to succeed. The window revealed what amounted to the front line. Archers were shooting from windows to my left, cutting into the Neemus climbing the barricade, flanking them.

Other men and women were moving in and out of the doorway in the opposite wall of the room. A fellow was trying to restring a crossbow and cursing, and a Fristle was methodically running a sharpening stone along the edge of his scimitar. I ducked back. At my side Brory whispered: "There's a door here—"

"Get as many lads through there as quickly as possible. This room must be cleared instanter. On my signal. I'm going in through the window. That's the signal."

"Quidang!"

With that I heaved up, took a last rapid glance into the room, and launched myself through the opening.

The Fristle sprang up, swirling his newly sharpened scimitar. The crossbow re-stringer dropped the bow and snatched for his sword. At the first blow my braxter snapped across. I didn't bother to waste breath cursing. The axe ripped free from its thong at my side and came around in a blurred arc. Down went the Fristle and the bowman yelped, and dodged, and the backhand swing took him across the top of his head. He collapsed.

The bowmen at the windows to the left were slow to react. By the time they'd turned about, yelling alarm, the room filled with Neemus at my back as I shot headlong through the door into the next room. Then it was a mad bedlam of hack and slay, dodging return blows, keeping a steady footing, and driving powerfully on.

Now we were committed. If we didn't clear these Volcanoes out very rapidly we'd be overwhelmed before our reinforcements arrived.

No time for niceties. Bash on, swing and hit, strike and bash on. Brory and his people supported superbly and we smashed our way through the enemy. The door to our left must—it had to, by Krun!—lead out onto the street abaft that confounded barricade.

In the lead, with a dripping axe in my fist, I catapulted through and the rest of the Neemus roared on after.

Torchlight splashed luridly over the action along the barricade. People were struggling like doomed wights in hell. Weapons flamed. The noises and the stinks beat maddeningly in our ears and nostrils. A massive yellow-skinned fellow hurled a trident at me and I batted it away. Brory was screaming orders in the tumult. We hit the defenders like a tidal wave. A bald-headed Gon called Garlash the Lips blew his trumpet. The notes rang clear and true above the hellish racket.

That was the signal for the final and triumphant onslaught of maddened Neemus outside. They charged in as we swept the wall clear from our side. Caught between two axes of attack the defenders crumbled.

When it was all over here and a screeching bunch of our fellows went hell for leather down the street chasing the remnants of the Volcanoes, I found Brory the Bold cleaning his sword and staring at a huddle of prisoners. Being still in somewhat of a hurry I did not properly clean the axe but wrapped the head in a chunk of cloth ripped from a corpse. The axe was so befouled cleaning would be a major task. And, I thought of improperly cleaned weapons and Vomanus.

Brory said: "Y'know, Kadar, I've been married four times. Each wife's been killed one way or another." He nodded his head to a strapping prisoner whose dark hair floated freely about a flushed face. Her leather breastplate hung askew and her pale body showed weals and blood streaks. "A beauty, hey? Yes, I think a marriage is next."

By the way the girl was slyly shooting looks the Brokelsh's way, might indicate the marriage would prove a success. It might also mean a dagger in his back on the night of the consummation.

I said: "I wish you well. I'll take a look down the end."

"My thanks, Kadar the Hammer. A true black Neemu, so you are."

I grunted, said something about seeing him later, and took myself off after our hunters of Volcanoes.

As I had indicated, this Nath Market Street was narrow. At the far end the streets leading off broadened out into Volcano territory. This rumble between gangs would be steered well clear of by the City Watch. Those Katakis were far too canny to embroil themselves to no benefit. A ponsho would get you a zorca they'd be sniffing round to buy as cheaply as possible any prisoners available to sell on to their disgusting slaver relatives. If Brory did marry that dark-haired beauty she'd be far better off than sold to the non-existent mercies of the Whiptails.

A wall-eyed chapter Jiktar called Nath the Seeing urged on his people as I came up with them. Nath the Seeing had taken over from Brory, whose folk were exhausted. By the same token the Volcanoes would have brought up reinforcements.

This looked like the end of the road for Nagzalla's Nasty Neemus here. But—oh, no, by Krun!—but not for Dray Prescot!

Nath the Seeing was not, as a grizzled old fighting man might expect, busily having a barricade built across the mouth of Nath Market Street. In any conurbation rules and laws must be worked out, written or unwritten. Between the two rival gangs this central crossroads forming a substantial plaza remained a no man's land. The reason for this reared up from the center.

From a rearing gray stone construction of squared masonry a lofting tower of cunning cross-struts reached up and up. In the darkness the top was not visible save for a warning light. A constellation of lights moved smoothly against the nighted sky over our heads, going towards the top of the tower where the cables between hills were supported. Up there, as I had thought before, the people in the cable car probably gave not a single glance down to the stews.

Much of the time people moved freely between the hills, for the gangs recognized the need for trade and barter. Food had to be brought in. Of course, the gangs took their own taxation. Only in times of trouble, as had happened this night, saw open warfare. Nath the Seeing cocked his head sideways to look across the kyro where only a few late folk walked home, thankful the fighting was finished.

"In Nagzalla's good time," he said with great satisfaction, "we'll have all three of 'em. Margayla, Homespun and Pin Streets. By Reder, yes!"

I said something politely in the affirmative. He cocked his head and focused an eye on me.

"You did well in the fight back there. Brory reckoned you were red hot. Good Neemu material."

What the devil was I doing standing shillyshallying around like this being patronized by a jumped up gang member! I told Nath the Seeing that if I ran Nagzalla's Nasty Neemus there'd be a lot of changes, mostly at the top. I finished by bidding him the remberees and walking off smartly, leaving him with his moist mouth hanging open.

The place I wanted was located in Margayla Street, directly across the plaza. On one side Pin Street was also Volcano territory. Homespun on the other was not, being controlled by the Skullbiters, a sub-group of the Hellraisers. Now the commotion had died away the Kataki City Watch would be on the prowl once more so it behooved me to keep an eye open. There were ale houses open. I licked my lips.

No. Duty before pleasure. Young Byrom must be thoroughly frightened, feeling sick, wondering what was going to happen to him. He must be my only concern. As for the Kataki Watch and the Star Lords, they must be pushed to the back of my vosk skull of a head for now.

Passing an ale house, open, with lights shining and men and women entering and leaving, some staggering, I reflected that ale was a food. This ale was thick and sweet and dark. Once they put hops in it and turned it into beer it became bitter and pale. I went resolutely on. Something was always going on through the night down here in the abyss and I was importuned for many a weird and wonderful product or service. Vibrant life, energetic and raw, pulsed all about me. The fighting was remembered but was now a thing of the past—until the next time.

Despite the dubious pleasures being enjoyed down here, you surely could feel sympathy for the folk trapped in the stews between the hills—but! But never forget these people owned slaves too.

Although Balintol is a nice warm continent, the temperature drops a few degrees down in the slots, naturally—one reason why the exposure of the wide-cleavage shamlak is not popular. Apart from the pestering peddlers no one offered to halt my progress and very shortly the end of the street came in sight sketchily illuminated by hanging lanterns. The next square had its cable car tower; there was a significant difference between this masonry construction and the last.

Here a guardhouse was built into the base. Here the notorious Kataki City Watch maintained what amounted to a police station, a precinct house, from which they could sally forth on raids and to which they could return for safety. A chair lift could hoist them to the platform at the top, where they could pick up a cable car.

There were quite a few of these Watch guardhouses situated in the runnels; most of the time the Whiptails would sail down in lifters to go about their nefarious activities and return to their barracks above.

I ignored all that and turned to survey my target.

The place was not a tavern as I had expected—oh, yes, there was a drinking saloon on the ground floor—but the lanterns and signs proclaimed the four-storey solid-looking building a house of ill-repute. It was well patronized and probably never closed its doors. Everything about it indicated it was a high class house. Some of the olive-green bunch had done well, then, and Prince Ortyg must be well satisfied.

Round the back, find a window, reach the top floor—that was the ticket. By the sticky nostrils and pendulous lips of Makki Grodno! The things a fellow has to do in this life!

The dolorous alley at the back, running in liquid filth, was lit only by a single lamp. This showed a window drowned in shadows. A cloth screen obscured the interior; but a cautious lifting of one corner allowed me to see a room piled with mattresses and bed frames, stools and benches. As I went in I just hoped that Naghan the Barrel was ready to play his part in this night's affair as arranged.

Out in the dim corridor the stair well showed me the way up.

The first floor landing above the ground floor had carpets and two doors.

One must lead to the front and the rooms above the drinking saloon. I took the other and found the expected passage lined with rows of doors. Judging by the sounds most were occupied.

They hadn't built the stairs going straight up, the flights were staggered. The end of the passage brought me out to a landing with a balcony on one side I had not expected. I looked over cautiously.

The room below was well-furnished, elegant in a tatty way, and there were even a few drooping palms in pots. Music played softly. Girls of different races of diffs in various states of undress sat or walked about and the customers were being looked after by an ancient and stunted little Och lady. Just as I started to move back and be about my business all hell broke loose.

The double doors to the room burst open. Three men flew through the air to land with bone-crunching crashes among the ornate furniture. Immediately the girls began screaming. When I saw what had flung the men through the doors I didn't blame them. Blind panic broke out in a bedlam of shrieks as everyone tried to run. I stared down, fascinated by the thing that smashed into the lounge.

It wore long robes of a deep and sinister red. It carried no weapons. But the face! It had once been apim, Homo sapiens sapiens, like myself. No more. That engorged face, bloated, distorted, the eyes like branding irons, the jagged, fang-like teeth, radiated such an aura of immanent evil I recoiled, physically revolted.

What on all of terrible Kregen was this nightmare?

The thing's hands were twisted into obscene claws, raking the air in uncontrollable anger. Spittle ran whitely down its chin. It was clearly insane, obsessed with the maniacal desire to kill and go on killing. It threw heavy furniture about like matchsticks. Its strength was colossal. It kicked anything in the way out of its path.

Those baleful eyes turned up, white crescents under bloodlust. It saw me. Instantly the thing, snarling incoherently, started for the stairs leading up to the balcony and to me.

Nine

I, Dray Prescot, Vovedeer, Lord of Strombor and Krozair of Zy, turned and fled along the balcony and went up the next flight of stairs like a mountain zerzy pursued by a mountain leem. Too true, By Krun!

Whatever that monstrosity from hell was, I wanted nothing of it, not one little tiny bit, by Vox!

On the next landing, four men, armed and armored, must have heard the uproar from below. As I belted off the top step I bellowed: "Trouble, doms! A customer's gone berserk! He's smashing the place up!"

"We'll sort him," snarled the leader with the golden sash about his waist. "By Salinchez, we'll have him. Come on!"

The four rushed off down the stairs and I didn't hang about but pressed on rapidly, very rapidly, by Vox! I had a single stab of pity for those four finely-dressed bully-boys, then I got on with my own business. Well, that was not strictly true. My business concerned the Star Lords, not rescuing kidnapped young princes, although this kind of affair is, as you know, unholy common on wonderful Kregen.

A Rapa popped out of a door in the corridor at the end and seeing me yelled: "Get away from here, you blintz!"

Continuing my charade I shouted: "There's trouble downstairs! A customer's gone berserk—"

The Rapa whistled his trident about. "That's nothing to do with us. You go and sort it." A second Rapa appeared, drawing his sword. His rusty black feathers bristled. "Schtump! Clear off!"

They both wore olive green, in addition each had a badge of a flame spouting triangle. I tried again. "They need all the help they can get. I've come to get everybody—"

The noise from below increased. Horrified screams knifed up. That must be those four unfortunates who had gone so uglily down. All the time I spoke I walked steadily forward, spreading my left hand in a gesture of appeal, my right gripping the braxter down at my side.

"For the last time, you blintz! Schtump!"

Now I was up level with them and they didn't mince matters. The one with the trident thrust viciously at me. The other Rapa's sword swished down in a lethal blow. I swerved avoiding the trident, slid the other's blow and hit him cleanly with my sword. The confounded blade broke close to the hilt. He was down but I did a foolish thing. In that split second I reflected that, knowing the poor quality in the steel of the munitions braxters, I shouldn't hit so hard.

In that fraction of time the first Rapa thrust again with his trident. One of the flank tines pierced my leather and I felt the smooth point stick into my flesh.

Instinctively I grabbed the shaft. I growled out in my old gravel-shifting voice: "I'll take that, dom," pulled the trident out of me, reversed it smartly, and struck him through his gizzard.

Both Rapas were down, and I glared back down the corridor. The unholy racket persisted. There was little time left before that apparition from hell raged up here. I looked into the room.

A Sylvie, all tinsel and tissue and curves, stared back at me with wide horrified eyes. On the truckle bed lay Byrom, just sitting up, his tousled hair over his eyes, his face streaked with tears.

Those Rapas were his guards, all right, and had tried to do their duty. I motioned with the bloody trident. "I shall not harm you, Sylvie. Byrom! Get up, do not make a noise, and follow me!"

There was no doubt I'd have to carry the boy. I wanted to have to do that as late as possible. If that red-robed monster got up here...

That was a fatuous thought. There was nothing between him and us to stop him. That was as sure as Zim and Genodras rose each morning.

The Sylvie remained absolutely still. She was, as they say in Clishdrin, scared stiff. Although far too over-the-top and voluptuous in their sensual female fashion, Sylvies are human beings and I couldn't leave her here with that uncanny monster lusting upwards. I grabbed her arm, and her scent gusted overpoweringly. "Come on!"

Byrom was a princeling; he behaved well. He was up off the bed and running out the door with me. Up I went, climbing the last flight of steps to the roof. So much noise boomed up from below, the echoes rang in my head. The Sylvie's tissue garments billowed revealingly about her figure as we ran. She was panting and her eyes remained wide and staring. Byrom concentrated his little legs on running as fast as he could. We tumbled out the trapdoor onto the roof and immediately I was searching the night sky.

Naghan Raerdu the Barrel had not been chosen by me to be my chief spymaster here without ample good reasons. A dark cut-out shape against the stars moved. The airboat turned and smoothly lowered down. She hovered and a dimly-discerned face peered down.

"Lahal! Swifter?"

"Lahal! With no Kink!"

With the password and countersign duly established, the airboat landed. Strong arms hauled Byrom in and there were plenty of volunteers to assist the Sylvie lady. I didn't smile. I vaulted up and Naghan snapped to the helmsman: "Take her up!"

As though arranged by some signal, the Maiden with the Many Smiles shot her first fuzzy pink rays over the lip of the hill. The radiance illuminated the roof. From the trapdoor exploded a titanic figure of malevolent fury. Red robes flailed in the violence of the thing's movements. It clawed its hands aloft, clear silent imprecations. It danced with foiled fury. Everyone felt the full blast of horror, of blood red violence, of chill foreboding, a maelstrom of terror.

Some of Naghan's crew called on their gods and spirits.

"What was that thing? Evil, evil..."

I said to Byrom, holding his shoulders: "You're safe now. Don't worry about any of that nonsense."

Naghan's helmsman swung the lifter up and away and we left that gibbering creature from hell raging far below. If I sweated easily I'd be running with it. Now we had to get on with our mission. Naghan had brought a needle lady with him, a nice Hytak woman, who cooed over Byrom. She took his head between her hands and massaged his scalp, turned his head this way and that. Naghan nodded.

"Yes, Drajak. Nessve is a larvan as well as a needle-woman." The best way to translate larvan is to say: 'A Layer On of Hands.' They can ease aches and strains by head manipulation, reducing tension.

I found I was still grasping the Rapa's trident. Well, he had no further need of it. It was not a Shank weapon. The tines were long and well-set and damned sharp. On the cross bar letters had been punched into the steel. I recognized them through the magic of the Savanti's language gift. They were Lohvian, ancient Lohvian. The word they spelled out was 'Prodigal.' I set the trident down in a corner and went to make sure Byrom was all right.

The horrendous experience through which we'd just gone affected me profoundly. By Opaz! That—thing—was the living embodiment of the worst nightmares imaginable. The inevitable reaction among the crew of the lifter set in and Byrom looked decidedly queasy. The puncture lady had stuck him and the Sylvie with her cunning needles. The Sylvie's name was Salarnie and eventually the puncture lady gave her a draught and sent her to sleep.

The flight back did not take long. Naghan had the lifter descend in moon-drenched darkness among shadows and I carried Byrom off to his mother's palace, calling a soft: "Remberee."

Well, as you may readily imagine, there was uproar and confusion, much running about and the flaring of torches, and bright tear-filled eyes as young Byrom was delivered back to his mother's arms.

When we were alone, Fweygo, in his calm Kildoi way, said: "You were lucky, Dray Prescot. The Everoinye have not spoken to me."

I just grunted.

"You—"

I interrupted. "All I want right now is some food and then to get my head down for a month of She of the Veils. I'll see you in the morning."

He flicked his tail hand by way of reply. So—I ate and slept. In the morning a new day dawned with all its anticipated evils.

They wanted to make something of a hero of me, and that I very quickly brushed aside. This was no fairy story. To add a grim and nauseating point to that, another poor young girl had been found overnight, disgustingly ripped to pieces in Cutler's Alley. Noni Seng, that had been her name. She'd been a sempstress, very respectable.

"The City Guard can do nothing," Ranaj told me, very somber.

The thought occurred to me that, should Tiri's bloody body be discovered in a gutter by her temple, I would not be surprised on Kregen. But I'd be angry. I'd be so angry that I would do something foolish in the best tradition of Dray Prescot, vosk skull, onker of onkers.

As for young Tiri herself, Dimpy had duly delivered her to her Temple to Cymbaro. She'd made him promise to make me visit her soon. There was something important and serious she wanted me to do. Dimpy shook his shock-haired head. No, he'd no idea what that could be, by Dromang.

There was no doubt that the succession of horrific murders made everyone jumpy. Girls were warned not to roam the streets alone. The City Guard announced they had doubled their patrols. There was even talk of employing some of the City Watch to patrol on the hills.

General opinion was divided on the reasons behind the murders. Bloodlust as a cause had its adherents. Sheer sexual frenzy was advanced by other people as the reason. Many whispered that the killings were ritual, that a maniac religious cult was at work in this ghastly fashion.

Dimpy said: "You know what I think of these stupid religions. Yes. Well, if it is one of them it won't be Cymbaro." He looked decidedly defiant. "Tiri wouldn't have anything to do with this stuff."

From what I knew of Cymbaro I fully agreed. From what I surmised of the cult of Dokerty, well, then, yes, it could be the maniacs in their red robes who killed and mutilated young girls to the glory of Dokerty.

The cult of Lem the Silver Leem must still exist, driven underground in places, but still disgustingly killing very young girls to the greater glory of Lem and their salvation.

I did not care to face the implications that these murders in Oxonium were the work of the Leem Lovers. They did not fit the pattern. The girls torn to shreds here were grown up into young womanhood. If this ghastly work was the foul hand of Lem the Silver Leem then my work here was ordained. The Star Lords abhorred the Leem Lovers as much as I.

Trying to think the problem through, I came to the tentative conclusion that the murders were not carried out by that monstrous—thing—encountered in the rescue of Byrom.

I certainly wanted to know more about the gibbering manic thing. Somewhat reluctantly I broached the subject with Fweygo. He just shook that golden head of his and indicated he knew nothing of anything like the thing I described, although he added that there were plenty of other hideous monsters on Kregen. That, I knew.

The problem of Dimpy was partially solved when, as Fweygo had suggested, Ranaj took the lad on in Princess Nandisha's household. I felt keenly for the rapscallion. Up here on the hill he could be near the object of his affections. Down in the warrens he could look after his mother and sisters. The dilemma was acute. As Fat Lardo said: "We can't bring every tatterdemalion and his family up here."

Asking Ranaj for the loan of a messenger, I sent word to Tiri at her shrine that I awaited her commands.

That evening Dimpy was not to be found in the palace. In addition a pair of braxters had gone missing from the armory. The Armory Deldar, scarlet, bristling, sweating, gave it as his considered opinion that young brats should not be allowed in the place at all and that he'd lose a swingeing great chunk of his pay in paying for replacements for the two swords gone from his charge.

Fweygo allowed himself a mocking smile when I paid up for the weapons.

I told him: "Dimpy will be back. Tiri's got her hooks into that young sprig of the warrens."

Princess Nandisha's puncture lady gave me a very annoyed look, tut-tutting with a most reproving click of her sharp little tongue. "An onker—that, indisputably, is what you are, Drajak."

"That I have been called many times. In this, though, I believe I'm right. Dimpy's passion for Tiri is—"

"Onker!"

I stared at her in puzzlement. "Mother Firben?"

A short, stout woman, she shook her head in perennial female disbelief at men's stupidity. She bustled forward. She whipped out a particularly long and vicious-looking needle and—snick!—in it went. At once the pain vanished.

She nodded with satisfaction and went to work on my wound. Mother Firben could not know that thanks to my dip in the Pool of Baptism in far Aphrasöe any wounds I collected adventuring around on Kregen healed with incredible speed. And, anyway, in my line of work pain is something you have to turn to your own advantage. Given a few days the wound would have healed of itself, and the pain would have vanished. I said, meekly: "Thank you, Mother Firben."

She just clicked that needle-sharp tongue around against her teeth and finished tying the yellow bandage.

As to the leather brass-studded jack, one of Ranaj's men had already taken that off to the armory for repair.

That, of course, made me think of the two swords that had broken in combat. Think, I may add, very darkly indeed, very darkly indeed, by Krun!

"The Kurin-forsaken blades," I growled. "I just hope the two braxters Dimpy took don't break so easily for him."

The steel of the trident that had wounded me was of good Lohvian quality, apparent at once. The name Prodigal within a frame of chiseled decoration, I recalled, appeared a mere part of that decoration and unreadable to any but those who had studied the old manuscripts out of the Empire of Walfarg—and to me equipped with the Savanti gift of languages. A kind of half-regret passed over me. The trident was lying about somewhere, unless, as was far more probable, one of Naghan the Barrel's people had picked it up as a likely weapon. At least, Prodigal wasn't going to snap in two at the most awkward time of a fight.

When Tiri's answer came and I found a silver Bhin for the messenger, I first went down to the armory. Ranaj in his open numim way told me to select the best weapon I could find. Fweygo came with me to offer sound advice. In the upshot I had to content myself with a couple of the ordinary braxters of the country, without a scrap of confidence in either.

Still, I still had belted on the rapier and main gauche, the Jiktar and the hikdar. Would they, I brooded uneasily, be of any real use if I confronted that monstrous red-robed thing?

Whatever uncanny manifestation it was, no reports of anyone sighting it came in—it might as well have ceased to exist. Word from the runnels seeped up to the hills well enough. Maybe, and the grisly thought chilled, everyone—apart from the folk in the lifter—had been torn to bits by the creature. I wasn't at all sure Byrom had seen it and I certainly did not want to question him quite yet.

That red-robed maniac monstrosity spelled trouble. Trying to push the Djan-condemned thing out of my mind, I hitched up my swords, and took myself off to the Shrine of Cymbaro and Tirivenswatha.

Now what did the little madam want?

Ten

They did not ask me to remove my weapons in the Temple of Cymbaro the Just. Had they done so in this cloistered sanctuary I would in the normal civilized way have had no objection. Remembering the attacks and the fights that had flowered in blood all along these arcades and flower beds the first time I was here, I might have remonstrated with the priests.

The young priest, who'd greeted Tiri and me on that occasion, called Logan, smiled. "You are welcome, Drajak the Sudden."

I acknowledged his greeting and we passed through the outer courtyards where the peace of this place could be felt as a tangible presence of the spirit. He conducted me to an inner chamber simply furnished where soft drinks and fruits lay appetizingly on a small table. "San Paynor and Tiri will be here shortly. Now I ask you to excuse me. I have duties."

"Certainly, San Logan. And thank you."

Whatever the young madam wanted, they were making an occasion of it, that was certain sure, by Opaz.

Presently San Paynor appeared and with him Tiri. The san was dressed as I expected, in a long brown robe. He did not lean too heavily on his curiously carved staff. Surprising me, though, Tiri, instead of her attractive shape charmingly displayed in a shamlak, wore a brown robe down to her feet. When she walked I noticed her feet were bare. Every scrap of her hair was covered by a brown four-pointed cap. She wore no jewelry of any kind.

After the polite greetings had been exchanged, San Paynor said: "I owe you not one but two thanks, Drajak."

"Oh?"

"We of Cymbaro abhor fighting but will fight if it is just in the eyes of Cymbaro. Your actions here were praiseworthy—"

"I chance interrupting you, san," I said, interrupting. "These thanks are entirely unnecessary. My actions were necessary."

His thin face betrayed a quiver of a smile. "Indeed. You know San Padria?"

San Padria I had met on the road with his protégé, Nath. A pair of shoes had exchanged feet. I nodded, guessing what was to come, and so was able to say: "Again thanks are unnecessary, as I indicated at the time. Rather, as I said, my thanks were due to San Padria for so graciously accepting the shoes."

Again he smiled. "I think Tiri has chosen wisely in you."

Some of the old Dray Prescot abruptness sharpened my words. "Yes. Just what is it you have in mind for me, young lady?"

Before Tiri could speak, Paynor said: "There are many things about us you do not know. Tiri is a temple dancer, true. But she has a higher vocation."

Very soon after meeting Tiri I'd sensed there was a lot more to her than appeared. From the way she was dressed I'd had a sudden startled thought she was to be the victim in some pagan sacrifice. Still, that wouldn't be in accordance with what I knew of Cymbaro the Just.

San Paynor went on to tell me that certain women had strange powers. Well, by Vox! All women have strange powers over men. Paynor indicated that Tiri could become a mystic, which didn't surprise me. He wouldn't say more than that about her actual powers.

Again I asked what she wanted me to do.

There was to be a ceremony. The way they explained it, Tiri would have to undergo some complicated and extremely arcane rites. In this ritual pain was involved. From past experience the priests were aware that these young girls could not stand that pain. So they had champions who, in some spiritual way, linked up and drew off the pain leaving the girls free to concentrate on absorbing the knowledge of the keys to unlock the powers within their brains and spirits.

"To choose as champion someone outside the temple is so unusual as not to have been heard of before. But Tiri insists."

"I do!" flared Tiri. So I saw there had been an unholy row before she'd got her own way.

The whole business was somber and serious. Paynor warned me that if a champion failed his lady, then: "The full weight will fall on her. Her mind and ib will be blasted forever. This is a most serious responsibility, Drajak."

Tiri turned her head to look up at me appealingly.

"You will agree, won't you, Drajak?"

There was no room in this place, it seemed to me, to call upon Makki Grodno or the Divine Lady of Belschutz. All the same—

"Yes, Tiri, and thank you for the honor."

And if you want to call me a creep, then a Herrelldrin Hell take you!

More surprises were to follow. The Temple of Cymbaro on the surface was indeed a small and insignificant structure compared to the grandiose temples and palaces around. I had penetrated into almost the whole of the ground area by now. A group of brown clad priests entered and bowed. They formed an escort for the san and Tiri as we left the chamber. We went down. By Vox! We went down all right.

Spacious rooms were here piled one upon another connected by wide staircases. This subterranean temple was rather like an inverted skyscraper, an earthscraper, perhaps. Everything I saw appeared tasteful. There was no vulgar ostentation, as Sjames would say. Soft light from samphron oil lamps illuminated and enhanced the decorations. The air tasted sweet upon the tongue. I followed on, silently, down and down.

Just about every hill in Oxonium was honeycombed with tunnels and secret chambers. In this the builders merely followed the custom of Kregen in providing palaces and temples with many secret passages. The color schemes soothed. Down we went. The gravity of the situation was not lost on me, yet I felt calm in face of the ordeal before me.

We reached a chamber draped somberly in earth brown. Lamps glowed in chandeliers. At the far end an altar reared a single black block. I could see no ominous bloodstains there.

There was no idol.

Six girls were waiting, all dressed in brown gowns, with flowers woven into their hair and in loops and belts about their waists. They carried Tiri off through a side door. At the door she half-turned and favored me with a smile that trembled her lips. I nodded.

A man approached San Paynor. His brown robe was tightly belted and he carried two swords and daggers. He was apim, with a face pale with passion, gaunt, the face of a man obsessed, driven by the needs of the spirit. His very intentness appalled.

"San." He bowed.

"I have tried, Duven, as Cymbaro is my witness, I have tried."

Duven's strong hands clenched, clenched and relaxed, shaking.

"But it is against all tradition, all we believe in. Cymbaro the Just is the only true force in all the world! We cannot gainsay him! We are of Cymbaro. We are of the Just."

"Some of what you say is true, Duven. But not all. We do not gainsay Cymbaro, for we follow the precepts. The chosen girl has the right to choose her own champion."

The trembling passion in this Duven struck out like a physical force. He was controlling himself only by the exercise of will. His dark eyes surveyed me with a distant, all-encompassing look.

"And this is the man, this is the champion. He is not of Cymbaro."

"He has proved himself."

"A pair of shoes!"

"Aye. And in the battle for us all here."

Duven lifted a fist, helplessly. "I was on my way back from Farinsee!"

"There is no blame attached to you, Duven."

San Paynor's words were calm and strong. He would not be deflected. He had asked Tiri and she had insisted on having me. This Duven would have been Tiri's champion had I not turned up. Then, and I felt with a genuine emotion, he acquiesced. He bowed his head.

"It is the will of Cymbaro, before which everything—everything!—must bow. Cymbaro the Just must rule the world!"

He took a few paces towards me and stuck out his hand. As we shook, he said: "I wish you well, in the sacred name. Bear yourself bravely. Tirivenswatha has the gifts. Do not fail her."

"All that I can do, that I shall do. I swear."

He nodded and stepped back, satisfied. His very fanaticism drove him on to the greater glory of Cymbaro, and in the grip of that over-riding passion he would do anything for Cymbaro.

The priests took up positions around the walls, and Logan and Duven joined them. Paynor and I waited in the center. He said: "Duven is so unlike his twin brother, Drendi. He went off to be a paktun when Duven joined us in Cymbaro. One is intense and passionate, thin, the other easygoing and stout. Sometimes twins are like that, totally dissimilar."

I did not say that any paktun worth his salt is not too easygoing, and stout mercenaries slim down after a few battles, until they become crumblies. I stood lightly, waiting for Tiri and what was to happen.

Presently more dignitaries entered the room. They moved with the deliberate motions of people who knew exactly what they were doing and the reasons for each action. Other priests high in the hierarchy joined Paynor. Priestesses, too, formed in their allotted places. Paynor told me I must remove all my weapons and clothes. They put a long brown gown over me which was wrapped loosely across the front. A small orchestra trooped in and took station to the side. The preparations were made. The silence rang profoundly in all our ears.

A trumpet blasted. The silver notes soared, hovered, died.

A bevy of flower clad maidens entered, escorting Tiri.

They opened out to allow her to glide gracefully into the central space. The music began, low at first, swirling, beating, growing in tempo and violence.

And Tiri danced.

She wore flowers. In any other circumstance the eroticism of her dance would have shrieked to the skies. Here, the dance expressed the true joy of Cymbaro, the flowering of life, of happiness, of a oneness with all created things upon Kregen. I watched as she moved, seductive, more voluptuous in her sinuous twinings than any Sylvie, enraptured within herself, beautiful.

When at last the dance ended and Tiri sank down, head bowed, one leg tucked beneath her, the other extended, her arms reaching out before her, I felt emotionally purified.

Not a sound disturbed the silence of that subterranean chamber.

Like the astonishing smash of a bolt of lightning a flame leaped up beyond the altar. The trumpet pealed. I was led forward to the altar where Tiri was conducted by her handmaidens. We met.

Stone steps were cut into the block. We two ascended. Many hands removed my gown and wove ropes of flowers about us. Tiri would not look at me. We stood, firmly pressed together, as the scented blooms formed their coils about us.

Music continued to play in a slow languorous melody. The priests chanted in sonorous levels and the priestesses joined their voices to soar above the melodies like larks ascending into the blue.

My surroundings became hazy. I knew I held Tiri in my arms, as she held me. I could hear the deep strong voices of priests chanting, and more felt than saw San Paynor and a sweet-faced woman laying their hands upon Tiri. The flame writhed silently. I felt heat, cold, dryness, dampness. Tiri moaned. Something like a red-hot sword drove cleanly through my midriff.

The world turned corpse white before my face.

I was standing on the quarterdeck of a little sixty-gun ship not fit to sail in the line and a monstrous great hundred and twenty-gun four-decker sailed effortlessly past our stern. In turn, gun after gun, he raked us. A stern rake, a destroying broadside that pulverized the ship, whirled in a conflagration of iron, smoke and flame.

The deck under me changed to that of a small swifter of the Inner Sea of Turismond. Spray-glittering, the bronze bound ram of a powerful swifter smashed splintering into our beam, flinging the broken bodies of oarsmen aside, wrecking us in blood and horror.

The background lurched and I saw Seg Segutorio drop his great Lohvian longbow and clutch futilely at the long black-fletched arrow through his throat. I saw Inch's head fly from his shoulders under the lethal sweep of a Saxon-pattern axe. I saw Turko ripped into bloody fragments by a black-furred many-armed monstrosity. I saw Mevancy's bindles ping harmlessly from plate armor and a swarm of flung darts shred her body. I saw Hap Loder trampled beneath the iron hooves of a stampeding herd of Voves. I saw—I saw...

My friends and family paraded before me, destroyed in many grue-some ways. The physical pains attacked my body as though I was being stuck through by a thousand red-hot lances, as though my flesh was being plucked from me by a thousand white-hot pincers. I shook uncontrollably.

But—but the physical pains were as nothing to the mental agony. I saw my children dismembered. My mind writhed and coiled and I lurched desperately close to complete insanity.

I saw Delia. I saw Delia...

"No!" I screamed, foaming. "No!"

Ghostly blackness descended, blackness drilled through by darting scarlet streaks, each shaking me, each driving me closer to the brink of despair. Some tiny portion of my mind told me that I could not sustain this terror. Told me that I must give in, relax all my willpower, surrender myself to the ultimate darkness.

In the roaring maelstrom I felt something move against me. I looked down, dazed, uncomprehending. Something pressed against my naked chest. Vaguely I made out Tiri's pale body squeezed against me. I felt her arms clasping tightly around my neck, her finger nails digging into my flesh. I felt her smooth bare back under my hands.

Even then no real comprehension hit me. The pain continued.

Delia... My Delia had been... This softly firm body in my grasp was not that of Delia. It did not fit properly, did not mold with me, was not the same. No, of course not! This was young Tiri. This was not Delia, Delia of Delphond, Delia of the Blue Mountains. No. This trembling form was Tiri's, and she was sobbing and shaking and the flowers draped us and light returned to the world and I could see again in reality. The grisly phantasms receded, dwindled and vanished.

Hands gripped me, held me, steadied me.

A soft yellow cloth was passed over my streaming body.

The flowers were removed, light from the flame died and the samphron oil lamps beamed their mellow radiance.

I just about fell rather than descended from the altar after Tiri.

A pure white gown was flung about her. That gown was no whiter than her face. The tears were wiped from her eyes. She would not look at me. Assisted by her handmaids she was led away. I stood there like a loon, completely drained of emotion. I could still feel the hellish agony of the red-hot lances piercing my flesh, an echo of pain, as though poison seeped through me. That was nothing, now.

Delia! I had seen and I had believed and I had welcomed insanity as a refuge.

San Paynor did not smile. His thin grave face regarded me, his head a little to one side, calculating. His eyes were those of a mystic. The sudden sweet waft of flowers enveloped us.

"In the name of Cymbaro the Just, I thank you, Drajak the Sudden."

"Is it over?"

"It is."

"Thank Opaz for that."

"Ah, yes. Opaz. Of Opaz we have heard. There is much in common between Cymbaro and Opaz."

With the suddenness of a rashoon of the Eye of the World my knees gave way. I would have fallen had not Logan on one side and Duven on the other caught me under the armpits and supported me.

"You must go to the Ibserrail Chamber for a time." He was talking about a room where the spirit might find resuscitation. I hung in the priests' grip.

"Willingly," I said. "And then I'd like to visit the Baths of the Nine."

They draped a cloak about me and led my tottering feet off to the Ibserrail Chamber. Every now and then my teeth chattered and I could not stop them. That was one experience I would never, ever, voluntarily undergo again.

Just suppose—

Delia...

Eleven

They told me that Tiri, having had the knowledge of the keys vouchsafed her, must now go to a place—whose name and location they would not reveal—where she would learn to use the keys to unlock the mysticism born within her. I lay back in the warm scented water, grunted, and got on with trying to forget what had just taken place. Since my dip in the Sacred Pool my memory was such that I did not forget things, although, thankfully, some of the more horrendous evils that have tormented me I have managed if not to forget completely then to push to one side.

When at last I felt as though I could face getting on with life once more I eased out of the water, donned a long yellow toweling robe and wandered off to the saloon.

Oh, yes, by Vox. I was still the same Dray Prescot as ever was. I could still wrap the brave old scarlet breechclout about me and go swinging about Kregen in deeds of derring-do wielding a great Krozair longsword—at least, I hoped I was.

But a fellow knows when he's been through something more than usually warm.

In the saloon Sans Paynor, Logan and Duven joined me. Also the priestess who had assisted Paynor with Tiri came in, looking serene. She was Sana Lally. At least, that was what she was called now. I learned she had been the Vadni L'Lallistafuros. When we settled down to a delightful repast served by attentive acolytes, I brought up the intriguing subject of these double capital-lettered names. They weren't exactly embarrassed by the remark as reserved. Eventually, by piecing bits of information gathered there and later, I now know that just about all the great families had the double capital letter. Some still used the form; some did not. Some said it was necessary for the dignity of their house, others that the form was old fashioned and cumbersome. In one vague sense it was somewhat like using a simple v for von.

I might have guessed, by Krun! Young Tiri was, of course and naturally, really T''Tirivenswatha.

"The fashion of use comes and goes," explained Paynor, and he smiled upon Sana Lally.

They talked upon inconsequential subjects for a time. I saw this small talk was designed to soothe me and ease me back into the real world from the nightmares that had nearly driven me insane.

Presently Logan chanced on the subject of the spate of horrible murders of young girls.

Sana Lally, a smooth-featured woman with a generous mouth, drew her eyebrows down, and lines appeared around that curved mouth.

"It is disgusting. If the City Guard do not find the killer soon, who knows what will happen?"

"The answer is plain enough." Duven's words ripped out like the sleeting hail of crossbow bolts. His intense face was drawn, hollowed, the eyes feverish. "Dokerty. It has to be."

"I do agree with that summation," murmured Logan.

Paynor nodded. "They practice revolting rites, it is true. But they take place in the privacy of their temples." He passed a hand across his brow. "Why kill young girls out in the street?"

"Because they are decadent and should be put down!" blazed Duven.

Lally sighed. "If only they could be."

They went on discussing the murders for a time, and it was noticeable that they ate very little. Presently I ventured to change the topic of discussion.

"You are religious, and have access to arcane knowledge. Your libraries must be extensive, your records comprehensive. Also, you know far more of Oxonium and Tolindrin than do I." I paused, not for effect—I swear!—but to take a sip of the excellent wine they had served. "I have seen a—thing—that puzzles and horrifies me." I went on to describe the red-robed manic monstrosity. I finished: "However, I doubt if this thing is murdering these girls."

They sat without moving, without talking, frozen. I could have tossed a freeze spell among them.

I gave my lips a tongue swipe. "If I have offended you, I apologize—"

"No, Drajak the Sudden. You have earned your nickname. It is just that..." here Paynor held a napkin to his lips.

"This thing—these things—are known." Logan looked distressed. He took a gulp of wine. "Perhaps, San Paynor, we could show Drajak the records?"

We all looked at the priest. He deliberated with himself for some time. Eventually, very somberly, he said: "You have seen an ibmanzy, Drajak, you are certain sure?"

"If an ibmanzy is a monstrous maniacal thing clawing people—"

"Quite. Very well. Come."

We went through the halls to a library. I say a library, for there were clearly other, ordinary libraries. Getting into this one behind its solid iron door was a rigmarole of keys held by Paynor, of bolts and bars, of literally opening up a most secure safe deposit.

Inside—! I knew that my comrade Wizards and Witch of Loh would give a very great deal to spend a few months of the Maiden with the Many Smiles in here, diligently perusing the arcane lore stored in hundreds of scrolls and enormous bronze-bound books.

"This is what we call our Black Library. It is not for those of feeble mind."

"I believe it."

Logan climbed the ladder to bring down the tomes indicated by Paynor. The priests together opened the vast pages and the leather binding creaked, dust and paper dust flew in a cloud. The page was smoothed out. Paynor pointed a finger, and, by Vox, that thin finger trembled.

"This?"

I looked. "Aye. That."

There it was, on the page, drawn and illuminated in bold colors. Red robes flapping, crazed eyes bursting from its head, arms stretched aloft with raking claws, the body shown in more detail than I'd appreciated. The pictured representation showed the ribs breaking through the skin, as though some superhuman force within was bursting its way out from the fragile human body.

"That!"

They told me that everything had its spirit, its ib, and the ibma was the materialization of the ib. Aeons ago researchers had discovered ways of uniting a human with her or his ib. In the nature of things there were evil spirits within the spirit world. They waited their chance to emerge into our world. Interfering with the balance one with another could, in certain circumstances, open the doorway within a human body for the ib to emerge. No doubt in the beginning the researchers were motivated by genuine desires to improve mankind.

"But, of course," said Paynor, "there were those who saw ends suited to their own dark purposes. A human being taken over by this horrific force, sometimes willingly, sometimes under duress, becomes more than human. Not superhuman, but an ibmanzy, the embodiment of evil breaking from a human body."

I saw something in these words, then, and I trembled.

"Tiri? When we were bonded, and you gave Tiri the knowledge of the keys—?"

Paynor drew himself up. "Yes, Drajak. The risk was there. An ibmanzy might have seized Tiri had we failed. Had you failed."

To think of that! Young Tiri, turned into a bloated screaming monster from hell, her lissom body being literally torn apart from within. She—rather the ibmanzy thing she had become—would have clawed and ripped and destroyed everyone until somehow or other it could in its turn be destroyed.

"I am glad you didn't tell me this before."

"These things are secret, hidden. There have been no ibmanzies for many seasons."

Duven in his brittle way said: "Let me show you this." He turned pages, helped by Logan. The picture they showed me was just as dreadful as the first. The thing wore a green robe. Another page and a picture of an ibmanzy wearing a brown robe.

Lally wrinkled up her mouth. "Yes. Even an adherent of Cymbaro once fell into evil ways."

"The reason I asked you to look at these others, Drajak, is obvious." Duven trembled in the intensity of his purpose.

Slowly, I said: "The red robed ibmanzy. The red robes of Dokerty."

"As Mabal and Matol rise each morning."

No one spoke for a space.

San Paynor did not so much heave up a sigh as let out a small breath of profound regret at the follies of humanity. "If what we now suspect is true, then we can look forward only to awful dangers. What insane fool would wish to meddle with these spirits of darkness?"

Duven's mouth curled in contempt.

"I can name you the top hierarchy of those blintzes of Dokerty-lovers. Any one of them or all of them together!"

They quizzed me more on my sighting of the ibmanzy, trying to establish the facts. Maybe, if some deluded fool of Dokerty was creating the monsters, then the murdered girls could have been torn to pieces by other ibmanzies. Now, that became a frightening possibility.

The tensions of these moments could not be sustained. I could feel the pressure on my skull. San Paynor, abruptly, said:

"Come. We will return to the saloon. A glass of wine."

As we went out I commented: "All this vast wealth of knowledge. All these treasures of wisdom." I shook my head. "All locked away."

"Necessarily so." Acid stung in Paynor's words.

"You are studious, yourself, Drajak?" enquired Lally.

"I like to know things."

"Some things," began Paynor. Then he stopped himself. Weird echoes of sententious words reverberated. I did not smile. But, by Krun, if a thing was necessary, then that thing must be known.

Something trembled up from my feet, through my legs, vibrated my backbone, shook me so that I stumbled sideways. Lally grabbed me to support herself. The ground moved.

The floor, the walls, the ceiling shuddered. The grinding sullen roar that accompanied this earth movement chilled the blood. The whole world gyrated around us.

"Earthquake!" Logan's yell was entirely unnecessary.

"Cymbaro will protect us." Even as he spoke so calmly San Paynor tottered and fell, thrown violently off his feet.

Duven leaped to his assistance.

The whole wall fronting the room fell away in a thunderous avalanche and chunks of rubble cascaded down around our ears. A chip hit me on the thigh and a larger piece struck nastily across Duven's skull as he shielded the san.

People stumbled through the roils of dust, screaming, trying to avoid the collapse at their backs. Priests, girls, acolytes, they disappeared with awful finality as the floor opened before them.

They were swallowed up as a leem swallows a lopy.

The shaking shudderings of the whole place abruptly ceased.

Dust hung smokily on the close air, choking us, bringing stinging tears. I shook my head and stood Lally up, making sure she understood that the immediate danger was past. This was a foreshock. There might be more before the big quake. That would be followed by the aftershocks. Perhaps, I hoped, this was a mere warning, and the main earthquake would not arrive. No one could tell.

San Paynor stood up. Duven, as I had with Lally, made sure the san was in possession of his senses. Then the young priest crossed to the newly-created crevasse. He peered down.

Joining him, I too peered down through the hanging dust.

"The folk are trapped on the ledge." Duven spoke flatly.

What he said was frightfully true. A huddle of people, those who so far had been lucky, clung together on a narrow ledge of the floor below. At their backs, the sheered side of the torn earth, reared a wall. Before them across the narrow lip of the ledge the black emptiness went on down and down and down.

Rather unhelpfully, I commented: "That looks like the entrance to the Ice Floes of Sicce down there."

Duven did not reply.

The sheered wall offered precarious hand and foot holds. I thought that even if we climbed down safely, we'd never get those frightened people to climb that vertical face.

The whole situation was one of deadly peril. Many of the lamps had fallen; but there was ample light—light from burning curtains and furniture. The oppressiveness of the scene, the sense of being deep underground, the pressure of the rock all about, the smoke and dust, the flickering eerie lights, the shadows, threatened to overwhelm us. We could all be buried alive down here.

And the next shock might occur at any moment.

When it did those trapped people on their fragile ledge below would be tossed into eternity.

Duven threw off his robe and stood forth in a brown breech clout. He flexed his muscles. He swung himself over the edge of the chasm.

"Cymbaro the Just is with me, Drajak. So fetch a rope."

Twelve

There was absolutely no question of protocol here. Duven had acted. I must respond immediately.

Running back I shook Logan's arm. He was staring about vacantly, trembling in expectation of the next shock.

"A rope!"

He looked at me, and he didn't see me.

What of curtains there might be in this windowless space were burning, their pullcords flaring with them.

San Paynor in his firm soft voice, said: "The serving hatch from the kitchens, Drajak."

I grasped his meaning at once and as he pointed I hared off to the undamaged wall. A small counter fronted a wooden hatch. I shoved this open viciously and, yes, there was the food lift with its rope. Wasting no time I hauled the rope in, flinging the coils back onto the floor. All the time I expected the next quake to bring everything tumbling down in final destruction about us.

I had no weapons, no knife. I bit through the rope where it was fixed to the food platform. Hauling the line abaft I raced back to the lip of the chasm. Dust still hung stingingly in the air.

Paynor was speaking to Logan in a quiet, almost cooing voice. He mentioned Cymbaro a number of times, and the love of life, and the utmost necessity of helping. There was no time to worry over that.

Looking over the lip I saw that Duven had almost reached the ledge. He descended with cautious and limited movements. I judged that he had done his share of rock climbing and knew what he was about, although just before he reached his goal he made two steps I considered risky, hanging from only one point before clamping onto a second. The situation was so desperate that I concurred with his judgment that the risk had to be taken. He was one tough bird, all right, by Krun!

Some of the trapped people were screaming, others sobbing, most were praying to Cymbaro. You could taste the stink of their fear. Duven climbed down to reach them.

Rapidly knotting a bowline on a bight I ladled the rope over the edge. "Rope below!"

Duven glanced up, his eyes white rinds. Bracing himself against the back wall he threw the loop over the nearest person, a mature priestess. He held the line, taking up the slack, and pulled her into position.

"Haul away."

Obediently, I hauled in, knowing the poor woman was being scraped and bounced against the wall and collecting more bruises. When she came in over the top her face was beet red, tears gushed, and her robe was ripped to her waist. She fell against me. Working as fast as I could I took the loop off and payed it out again.

"Logan!" I bellowed, without turning around, supporting the priestess with my left arm. "Brassud, dom! Come and help."

What San Paynor said to Logan I didn't know; but they both came across and took the woman away. I looked down into the chasm.

Duven yelled: "Hurry up, Drajak!"

The next was a girl who came up surprisingly lightly. Her bright black face with the cut glass features composed. "Thank you," she said, as she pulled the loop from around her and tossed it down. She needed no help from the two sans at my back. She was a splendid example of the best of the Xuntalese women allied to her faith in Cymbaro. So, one by one, I hauled them up.

Whether or not they were being pulled to safety was entirely another matter, by Krun.

By the time there were only three priests left I began to hope that the quake had been an isolated shock. The crowd in the shambles of the saloon were quietening down. Logan had recovered from his first terrors and worked like a hero.

One more came up, then the penultimate one and the rope went down for the last.

With the bight safely around him I leaned back and hauled away and the ground shuddered like a beast in torment.

It was very necessary to spread my legs wide and to lean back and not to lose my balance and to haul like a madman.

The world vibrated all about me. People were screaming. Rubble fell and the noise hammered mercilessly. I slipped and recovered and clawed at the line and so brought the last priest inboard. Then I looked over the edge.

The ledge had vanished.

Duven was still there.

He clung to a knob projecting from the face, legs dangling. The look on his face was one of ecstatic joy.

Any second and he'd be gone, slipping down and away and vanishing in the turmoil of dust boiling in the abyss.

The reason for his heightened sensory state was obvious. He had performed a great deed in the service of Cymbaro and now he was about to die. His name would be remembered. Cymbaro would welcome him. There would be no long and painful struggle through the Ice Floes of Sicce, through the mists and the perils to the sunny uplands beyond. He would die a hero and a martyr to the dread forces of evil that lurked deep within the earth.

Well, by the disgusting diseased eyeballs and putrescent nostrils of Makki Grodno! He'd proved himself. He shouldn't have to die now. Not if I could prevent it.

I yelled at Logan and Paynor as the shocks ceased abruptly.

"Get some people! Tail onto this line!"

Give Paynor his due. He was the first. He marshaled the others and a party tailed on. Over and down I went like a grundal.

Twice the line jolted and swung down savagely as those above relaxed their grips. If those people up there let go I'd be taking a swallow dive out and down headfirst into the Ice Floes of Sicce.

When I reached him, Duven said with a twist to his lips: "You needn't have—"

"Get this bight around you, dom, sharpish."

The old Dray Prescot intolerance must have blazed out then for he did as I'd bidden him. I had a hand over the projection; but my feet had no support. Between us, one hand each, we got the rope around him. I thought back grimly to my assessment of the risks he'd taken first climbing down here.

When we were settled, he in the bight and I with a fist clutching the line, I leaned my head back and hollered: "Haul away!"

They'd make heavy work of it, the frightened folk up there. I did not wish to contemplate sticking to the sheer face like a fly whilst they pulled Duven up and then lowered the line for me.

But — if they couldn't haul both of us, then, by Vox, that was precisely what I'd have to do.

We lurched away from the wall, swung, and then started to inch up and at that self-same instant the next shock struck.

I swear blind the wall before me danced a saraband. We were swaying and swinging, swinging and swaying, as though perched in a swinger of far off Aphrasöe.

We'd have been all right, too, for the people up there stuck bravely to their task. They did not let the rope slip.

The sense of tons of rock poised above my head ready at any instant to come tumbling down in an avalanche that would bury me for good and all gave me a most queasy feeling, most queasy, by Krun.

Duven was gripping the rope just beneath my fist and my other arm wrapped about his body. We swung out, away from the face as the world went crazy, the ground tormented by forces powerful and violent. We swung in catastrophically.

The smash as our bodies hit the rock jolted me clear and I felt my fingers slipping from the line. A desperate clutch, a heave, the harsh line tearing at my skin, a final exhausting grab — and I was clear, free, floating, spinning over and over and falling headlong into the boiling turmoil of dust in the abyss.

Thirteen

Dust choked up into my nostrils, stung my eyes half-blinding me, scoured in ribbons across my face. Over and over I went hurtling, down and down and down.

I really began to think this colossal cleft in the earth went all the way down to the center where the fiery sprites worship their demons of flame, where Imphlor'tain pours rivers of molten lead that hold Kregen's course steady among the stars they can never see.

The dust thinned at last and with streaming eyes I could see below the sullen redness nearing as I fell all askew. Getting a few breaths of dust-free air into my lungs came as a blessed relief. With the relief, fresh alarm, as the unmistakable stink of sulphur, mixed with tar, pitch, and an acrid unfamiliar stench, billowed up, making me visualize the enormity of my perilous situation.

Down below probably bubbled a lake of boiling pitch. Even if I fell into a lake of clear water, and there are plenty of those beneath the earth's crust, I'd be done for. If I hadn't already reached terminal velocity I would very soon do so. I'd smash every bone in my body.

I let rip with a ferocious roar—and out croaked a husky little voice: "Star Lords! Everoinye!"

May Opaz make them hear! I said to myself. "Star Lords! Get me out of this! Put me back on duty guarding the numim twins!"

Of reply there was none. I continued to tumble helplessly down towards the redly glowing radiance beneath.

Well, if this was the end, then this was the end.

So much for the Star Lords' grandiose designs for me to become the Emperor of Emperors, the Emperor of All Paz!

When I scrunched into a bloody mess the joke would be on them.

Something fine brushed across my face. Like spider silk a strand drew tight under my nose and broke. Another filament caught at me, and another. I stopped thrashing my arms and legs about and spread them out like a star.

Whether or not this was the work of the Everoinye I did not know. They would not tell me, as was their custom, until such time as in telling me they could make a point and put me in my place.

The strands thickened. They were difficult to see except in mass, where they bunched. Down I plunged through a gathering collection of filaments, fine as gauze, streaming them back as a seed streams back its silky coverings. Was my speed slackening?

There must have been other earth shocks as I fell. Rubble tumbled from the one wall I could make out in the lurid light, the sheer rock flashing up past my ear. That debris pitched in long streams down below me, going faster than I was. I had to be slowing this crazy descent; rather, these clumping streaming strands were slowing me down, acting like a drag parachute.

Wrapped in a gossamer cloud I fell. I just hoped that would not be a gossamer shroud when I landed.

The gory glow below shone to one side. Slower I went down, slower and slower, the silken strands wrapping me and tailing away aft so that I must have looked like a comet. The redness poured up from a veritable boiling lake of lava and the heat started to stifle into the close air. Underneath my falling body the spider silk clumped thickly. I readied myself for one almighty crash. When I did touch down the end swooped up with unexpected swiftness.

Flat on my back I hit the piled fluffiness. The experience was weird, as of falling listlessly in a dream. Strands covered me everywhere and I plunged beneath them. At once I started to thrash a way back to the top. I could be suffocated in here, by Krun!

The combined downward movement and my efforts succeeded in driving me into a slanting course, through the mass, still downwards but at an angle.

Eventually, breathless, panting, slapping clinging strands away, I tumbled out onto a moss-covered slope.

I staggered up. The air shimmered redly. The piled mass of spider silk reached up a long way, between me and the lake of fire.

"Thank Opaz!" I said, and to a Herrelldrin Hell with any futile thoughts I'd been saved by the Everoinye.

As far as I could see in the direction away from the silk and the lake of fire the rocky walls stretched into a horizontal cleft. They reflected the crimson glow. The moss underfoot was a sickly pallid off-white, springy, and quite pleasant walking.

There was only one thing to do in all of Kregen. So off I set, walking resolutely along the slot in the earth, seeking ways up.

An eerie blue column of fire grew abruptly directly before me. I stopped. The blue wavered, distorted, changed shape, almost died and then grew and thickened.

I felt a great leap of hope.

This must be a friendly Wizard or Witch of Loh, come to save me!

The uncertainty of the apparition convinced me this was not Deb-Lu or Khe-Hi or Ling-Li. No, this was our apprentice sorcerer Rollo. Good old Rollo! One of these fine days he'd master completely the arcane art of going into lupu and scrying on people at great distances. I waited, somewhat impatiently, for the figure of the wizard to appear fully formed.

A face stared from the blueness, vanished, returned. That face was not that of any of my friends.

The eyes were closed. The nose was sharp, the mouth thin, and deep lines of concentration furrowed his brows. This, then, was a Wizard of Loh whose powers were not fully developed. That he was a Wizard of Loh I did not doubt, quite apart from the red hair hanging untidily from beneath a flat crooked cap.

He opened his eyes.

He gazed upon the scene all about, at the redness, the caverns, the piled mass of spider silk—and at me. A look of absolute horror crossed that disembodied countenance.

The thin mouth opened and words must have spilled out; they were quite inaudible. He had not yet learned the art of speaking when in lupu. I said: "Who are you, san?"

By his reaction he could not hear me. He looked about him in terror, eyes wide.

Then he vanished.

"Well," I said to myself, "and bad cess to you, too, dom."

So, on again I went, walking stoutly along from cavern to cavern. Any second now I expected to meet the creators of that silken mass. Spiders, like as not, giant spiders, all legs and stings and eyes on stalks. And here I was, the so-called puissant Dray Prescot, clad only in a brown breechclout, the yellow robe long since gone, and not a steel weapon to my name.

Light from the lake of fire gradually faded as I advanced, to be replaced by the pervading radiance of the lichen clothing the walls. Dimpy had told me of this phenomenon and I was greatly pleased to have it. Yes, it is true the Star Lords enhanced my night vision so that I can see remarkably well in the dark; all the same, a little light does wonders for a fellow's morale in spots like this.

Twice I saw small scuttling creatures that skidded off at top speed the moment they were aware of my presence. I walked silently. Whenever a choice of direction presented itself I went up. Two or three times I came to dead ends and had to backtrack; but slowly I made my way along the crevices in the earth going steadily up towards the surface. There was the problem of just which surface that would be. I could come out onto a runnel; I could be climbing up inside a hill. Djan knew, they were riddled with holes like cheese.

Some of the passageways were narrow, damned narrow, by Krun, and I had a bit of a squeeze from time to time.

Anyway, just who the hell was that incompetent Wizard of Loh?

He'd been intending to spy on somebody. Instead, he'd wound up having a look at me in my predicament. Just what was he up to?

There was absolutely no use in expecting my own comrade sorcerers to pay me a visit. They were eternally busy, never having enough burs in one day to do all that they considered had to be done. We were fortunate that they were our comrades, and deigned to assist us from time to time.

A shape lumbered from behind a fallen boulder.

I stopped. The thing looked like a skinned ape, having two muscular arms and two stunted legs. White bone coverings obscured its eyes. Sinuous tendrils sprouted from its forehead, turning, searching, locating, finding—me.

Its clawed hands were busily stuffing the remains of a small creature, similar to those who had run from me, into a gappy and fang-filled mouth. With a last convulsive swallow the poor little beastie went down at a gulp. The skinned ape turned its attention to its next meal.

It stood perhaps a hand's breadth taller than me. It looked compact and muscular. That it was blind meant nothing down here; once it fastened those hooks into me, he'd have me, so all his previous experience told him. I stood motionlessly.

The silence was broken only by the thing's heavy breathing, by the pad of its feet on the ground as it shuffled forward. The moment he leaped...

When he surged forward with arms outstretched and claws extended to rip and rend, I swayed sideways. Instantly, he followed my movement. Snapping back the other way I laid a knobbly fist alongside his head, scrunching into his ear, and then dived on and flat.

He wasn't fazed in the slightest. As I jumped up, the stench of him fouling my nostrils, he drove in again. This time I hit him harder. He shook his head, no doubt puzzled.

He did stink, too, rotten. This time I kicked him betwixt wind and water. I had no desire to kill him. After all, like the scorpion, he was only doing what he was created to do.

Blind though he was, he was damned quick. So I leaped in, avoided the flailing claw-armed hands, and grabbed his tentacles.

All the time he had made no sound apart from his breathing. Now he let out a keening whine, most distressing, as I yanked savagely.

Gripping and twisting his tentacles, inside the reach of his arms, I laid into him, kicking him repeatedly. His screech shrilled higher in agony. Oh, yes, by Vox, I felt sorry for him. I kicked him good and hard and then with my left hand dragging his head forward by the tentacles I gave him a cracking blow on the jaw with a right. He went down, thump, and as I released him rolled over and so lay still. I stared down at him, impassively. He'd recover.

Shaking my shoulders, I walked on.

By the time I reached clear signs of the handiwork of people my insides were like the money-pouch of a fingerless pickpocket.

I gave a sigh of relief as I saw the palisade across the tunnel. The next step would have been to capture one of the creatures living down here and eaten the little fellow. I examined the barricade.

Clearly it was meant to stop people from going down into the depths from which I'd walked. When I'd taken down enough to allow me to pass through, I carefully re-erected it. Then I went on.

The exit was only a few paces on. I stepped out into the familiar dimness of the warrens. I was at the end of a side street where already the torches were being lit.

The torch lighter looked at me in amazement, mouth open and light held high.

"What? Where'd you come from, dom?"

"Oh," I said, off handedly. "I just dropped in."

He'd lost most of his front teeth, so he splashed and mumbled when he talked. He was a slave. I decided to put a hangdog look on my face, and hold my head down, and with the brown breechclout pass along as a slave. I obviously had no weapon, and no money, either. That, I felt, would be the safest course to prevent being jumped and unnecessary agro of that nature.

He was still staring after me and scratching his head as I shambled on. One of the lesser Moons of Kregen shot past in the evening sky, in view for a short time only between hill and hill.

I stopped and turned. "Oh, dom, whereaway is this?"

"Ravelstan Street. You'd better watch out. The Alley Leems are out tonight, hunting."

"My thanks. 'beree."

He mumbled and I walked along the unlighted side of Ravelstan Street. People were about, doing what they did down here. Then I made another decision, a more delightful one this time.

Dimpy's address was not far, a couple of warrens away. I'd go and see what the young Imp of Sicce was up to. Anyway, I ought to put my outsides around some food to stop my insides complaining.

Nothing was to be seen of any trouble being caused by the Alley Leems gang. They all had their rackets. Some of the more lurid establishments were opening for the night, lanterns shining invitingly over tawdry porticoes. The young bloods from the hills would be down, indulging in what they fondly imagined to be the height of decadence. No doubt the usual couple or so would be hit over the head and robbed. They'd have their private guards. It all added to their conception of fun.

Sentries from the Hellraisers stood alertly at the crossroads that marked the beginning of their territory this side. No doubt they'd heard the Alley Leems were looking for trouble. As a slave I just shambled through and no one took any notice.

I'd expected to have to ask for Dimpy's house. I did not.

There was no mistaking what was going on. Dimpy stood in front of the sagging door to his hovel, a whole braxter in one hand and a broken one in the other. Facing him a yelling, taunting crowd of young hooligans were working themselves up to rush him and overpower him. From the windows the faces of two young girls and their mother stared in terror upon the scene and what was about to happen.

Fourteen

"The Watch! The Watch! Run! Run!"

The bellow burst over all the noise of the mob. Then, in an even louder roar: "Run! Katakis!"

That old foretop hailing voice struck immediate terror into the young hooligans. For a single moment only they stood, petrified, suddenly silent. They all knew that the infamous City Watch rarely interfered with big gang fights. In a small local disturbance like this, a petty rumble, the Katakis would come leaping in like leems, arresting anyone who looked likely. They'd be out for slaves. There'd be a nice profit to be turned here.

Again I yelled, running up and waving my arms.

"Run, you famblys! The Kataki Watch!"

That did it. Like a bunch of terrified ponshos as the werstings close in, they turned and ran. They ran in a helter-skelter bunch away from Dimpy's house.

Crossing swiftly to him I snapped out: "You're not safe here, Dimpy, that's obvious. You'll have to—"

"Drajak!" He gasped it out in shocked amazement.

"Aye," I said. "We've got to get your family out of this."

"But—but where'd you come from—?"

"No time for that."

The noise of the hooligan mob was not decreasing. Rather, the shouts were coming back again. In the forefront of the canaille the boy who'd so basely tricked Dimpy with the sword had been urging them on. Now, in the uncertain light of torches, here he ran again, charging back up the street, waving his arms. The mob followed.

"Inside." I grabbed Dimpy and fairly hurled him in through his open front door, back-heeling it shut after us.

The girls were clasping each other. They were not screaming. His mother, pale, worried, stared at me in apprehension.

From the windows we could see the mob, led by the trickster, haring back up the street. They ran gasping, with open mouths and staring eyes. Following them in full cry chased the Kataki-led Watch. Cudgels rose and fell. Some of the hooligans dodged, yelling; others fell with bleeding heads.

And I, Dray Prescot, laughed.

I'd chased them off with a false cry of the Watch, and they'd run slap bang into the real Watch out for blood and slaves.

I relished the joke.

"Sleed the Slick." Dimpy sounded angry and contemptuous. "I hope the Watch take him."

Now in the normal course of events in a situation like this, one could go into a police station and request assistance. Down here with the Watch, a gang of little better than masichieri led by Katakis notorious for their hunger for human bodies to be collected up as slaves, such an open course would be disastrous. All the same, I had to get myself and Dimpy and his family up aloft out of this.

The pursuers and the fleeing disappeared off into the dimness along the street. Dimpy's mother said: "I do hope—" She put a hand to her forehead. "This is all so—so dreadful."

"It'll be all right, mother." Dimpy turned to his sisters. "Did you see Big Balla?"

They shook their heads—no.

I said: "Perhaps you'd care to introduce me, Dimpy." By this I hoped to restore some normalcy to a fraught situation.

"Of course." His mother was called Velda, the two girls were Samphron and Melly. They all bore the marks of living down in the warrens where existence was a daily struggle. They shared Dimpy's independent toughness, his resilience, his—not to put too fine a point on it—his bloody-mindedness. I liked them at sight.

"We can't stay here now." Velda sighed, I guessed, at having to leave what, however ramshackle it might be, was her home.

Some vague kind of plan was already forming in my old vosk skull of a head. I nodded and told them to gather up what possessions they valued and could carry. With a careful survey of the street, carrying bundles, we slunk out. They turned for a last look back; then we set off.

"Once that tanzy Sleed shakes off the Watch, he'll be back." Dimpy's voice was ice cold. "I just hope they take him."

I wanted to know if they had anywhere they could hide and be safe for half a day. They were uncertain. Since the Hellraisers had taken over Roaring Fifties territory everything had changed. Their old friends had either died, been killed or had disappeared.

Now how the blue blazes was I going to get this parcel of folk up out of it?

If they could be stashed away somewhere safe, fine, I'd get myself aloft and get a lifter to come back for them. As it now appeared they had nowhere to go, that simple plan was squashed on the head.

The evening was gathering momentum, with people moving about, stalls with flaring torches and shouting barkers at every vantage point, places of entertainment gearing themselves for the night's first performances. The noise was bearable, even with occasional odd echoes bouncing off the sides of the hills. If fights erupted, they'd be personal. The gangs were not out tonight—yet.

Dimpy was not dressed in the decent clothes given him from Princess Nandisha's bounty; he wore a shabby old tunic. The ladies of his family wore the dress common down here, scooped as to neck and plain as to hem, in materials woven to give pretty patterns—flowers, birds, animals. They looked what they were, common folk from the warrens.

Among the throngs now out for the evening there would be eyes searching for Dimpy and his family.

My vague plan jumped a notch as I spied the place I needed. It didn't matter to me what kind of decadent entertainment was being offered here, just as long as it attracted the clientele I required.

The front was built out of stone from the cliffs but you were left in no doubt as to the amphitheater's capacity by flaring notices proclaiming the fact it was cut back into the earth. At the left side a narrow alley led back, on the right a wider road was obviously provided to afford access to carts. One such cart ground past now. We shrank back. The cage contained a muzzilla, all hair and fangs and claws, with a whiplash tail. The promoters of the fight might strap a dagger to that tail, if the muzzilla had been trained in its use. They were cantankerous beasties at the best of times.

Lanterns swinging on poles heralded the arrival of a party of young bloods. Their morals were none of my business. If they fancied that venturing down here, well-guarded, of course, to witness a wild animal contest was adventure, then they were welcome to that, the famblys.

Jewels glittered and glistened from sumptuous clothes. Faces shone in the lights with gluttonous expectations. Lace handkerchiefs were waved in airy gestures, strong scents battling the various and dubious aromas pervasive on the air. Oh, yes, by Krun, they were a right dandified bunch. In they went to their play.

"Down here." I led my party into the narrow left-hand alley. The ladies were bearing up in a wonderful way. I found a niche for them at the end, against the face of the cliff, and told Dimpy, in most stern and measured tones, to stay on guard. He nodded, started to speak, changed his mind, and nodded again.

Then I took myself off to pluck my chicken.

In my present condition, naked save for a brown breechclout, I'd never be let into Nalimer's Iridescent Faerling, even if I had the money to pay the entrance. The proprietor, Nalimer, hired plug-uglies to stand on the door and throw out people like me.

The uncomfortable feeling was that my friends in the alley were more than likely in for a long wait.

Now down here in the gullies life might be red raw and gang-ruled; the fact remained these were real people. I couldn't just hit somebody at random over the head and steal his clothes and money. That antisocial and criminal activity might suit a fairy story or an improbable romance, it did not suit me. Maybe at times in the past something like that had happened; then I was young and new to Kregen, hot-headed and intemperate, and desperately put upon by the Star Lords and various slavers of several evil kinds.

Mind you, by Krun, if I ran across a Kataki...!

The dandies allowed their guards in to see the show. They'd have high seating at the back, to be sure; but they'd be in and part of it all. One has to keep one's guards happy, you know.

When the noise burst up in crescendos of beast roars the fight had begun. Idly I wondered what the muzzilla was fighting. A couple of beautifully-dressed men came out to visit the house at the side and a single look told me they'd be useless. I didn't like the cut of their jibs one little bit. Eventually a fellow came out and I decided that this was it, now or never. He was a cadade, kitted properly in armor, wearing swords, a Hytak.

One can tell a great deal about an employer by the condition of his guards and particularly his guard captain.

"Llahal, dom," I said politely, standing beside him. "I'm in a spot of difficulty." I spoke precisely, hardly, as a noble would speak—not as a slave or commoner. He was attentive at once.

I explained that I'd been down to buy servants, had concluded the deal, and had then been hit on the head and robbed of everything. The servants remained with me. I wanted to know if he thought his employer could guarantee me safe passage aloft, as, in my present condition the Katakis would—"

"Aye, dom. They would, the blintzes."

He gave me a good hard stare under a lantern. I returned his gaze, hard, unyielding, but not unfriendly. He seemed satisfied. He was Jiktar Zonder ti Rannellden. He had the pakmort at his throat.

He seemed in no hurry to return. Taking a chance I commented on the beast fight. His remarks were choice. He found the spectacle degrading and disgusting. Before I gave him my name I needed to know who he worked for. This turned out to be a Strom Logan. I'd not heard of him. Clearly I as yet didn't know all the nobility of Oxonium, let alone Tolindrin.

"Drajak the Sudden. I work for Princess Nandisha."

I held my breath. But he smiled. "Old Ranaj, eh? He's a bonny lad in a fight, by Hartagas the Marvel."

So, that was all right, then.

Jiktar Zonder had heard of Nandisha's troubles. He confided in me that Strom Logan had all along supported Tom. He'd be glad when the coronation was over and out of the way. We talked about the ghastly murders of young girls. Without any embarrassment at all I touched him for a silver or two to buy some food and a wet at a stall under its swaying lanterns. I was famished. When Zonder went back into the amphitheater to resume his duty I took the food round into the alley and we had ourselves a little feast. I reassured my new friends that everything was going well and a little more patience and we'd be off and out of it.

"And then what, Drajak?" sighed Velda. "What will happen to us on the hills?"

"Oh," I said, firmly. "Don't worry over that. I've plans you can't dream of." Dimpy gave me a quick almost hostile stare. I wasn't yet going to tell him that Esser Rarioch was where they were bound for.

This section showed no signs of the earthquake, although Zonder mentioned that there had been damage on Grand Central. I concluded that the quake shocks had not been succeeded by the big one, for if they had I would probably not have still been around in the land of the living. I just hoped my friends up there were all right. The numim twins most certainly were; the Star Lords would have had something to say otherwise, by Vox!

After that everything went off without a hitch. Strom Logan turned out to be a portly Hytak, an old paktun who'd served his time and saved his money and been rewarded with a small stromnate. Soberly dressed, he was accompanied by a couple of dandies for whom he had the same politeness as he showed my party. The young bloods were up from Laconden and in his care, to be shown the sights. We went up in the basket from the watch tower, hoisted to the waiting cable car. Whisked through the clean upper air under the stars we went our separate ways with my thanks and promise to repay Zonder.

As I had expected, there was surprise in Nandisha's palace that I was still alive. I'd fallen into the bowels of Kregen and the devil fires had swallowed me. That was swiftly sorted. I was not tired enough to miss what the news in the palace was.

Ranaj, on my solemn promise that Dimpy's family would be gone in the morning, found them sleeping quarters. Fweygo just stared daggers at me. Nothing, I gathered, had been heard from the Everoinye.

We sat to a proper meal before we slept.

Ranaj said: "Whilst you have been away, Drajak, we have had a visitor." He brushed his golden whiskers. "Rather, a visitation."

"Oh?"

Fweygo said: "A damned sorcerer. Probing and prying about the palace. Scared the princess and the children half out of their wits."

"Yes." Ranaj looked wrought up. "A damned weasel-faced fellow, sharp-nosed, thin-lipped. Red hair. Blue lights all about him enough to bring out any honest man in goose-pimples."

Fweygo finished: "A spying Wizard of Loh!"

Fifteen

"And will Drajak make us slaves?" Samphron gave a decisive jut of her rounded chin. "If he does I shall kill myself first."

"Oh, don't be silly!" said her twin.

"You're going to a land where they don't allow slaves."

Dimpy laughed. "There's no such place in all the world."

Very drily, Fweygo cut in. "There is. It's called Vallia."

"Never heard of it!" quoth Melly defiantly.

"The first thing you two misses will do in Vallia is go to school. Reading, Writing and Arithmetic."

"Oh!" in a chorus.

"And geography."

When I spoke to Dimpy about his plans I already half-guessed what his answer would be. Much though he longed to be with his family, the thought of Tiri obsessed him. I gave him absolute assurances that his family would be safe, well-cared for and happy. He elected to stay in Nandisha's palace, working for Ranaj.

"After," he said in his truculent way, "I've been to Cymbaro's temple and seen Tiri."

"What's left of it," I grunted. "And Tiri's gone away."

I didn't tell him I thought the young madam had gone to Farinsee because I wasn't positively sure. It was most likely.

So that all turned out well. Without revealing who I was, arrangements were made by the Vallian Ambassador. There was a tearful farewell. The remberees were called as the Vallian voller lifted off. It was quick and sudden, a clean break, which was absolutely the best thing. Then, with Dimpy, I went off to Cymbaro's temple. Duven was not there. I'd wanted to congratulate him on his actions. Workmen were already trying to make sense out of the mess. The giant cleft in the ground had closed in the subsequent shock. The temple would be rebuilt. San Paynor was positive on that point.

When I mentioned the mysterious Wizard of Loh he looked grave but had no information.

The interrupting noise of banging workmen hammering and smashing away distracted the conversation. Workmen love to make a hideous noise. I don't doubt they're all deaf in no time. Have you noticed how workmen on a building site always shout at one another? It makes trying to work extremely difficult. By the disgusting dangling eyeballs and lacerated liver of Makki Grodno! Wouldn't it be wonderful if workmen were issued with rubber hammers to do their banging with!

Collecting my gear, which had been saved, I bid remberee and Dimpy and I took ourselves off.

We stopped off on the way back at a little corner shop for refreshment. Naturally enough, and there is probably no need to mention it, with a voller flying direct to Esser Rarioch I'd taken the opportunity to write letters. One of them requested one of our resident Wizards of Loh to contact me as soon as possible.

Watching the busy bustle all about I was once again struck by the vivid contrast between here and down there. There was bustle down there, all right; the differences remained startling.

Naturally enough the twin topics of discussion were the earthquake and the coronation. One affected the other. Oh, yes! Many people were openly saying that the quake was a bad omen. Should not prince Tom delay his crowning? In a religious community the wills of the various gods are considered to be expressed by forceful happenings. Natural disasters have to have an origin, surely? And who else but the gods possess the powers?

Sorcerers?

Don't make us laugh! the folk would scoff. That's why the old king practically banned wizards from the kingdom.

As you will readily appreciate, the earthquake had a profound and immediate effect on the course of history in the making, and of my plans in particular. Any delay in the coronation, I believed, meant continuing peril for Princess Nandisha. That, in turn, meant the numim twins remained in danger. And, by the pelvic monstrosity of the Divine Lady of Belschutz, that meant I had to lollygag around in Balintol instead of shooting off home to Esser Rarioch and to Delia.

As if to point up the somberness of my expectations, a nasty brawl broke out along the road before us. Many people had come into the city for the coronation and Oxonium was bursting at the seams. Cudgels rose and fell. Women screamed and stumbled away.

Dimpy half-rose. I put a hand on his shoulder and pressed him back into his seat.

"Let 'em get on with it, the hulus."

Differently colored and stylized badges marked the combatants. What they were brawling about could be anything. It was no business of mine. At the moment, unfortunately, at the behest of the Everoinye, Fweygo and I had to look out for the numim twins. That was my business. So I'd better get back to the palace and get on with it.

Naturally, as this was taking place on Kregen, it wasn't as easy as that.

The brawl spread. Half a dozen struggling men sprawled across the ground before us and another battling group crashed into the pile. They were all yelling blue bloody murder and calling on their respective gods and goddesses and patrons. The tumbled mass hit our table, upended it, and bore Dimpy and me over backwards.

Makki Grodno's blessed name escaped my lips as I struck out and fought for air and space. Dimpy's fist hit a squat nose which burst and sprayed claret. I chucked a polsim away, staggered up and brushed off a Fristle who was trying to bite my legs.

My fist gripped under Dimpy's armpit and, struggling like a newborn Wersting, he was hoicked up out of the ruck.

"Come on, Dimpy. Let's get out of this!"

We span about, ready to run, and a damned great Rapa, his feathers all bristling, jumped in front of us from nowhere and hit me over the head with a monstrous great wooden billy.

I let out a yell—by Krun, I yelled!—and staggered back and tripped over an unconscious form on the ground. Dimpy fell all asprawl on top of me. I caught a frenzied glimpse of the Rapa lifting his club to smash Dimpy in the back of the head.

There was just time to haul Dimpy out of the way and so make this cramph of a Rapa miss with his savage blow. There was a familiar feeling of wetness on my forehead. Lumbering up as the billy swung for another blow I slid the descending strike. The wood was hard and polished with much usage and it slipped easily away off my right arm. I reached out and took the Rapa's scraggy vulture neck in my left fist. I clenched my fingers and thumb. I shook him.

His beady eyes popped and his beak clacked up and down like a pair of fool's clappers. I shook him some more, hit him between the eyes, and so threw him away. I was, as you will perceive, a trifle wrought up.

Dimpy screeched: "Look out!"

I ducked.

The flung knife went zzinngg! past my head.

Another Rapa charged at me. He was bigger, uglier and altogether more unpleasant than his comrade with whom I had just passed a few fraught moments. He tore out his sword, a slikker, and bore in with every intention of skewering my guts.

The petty brawl had, on a sudden, turned deadly.

Dimpy yelped out: "Come on, Drajak. Let's go!"

I wasn't prepared to turn my back on this rast so I didn't bother to reply. The slikker, halfway between a shortsword and a braxter, was held in a fighting grip and the Rapa was clearly skilled in its use. My reluctance vanished and I unsheathed a braxter and put up my blade.

The noise of the brawl all about spiraled, as it were, into another dimension. The stinks, the noise, all vanished into a single all-encompassing concentration upon the Rapa's eyes and sword.

All the same, fine though that is in swordsmen's jargon, I remained Dray Prescot, a cunning old leem-hunter, a fellow who's had more fights—to his shame—than most. So, centering my attention on the Rapa and the fight to hand, I still had a wary eye open for anyone else likely to jump me. It is a knack, and it keeps one alive.

The Rapa was good, a solid fighting man, and I determined, however base he might be, not to slay him. We foined, I did this and that, sent him one way, flicked his slikker out of his hand into the air where it span and glinted in the light of the suns, and put the braxter's hilt into his beak.

He fell down.

"Now you've had your fun, Drajak, will you come on!" The clear young voice was sharp above the clamor.

I scabbarded the unbloodied sword. I walked stiff-legged over to the young imp. I glared into his eyes.

"Fighting is not fun, Dimpy, not fun at all."

"Well, you could have fooled me."

Cheeky young scamp!

The idiots were still hard at it as we left, still yelling for their gods and goddesses and patrons, knocking hell out of one another.

By the time we'd reached the cable car terminus the City Guard were descending on the brawl in force. Putting all that nonsense out of my head, once again I mused on the people festering in the warrens below as the calimer passed so grandly by high above. There was time as we sailed along suspended from the cable over thin air to ponder on what had transpired over the past few days. The great nobles in contention had not given up their hopes of placing the crown upon their own heads. Those poor folk down in the canyons below were being used as mere pawns in the game. Prince Ortyg had his olive-green clad bully-boys. Khon the Mak would be busily at work recruiting for the showdown to come. All Oxonium, all Tolindrin, could run red with blood.

The car jounced into its retaining guides and we alighted. There was another call to make before I could get back to the numim twins and try to explain it all to Fweygo.

At least Fweygo supplied funds. A careful choice had to be made between one wine and another, for in our conversation Zonder had mentioned in passing that his favorite wine was Xalanx, a perfumed vintage out of Xuntal. Finding a satisfactory vendor I purchased a case of a dozen, hired a porter, and sallied off to Strom Logan's villa.

In his comfortable quarters beside the guardhouse in Logan's relatively modest residence, I said to Zonder: "Yes, I was badly robbed on the road and lost my pakzhan. Employment with Ranaj was most welcome, as you will understand. Replacement is most difficult."

He said: "There is no need to repay the silver, Drajak—the wine alone—"

"Is a paltry attempt to say thank you. I tell you, dom, it is most unhealthy down there in the stews."

He nodded in his Hytak way. We drank a little parclear. Dimpy kept a most unusual silence. The conversation was of the coronation and the earthquake. There had been no more murders of young girls, although deaths through street fights had increased.

Presently we said the remberees and just as Dimpy and I went out, Zonder called after us: "And you will be most welcome to visit again."

Walking quietly along, Dimpy suddenly came out with: "You know why he wants to see you again, Drajak? It's obvious. He wants you to leave Princess Nandisha and go work for him and Strom Logan." He cocked his head up. "Will you?"

"Nope."

We walked along thereafter in a pool of silence between us.

The disparate events that had been happening all about me were, I felt, interconnected in some mysterious way. The very absence of interference from the Star Lords pointed up the seriousness of the present situation. The long-term plans of the Everoinye must look many seasons into the future. Their concern was for the numim twins. They'd said they had little interest in who won the crown so long as the lion maid and lion lad lived.

Just what was to be their role in the future of Kregen? As always, I had no way of knowing, and only the passage of the years would provide the answer.

A blare of trumpets on the warm air, harsh and commanding, drawing closer, was followed by a scattering of the crowds. They flew apart like chickens in the farmyard when a horse and carriage thundered through. Dimpy and I hopped off to the side where, perched on a plinth, we saw what was toward.

In front of the trumpeters marched armed men who made sure no one was left gawping and standing in the way. The trumpeters were gorgeously attired; over-decorated jackanapes was the thought that jumped immediately to mind. Next marched a bevy of men carrying standards and flags. Mostly the colors were red and combinations of red. My face did not move a muscle as I stared. Young boys pranced along distributing perfumed water in graceful jets, glinting rose red in the lights of the twin suns. Whatever this procession was in aid of, it had its own Perfume Patrol.

All this grandiose display of wealth and power made me assume a long and tiresome procession would follow. Restless, I started to look about for a way to slip off out of it.

A troop of zorca cavalry, lance-armed, glittering, trampled past guarding a palanquin. The gherimcal was ornate, laden with gilt encrustations, silk-curtained, feather decorated. The slaves carrying it were all big muscular fellows, eight to each end of the two poles. Oh, yes, it was impressive, no doubt of it, if you were witless enough to be impressed by such tawdry signs of power.

"Who's he?" demanded Dimpy.

A pale face was discernible at the gherimcal's silk-clothed window. A languid hand was raised in acknowledgement as many of the watching crowds fell to their knees, hands clasped before them.

Just before our plinth a hairy Brokelsh wearing the floury clothes of a baker fell to the ground. He shook his clasped hands, mumbling prayers. A fat little Och beside Dimpy looked down in contempt. The Och waved his middle left at the gorgeous procession.

"That, young fellow, is San Volarminanster, San Volar, the chief priest of the ridiculous cult of Tolaar."

Dimpy uttered what was in my mind. "I thought Tolaar was the chief religion."

The Och spat. "Biggest, yes. Biggest bunch of onkers. Not the best, though, oh, no."

The Brokelsh was trying to kneel down and express due reverence, and at the same time twist around to stare with baleful hostility at whoever was contuming his chief priest.

I nudged Dimpy.

"There's going to be another fight. Come on."

Armed men brought up the tail of the procession. As they passed people began to gather in a knot about the plinth. I pushed through, fairly dragging Dimpy along. Angry voices raised. Shouts, threats and counter threats flew thickly. We two just ran off.

Before we'd gone a dozen paces the meaty sounds of blows and yells of pain lifted at our backs.

"Onkers," I said.

We slowed to a brisk walk. That young devil Dimpy would cheerfully have gone wading in, breaking heads, even though he had no interest in the rights or wrongs of the argument. I sensed he was still wrought up, craving to see Tiri again, perhaps still a little apprehensive about the fate of his family despite all that had been promised. Without being consciously aware of his attitude, Dimpy just wanted to get into a fight to work off some of the bile. My plans—such as they were—called for a low profile.

Fweygo had not balked overmuch at my continued absences. He was content, more than content, to remain in Nandisha's palace. He had not told me himself, for I'd had it from Fat Lardo, about his charming if odd romance. No names had been mentioned. But there was a stunning girl somewhere in the palace who had taken Fweygo's amorous attentions. As is the nature of these things, everyone wanted to know who the girl was, for there were, as far as I knew, no other Kildois among Nandisha's people.

Well, whoever she was, she was damned lucky to find someone like Fweygo to care for her, that was for sure, by Vox!

So I had no hesitation in trotting along to make the next call on my appointment list.

Milsi the Slinky had arranged for me to see Naghan Raerdu at a middling tavern, The Flying Vosk, where we would attract no attention. I wanted to arrange a visit back to the house where I'd seen the ibmanzy. If events turned out in such a way that I could not go in person, then Naghan would detail some of his people to find out. Surely, news of the monstrous thing must be common knowledge down there? What had happened to it after we'd left it dancing in frustrated rage on the rooftop?

Dimpy stopped suddenly. I hauled up alongside and a skinny polsim cannoned into me. He mumbled an ungracious apology, for he, too, could see why we'd stopped.

"Not again!" Oxonium was turning into a mere bear pit.

A mob of people were running down towards us, shrieking, waving their arms, terrified. A couple of lads of the Perfume Patrol threw down the implements of their trade and fled. Bedlam bore down on us like a bursting volcano.

We stood aside very smartly to let the panic-stricken horde trample on. The polsim fled with them. Dimpy cocked an eye up at me.

"When we see—" I began.

Dimpy yelped and pointed. "Look!"

No wonder the people had simply fled in sheer unholy terror.

Now—the earthquake through which I'd gone in the shrine to Cymbaro had in reality been more of a local earth tremor, a movement that had opened the chasm and subsequently closed it. There was practically no real damage to the other buildings on Grand Central. By some freak of the earth's structure, a fault line, a tremor had shaken three or four of the buildings here. Rubble lay across the street. A house had been gutted and workmen were putting back windows and doors. As usual, they were making a hell of a noise, clattering and banging, shouting and—oftentimes—singing among themselves.

The workmen's annoying uproar stopped as though guillotined.

One poor devil, for all his noise, fell off the scaffolding. He hit the ground head first and burst in blood.

Others were tumbling down the ladders, shrieking. Some fell back into the building, disappearing. The workmen were utterly destroyed.

Dimpy still stood, rigid, pointing.

Whatever the thing was, it was not human.

It may have been human once. Or even twice. It looked like a cross. One arm was that of the head of a beautiful girl, blonde hair swirling, blue eyes wide, red lips moist and full. Opposite her the head was that of a monster from nightmare, squamous, dripping with ichor, three red eyes glaring in mad passion. Its fangs lapped its lower and upper jaws to form a vice of death.

The crosspiece's arms were those of a reptilian monstrosity with lashing barbed tail and a gigantic hairy spider, all legs and antennae, writhing uncontrollably.

"By Makki Grodno's maggot infested intestines—" I started to say. I stopped. Makki Grodno had stiff competition in this unwholesome and unreal chimera.

But it was real.

The red blood and green ichor dripping from it stained the flags of the pavement. It stank. Its putrescence fouled the air all about. It moaned. It keened. It lashed its reptile's tail and stretched and withdrew its hairy legs. The blue eyes of the beautiful blonde woman seemed to drill into me, imploring, pleading. I felt a chill thrill through me as though I stood among the Ice Floes of Sicce.

The thing floated head high. It dribbled its puss onto the ground and drifted along leaving a trail like a snail's.

But it was real.

Dimpy lowered his arm. He panted. He didn't look at me.

The thing drifted along the street and terrified uproar surrounded it. Its stench nauseated. Slowly it floated past.

Four beings, squashed blasphemously together, joined in blood and ichor, a star of agony—oh, yes, that was one sight it were best to forget.

Sixteen

If I had expected news of the ibmanzy to spread throughout the city and been disappointed, I most certainly was not in respect of the hideous four-creature object that drifted in the air and dribbled blood and slime. The news of that unholy monstrosity spread as the fires spread in the dry season among the grasses of the Pomongo Plains.

Every religious order immediately put out statements denying any association with the thing, which folk were now dubbing the leygromak.

No one doubted it was the work of sorcery.

Despite the old king's laws restraining wizardry in his realms some thaumaturges still practiced the minor crafts. This was tolerated provided they did not presume too far in the arcane arts. Khon the Mak, no doubt due to his exalted position, had maintained his own private Wizard.

One of these minor sorcerers had been employed by Naghan Raerdu the Barrel when he'd taken me out of custody in a cloud of magical smoke. Now Khon the Mak's wizard, Wocut, had gone off to Vallia, who was there in Oxonium able to fabricate such a devilish thing as the leygromak?

The only answer was, of course, the Wizard of Loh who'd spied with so much terror on me down in the fire chasm, and who'd scryed Nandisha's palace. This meant, I was sure, the idiot had been attempting a spell, had fumbled, and wound up by creating the leygromak.

Yes, all well and good. But what had been the import of the spell, what was he up to, and who was paying him?

Hyr Kov Khonstanton, known as Khon the Mak, that's who, as sure as Zim and Genodras rise each day over Kregen.

With Wocut gone to Vallia, Khon the Mak had hired himself a Wizard of Loh. He'd found himself an incompetent, that was for sure, too, by Krun.

So, now there was another burning topic of conversation buzzing in Oxonium.

Naghan the Barrel informed me he'd send to find out about the ibmanzy. Naghan was a fellow who liked to know everything there was to know, and relished mysteries only if he knew the answers. As to the leygromak, he shrugged his fat shoulders. Who could say as yet?

Dimpy remained uncharacteristically quiet. He was pining for Tiri, worried over his family, unsure of what future lay ahead for him.

Taking him off to Nandisha's salle d'armes I foined with wooden blades with him. I let him clout me over the head a couple of times with the rudis, hoping thereby to cheer him up a trifle. He was quick and nimble and I was happy to show him a few tricks of the swordsman's trade. Fweygo came in to watch us, beaming with his inner satisfaction. He, I knew, would not welcome a release from the Star Lords in our guardianship of the numim twins.

As the day of the coronation drew nearer, Nandisha became more and more preoccupied with just what she and her children should wear for the various great occasions of the fortnight's events. As to that, the whole seething mass of the population of the hills became gripped by coronation fever. Tailors and jewelers and tradesmen of that ilk were run off their feet filling all their orders. Such a pother, such a commotion, such splendid extravagance, and all for young Tom who really didn't want to be king at all.

When news arrived that part of one of the towers of Khon the Mak's palace had fallen down I had to laugh.

By Zair, yes! This damned incompetent Wizard of Loh was at it again. This time he'd blown the palace roof off. It was given out that the tower's fall was a late result of the earth shock.

Now, along the routes the coronation procession would take, stands were being erected. Workmen were everywhere. The confounded noise of banging and hammering went on from dawn to dusk—and well into the night, too. The racket made a fellow's head ache.

Nandisha outfitted her guard with new uniforms. Of a tasteful pale blue, they were well enough. I was glad most of the color was obscured by a good quality brigandine. Not of iron but bronze, the plates were riveted to stout buff leather. We all had new helmets, too, a type of pot helm of iron with a nasal and crest. Naturally, in that crest a whole mass of floating feathers were fixed to give us the imposing impression rightful to a lady of so exalted a position as the Princess Nandisha. Well, she was a good soul, and I could not find it in me to mock her too outrageously. For all she was a princess, she had a hard enough life. And she and her children remained in peril.

A couple of mornings later we had altogether grimmer news to chew over at the first breakfast.

A young girl, Jenni Farlang, who worked in a jeweler's shop, had been discovered in Ruby Alley torn to pieces. Her body was ripped apart, scattered, the hideous work of a maniac.

The murders in Oxonium had begun again.

In one of her hands—discovered some fifty or so paces from other parts of her pitifully shredded corpse—had been found a scrap of red cloth. This had clearly been torn from the hem of the clothes worn by her murderer. This was the first clue the City Guard had. It pointed up the correctness of the theory that the murders were the work of the adherents of Dokerty.

Having to relieve Fweygo on duty might be a nuisance, but it was entirely fair. After all, hadn't I been swanning off a great deal lately? He had, this morning, a rendezvous with his mysterious lady. I took myself off to the solarium. Two competent lads, Nath the Frogenstal and Herpato Froth, both apims, were already on duty. They greeted me cheerfully enough, for Fweygo and I had, as it were, pushed in to comfortable positions in the household guard. Paktuns all, we accepted good fortune in others.

Presently the young prince and princess accompanied by the numim twins came in. There were servants in attendance. The glass-roofed solarium was pleasantly warm and soon the youngsters threw off most of their clothing. We guards sweated it out in our armor.

There was nothing to do save stand and watch. I was looking forward to the end of the watch when a dark shadow abruptly hovered over the glass roof. In a rending shriek of timbers and the shattering of glass, the whole lot caved in. A lifter smashed down and settled on the floor.

An arrow sped towards me from the bow of the first man over the side of the airboat. I swayed aside and the arrow hissed past.

Herpato Froth was not so fast, and he was certainly unlucky, for his arrow took him clear through the eye. He went down, jerking. Nath the Frogenstal jumped and the shaft intended for him missed.

At once he ripped out his sword and charged headlong for the men leaping from the lifter. In that action he followed me. Uproar broke out. The servants were trying to pull the children out of the room. Young Byrom had drawn a little dagger and was struggling not to be carted off. As for young Rolan, the lion boy was running forward with us, a dagger in his fist.

"Keep out of it, Rolan!" I shrieked.

Opaz forfend! If he was slain, now—I'd be back on Earth for how many miserable years, if not for ever.

The fight blossomed into a red roaring insanity.

My braxter flashed this way and that, and all my efforts were directed to keeping Rolan's head on his shoulders and the life in his brave body. Naturally, after a few of the attackers had been knocked over my braxter snapped.

I flung the hilt in the face of a Rapa, kicked a Fristle, whipped out the second braxter and laid to with that. Blood splashed Rolan; thank Opaz it was not his. He fought as numims fight—well.

Yet he was not fully grown. He could not expect to stand against professional assassins, stikitches cunningly trained in the arts of murder.

Nath the Frogenstal was wounded, a nasty gash down his thigh; but he went on battling like a leem. There was no time to take stock of the airboat or of the commanding figure in the bows gesturing his assassins on. He stayed back and did not join the men he so ardently drove on with signs and imprecations.

Keeping Rolan out of trouble as much as possible meant that the Prince Byrom ran more risk than I liked—or that he should. Here was where the cruelty of having to choose from selfish motives made me revert to the old madcap, reckless, intemperate Dray Prescot ways of carrying on.

The blow with which I hit a polsim was far, far too powerful. His head jumped off his shoulders, true, trailing bloody streamers. But my blessed braxter broke.

A Fristle saw that and charged me, scimitar glittering.

"Sink me!" I snarled. "I'll have you, catman!"

I slid his blade and kicked him. A blur in the corner of my eye made me swing violently away. The rapier hilt was in my fist, the blade half-drawn when the blur turned into a Brokelsh, burly and hairy, mouth agape, swinging in with a rush.

He wielded a kunsan, the short spear very like a Zulu assegai, very like the similar weapons used by my Clansmen of Felschraung. In the right hands they are more deadly than they appear. He thrust and I avoided and drew the rapier fully from the scabbard. The Brokelsh brought the butt end of his kunsan around in a vicious arc. He hit my hand with stunning force. The rapier span away across the floor.

"Now you are dead, apim!"

I ducked and surged forward. Our bodies collided with a thud and before he could recover I clouted him across his hairy jaw.

Before I could chase after either his kunsan or my rapier a Rapa slashed at me with his sword and I had to skip and jump. Facing him I got myself in front of Rolan who was just reaching down to pluck his dagger from the eye of the man he'd just downed.

My right hand was numb.

With my left I drew the main gauche and fronted the damned Beaky. He laughed his peculiar Rapa cackle and charged in and I had to swerve and thrust the left hand dagger into him as he went past.

The confounded onker took the dagger with him embedded in his feathered body.

After that everything becomes a blur. Scarlet flashes of faces, of blood, of wretches falling away with their arms ripped off, their faces smashed in, of wights doubling up in agony, flashes that bring some memory of that horrific fight.

I really thought we were all done for.

In the end it was with the wonder of a snow filled morning unexpectedly seen from the window that I saw crossbow bolts sizzling past us. The quarrels dug their cruel steel heads into the bodies of the assassins—and very few of them there were left, by Krun!

Nandisha's guards trampled in and the stikitches, what was left of them, scrambled the lifter up and away through the hole she'd made in the glass roof. Crossbow bolts followed them.

"Well," snapped Ranaj, crossly. "What a mess!"

"Aye," said Fweygo in his calm fashion. "You have to give credit to that blintz Prince Ortyg for trying."

There was no doubt this was the handiwork of Ortyg—the commanding cramph in the bows of the lifter was recognized as one Nath ti Fangenun, by his insignia holding the rank of Jiktar. He had recently been taken on by Ortyg. Ranaj's sources of information were positive on that point.

"So why send a man in command we would know?" demanded Ranaj.

"The little fool must be getting desperate," said Nandisha, her children clinging to her skirts. "I do not like this turn of events one little bit." She was badly shaken.

Ranaj stroked his golden whiskers. "We shall double the guard on a permanent basis, princess."

As for me, I brooded on the miserable quality of Tolindrin steel. As you know, during all my hectic career on Kregen I had never depended on one single favorite—and named—weapon to the exclusion of all others. A veteran fighting man will use any weapons that come to hand. As an example, young Tiri's handbag had dealt a doughty blow in combat. No. I'd have to get Ambassador Larghos Invordun to send to Vallia for a proper fighting man's sword. A great Krozair longsword in my fist—aye, by Zair! That would make a few eyes water!

Of course, really and truly, if I was honest, I'd have to admit that the fault lay with me. I just hit too damned hard.

During the course of the day Ranaj hired on a wersting pack. Their controller was Hikdar Nalan C'Cardieth, whose last employer had embarked upon a hazardous overseas holy pilgrimage to the birthplace of Benga Prodacta, one of the patron saints of sandal makers. He gave the Hikdar a glowing reference. We were very quickly left in no doubt that C'Cardieth was enormously proud of his double-initialed name, as a cadet branch of a famous family. Fweygo and I did not tease him on that score.

Anyway, his pack of werstings were a most ferocious bunch. The four-legged black and white striped hunting dogs, vicious, always in turmoil, should prove a most efficacious deterrent to further assassination attempts. These animals were dogs, yet I knew that, like the hyenas of Earth, they were born with fangs, and the moment their caul was licked clean by their mother they'd fight savagely amongst themselves for subsequent supremacy among their fellows. I was glad Hikdar Nalan and his assistants kept the animals on strong leashes.

The very next morning as ever was another murder was reported. Tansi the Lily had had her throat cut and been disemboweled on the steps of the somber Temple to the red god of blood—Dokerty.

Seventeen

That day Naghan Raerdu sent word that the body of an ordinary man had been stumbled upon in the gutter perhaps half a hundred paces from the house where the ibmanzy had caused such confusion. The fellow was thin to the point of emaciation, as though the life had been drained out of him. He wore a red robe. Pieces of skin were dislodged from his fingernails, and he was smeared in blood.

Down in the warrens where life in the favelas was cheap no one took much notice of another dead body in the gutter. The Watch had him taken up. He'd probably end up in the crematorium where the ovens disposed of corpses properly, under strict supervision. There was little room for burial grounds down in the canyons and the poor folk could not afford to avail themselves of the cemeteries outside the city.

No one claimed him before the funeral service. It was certain sure no one would claim his ashes.

He was, I felt convinced, the poor devil who'd been turned into the ibmanzy.

Also on that day the familiar blue radiance formed as I practiced alone in the salle d'armes. A face looked out from the blueness. This was not the face of Deb-Lu nor yet of Khe-Hi. It was not, and for this I was profoundly grateful, it was not the face of the fumbling sorcerer recently imported by Khon the Mak.

There was little color in the features, save for the scarlet mouth. The hair was red, as any self-respecting wizard from Loh should have. Blue were the eyes in that sculptured face, formed as though by the hand of a master craftsman from the ivory of Chem, firm of rounded chin, with not a single trace of sagging skin anywhere. The scarlet mouth widened and now that was not a mere movement of the lips but a genuine smile, warm and affectionate.

"Ling-Li!" I said. "Lahal!"

"Lahal, Dray. Everyone is so busy these days; but we are anxious to do all we can whilst you—ah—potter about here in Balintol."

I felt my lips start to rick into a grimace, and so stopped that betrayal to what I had to do here.

"There's a new damned Wizard of Loh poking and prying about in Oxonium." I went on to tell her what had happened and she promised to make immediate enquiries. The Wizards and Witches of Loh like to keep track of what their associates are up to.

I asked after her husband, Khe-Hi, and the children and she gave me the latest news on the folk at Esser Rarioch that I so hungered to learn. Delia was off somewhere, and I knew she was, as was I, about the business of the Star Lords.

Just before we parted, I mentioned casually: "Oh, and Ling-Li, you might let Deb-Lu know I found an object of antiquity that should interest him. It's a trident engraved with the old signs and language of Loh. I—"

She interrupted. "You have it?"

"Nope. It was left lying about when we had trouble with that blasted ibmanzy."

She pursed those red lips. "Deb-Lu will be interested, yes, and cross because you lost it, Dray."

"It was very old and I was busy and I didn't give another thought to it."

Among the information she gave was the satisfying fact that Dimpy's mother Velda and his sisters were safely in Valkanium. A letter would follow. Among many of the cultures of Kregen where there are people who cannot read or write a somewhat more subtle system of making one's mark at the foot of the paper against your name written by the scribe is in being. Signet rings which, instead of being impressed in a wax seal, are smeared with ink and then stamped alongside the written name. There are millions of different identification rings, called queyfors, and whilst forgery is a fine art on Kregen, the system does give some guarantees.

Dimpy would recognize the mark made by his mother's queyfor.

The various knocks and cuts I'd been taking recently all cleared up with the miraculous speed conferred by my dips in the Sacred Pool of far Aphrasöe. Mother Firben, clicking that needle-sharp tongue of hers, had rubbed garlic into the wounds, a sure preventative of gangrene. Mind you, if I'd had decent weapons in my fists I might not have been so easily cut up, by Krun.

As Princess Nandisha told me, briskly, she was pleased I was healing. She wanted Fweygo and me near her with Ranaj, and she was not too enamored of plug-uglies with unhealed wounds in her vicinity.

This was as we set off for the palace of the Kings of Tolindrin. Apparently there was some argument among the priests connected with the earthquake of unhappy memory. Just about everyone went. Ranaj did not intend to leave any of his charges as hostages to fortune. Hikdar Nalan C'Cardieth and his pack of snarling werstings preceded us through the streets. I, for one, was glad they were there and on our side. Too right, by Krun!

When I discovered the reason for this conclave I lost a great deal of interest in the proceedings. Instead, I took note of the people gathered here, in a sizeable chamber of Tom's palace. The debate, hotly contested with much rhetoric and waving of arms, consisted of the chief priests of Tolaar and Dokerty claiming the right to crown Tom king. It was generally conceded that the earthquake was a direct reproof, a sure sign that the priests of Cymbaro were unfit to place the crown on Tom's head. Some went so far as to suggest that no one of Cymbaro should be anywhere near the coronation.

On the way we passed two mobs, all shrieking and waving cudgels and throwing brickbats. One gang shrilled abuse outside the Temple of Dokerty, accusing the red-robed priests of committing the series of horrific murders. The other gang was yelling outside the Temple of Tolaar. Among them, I suspected, were very many agitators paid by the Dokerty hierarchy to draw attention away from themselves.

Now, in the meeting, San Volar, with some pretensions to authority as the chief priest of the largest religion, suggested in his languid way that perhaps Dokerty, too, was not fit to conduct the ceremony. The chief priest of Dokerty—a large, almost bloated man, with the flushed face and breaking veins of one who indulges too freely in the good things of life—violently objected. He was clad in a red robe from neck to feet. His shoes were red. His hat was red. He was all red.

"I categorically deny that these murders are anything to do with Dokerty!" He was passionate, wrought up, seeming ready to burst into flames.

"Everything, San Cronal, points to the opposite." San Volar spoke in his quiet, lisping way, vastly enjoying making this huge red-bloated fellow squirm.

There were a few other priests there, representing some of the minor cults. They appeared a timid bunch, seeking only to secure a small place for themselves in the rituals.

A single look at Khon the Mak's entourage told me that my engaging sparring-partner, Dagert of Paylen, a most rascally gentleman, was not in attendance. Khon the Mak and Prince Ortyg spent the time glaring daggers one at the other.

With red jowls all aquiver: "My name, San Volar, as you very well know, is San C'Cronal."

Tom, sitting tiredly in a chair overseeing this quarrelsome gathering, raised a hand for silence. He tried to calm them down and to apportion certain parts of the ceremonies to various religions. I stopped listening and took stock of these great ones of the land, with their entourages backing them, as we backed Nandisha. Our werstings, of course, had been left outside, and as others had their own packs of savage dogs the leashes would be severely strained.

With San Paynor and the Cymbaro delegation I was surprised and pleased to see San Duven. He looked fit, slightly tanned from his travels, very upright. The way the meeting was arranged, with the principals in a circle around Tom and we supporters to the rear, meant I had only occasional glimpses of everyone. Hyr Kov Brannomar, after Tom the most powerful man in the kingdom, said very little. He knew I was Dray Prescot. He gave me a look when he spotted me among the crowd, a raised eyebrow, a half-smile, and then a turn away.

The wrangling went on. I shifted my feet, bored to tears. In that, as on many previous occasions on Kregen, I was very wrong.

Standing belligerently in the forefront of Prince Ortyg's followers Jiktar Nath ti Fangenun scowled at us. A large, florid man, with the shoulders of an ox, he looked like and was—as we knew to our cost—a great deal of trouble.

Presently the time came for the private part of the conference. All us followers trooped out and there was a lot of petty bickering as to precedence, a certain amount of shoving. Protocol and the importance of rank duly observed were vital facts in the lives of these high flown folk and their retainers.

I didn't give a damn where I landed up in the mob surging out. Ranaj said, curtly: "We take our proper precedence, Drajak. We owe it to the dignity of our mistress."

Well, by Krun, you couldn't say fairer than that.

The parties lounged about outside. Jiktar Nath ti Fangenun sauntered over. He eyed us and then focused his gaze on me.

"I shall know you again, blintz."

Fweygo did not stir at my shoulder. Ranaj started to say something and

I cut in, sharply, with: "You and your men slew our good comrades. If you want to make something of it, step out into that garden. I am at your disposal." He wore rapier and dagger.

Slowly he shook his head, face mottling.

"I think not."

"Then," snarled Ranaj. "Schtump! Clear off, blintz."

There was a much more pleasant reunion as I spoke to Duven. He looked fit, bursting with energy, his every word indicating his absolute dedication to Cymbaro. I congratulated him on his courageous actions during the earthquake in brief soldierly words, not in any sickly fashion. Everything, he declaimed, was done at the behest of Cymbaro, who gave him the strength and purpose of will.

I said: "You went and returned from Farinsee very quickly."

"Oh," he said. "I took a lifter."

"And Tiri?"

"I unfortunately did not have that pleasure."

"A pity."

He excused himself and went off and the moment he'd gone a lithe slip of a girl glided up to me. She was not slave, for she wore a revealing dark green shamlak and flowers in her corn gold hair.

As she passed she pressed a note in my hand. Then she was gone, skipping away with her long slender legs splendid in the lights.

Being a fellow used to wearisome intrigues I waited until I was sure no one observed me before opening the note. It was from Hyr Kov Brannomar. It requested an audience. Would I meet him at The Golden Zorca, a very private and high class establishment.

Now, having boasted of how wonderful I, Dray Prescot, was at the intrigue business, I now found myself slung by my own varter, as they say in Clishdrin. I'd stepped away from the crowd to the ornate gate to the little enclosed garden. A net descended over my head and I was brutally hauled in like a catch of fish, flung headlong to the ground beyond the gate and wall. The gate slammed shut.

"Right, you blintz!" came the voice of Nath ti Fangenun. "You asked me to step into the garden." I rolled about in the net thrashing helplessly. "Here I am!"

Eighteen

He wasn't alone.

Well, he wouldn't be, would he, the cramph.

Nets are devilish things to get out of quickly, as I knew only too well. Useless to try to draw my knife and cut through. I took a strand in each fist and in the instant I savagely burst them apart a cracking great clout laid alongside my head and over I went. Instead of trying to rise, as these bully boys expected, I went on with the roll. Two of the net's strands parted and I started on the next square. A hard-toed boot crashed into my ribs and I let out a gasp. By Krun! These plug-uglies meant business!

More net strands parted and I fixed a most malicious eye on my attackers. A big Rapa jumped in to kick me again and I rolled away. On the other side another Rapa brought a damned great cudgel down. Going on with the roll I collided with his legs and swept them away from under him. He fell on top of me and before I could heave him aside his mate kicked him in mistake for me. That was quite pleasant.

My head was free and the last couple of bits of net dangled as I stood up. I gave the second Rapa a good kick as I did so.

They'd been kicking me and hitting me with bludgeons. This did not mean they did not intend to kill me. They wanted to have their perverted idea of a bit of fun first.

By this time I was so bitter and frustrated about the whole lousy situation in Oxonium I had no such inhibitions.

In a scrap of this kind the rapier would be the best weapon.

Out came the Jiktar with that sliding snick of a professional fighting man and the companion hikdar followed, snugging into my left hand.

I jumped for my attackers.

Standing at the back waiting their turn to kick and beat me, a polsim and a Brokelsh saw my face. They turned and ran.

The two Rapas were not so quick.

At the very last moment I deflected my blades so that, instead of killing them stone dead outright, I pinked them where it would hurt. They yowled, feathers extremely ruffled, and ran off.

Blades up, I faced Nath ti Fangenun.

Give the rast his due, he hadn't run off. He stood there, rapier and main gauche poised, watching me.

"I see, blintz, you have some skill—" he started to prattle on.

I just jumped in, slid his blades with the dagger, and hit him an almighty clout around the head. He toppled backwards, a glazed look sweeping over his eyes. He dropped his sword and dagger. He fell down. And I, Dray Prescot, drew back my foot to let him have a good one in the ribs.

I stood there, balanced on one foot, still feeling the blood pounding in me. By the disgusting diseased nostrils and dangling eyeballs of Makki Grodno! Was this what all this nonsense was bringing me to? Nasty little brawls in quiet gardens. Kicking a man when he was down? The rast wasn't worth soiling my boot on.

Thrusting the unbloodied weapons back into scabbards I gave a last malignant look at the unconscious Jiktar, and took myself off.

Mind you, a little brisk exercise gets the old blood tingling around the veins and arteries again, by Vox!

Nobody appeared to have heard the fracas, and in truth there had not been a great deal of noise. By the time our principals emerged from their secret conclave, Fangenun and his cronies were back on duty with their fellows. The two Rapas were wearing bandages. Ranaj gave me a long look; but said nothing. There was a great deal of hubbub which quietened down as the great ones took up their positions with their retainers.

With the werstings snarling and growling before us we wended our way back to Nandisha's palace.

When Dimpy heard there was no news of Tiri he looked morose. He was most restless. So I suggested when I got off duty late that evening we went along to the Temple of Cymbaro to see if anything had been heard of our dancing lady friend.

Dimpy brightened up at once.

After the hour of mid the young princess Nisha decided she wanted to go shopping. Naturally the lion maid, Rofi, would accompany her. I was detailed as part of the escort whilst Fweygo remained with the others at the palace. The princess was in a most playful mood and she and Rofi chattered like parakeets. I own I sighed for them, two young scraps of humanity trying to be cheerful and grow up into the hostile environment of Kregen. As a job, protecting them was not unwelcome, save—save for the ache for Delia and Esser Rarioch.

Thankfully, nothing untoward occurred during the shopping expedition. When I spotted a handsome red shamlak on a stall in the market I weakened. The loops and embroidery were a dull yellow, and the whole garment was in the best of taste. I could wear it off duty. So I bought it. Then we all trooped back to the palace for tea.

Although I say nothing untoward happened there were, of course, a couple of the quarrels erupting into fights going on in the market. We guards kept our charges well clear. The sense of oppressive thunder hanging over Oxonium portended worse and worse outbreaks to come. And, through it all, we had a fellow who did not want to be king, broodingly awaiting his coronation.

What the result of the meeting of the high ones might be was not at this stage revealed to us common folk. After trying to sort Dimpy with news of Tiri at the shrine to Cymbaro I'd have to go along to The Golden Zorca to meet Brannomar. He might vouchsafe the information. All the same, it meant little to me.

When, at last, I came off duty I put on that splendid new rose red shamlak. It fitted well. Hitching up my weaponry and with Dimpy in tow, off I sallied to see San Paynor. If Duven was there we might have a jar or two.

Logan met us and after a little time we were admitted to San Paynor's outer study. The temple lay quietly at this time, for the banging, slamming, shouting workmen had all gone home. It was very peaceful. Paynor looked up from architect's plans to greet us.

"Some of the old passageways were brought down and others blocked," he told us. "We're worried in case the foundations are faulty." He went on to say that, like all the buildings, a maze of tunnels existed under the temple. Many had odd exits long forgotten. We drank a fine pale wine, Dimpy as well; but there was no news of Tiri. Dimpy sat silently, his glass clutched hard between his fingers.

"Duven?" said Paynor. "Ah—you've just missed him. He's gone out to minister to a sick parishioner, a vegetable merchant in Momolam Street."

I looked a question. Unexpectedly, Dimpy piped up. "I know that place. The Hill of Dancing Ghosts."

"We generally call it Barter Hill," smiled Paynor.

There was some time yet so I suggested we went across to The Hill of Dancing Ghosts. We might bump into Duven. In any event, the places would still be open and we could have our jar. Dimpy agreed and we said the remberees.

Taking the cable cars we soared out over the lower spaces. The lights were just coming on in the city and glowed like fairy lamps from the hills. Down below spits and sparks of light glimmered up. The young bloods would be decking themselves in their best and venturing down for their dark enjoyments. The cutthroats would be sharpening their knives. The cutpurses would be making sure their cunning curved blades were ready for the lightning slash. Was there in all this busy anticipatory activity some innocent young girl somewhere walking home destined to die, to be ripped to shreds this night?

One fact could not escape notice. Not one of the murder victims had been a devotee of Dokerty.

Momolam Street ran at the back of an avenue leading to the Kyro of Nath the Haggler. Dimpy glanced quickly up at me in the lanternlight. He must be thinking what I was, that here was the place we first met.

Everything was running flat out, the last of the day traders still hoping for last minute sales, the night hawks opening up. We passed a patrol of the City Guard, hard-faced, grim in armor. They could not be everywhere. They'd cut the size of the patrols down in order to increase the number. The vegetable shop stood at the corner of an alley evilly lit. Beside it lanternlight showed the facade of a temple to one of the minor cults, The Most Puissant Nethized, and as though to mock the very insignificance of Nethized, a more imposing frontage of a temple to Dokerty rose opposite.

The worried woman who answered our knock told us that her husband was very ill, the needleman was with him, and San Duven, may Cymbaro be praised, had spoken powerful words on the sick man's behalf. As for San Duven himself, that great man had just left.

"He went down Cabbage Alley past the grading sheds."

We thanked her and then decided to follow Duven. Cabbage Alley smelled of the obvious. The lights were few and scattered. At the end where the alley joined the main avenue, lanternlight splashed a streak of brilliance into the dimness. From that direction came the muted hubbub of people about their various businesses.

We walked along steadily. Perhaps Duven had gone this way to take the opposite cable car to a different destination. He must be kept busy doing the visiting rounds for the folk of Cymbaro.

A thin bubbling scream scythed into the air. That shriek held all of terror and doom and death in its unearthly screech. At once it was cut off. The silence seemed to fall in after that hellish sound.

Dimpy and I sprang forward. "Stop! Murderer!"

Against the avenue lights the dark contorted silhouette of a man scrambled away, robes flapping. We followed—fast.

Dimpy fell over the body.

The silhouette vanished around the corner into the avenue and I stumbled as Dimpy crashed into me, so violent was his reaction to get away from the corpse.

I looked down.

There was light enough to see the gash in her throat, the dark blood, the terror branded on the pretty, innocent face. She must work at the grading sheds. Poor thing; there had been warnings enough about young girls walking alone at night.

Straightening up, I said: "Come on. We might catch the blintz along the avenue."

That heart-rending scream had attracted other attentions besides ours. A patrol of the City Guard debouched into the alley from the avenue. Their lantern light flared upon the scene, upon the dead girl, on Dimpy, on me just straightening up from the dead body. The guardsmen let out a snarling growl of anger.

Many of the great ones had detailed members of their personal guard to assist the City Guard. One of those armored figures ahead recognized me.

"Stand still! Drajak known as the Sudden! Bloody murderer! Stay where you are!"

"Not likely!" I ripped out. There'd be no mercy from those men. I doubted if I'd reach their headquarters in one piece. The case was open and shut.

The guardsmen started down towards us, armor clanking.

"Come on, sunbeam," I said. "Run!"

Nineteen

"I'd never have believed San Duven could've done these 'orrible murders," said Dimpy.

I felt the shock. "Dimpy! You can't really believe Duven is guilty!"

We crouched in a dark doorway. We'd thrown off that first pursuit and now we were getting our breaths back.

"We saw him! Didn't we?"

"We saw a dark figure—"

"And the vegetable lady told us he'd gone down Cabbage Alley."

"All the same—" I shook my head. "If the murders are not the work of Dokerty, then my guess was that Prince Ortyg had put some of his gang up to it. That way he'd hit directly at Khon the Mak who is a strong Dokerty supporter."

Dimpy didn't reply. He had a tough and resilient young mind and he'd seen plenty of unpleasant things in his seasons on Kregen. It was easier for him to believe in Duven's guilt.

He spelled out the obvious when he said that now the City Guard had me down for the crimes, they'd block all the cable car exits. Any known way off the hill would be guarded. All lifters would be watched. They had me trapped.

I didn't tell Dimpy that if I could reach the Vallian Embassy I'd be safe. Then I'd contact Kov Brannomar and he'd straighten out this mess.

Also, if I could get word to Naghan Raerdu the Barrel, probably through Milsi the Slinky, he would be a tower of strength.

So, it wasn't all gloom and doom in this desperate situation.

Dimpy brought those daydreams down to earth with a bump.

"They'll never give up till they catch you. I'll tell 'em you didn't do it, in course. But they won't believe me."

Would Brannomar believe I was innocent?

"And you ain't going to get off here easy, I can tell you that."

"No," I half groaned. "You're right."

"I gotta idea."

His voice hardened. I supposed it had occurred to him that if the City Guard caught us, Dimpy would be judged as guilty as was I, for he'd been there, standing over the body with me.

"Come on, Drajak. Lessee what we can do."

So off we went, skulking like a pair of ghosts on the Hill of Dancing Ghosts. Dimpy knew his way about here, for, as he'd told me, this was a favorite stamping ground of the robber gangs.

Inevitably, we were spotted.

We'd just cautiously crossed from one alley to another. My description must have been broadcast by the patrols, for a shout lifted, high and shrill.

"That's him! Drajak the Sudden! Murderer!"

By the pendulous purple jowls of the Divine Lady of Belschutz! What a stinking mess we were in! We hared off at once into the shadows and in no time at all a howling mob formed and roared after us like a pack of werstings on the loose.

One of the many problems besetting me now was that if a person tried to stop me he would be an ordinary honest upright citizen helping the guard to arrest a despicable mass murderer. He'd be trying to do his civic duty. I certainly couldn't kill him.

We shot across the next street like two bolts from arbalests. The yells at our backs intensified. The next alley, ill lit, showed a line of dark back entrances. Dimpy spotted a broken window and hared across to it. I hesitated. Then I followed him.

If the mob sussed out we'd ducked in here we might find ourselves completely trapped. But there was a chance they'd go storming on and out of sight.

The window eased open under Dimpy's professional expertise. We squeezed through and the window closed at our backs. Utter darkness stretched ahead. There was a strange smell on the air.

Dimpy sniffed. "Kaff." He spoke in a disgusted tone.

We groped forward. The racketing noise of the mob swelled at our backs, crescendoed—and then, blessedly, faded.

A wall came up and hit me on the nose. I did not swear. Feeling along, my fingers encountered a handle. I couldn't see Dimpy; but I could hear his light breathing. Quite an athlete, young Dimpy. Taking a breath, I turned the handle and pushed the door in.

A low pinkish radiance from a shielded lamp revealed a double row of low beds. Each bed held a man. They were not in this world. The stink of Kaff invaded my nostrils. They were all stoned to the eyeballs.

Dimpy, like a sinuous wraith, glided ahead between the rows. At the far end a door stood ajar and we peered around the jamb.

A hulking great Undurker, his borzoi nose in the air, was reading a book. He looked up, eyes widening. I leaped. He went to sleep and I trusted to Djan that he was not too injured.

"'Orrible stuff, Kaff," quoth Dimpy. "You should have hit him harder."

"You have to feel sorry for folk who indulge. It's their funeral."

"Yes. Come on. It's not much further."

We exited through the far door onto a street where the torches flared, and skulked along. On the next turning Dimpy turned down it and a few doors along stopped before a shopfront. The establishment was a carpet store.

"This is where the Hellraisers came up that day."

I looked at the shop. It was nondescript, a likely place for the gang members to leave when they'd made the ascent. Dimpy tried the door. The place was in darkness and naturally the door was bolted.

"Give us a moment."

He worked busily. Then the door creaked open. In we went.

I fell over a carpet, and cursed. Dimpy produced a tinder box, and when we had a light, we explored. Dimpy spent some time prodding and prying at the floor. By his face I knew the news was not good.

"They've sealed it up." He sounded exasperated.

"I'm not surprised. You were being chased and they must have reasoned you were arrested. You'd tell where this place was."

He looked murderous in the lamplight. "That Sleed!"

"Don't fret—"

"I'm not! Come on. There's still a chance."

He extinguished the light and we went back out into the street. My splendid new red shamlak had been partly the cause of my predicament. The red of the shamlak had been immediately equated with the red of Dokerty, the red of the scrap of cloth found in the hand of Jenni Farlang, who'd worked in a jeweler's shop.

Although I'd so coolly told Dimpy not to fret, I was, myself, seething with frustration and disappointment. We could so easily have gone down the way Dimpy and the Hellraiser recruits had come up. I kept my futile anger to myself. Dimpy was doing splendidly and I did not want to jeopardize his confidence.

There were two obvious courses of action that might be followed, one initiated by me, the other not.

Using the skills taught by Deb-Lu I could change my face around. I could grab some fresh clothes, discard the braxters. I was enormously reluctant to abandon the rapier and main gauche; but if it came to a choice between those and my life, the decision was obvious. Even then, there'd be no cast iron guarantee of success. And Dimpy in that scenario?

He was the reason the other course of action could not be followed. The Star Lords might—might, ha!—reach down and hoick me out of this mess. They'd probably want to talk to me and to discipline me. I'd not had so much of that lately as in the old days. Then they'd hurl me back to guard the numim twins. I did not want that to happen; I didn't want to leave Dimpy alone, and hunted.

Anyway, even if the Everoinye returned me to duty, that fact would soon be known and the City Guard would be around Nandisha's palace seeking my hide.

Mind you, if my plan succeeded and I reached Brannomar first, everything would turn out for the best. I'd just have to convince the Hyr Kov that the Emperor of All Paz didn't go around murdering sweet young girls and chopping them up.

Dimpy leading, we scuttled through the mottled shadows.

You could say this for Dimpy—he was the complete expert at keeping a low profile, of stealthily creeping along, of avoiding observation, of taking full advantage of every shadow. By Vox, you could say it, and it was true! Mind you, as an old leem-hunter I'd been at this game longer than he had. So we skulked along the streets, using the shadows, halting at the slightest sound, two fugitives from justice.

Waiting patiently for some time at a corner, he took careful stock of the street and of the shopfronts lining it. Eventually he motioned and we padded across to a cake shop. It was a middling establishment, emblazoned with the name Nath's Cake and Bun Emporium, and, of course, it was locked up for the night. Dimpy had us in there in no time.

The place was not abandoned but in business and Dimpy said they'd be new owners. We went down into the cellar where Dimpy prodded and pried as he had before. He grunted as he heaved up a trapdoor. A ladder led down into darkness.

"We Roaring Fifties used this." He sighed. "Them was the days." A lamp on a shelf was quickly lighted. We went down into the depths. I, for one, wondered just what I was getting myself into.

Very soon the way down changed from a ladder to a stone-walled passage, past an iron-barred door, into rough-hewn tunnels. The way was steep and treacherous. Nitre shone on the walls. The air smelled musty and stale. There was the stink of sulphur.

Dimpy was trying to go along at a breakneck speed.

"Apart from lack of food and drink," I told him, "we're not in any tearing hurry. The longer they can't find us aloft, the more they'll slacken their search."

He slowed down a trifle—not by much, by Krun!

The adventure down the tunnels was accompanied by many alarms and excursions. We met none of the skinned apes. We did run into a prowling praxul.

The thing's warty scaled hide bulked shoulder high for it was a full grown adult. Its three stalked eyes surveyed us in the luminosity of the lichen, and writhed away as the lanternlight fell across its head.

It hissed, its claws slicing the musky air.

Dimpy hauled out his braxter. I did likewise. Side by side we confronted the praxul.

I had the light. I swung it violently forward and the praxul backed, hissing.

"He stinks like garbage left in an alley for a sennight," I said. "Phew!"

Even as I spoke Dimpy leaped in and slashed. He missed the eye and jumped back, avoiding the return slash of the lethal claws. Watching for an opening as the thing weaved from side to side, I saw a chance, slid in, slashed, missed, and managed to skip back. The lights and shadows writhed madly along the walls and roof.

The lamp might not be essential now we had left the darkness of the ladders down and were in the luminance of the lichen. Stepping back I placed the lamp carefully down, keeping my gaze fixed on the praxul. Had our light been a torch, of course, we'd have singed the beastie to a nice crispy toast.

Unencumbered and using two swords I attacked again as Dimpy put in a distracting side feint. Two stalked eyes flew up into the air.

As always, as always, I felt sorry for the poor thing. It screeched and stank and turned around. Whining and howling it scuttled off into the confusing shadows.

We went on and down resolutely, alertly. All the time I kept wondering why the Everoinye had not plucked me up out of the tunnels and set me down to my duty. Why?

When the blue radiance formed Dimpy remained in complete ignorance of the phantasmal presence of a Witch of Loh. He could not hear Ling-Li or me. Her Ivory of Chem face looked as gravely beautiful as ever. "Gron-Arm-Chenlang. That's his name. Recently graduated."

"I supposed," I said drily.

"Deb-Lu at first was concerned he might not be a true Wizard of Loh—of Walfarg. Khe-Hi, too, was worried lest he was a—"

"Yes?"

She touched her lips with an exquisite finger. "Balintol is famous for sorcery, Dray. The old king in Tolindrin tried to suppress some of them because they were becoming too powerful."

"I've only heard of low level mages here."

"Quite. It is better that way. Oh, and the trident. Deb-Lu is looking into that matter."

When I suggested she might like to give us directions as to the best way of getting out of this maze, and of contacting our ambassador when we did, she gave an immediate assent. Her directions were lucid and easily followed. After she had gone and Dimpy was with me again, as we went on down I saw that he was following Ling-Li's suggested route. We met a couple more nasty moments. But working together we came through unscathed and, at blessed last, debouched from the hole in the cliff face leading onto a side alleyway.

The mingled and wonderfully exotic aromas of the warrens wafted into my nostrils. There was little noise for it was near morning and the dopa dens and their ilk had at last closed. We crept out.

"This was all Roaring Fifties territory. Now it's Hellraisers'." He sounded bitter. We paused at the corner of the street.

"Can you guide us to Skullbiter territory, Dimpy?"

He looked his surprise. "Why? Yes, of course I can; but—"

"Homespun Street."

"Yes. Off Umpitor Kyro. The Katakis have a watchhouse there."

"Nagzalla's Nasty Neemus. They'll help."

He looked more than a little incredulous. He started to say something, shook his head, and didn't.

At this hour the gangs would not in the normal way be active. We had to be carefully on the lookout for the City Watch. That rabble would be only too happy to take up unwary pedestrians. The Kataki officers would gloat at the chance of a few more slaves. We went along the darkened streets between the hills with extreme caution.

One of the lesser moons of Kregen shot past above, a glinting spark one moment, gone the next.

There was little traffic along the cableways overhead. The place was not completely silent—what great city ever is?—a dog barked, carts rumbled complainingly, and a couple of late roisterers staggered past. I didn't give much for their chances, the famblys.

Although we'd rested on and off in the descent, Dimpy was obviously tired. We were both famished. We were still in one hell of a mess, and far from safely out of it yet.

Umpitor Kyro with its watchhouse was a major obstacle.

Dimpy tapped his foot nervously on the ground as we peered across the square. Homespun Street at our backs was beginning to think of coming to life for the next day. The Suns of Scorpio would not shine down here for a long time yet; people were up and about by the lights of lamps and torches. The whole place held that hushed air of expectancy ready to herald a fresh beginning.

A light voice at our backs said: "I've been following you, Dimpy. What you up to, then? And who's your big friend?"

We spun about. I'd been so watching out for the Katakis this young girl had followed us completely unobserved. I crushed down my annoyance at the mistake.

"Come on, Dimpy! By Ferzakl, I didn't expect to see you again!"

She was a Hytak, a fine strong girl with good features and a splendid body. She fingered the sheath of the dagger at her belt. Dimpy swallowed.

"Big Balla! Well—it's a long story."

I cut in, and to Dimpy's surprise said my name was Kadar the Hammer. Very forcefully, using that sometimes hateful power of the yrium, I explained some of the situation, and told Big Balla we were going up onto the hill. Her reply, I suppose, shouldn't have surprised me. Not when all the circumstances were taken into consideration. Dimpy's response was immediate.

"Can she come with us? I mean—what with Sleed the Slick—"

"He's worse than being chased, is he?"

"Too true, by Ferzakl!"

This Sleed clearly was an unpleasant character, and I could see Dimpy was fond of Big Balla. If only for his sake I'd have to accede. All the same, it could prove an inconvenience, to say the least, by Krun.

"We have to get across to Nagzalla territory."

"Nath Market Street," said Big Balla. "They just took it."

"Aye."

So, the blessed fates had taken a hand again, for Big Balla simply organized our expedition to cut through an alley and then go through a house whose occupants she knew. An advang family, they were up and preparing themselves for the day's labors. They let us through without fuss, Big Balla thanked them, and we walked smartly along to Nath Market Street.

All the time the nagging sense of this whole scenario being, as it were, wrong, oppressed me. Why, for the sweet sake of Jaz the Impedimenter, hadn't the Star Lords taken me up and slapped me down again to my duty with the numim twins? Why? Had we failed? Had Fweygo been slain and the numims slaughtered? Was that the reason my presence there was no longer required?

Once into Nagzalla territory a very few enquiries brought me face to face with Brory the Bold. He came out from an inner room rubbing sleep from his eyes. As the curtains swished to there was just a glimpse of the maiden he'd claimed in marriage sitting up in bed. Her hair was ruffled; her face looked happy, which pleased me.

"Kadar the Hammer! By Reder—where've you been?"

I gave him a garbled account of being trapped in the hill and went on to request his help in getting us away. He looked undecided. A fresh round of the war against the Volcanoes was about to begin. He'd appreciate it if I'd help. So, once more, that imperious Dray Prescot yrium had to flash forth. Overpowering him, I demanded assistance.

The Neemus had their entrances and exits. There were ways up.

Both Dimpy and Big Balla remained subdued. Here they were with a gang with whom, in the not too distant future, their own gang might be at war for territory and control of the rackets.

The first priority was food and drink. We sat down to a good Kregan meal. If Ling-Li could organize it with our ambassador a voller might fly down for us. That would be nice. I did not count on it. Big Brory would have to come through.

We needed sleep and quarters were found. Dimpy said: "Can we trust these Nasty Neemus? They looked at our shamlaks a bit hard."

"My wonderful show-off red shamlak," I said, with more self-mockery than useless bitterness. "That contributed to our misfortunes."

Dimpy grunted and curled up in his blanket.

If the Everoinye didn't call for me then there was no breakneck rush on my part to return up top. A good sleep, some more grub, and with a hitch to my belt I'd be ready. I slept.

That evening when we awoke Brory reported he'd organized a party to go through the hill. It was not safe for a few people. He was humming a little song, "Nandy Nath's Blind Pilgrimage" which, given the circumstances, was either in very bad taste or was grimly prophetic of disaster within the hill. His new wife came in and, in truth, she looked happy. We ate again, and drank sparingly, and then it was time for the off. I thanked Brory sincerely; but I also left him in no doubt that I had other fish to fry than joining the Neemus.

He'd put another Brokelsh, Brango the Toriner, in command of the party, a fellow with a bent nose and an oddly high-pitched voice.

We went through a quiet dormitory section and came out onto a cross street with its cable supporting tower without a Kataki watch house. Across the way the torches flared, people shouted, the night's doings were well under way. The noise increased alarmingly.

A mob abruptly materialized. Helter-skelter they ran madly past us, screaming. Brango grabbed a Gon and shook him. "What!"

"The Screaming Leems!" The Gon was almost incoherent with fear. "They've busted through the Cherry Chavonths! We're all doomed!"

"By the Resplendent Bridzilkelsh!" Brango looked wild. "The Screaming Leems have had this planned all along! I've gotta get back and warn Brory!"

As he spoke the ground moved beneath our feet.

Chunks of stone dislodged from the sides of the canyons began to fall about our ears. The noise boomed up drowning the pitiful shrieks of the humans trapped in their slots of darkness.

The tremor shook everything savagely. We staggered as though dopa drunk. A zorca-sized slab fell on a polsim who vanished save for arms and feet and spraying blood.

"Come on!"

I yanked Big Balla by the arm and with Dimpy we fled for the side wall, lurching as the ground lurched.

"By the slime-infested intestines and the maggoty eyeballs of Makki Grodno! This would have to happen now!"

The whole of Kregen, it seemed, roared and rattled and rumbled about us. Dust swirled madly everywhere. We crouched hard against the side wall as the hill above our heads disintegrated.

Mites of humanity, we waited for the end of the world.

Twenty

With Dimpy at one end and me at the other we heaved the slab up and toppled it aside. The mess of black blood and splintered yellow bones underneath had been a woman and her child.

The world had not come to an end. But it seemed not far off to the folk down here working like ants to clear away debris. There might still be people trapped. We found some alive; a couple of days later we were uncovering only dead bodies. We worked, ate and drank, slept when we fell. We wore scarves over our mouths and nostrils. The sights were piti-ful, ugly, depressing. The spirit of the folk of the warrens was splendid. They toiled without stint. Members of opposing gangs worked side by side, enmities forgotten. Oh yes, in bringing death and destruction, the forces of nature can also bring out the best in humanity.

There was looting, of course. Looters who were caught received short shrift.

The cable car tower had fallen, trailing lines. One odd and interesting, if expected, fact of note was the complete absence of the City Watch. The Katakis and their masichieri scum had all been summoned aloft to assist the great ones as they cleared up.

Still, through all the horror, the Star Lords had not summoned me. What in a Herrelldrin Hell had happened to Fweygo, Nandisha, the chil-dren? It had seemed to me the only honorable course of action to stay and assist these people who had shown friendship to my friends and me. Dimpy and Big Balla slaved as we all slaved. Loyalty to new friends down here and to be shown. All the same, what was going on up there, above our heads, among the palaces and temples?

In some countries of two worlds the houses of the poor folk fall down of their own accord from time to time without the assisting nudge of an earthquake. The swathes of destruction along the streets was heartrending; rubble, shattered timbers, odd angles of wood and stone, all jumbled in dust-clogged piles. Three days after the shock Dimpy and I, smothered in dust and dirt, turned over a slab and to our consternation heard a faint cry. Frantically we dug, hauling blocks away, carefully making sure nothing would tumble down. We found a young girl about Tiri's age with smashed legs under a beam. She held a dead baby in her arms, and her granny lay in a black-blood pool at her side. She was not quite mad yet. Her face looked like a shriveled leather shoe. We carried her out. What else was there we could do? What was her life to be now?

The gangs organized food supplies. Brory told me with grim satisfaction that he'd led a raid that had taken up some of the rich farm produce destined for the hills. The carts had been intercepted, the guards slain or driven off, and then galloped into the dark slots between the hills. We all fed well that day. A few days after that, a very brief visit from Ling-Li told me Ambassador Invordun requested me to be at the center of the ruined kyro at the hour of dim.

I heaved a sigh of relief. We had done what we could to assist down here. Now I must find out what had been going on in the world above.

So it was with something of a tremble of apprehension I observed the fantamyrrh boarding the airboat. Dimpy and Big Balla followed. For them this was a fresh adventure. For me it might be the end of all my adventuring on the terrible and mysterious world of Kregen.

The red eye-patch looked like the black eyesocket of a skull as Nalgre ti Poventer greeted me. She of the Veils was up, riding the night sky between the stars. A gleam of roseate light struck a long curved shine from the Gon's shaven head.

The voller lifted and soared up and out of the chill horrors of the warrens. Nalgre told me that much of Oxonium had been knocked down by the tremors. There was important news, but: "I must allow the ambassador to tell you, Drajak."

So I had to contain my curiosity until we were ensconced in Elten Larghos's inner sanctum. Dimpy and Big Balla sat silently, sipping wine and stuffing themselves with good Vallian food. When they went off to rest and Larghos and I sat alone, at last, I asked about the immaculate state of the Vallian Embassy in Oxonium.

He smiled. "Sana Ling-Li-Lwingling was here about our business when the shocks began. She recognized sorcery at once and was able, therefore, to counteract the effects here."

"That confounded Wizard of Loh of Khon the Mak's."

"Precisely. Interestingly, you will remember Hyr Kov Brannomar's sister, Sana Besti—"

"I'm hardly likely to forget," I said, thinking of that nightmare ride through other dimensions.

"Quite. She managed to save most of Brannomar's palace."

He went on to say that as a result of the sorcerer Gron-Arm-Chenlang's thaumaturgical upheavals at the orders of Khon the Mak, Prince Ortyg's palace had erupted like a volcano. The prince had barely escaped with his life. He had left the city at once. Princess Nandisha and her people had also left. Many, many citizens had fled. The only great ones left were Tom and Brannomar.

Well, by Zair, I said to myself, thank Opaz the numims are safe. But why hadn't the Star Lords sent me with them?

"The fury at Khon the Mak from everyone was quite remarkable. He had to fly for his life. Everything has changed in Oxonium."

After he had given me information to fill out the details, I said: "Well, the murders have been pushed into the background. I must still go and see Brannomar. I want the hunt called off."

"I saw him and he assured me he did not believe you were the mass murderer. But—well, the proof seemed pretty damning to everyone and the City Guard were determined to pull you in."

"Bad cess to 'em."

After that it was a matter of having my clothes washed and ironed as I slept, of eating a massive breakfast, of telling Dimpy and Big Balla to stay in the embassy and keep out of mischief, and being chauffeured by Nalgre to Brannomar's palace.

Dimpy, of course, wanted to go to the Temple of Cymbaro. The cable cars were down so I asked Nalgre to take Dimpy when he got back. I wouldn't put it past the young scamp to persuade Nalgre to take him all the way to Farinsee. He was really missing Tiri.

Now this may sound farcically out of proportion in a normal man's perception of importances. But, by the Blade of Kurin! To me, plain Dray Prescot, Vovedeer, Lord of Strombor and Krozair of Zy, swordsman, the feel of the great Krozair longsword handed to me by the ambassador felt like—felt like—well, by Zim-Zair! I felt that perhaps now I might fight in the old wild Dray Prescot way without having blades snapping left and right under my blows.

As we flew over the city Oxonium presented a wretched sight. The fires were out but smoke still hung sootily here and there. I experienced a vivid flash of recollection of the time Delia and I flew out of the blazing pyre of Vondium the proud city. Still, we'd rebuilt. I did not doubt that the Tolindrinese would rebuild too.

They were digging out dead bodies. Rubble was carried away by the cartload. Provisions of all kinds were coming in, for the country folk had rallied to help the city dwellers. We swooped across Grand Central. The cable car between the king's and Brannomar's palaces was down. Both structures, apart from the loss of a tower or two, looked intact. Nalgre brought us down onto a lawn where the fountain stood dry and the garden walls lay strewn across the flower beds. At the moment no one was about.

Nalgre shouted down the remberee and took off. The landing of the voller would not have gone unnoticed and guards would be along at any moment. I had my story ready and had no doubts of seeing Brannomar quite easily.

Ahead stood a lenken door adorned with bronze chavonths. I pushed it open and went through. The entrance hall was wide, flanked by black marble pillars. Black beams stretched across supporting the ceiling. The floor was a blinding white. I started off striding along. A faint trace of jasmine perfumed the air. The silence was profound. This entrance hall was hugely impressive and it went on and on. All this, I marveled, inside a hilltop palace!

Eventually in the lamplights shining between the pillars a door showed up at the far end. Golden animals of mythological significance that escaped me writhed upon the ebon surface.

Beyond that door the silence struck ominously. There was absolutely no one about, not a living soul to greet or challenge me.

The room was octagonal, draped in crimson, lit by golden lamps. Gilded furniture stood here and there on the faerling carpet.

I knew what this was all about in the instant before the ghostly voice with the edge of steel rustled in the air all about.

"Come in, Dray Prescot. Sit down. There are refreshments and wine." I looked at the wine bottle regretfully. It was a top quality Jholaix.

"It is too early for me for wine. If you have some sazz—"

On the word a bottle of sazz shot into being alongside the Jholaix. Pale rose, sparkling, it was delightfully refreshing.

"So this is where you attempt to discipline me?" Even as I spoke those foolish words of bravado I could feel my heart thumping.

"Your duty to the numim twins is finished."

Quickly, I shot out: "They are safe? Fweygo—?"

"Safe. Another kregoinye has been appointed. Your duty, as you know full well, is to become the Emperor of All Paz."

The nonsensicality of this did not warrant a reply.

"The Shanks have left Mehzta. They strike south. Many Chuliks are returning home in anticipation of an attack. The Shanks will bypass the Chulik islands. They will strike Balintol."

"That is grave news."

"Your duty, Dray Prescot, is to unite all of Balintol to resist the Shanks' invasion. You must use your powers. This task is laid upon you. You will not fail."

I sat silently. Not fail? The Star Lords must be going completely senile—or insane. "I recall Phu-Si-Yantong, the Empress Thyllis, King Genod Gannius—and others. They were mad with this phantasm of world conquest."

"You will use your powers, Dray Prescot."

Although I had this new relationship with the Star Lords, I still had to be circumspect. So I did not say aloud what was in my mind. "Whom the Gods wish to destroy, they first make mad."

The rustling voice of the Everoinye that could be millennia old went on to give me details of the movements of the Shanks. Those fish-headed reivers from over the curve of the world were recovering from the reverses we had inflicted on them. And I, plain Dray Prescot, had to unite the sub-continent of Balintol to resist them. And that was only the first step, for I then had to unite all of Paz. Dear old Makki Grodno's gross appearance flowed unhappily in my thoughts.

The mystery of the serial killings of young girls entered the conversation when the Star Lords informed me that my suspicions about Duven were, indeed, correct. His motives were quite clear. He sought to discredit the Dokerty cultists. I felt sorry for the idiot and also angry at him. His actions were just as mad as any real maniac who went about mass murdering without any lofty ideals. This also meant the Dokerty people were not as bad as was thought.

When the blue radiance dropped down about me and I looked up, there, hovering, immense, the Scorpion took me up into cold and darkness. The sensation of madly rushing through space, of being hurled down blindly into danger—oh yes, by Vox, these were the familiar sensations of my transactions with the Star Lords.

I'd had my fill of being an emperor. I'd been the Emperor of Vallia. Delia and I had abdicated in favor of our son, Drak, and his wife, the lovely Silda, daughter of our blade comrade, Seg Segutorio. The Star Lords were damned demanding. Of course, by Krun, they could afford to be. Their powers remained unknown to me; I did know they could banish me back to Earth, four hundred light years away, and there let me rot.

Mind you, making myself some kind of puffed-up emperor was one thing. Uniting the various countries of Balintol to resist the Shanks was quite another. That was a deed worth the doing.

My feet hit marble. The giant Scorpion disappeared. The blue misty radiance cleared.

I stood in an entrance hall with white marble floor, flanked by black marble columns. Jasmine blew on the air. Lamps burned mellowly. Ahead a lenken door stood ajar, near enough to be reached in a dozen strides.

On the floor at my feet lay the ripped body of a guardsman. Screaming in a futile effort to scrabble away across the marble, a woman shrieked for help. Savaging her was a black and white striped wersting, snarling, fangs dripping, shaking his head from side to side.

The Krozair brand ripped free. A single precise blow took the Wersting's head off. It span away trailing blood.

Lifting the woman tenderly I saw her legs were torn and bleeding but that she was otherwise unhurt. She was Sana Besti, Kov Brannomar's sister.

She shrieked again, unintelligibly; but what she was trying to say was abundantly clear by the racket roaring from beyond the door. Through her pain and fear she gestured impatiently towards the door.

The scene beyond the door was ugly. I hardly took notice of the elegance of the chamber. Brannomar's guardsmen were being ferociously attacked by a wersting pack. The black and white striped hunting dogs, snarling, yellow fangs lethal, leaped and bit, were cut down, and writhed in agony—but more and more leaped. The guardsmen were going down in the welter of their own blood.

To the side the controllers of the pack were taking no part in the combat. They were laughing and urging their dogs on. Whips in right hands and the leashes coiled up along their left arms, they were thoroughly enjoying this hideous spectacle.

The werstings first. Then the controllers. Chief among them the florid face and bulky shoulders of Jiktar Nath ti Fangenun stood out. That cramph saw me and his laughter changed to mean hatred. He had no whip. He drew his sword. I ignored him—for now, by Krun, for now!—and went hell for leather into the werstings.

Laying about me with a will I cleared a way through the black and white bodies towards Brannomar. The scar across his bronzed face looked like a vivid weal. He fought well, keeping his footing, using his sword with skill.

The noise of snarling dogs, of screaming men, the stink of blood, the raw choking stink of the whole combat, all blended into a bloody turmoil.

Brannomar was a great noble. In all the ferocity of the combat he saw me and panted out: "Lahal, majister. You are well met."

"Lahal, kov." I sliced the Krozair brand into a dog's body and he shrieked and dropped. Like our hyenas of Earth, these werstings' jaws could exert a pressure on their rear teeth of seven hundred pounds per square inch. They crunched bones into splinters. If they fastened those fangs into you, well then, by Krun, you were in deep trouble!

Slashing and slicing away, keeping the ring, we formed a group about Brannomar. His guards fought well. The numbers of dogs lessened. These poor beasts by nature and training were intent on killing. Pity for them, oh, yes, I felt that. They were like the scorpion and did what they did because that is what they did.

They were not going to chomp me up, no, by Vox, and whilst I stood they weren't going to savage Brannomar.

Fangenun and his wersting handlers saw which way the fight was going with my entrance onto the scene. Weapons in fist they closed in to finish what their dogs had begun.

Well, then, if this was the last great fight then so let it be, so let it be. A Krozair of Zy knows how to die.

The clash of blades grated in that ugly menacing scrape so familiar to me. Fangenun joined in the fight now, thinking it won, instead of hanging back as he had in Nandisha's solarium. He struck with savage force, streaming sweat, scarlet of face, bulging of eye.

The paid swordsmen fighting alongside him were professionals, stikitches, and their style of fighting was altogether more compact and economical. I just managed to interpose the Krozair longsword between a guardsman and a braxter seeking his internal organs. A twist and an instant thrust and the stikitche went down with his guts instead of the guardsman's hanging out.

Shouts ripped through the chamber. Calls for assistance, brittle warnings of backstabbing, screams as the steel brutally slashed down, all jumbled into a cacophony of death.

I began to think we might prevail. Most of the werstings had crawled off, dragging bleeding bodies on trembling legs. The men pressed and we fronted them. The grating clang of steel on steel, the screams of anguish, the spouting blood, the stink of it all, sickened me.

A voice ripped through the turmoil.

"Notor! Hold on!"

Lord Jazipur, Brannomar's right hand man, led a rush of new combatants from the door. Immediate confusion embroiled us all as stikitches tried to switch their weapons around to meet this new peril, we hurled into them with vengeful brands, and the newcomers sought their targets.

After that the fight did not last long. An eerie silence fell.

We gazed around stupefied on the hideous scene of carnage. A few bodies twitched and writhed. Slowly the shrieks and moans of the wounded splintered into our consciousnesses and we realized the silence had only been in our heads, a reaction from the battle clamor.

Some of the survivors sank down, panting, white-eyed, overjoyed still to be alive. Brannomar stood straight and tall and splashed with blood. He stared levelly at Lord Jazipur.

"You are welcome. I expected you before this."

Jazipur made one of his gracious gestures. He indicated the men he had brought to our aid. They were a patrol of the City Guard.

"There was no one else, notor. I was fortunate to find a patrol so quickly. I am happy to see you alive."

Brannomar nodded. "Where is that scoundrel Fangenun?"

A Jiktar spoke up smartly, still wiping his sword. "He is not among the dead or injured, notor. He must have escaped."

"His day will come."

I said: "He is Ortyg's man. The young prince is a fool if—"

Brannomar interrupted very gravely. "Yes. But he has outrun his patience. His palace falling about his ears decided him."

"And Khon the Mak?"

"He was forced to leave the city after the disastrous earthquake he and his sorcerer initiated. He has at last shown his hand."

So—events were moving swiftly. My task for the Everoinye remained. At Brannomar's next words I felt a deathly chill grip into my blood and choke up my breath.

"Hyr Kov Khonstanton has gone to the Chulik Islands to recruit an army. Prince Ortyg has treacherously thrown in his lot with the King of Caneldrin in return for his aid. Both of them will lead armies against King Tom, against me. They have taken the final step to outright war."

I felt the horror of an undeserved fate crushing me into a darkness like the cloak of Notor Zan.

Southern Balintol was about to be ripped apart as armies and factions clashed in a megalomaniac desire for power. Wars and Civil Wars promised a ghastly red-lit future.

And the Star Lords had ordered me to unite the continent! Failure would send me hurtling back four hundred light years—no. Oh, no! By all the deformities and defects of Makki Grodno and the Divine Lady of Belschutz! I wasn't having that.

Somehow, I, plain sailorman Dray Prescot, had to save this situation. These idiots must be talked to, their heads knocked together to make them co-operate instead of feud. A way must be found.

My Val! My future was one of near impossible tasks that must be accomplished. For my sake, and, supremely, for the sake of Delia without whom everything was dust and ashes, whatever might be needed, that must be done.

"Selah!"

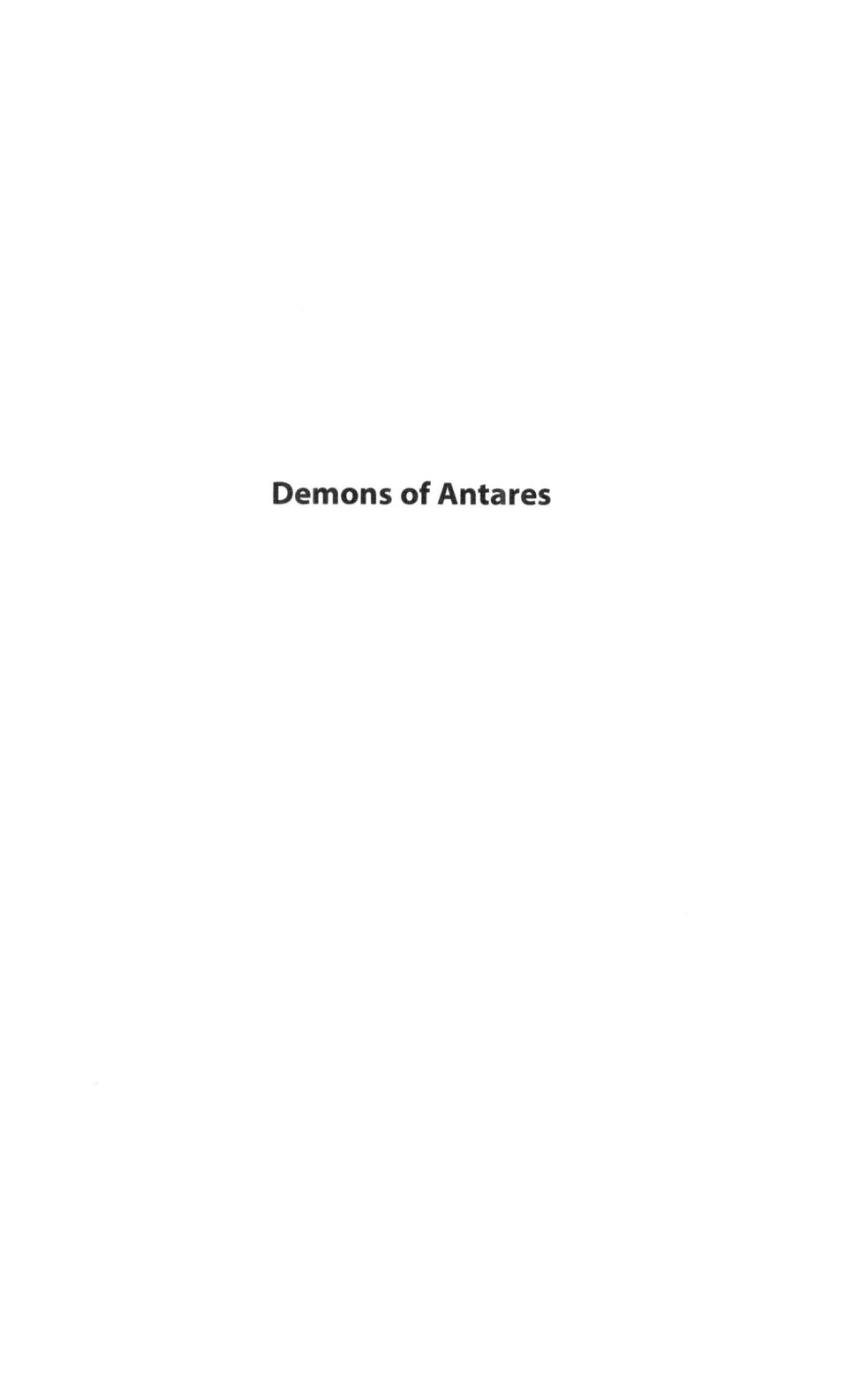

Demons of Antares

A note from the publisher

Although the first 37 books of the saga of Dray Prescot were published in English, books 38 to 52 were previously published in German translations only. They were written in English by Ken Bulmer (writing as Alan Burt Akers) and the current Mushroom eBooks and Bladud Books editions are published from the original type-written manuscripts. Unfortunately, the original manuscript for Demons of Antares could not be found, and the decision was made to attempt to retranslate it into English using the German translation as the source.

A project like this would not normally be attempted, because translating from English into German and back again would result in the loss of too much of the author's voice and style. However, we had the advantage of forty-five previous volumes in the series to refer to, and a vast pool of in-depth fan knowledge to call upon. Also, the German edition is a very faithful and accurate translation by Andreas Decker, who translated the entire series into German for Heyne Verlag.

Translating into a very rough and ready version of English proved to be ridiculously easy, thanks mostly to Google Translator Toolkit. A number of volunteers then worked hard to tidy this "machine" translation into readable English. More volunteers then brought their extensive knowledge of Dray Prescot and Kregen to bear, honing the text into a style hard to distinguish from the rest of the books in the series.

After reading and re-reading, checking and re-checking so many times, I feel confident this book closely represents Ken Bulmer's intent. I am also confident that there are mistakes.

I would like to thank Ken Bulmer's family for allowing us to even attempt this, and Andreas Decker and Heyne for producing the German edition. Thank you to everyone who contributed time and energy and encouragement, including Michael Victor Bassett, Helen Folkes, Simon Maybury, Sven Paulik, Stephen J. Servello, Michael Sutton, Tyketriker, Els Withers, and many others...

And thank you, Ken, for Dray Prescot.

Martyn Folkes

Dray Prescot

Lit by the ruby and emerald fires of Antares, the planet Kregen, four hundred light years from Earth, is a world harsh yet beautiful, terrible yet alluring. There any man or woman may achieve what their heart desires if they plan and struggle and keep faith with their innate purpose. The Star Lords have brought Dray Prescot to this place and plunged him headlong into danger and adventure, and he must cope with tasks in their service that at first glance seem insurmountable.

Dray Prescot, as described by one who has seen him on this Earth, is a man above middle height with brown hair and level brown eyes, brooding and dominating, with enormously broad shoulders and a powerful physique. There is about him an abrasive honesty and indomitable courage. He moves like a savage hunting cat, sudden, silent and lethal. Reared in the harsh conditions of Nelson's Navy he is a man who, relatively unsuccessful on Earth, is ideally suited to the new life to which he was called by the Star Lords.

Currently, he is on the subcontinent of Balintol where he has the task of uniting the disparate countries so that all Paz can defend itself against the predatory, fish-headed Shanks from the other side of the world. This undertaking is complicated by the megalomaniac desires of certain princes and nobles who are determined to win the crown of Tolindrin for themselves, and are willing to destroy anyone who gets in their way. For this reason they have hired mercenary armies and allied themselves with the traditional enemies of the country.

Dray Prescot has to use all his strengths and all his scheming and tricks to achieve his goal with as little bloodshed as possible. The Star Lords have thrown him into new danger that is all too familiar to him as a Kregoinye. For the sake of his love of Delia, Delia of Delphond, Delia of the Blue Mountains, Dray Prescot sets everything else aside and throws himself into new and deadly hazards under the streaming mingled lights of the Suns of Scorpio.

Alan Burt Akers

One

One of the best ways to survive on Kregen is to know at all times exactly what is going on behind your back. The cat-man, his whiskery face distorted with rage, turned towards his adversary and exchanged blows, but apparently forgot in the heat of battle this essential habit that makes for an unabbreviated life.

As the airboat swayed in the sky, a hulking fellow stormed up behind the Fristle and clubbed him over the head. The Fristle let out a short, surprised, pained cry, and fell helplessly out of the lifter.

His two attackers leaned over the rail to watch him fall.

The Fristle was clinging on with one hand, his whiskery face contorted with pain and fear.

"No, doms!" he shouted. "It was all a misunderstanding!"

They laughed. They were Rapas, with heads that bore a close resemblance to black vultures. They carried swords, but for the Fristle the cudgel had been sufficient. They mocked him.

"Doms! For sweet Tolaar's sake!"

This was another mistake that could quickly bring death.

"Tolaar!" The Rapa's anger was frightening. "Dokerty has no time for blintzes who worship Tolaar!"

With these words, he raised his cudgel to smash down on the Fristle's hand.

I stepped forward and intercepted the downward blow.

"All right, doms. You've had your fun! Pull him up now."

They turned around. I held the cudgel in a grip that I judged would prevent any further use—either against me or against the Fristle.

"Clear off, blintz!"

"Schtump, you rast!"

I was in no mood to be overly polite, nor even to have sport with them. With a sudden jerk that surprised both of them the cudgel came into my possession and I brandished it first under one beak and then under the other.

"No. You are the ones who will clear off."

"Are you one of those damned Tolaar followers?" one of the Rapas rumbled.

"No. And I'm no Dokerty cultist either."

For a moment, nothing happened. The airboat, a quite ordinary passenger lifter, was flying above the clouds on its way to Oxonium. An invitation from San Paynor, the high priest of Cymbaro, had taken me to Farinsee where I paid a visit to young Tiri who was progressing well in the studies that would eventually confer strange and mystical powers upon her. It had gone well. Now the next task awaited me. Young Dimpy had remained in Farinsee.

All of us wore ponsho fleeces over our fashionable shamlaks because at this height the bite of the cold could be considerable.

The brief, breathless moment came to an abrupt end. I reached down with my free hand to heave the trembling Fristle aboard—and both Rapas threw themselves on me.

A strange cloud blocked my view. Either the Rapas were damned fast, or I was incredibly slow, because they were instantly on me, by Krun! The first threw himself against my legs. His sidekick aimed at my head with his cudgel. He hit me but I did not feel the impact. Somehow, I was hanging onto the railing, holding tight with one hand while with the other I tried to protect my head. Of the Fristle there was no sign. No cry of despair could be heard. If he had fallen to the ground, he'd had the courtesy to do it quietly.

The cudgel struck my hand. Again I felt nothing. But I fell. Of that I was sure. The strange cloud that impaired my vision blotted out the leaf-shaped silhouette of the flier. Instead I saw treetops, the glint of a river and a red roof.

I fell head over heels through the air. I remember that I had the ridiculous idea that Dray Prescot's end had finally come, and that this was my last fall.

I plummeted downwards, and could do nothing except wonder if the Star Lords would hoick me out of mortal danger at the last minute.

Strangely, the trees, river and roof beneath me dissolved. I hurtled past steep rocky cliffs bathed in a gloomy red light from the fiery lava lake lurking at the bottom. Everything around me was red.

The impact was hard. I opened my eyes. Everything was dark.

A voice growled: "Keep still, you blintz!"

For two heartbeats, I wondered if these were the hellish mists that veiled the gateway to the Ice Floes of Sicce. Or maybe it was a Herrelldrin Hell. Then I came to my senses.

It had been merely a dream—in the best tradition of Victorian ghost stories.

By the ruptured eyeballs and dangling entrails of Makki-Grodno! I had dreamed it all. I was staying overnight in a caravanserai north of Oxonium, which was recently hit by an earthquake. The owner of the gruff voice was a traveler like me. I did not sweat, but I felt a shudder, by Krun! That dream had been too real in a very unpleasant way.

Granted, it had vividly demonstrated one of the many problems with which Tolindrin in the subcontinent of Balintol struggled. The two religions of Tolaar and Dokerty, opponents in a religious war, were the cause of riots and civil commotion all over the country, and nowhere caused more damage than in the capital Oxonium.

To my way of thinking the superior religion of Cymbaro was being pushed to one side. I pulled myself up from the floor without making any effort to reply to the unfriendly remark, and crawled back onto the bed.

The obsessive attempts of powerful nobles and princesses to overthrow King Tom, and even to lay claim to the crown, already gave the country enough problems to cope with—and it could well do without a religious war, by Vox!

Someone was snoring softly. The dormitory was not at all full; there were only half a dozen travelers staying here.

Of course it occurred to me to wonder what Delia would say when I told her I had fallen out of bed.

Her beautiful nose would turn up, her magnificent eyes would flash, and her rose-red lips would pucker up into a laugh. Confound it! I said to myself. Could this state of affairs in Tolindrin have even the slightest importance when compared with Delia, Delia of Delphond, Delia of the Blue Mountains? Of course not. Not at all!

And yet there lurked in the background, driving me on as always, the ghostly, ubiquitous presence of the Star Lords. I had to unite all Balintol to resist the predatory Shanks from the other side of the world whose greedy fish eyes had already fixed on their next prey.

Hyr Kov Brannomar, the most powerful man in the kingdom, next to King Tom, was of the opinion that the greatest threat to the country came from the intrigues of the treacherous young prince Ortyg. The prince had fled to Caneldrin, Tolindrin's immediate neighbor to the north, to assure himself of the help of the king there.

The armies of Caneldrin would roll over Tolindrin and spread fire, death and destruction.

Hyr Kov Khon the Mak had gone to the islands of the Chuliks off the south coast of the subcontinent. He would be able to recruit an army there now that the Chuliks were sure that the Shanks would pass by their islands and attack Balintol directly. The Shanks had already tried their luck against the Chuliks and had suffered a crushing defeat. Now they would attack by a different route.

So King Tom, Brannomar and myself agreed that the greatest threat to Tolindrin came from the north. We came to the conclusion that Caneldrin would use the impetuous Prince Ortyg's money and troops for an attack, after which they themselves would try to take control of the country. It was an old and ugly story.

The plans of Ortyg had to be thwarted, and sharpish. Only then could we take care of Khon the Mak.

And so it was that I, the unimportant Dray Prescot, was on his way north to do a bit of spying. We must have knowledge of Ortyg's plans.

Brannomar had other spies on the trail of Khon the Mak, of course. He had mentioned that he had also put a few of his men on Ortyg. I preferred to keep my plans to myself, for the obvious reason of security.

When the travelers came together for the first breakfast, the threatening storm that had forced a premature landing the night before could still be seen on the northern horizon. The captain of the lifter, Llanili the Stout, was clearly doubtful. Many of the passengers watched the menacing black stripe on the horizon and shook their heads. No. They would not travel today. They would wait for a clear sky.

A bright, firm female voice rose above the quiet discussion.

"A bag of one hundred gold pieces, Captain Llanili, if we continue our flight."

An abrupt silence fell, and we all turned curiously to look at the woman.

She rose from her chair and stood up straight. She was tall and wore a long, gray-green dress. Here and there a few embroideries sparkled. A simple belt of silver rings circled her narrow waist and held a useful-looking sword and a small dagger. Her face was not one you would immediately call classically beautiful. Her well-proportioned features—a purist would probably have complained that her lush mouth impaired her looks—told of serene determination and suppressed passion. She wore her hair cut short. It was, as they say, as black as a raven's wing.

She lifted a leather pouch. "One hundred pieces of gold."

Llanili wet his lips. As his name suggested he was fat, and his indecision made him sweat.

"It's not worth the risk," someone called out.

"I will fly with you!" said another.

Two attendants stood dutifully behind their mistress. They were neatly dressed and wore ponsho fleeces. This was a lady who was not to be trifled with. Her expression hardened. "Well, Captain Llanili? What do you say?"

"My Lady Q'Quensella, I..."

"Well?" she asked. "It is not necessary that you use the double initials," she added sarcastically, as if she was swatting at an annoying fly. "I am Quensella."

"Certainly, certainly, my lady."

He put his hands together. They were shaking. Finally, he nodded. "I will fly."

"Good." She was pretty forceful.

In the end, only four of the half-dozen men from the dormitory ventured onto the flight: two Fristles, a Rapa, and a small Och. Oh, and of course me.

After breakfast we all hurried outside.

The caravanserai was not large, little more than an outpost. Llanili's airboat was a simple, robust flier with a cabin in the middle of the deck and an acceptable turn of speed. I glanced to the north and saw that the dull horizon had not changed much. Perhaps the storm was moving away from us. We would soon find out.

Another lady decided to join us. She was wrapped from head to toe in a simple hooded cloak, which revealed only two bright eyes and the tip of a perky nose. The pointed protrusion near the back hem of the cloak betrayed the presence of a hidden weapon. She spoke rarely, and then with a hard, unrelenting voice. She called herself Froisier, which in my opinion was not her real name.

A burst of energy from the two silver boxes, which provide the lift and movement, raised the flier. We climbed up into the air and once again wrapped ourselves in our furs and ponsho fleeces.

The Och sat on a bench and buried himself in a book.

The two Fristles laughed, their cat faces distorted with excitement. Both rested their left hands on their sword hilts, and had cudgels dangling handily from their belts.

The Rapa gave them suspicious looks. He had a pile of luggage with him; to all appearances he was a traveling merchant. He wore neither sword nor cudgel, just a simple dagger. He seemed nervous.

Then he took out a book and began to read.

I could see that this was a religious book, dedicated to Tolaar. He kept his beak lowered. His feathers had a greenish-black color.

The ladies had retired to the cabin amidships and so I sat there and strained my old vosk-skull, thinking about how I could bring some order to the deadlocked Tolindrin.

"Tolaar!" hissed an unpleasant Fristle voice. "You might as well worship the nine demons of Narfreal!"

The Rapa said nothing. He kept his beak lowered.

"In the eyes of Dokerty, Tolaar is an abomination!"

An uncomfortable feeling crept over me concerning this situation. The obvious thought occurred to me: was I still dreaming?

Was I on the hard beds of the caravanserai, and was this the second part of my dream? Except now it was not two Rapas provoking a Fristle, but the reverse? Or was it all real?

I got up and sauntered towards the bows of the lifter. The headwind was fairly benign, and Llanili flew straight and fast. We floated over a flat landscape with trees and rivers. The villages were few and far between and clung to the curves of the rivers. A few boats were moving slowly over the surface of the water. Beneath us an assortment of birds flew through the air, and a white bank of cloud in front reflected the splendor of the Suns of Scorpio. At our current level and course we would fly over the clouds.

I strolled back just as the cry sounded.

Was it a dream? The Rapa hung in the air. With one hand he clutched the railing, with the other he tried rather unsuccessfully to protect his head.

The Fristle raised his cudgel. In the next instant, the fingers of the Rapa would be shattered, he would cry out, let go and plunge to the ground.

Whether this was a dream or not, I stepped forward and grabbed the cudgel. "All right, doms. You've had your fun! Pull him up now."

"Clear off, you rast!"

"Schtump, blintz!"

In my dream, it had been the other way around. I took the cudgel from the fellow. The flier shook and we all stumbled. The Rapa was still screaming and pleading to Tolaar for help. I took a step back, flung the cudgel and reached out to grab the bird-man.

The Fristles reacted. They threw themselves at me with a feline determination that, too late, I realized was deadly.

I yanked the Rapa upwards with a quick jerk, which normally would have brought him back on board easily. But the fool clung on more tightly to the railing and would not let go. He dangled in the air.

The Fristles hit me with brutal force, and I crashed overboard. Now I had to hold on to the railing myself. Suddenly, between my body and the hard surface of Kregen there was only thin air.

"Doms! Doms!" shrieked the Rapa. "Please!"

Somehow, the Rapa managed to continue holding on to the railing. The first Fristle slammed his cudgel down on my knuckles. I let go with my other hand, reached upwards to grab the cudgel, and missed. A vicious pain shot through the hand that clung on to the railing. I did not cry out.

I let go—and plunged into nothingness. I rushed headlong towards the ground. A swirling panorama of trees and rivers raced past my eyes.

My mind raced. It was time to say farewell to Kregen. I plunged into the darkness of the enveloping black cloak of Notor Zan.

Two

Any attempt to appeal to the Star Lords for help would almost certainly be futile. If I was still dreaming an enormous chasm would swallow me up and with a little luck I would miss the lake of fiery lava.

The force of the wind was a clear indication that I was not dreaming. Funnily enough, I remembered that in my dream I felt no pain as the cudgel hit my hand. In actuality, I felt the pain, and keenly, by Krun!

Out of the corner of my eye I saw a darting shadow. Wind buffeted me, and it was deuced difficult to see what was going on. The ground was approaching very fast. I managed to turn my head, and there was the flier, almost vertical and diving nose first towards the ground. With the power of its silver boxes it sped downward faster than me.

I wanted to look down; but I should have saved myself the effort since the wind whirled me around so that I had to squint through my hair to be able to see the ground.

The flier did a wonderfully controlled nosedive, pulled up so abruptly that everyone on deck must have been thrown off their feet, and then positioned itself directly under my falling body.

"If Delia were controlling this flier..." I mumbled, but then stopped because this was not the time for reminiscences.

The lifter beneath me adjusted to horizontal flight. Everything was indistinct, confusing and vague. Figures were moving about on the deck. They were doing something with great haste but I couldn't work out what it was.

The airboat plunged downwards below me, matching my speed at first and then slowing somewhat. I rushed with flailing arms and legs towards the deck and landed with a thud in a huge pile of pillows and fur capes. The breath was driven from my lungs, and I lay there like a beached fish gasping for air on the shore.

Hands grabbed me. Voices rang out, and merged. They rolled me off the makeshift landing pad. I tried to speak, but could manage only a croak. I sat there, my head lowered between my knees, while all around me Kregen whirled, and as my numerous bruises and cuts made themselves felt for the first time, I slowly realized that I was still among the living.

They dragged me into the deck cabin and laid me down. Then they held a cup of heated wine to my lips, and I drank gratefully.

Captain Llanili's helmsman turned his gaze from the controls and looked abaft. He was not staring at me, although that would have been understandable; no—his gaze focused on Lady Quensella, and he seemed to be a little pale around the gills. As she arrived at the bench on which I lay, she turned and said in her forceful manner over her shoulder to the helmsman: "Well, Goron, you can take control again. Keep a steady northerly course."

"Quidang!"

So that was it! This wonderful lady had steered the flier to rescue me. She leaned over me, lifted one of my eyelids, and tutted. "You will recover. Get some rest now."

I rested. When I finally went back on deck the storm was much nearer. However, the first thing my eyes fell upon was of more immediate interest—the two Fristles were bound together expertly. They looked like they were drowning in self-pity. The Rapa must have managed to climb back on board using his hands and feet, for he sat there patting his dagger blade and staring at the two Fristles angrily.

It was obvious what had happened. Lady Quensella had taken command. Everyone clung on determinedly as she steered the flier in a nosedive into the depths to save me. Froisier, the other lady, stepped towards me and gave me a warm jug of wine.

"Thank you, my lady."

"It is Quensella you should be thanking."

She gave off the pleasant scent of lavender. I could see only her two sparkling eyes, her pert nose and a hint of a pale face. Her hands were hidden in black silk gloves.

"I'll do that."

She gave a short laugh. "You have been saved, Horter. But perhaps we will all die when the storm breaks."

"Perhaps."

She looked at me from under her hood. "You are a strange fellow."

"I have heard it said on occasion," I said. "Now I must give the lady Quensella my thanks."

No sooner said than done.

"That aerial maneuver posed an interesting challenge. For your sake I am glad that it worked," was all she said in reply.

"Who took care of the Fristles?"

It turned out that it was the little Och and Llanili's three crew members who had overpowered the Fristles. Moreover, Quensella's servants had brandished their daggers.

You should know that Kregen is populated not only by villains, scoundrels and cutthroats, but also with many good, decent people who make life worth living.

This profound and comforting fact of Kregish life gave me a warm feeling, and I looked forward hopefully. In recent times my experience of sailing was limited to skyships rather than on ships which fought against the surf, but storms were still storms, and before us a far from gentle breeze was brewing. We were likely to get caught up in it.

Llanili was of the same opinion. He stood beside Quensella and spoke insistently to her. She shook her imperious head. Llanili gestured with his hands.

"I'm beginning to think we'd better land," said the Och, a man named Nath ti Lernerzun, to the Rapa, who was guarding the Fristles.

The Rapa, Ragaran the Ordsetter, grunted. "The main thing is that this pair doesn't get away."

"Oh, that will not happen, of that I am sure."

Ragaran turned away, running his knife blade over the back of his hand. Llanili stormed onto the deck. "Women!" he said.

I went to the bow, stood by the railing and peered out carefully at the horizon. The dark band stretched from west to east. It had to be an approaching storm front, bringing rain and wind with it. If there was a blocking high-pressure area, the low-pressure area could create problems for some time. Perhaps waiting it out on the ground would be the wisest course of action. That was the obvious conclusion. In fact, there was no question in my mind that we must land as quickly as possible and seek shelter. There was no perhaps about it.

Apart from the determination of the lady Quensella.

I knew that I risked a sharp rebuke, but I decided to talk to her.

She received me with a cool look, and I realized at once that she knew exactly what I was going to say.

First, I thanked her again—which she impatiently brushed aside—and then I commented that someone with her flying skills certainly must have flown a lot. With so much experience, it was safe to assume that she had accumulated a great knowledge of weather conditions. Squalls were...

I got no further.

"We fly on. It is of vital importance. Queyd-arn-tung!"

No, she truly was no beauty. Even with her cheeks a little flushed and her full lips pursed, her face lost none of its severity. She would not be characterized as pretty. She stared at me like I had just crawled out from under a rock. "My father has flown through much worse weather than the storm ahead of us, from Opus Mountain to Tjorus Mountain," she said suddenly. "If the lifter can withstand it, then I can fly through it."

Why did she say that? Maybe the old Dray Prescot devil look had flared up on my face. She turned away abruptly. "We fly on!"

I felt a feather-light touch on my arm, and I turned around. "So we will fly on," said Froisier in her imperious way.

"Aye."

Each mur that elapsed brought us appreciably closer to the storm. When it was upon us, we must get through. Therefore, it was of vital importance that everything was shipshape and Vallian fashion.

Something about this arrogant and demanding Lady Quensella was extremely strange! Why was she on this flier? She was obviously a high-ranking noblewoman, but where was her entourage? Where were her guards? Where was her cadade? The two servants certainly knew how to use their daggers, but if the other passengers and crew of the flier decided to land, could they prevent it? Probably not, by Krun!

Quensella had come across the border aboard Llanili's flier *Sparking Thunder*. I booked my passage from the border to skirt the rugged mountain ranges that rose in northern Tolindrin and stretched beyond Winlan. I had left Oxonium in a northeasterly direction. This route skirted the yellow deserts of Caneldrin which were just east of the mountains. Kildrin lay to the west, towards the coast.

There had been no trouble at the border. The rivalry between Tolindrin and Caneldrin had always been subject to fluctuations, with both good times and bad, and it seemed pretty certain that a bad time was lurking just around the corner.

The arrogant Quensella was in a great hurry. Was her haste in any way connected with the problems that the future might bring? I looked again at the bank of clouds on the horizon. I was in a hurry as well, but not even Prince Ortyg was worth this mad flight through the hell approaching us.

The lady had done me a great service, so I decided not to take the matter into my own hands and land the voller. By the Black Chunkrah! That would have been a dishonorable repayment of her kindness!

Everyone was now squeezed into the deck cabin and the helmsman was tied firmly to two posts. We all found a secure place to ride out the coming storm. The anticipation of our impending destruction created an atmosphere in the cabin that could be cut with a knife. We avoided eye contact with one another. We were tense. The two Fristles were tied together securely, and I reflected on the causes of the conflicts between religions throughout Balintol.

San Duven, who as a fanatical supporter of Cymbaro had cruelly killed innocent young girls so that blame for the murders would fall on the cult of Dokerty, was a sad example. Brannomar had ordered his immediate arrest, but the guard of Oxonium had been unable to find him. He had vanished. I knew in my bones that I had not yet heard the last of him.

Politics was also a constant source of discord. The Och, Nath ti Lernerzun, had nothing good to say about the King of Caneldrin. "A first rate blintz! Should have been drowned at birth!"

"Expressing opinions of that kind too loudly, tikshim, can easily cost you your head," Quensella said sharply.

Nath waved his middle left hand. "I don't think I have anything to fear in that respect, my lady, as we're all likely to die in this storm."

"We are all in the hands of Croken of the Rainbow," said Captain Llanili. He buried his head in his hands, slumped to the deck, and fell into a sullen silence.

One hard look through the forward hatches told me that the storm was right in front of us. I was not of Nath's opinion, although Quensella's remark about the lifter breaking apart had been less than reassuring.

The first gusts broke upon us suddenly and with devastating force.

We shot up like a thrown spear, we plummeted into the depths like a stone. We were tossed about. In the cabin there was chaos. People screamed and clung on tightly as best they could. The noise was tremendous. The wind howled and the flier shook. Heavy rain lashed and ran down the side window.

The helmsman was thrown violently against the ropes that held him, and he struggled gamely with his levers and instruments. He should have saved himself the effort. The storm held us in its grip, and it shook us like a wersting with a rag doll.

Lady Quensella's expression hardened into one of complete determination. Her jaw muscles tensed as she gritted her teeth, and she extricated herself from the supportive hold of her servants. She stood up, stumbled a few steps forward and then staggered back. She worked her way forward, bit by bit, until she reached the lifter's controls. There, she simply took the rudder from the dazed helmsman's hand, squeezed herself between him and the console and tried to force *Sparking Thunder* to an even keel and ride the winds.

I sighed. Now it was up to me to do something. This was about saving my own skin as well as about the fate of all those assembled here. I stood up and was immediately thrown to the other side of the cabin and back again.

But if she had done it, I could do it too.

By the time I reached the controls, Quensella had forced the flier onto an even keel. We still moved up and down like a yo-yo, and it was impossible to estimate how fast we were moving.

I put my hands over the lady's, and together we forced the stubborn, shaking lever forward. Before us stretched a dense dark mass. Heavy rain drummed against the portholes. In some places they had sprung leaks that let water through, soaking us. More than once our feet lost contact with the deck planks and we clung tightly onto the levers until the airboat had caught up with us.

The passengers were overcome by nausea and the stench of vomit made our misery worse.

Quensella stared straight ahead, her face hawk-like.

"Come on, you beast! Come on!" she gasped. For her, it had become a personal struggle. Her pride demanded that she bring this lifter under control. It occurred to me that she thought she felt the scrutiny of her father.

How she stuck with it so long, Opaz alone knows. Her stamina and strength encouraged me. She was a tough woman. In the darkness a few bright flickering streaks of light flashed and then disappeared immediately. I was confident we would make it.

Abruptly, an infernal thudding sound fell about us. The lifter shuddered with every blow. The brutal buffeting drowned out the fury of the wind and was directed against the side of the lifter and thus against us.

Quensella peered with narrowed eyes through the rain washed porthole.

"The mast is broken. It will smash the lifter to smithereens."

I took a good look. She was right. The mast from which the flags waved on nice days was broken, but it was hanging from its shrouds and would smash the lifter into kindling.

I sighed once again. So now I, Dray Prescot, was being asked to prove my right to be called a sailor.

"Can you keep the flier on course?" I asked firmly.

"Of course!"

I took a deep breath. Venturing out onto the deck was sheer madness but someone had to cut the mast free or it would smash the deck and eventually reach the silver boxes. If they were damaged—well, then there would certainly be no future for the travelers on board.

"If you go outside, you'll die..." Quensella gasped out as I went forward and held onto the door.

"That is quite possible, my lady. Try to keep it steady."

So I asked her to accomplish a nearly impossible feat.

Somehow I managed to open the door. The shriek of the wind increased in its intensity. I fought my way through the door and immediately ducked my head. The storm robbed me of air. I took a laborious damp breath and made my way forward again.

It was a perilous business trying to reach the side. I made a start twice and was hurled backwards both times, slipping on the soaking wet deck as the storm and rain pounded me.

I was soaked to the skin. This had to be done, and fast.

On the third attempt I was thrown forcibly against the railing. The top cross-beam splintered, and only the fact that the flier jerked in the other direction kept me from going overboard. I clung on tightly, pulled my old sailor's knife from its scabbard on my right hip and set to work cutting through the rigging.

The whole undertaking was a nightmare. I had to hold on and at the same time move with the jerking of the flier. Freed from the pressure, the ropes whipped around and I dodged about like a crazed violinist with a saber on the rigging.

If the ropes here were all severed, the mast would twist in my direction, and could splinter and crush me like a fly under a boot. I'd have to be pretty damn fast. The heavy mast snapped the last shroud, and almost threw me to my death. A successful last-minute leap forward, which ended in a roll and a hard collision with some Opaz-provided railings, saved me. I took a gasping breath. By Djan! Such work could get confoundedly warm!

The freezing rain and darkness made a clear view almost impossible. The mast was bolt upright again. Then, in an instant, it swung around madly. Finally it toppled over the side, and the shrouds tore away. Phew!

A long shudder reverberated through the hull of the lifter. The deck planks under me jumped. A groan rose to a shriek that faded to silence as the airboat gained altitude again. We had come into contact with the ground and skidded along a bit until Quensella managed to gain enough lift. We still flew much too low! At any moment we could smash into the ground.

I put my sailor's knife away again while I continued to hold on with the other hand. Trying to cut through the rigging with the two-handed sword would be pointless; I would have laid into the rigging with little success and it would have gained me only half a dozen stumbling steps across the deck. The way back to the cabin was going to be just as difficult as the way out.

The raging storm roared relentlessly in my ears. The rain beat down on me without mercy. Breathing was difficult. Around me everything became blurry.

I did not want to think about what Quensella was going to do. Again a shrill groan rang out as the keel scraped along the ground. We climbed up into the air, jumped and swung around. I clung on tightly and waited for an opportunity to sprint to the cabin.

All sorts of disjointed thoughts raced through my head. The only reason I was in this mess was because I wanted to spy on Prince Ortyg.

The nightmare of falling overboard from *Sparking Thunder* had almost come true. Had that dream been a warning to me of the danger? We had to ensure that the flier survived the storm unscathed. The thought of Quensella at the helm was a consolation in all the chaos.

I could not tell how fast we were moving, the rain made it impossible to judge. Quensella had to gain altitude! If we hit the ground...

With that thought I was struck in the side by something extraordinarily hard. I was crouching there, facing the cabin, ready to rush to it, when the blow sent me sprawling in a daze across the deck.

I found no way to hold on and could not prevent what happened next: I was catapulted over the side.

I fell head over heels, the storm howling in my ears and the rain soaking me. I felt a tiny, blood-red moment of pain. Then the midnight-black cloak of Notor Zan enveloped me.

Three

Screams of fear and terror echoed in my ears and penetrated sluggishly into my slowly waking consciousness. The famous bells of Beng Kishi clanged somberly and incessantly in my head. I struggled to open my eyes and saw an indistinct shimmering blue light.

A glance around told me that I was in a long, spacious and sturdily built wooden hut. Pillars spaced at irregular intervals supported a leaf canopy; the construction material was reminiscent of papishin leaves. In the center of the hut a smoldering fire surrounded by stones filled the stuffy air with an all-pervasive smoke, which explained the ubiquitous blue haze. The smell of fruit, vegetables and cooking food intermingled. A wide variety of household items hung on the pillars, as well as peculiar objects, feathered dolls and firewood. I was lying on a cot, cushioned with grass, and when I turned my head to one side I discovered a clay jug next to me. I picked it up and drank gratefully from the crystal clear water.

The terrible noise outside continued. I had to find out what was going on. I wanted to sit up, but I could not manage it; pain gripped me like a pair of pliers.

Then I heard a word that I hated like no other, a word that was accompanied by malicious whip cracks. "Grak! Grak, you blintz!"

Shadows filled the door opening. I blinked.

Men in armor trooped in with purposeful strides, then spread out and poked beneath the sleeping places with swords. They saw me.

"Hai!" said one and stepped towards me with his coiled whip. "Here's one just waiting here to be taken."

"And he's apim. Peculiar, you don't usually find other onkers with the Fleurese." I knew who they were—hateful and despicable slavers. Katakis. They looked down at me with malicious satisfaction. I made another attempt to sit up; I lifted myself up a little and fell back onto the bed with a groan.

"Look," said the first through gritted teeth. "He is sick. He is worthless."

The second Kataki raised his sword. "I'll kill him."

"Wait, Rakif, wait. He may be sick at the moment, but by the Triple Tails of Targ the Untouchable, he will be healthy again and ready to go when we return."

"How true, Krando, how true." The sword fell, albeit reluctantly.

The hut contained nothing to interest them, apart from the handfuls of fruit that they took and stuffed themselves with, loudly smacking their lips. Then they left, their bladed tails held high. I could only lie there and feel like the most useless onker on all Kregen, ever.

The horrific sounds outside grew fainter and eventually died away altogether. I knew from the crack of whips and shouts of "Grak!" that the Katakis were driving their prisoners to the slave markets and a fate that they did not deserve, to judge by the level of cultural development revealed to me by my glance around this hut.

After some time I heard a couple of quiet voices approaching outside.

"Next time you must be faster with your warning, Lazlo."

"It's all my fault, father, and I accept my punishment."

"You are punished enough by what has happened."

They entered, despondent, dejected, and crouched down by the fire. They wore a minimum of clothing, only loincloths, and their bodies were painted with a series of delightful patterns. A young woman, almost a girl, leaned over me. In the dim light of the hut her hair appeared dark and untamed, and tears glistened in her eyes. She wore a dangling necklace of pearls.

"He's awake!" she cried. "The visitor from the trees is alive!"

In that cheerful face with wide-apart eyebrows and a narrow chin her eyes were speckled gray-green. Her soft mouth trembled. In the background these people lamented their losses with silent sobs, and it touched me that this girl was concerned about a stranger.

An older man came up and leaned over me. I can't say that his face wore a friendly expression, but it was open and showed none of the telltale characteristics of greed and lust for power that so often disfigure the faces of the mighty of Earth and Kregen.

"I am pleased you are alive, stranger. I must ask you to forgive us leaving you here when we sought refuge in the forest." His eyes looked tired; they were ashen gray. "We lacked the time to take you with us. They surprised us..." He shook his head. "They were not the ones we expected; they were not the men in red."

"No," I grated out with difficulty. "It was the damned Katakis."

He handed me a bowl made of a leaf held in shape with bramble thorns. It contained a mixture of fruits and nuts. I ate. The Fleures were vegetarians. As I discovered in the days that followed, they lived along a secluded tributary of the great river. The tax collectors of the king visited the Fleures once a year, and their tribute was now due. However, I was told by Fandon, their leader, that the men from the town often demanded more than their due. The privilege to levy taxes attracts unscrupulous collectors, and one must expect that they will demand far more than they are actually owed. Ultimately, they want to make fat profits. Such things have happened before, in Vallia at any rate, by Vox!

I recovered slowly. A branch had swept me from the deck of *Sparking Thunder* and they found me hanging in a tree. When I asked after other survivors of the flier, I was met with a shake of the head. No, they had found no one but me and no wreckage of a flying boat.

I walked slowly through the village, which was made up of several long huts with roofs of leaves. The river flowed past nearby. Although they did not eat meat, they had a collection of long spears. They were made from branches that had been selected and cut so that half a yard along thick knots served as a backstop behind the fire-hardened tip. I could think of the reason. The primitive weapons were like pig-stickers. Somewhere in the forest, dangerous animals were lurking.

Although I was still a little weak-kneed, I was getting better quite quickly, and one beautiful day I offered to go into the forest with a group of berry and fruit collectors. I had two reasons. I needed to travel northwards, since my mission was waiting for me, and I wanted to express my thanks to these people by helping them.

The forest wasn't gloomy; it was dotted with many clearings, and the profusion of flowers and sweet fragrances made it a peaceful place. At least until the Linomin appeared, all bristling fur and pawing at the ground, its curved tusks directed towards us ready to attack.

The Fleures cried out in alarm. They lowered their long spears and formed a wall. These people were about a head shorter than me. They all had graceful muscular bodies and smooth skin. The contrast between them and the Linomin could not have been any greater.

The beast attacked, its tusks yellow and deadly.

The Fleures skillfully kept the poor animal at bay. One stabbed at it, making it hiss and leap into the air, but it hesitated to oppose the spear tips. It did not run away. Four more Linomins appeared.

Our small group was surrounded. "They will keep us here until more of them arrive," said Finul, the leader, a young carefree guy who laughed a lot. He did not laugh now. "We are trapped in the forest, and I must apologize to you."

"Then we have to break through their circle right away," I said.

I stepped out of the group, leaving the wall of spear points behind me, and pulled out the Krozair longsword.

"Stay where you are! They will impale you!"

I did not answer, but went with a steady step to the nearest Linomin. It stomped its hooves and lowered its head, tusks sparkling in the light of the sun shining through the leaves. It decided to attack.

It was fast. By Krun, it was pretty damn fast! At the last instant I stepped to the side to avoid the tusks and slashed with the Krozair blade. The Linomin stormed on and then collapsed with his head held on by only a piece of fur.

It was a repulsive job. But I had a duty to stay alive, firstly to repay the folk who had helped me, and secondly, naturally of course, for Delia.

The next Linomin stormed forward and suffered the same fate as its predecessor.

"Hai!" I called. "Come on, doms. We attack together!"

They responded quickly. I marched to the front of the wall that they formed, and we moved quickly through the trees. Another animal was attacked and killed, and the remaining two pawed at the ground and hissed. They did not attack.

The whole episode served to explain how the Fleures lived. They ate no meat, so they did not aggressively hunt down the beasts that wanted to eat them in turn. They could only defend themselves. I led them back. We collected our baskets filled with produce from the forest and returned in triumph to the village.

That evening there was a huge celebration. However, it felt strange and unfamiliar to wait in vain for the appetizing scent of frying hams while three succulent carcasses putrefied in the forest.

I asked about the aforementioned men in red and learned that they raided the villages along the river just like the Kataki slave hunters. But that was about all that made sense to me. Presumably my red shamlak and the red breechclout caused quite a stir when they rescued me from the tree. The fundamental kindheartedness and simplicity of these people was clearly demonstrated in their good-natured action.

However, they had no good words left for the King of Caneldrin. The taxes, which they paid from the natural bounty that the forest had to offer, were higher each time they were visited. Although everything in the forest grew lushly, it nevertheless took a great deal of work, sweat and toil to bring in the harvest.

Later than I wanted I felt ready to travel, even though I still did not have full command of my powers. Pansy, the young girl who epitomized the village beauty, gave me a garland of flowers. She hung it around my neck.

"The garland will bring you good fortune in the forest."

"Thank you, Pansy." I did not know what else to say.

I decided not to take a lot of provisions because the forest would provide. I had to go north. Somewhere out there—the Fleures had no idea how far away—there was a large village. I was convinced that it was a proper settlement and I would find a means of transport. I still had my money. Although the Fleures knew what money was, they did not use it between themselves.

After our Remberees had echoed through the dense deciduous forest, I departed.

I did not give myself the option to travel on the river. Although the Fleures lived near a stream which teemed with fish they remained confirmed vegetarians. They had three primitive canoes that were used only for rare visits to the other villages. To take one of them would not fit with my idea of how an honorable Krozair of Zy would behave.

So I started the long walk.

The mingled streaming ruby and emerald light of the Suns of Scorpio shone down and the forest was transformed by the canopy of dancing patterns. I inhaled deep breaths of the magnificent Kregen air. Ah! How sweet the air of Kregen! I walked with long strides, and except for the depressing thoughts of the various tasks that I had to perform, I enjoyed the experience wholeheartedly.

When I reached a clearing after a long time in the forest, I saw the outlines of a flier, which turned mid-flight and landed at the further end.

The hope that rose in me at first quickly went away. I did not know who or what this flier carried. I dove back into the forest and moved on with extreme caution; the sounds of voices were the first indication that I was near to the landing site.

In the general murmur of voices, a few words jumped out at me.

"May Dokerty grant us generous support in our mission."

I crept on, still cautious. I peered through the leaves at the camp that they had made. A few tents, a roast turning over a campfire—the scent made my mouth water—men approaching carrying wood and water. They wore red robes and cowls that were similar to the followers of Dokerty. I could feel my lips pursing with anger.

By the dangling eyeballs and festering tongue of Makki Grodno! These were villains who should dangle from the gallows, men who had turned normal people into horrible monsters. They unleashed demons from a sinister netherworld, who then took over the bodies of their victims. These unfortunates were ibmanzies, monsters ensouled by murderous rage, who felt no pain as long as they destroyed everything that stood in their way until their bodies gave up. Then the demons departed, leaving behind only a corrupted shell.

The reason for the presence of Dokerty cultists here in the forest was obvious. These were the men in red, who my friends the Fleures were so afraid of.

There was only one thing to do. I, Dray Prescot, Vovedeer, Lord of Strombor and Krozair of Zy could rant against the interruption to my mission as much as I wanted, but it was very clear what I had to do. I had to turn back at once and warn my new friends about the danger.

Before I set off, I looked carefully at the Dokerty expedition once more. Then I hurried back in the direction from which I had come, and just hoped that I did not meet any Linomins on the way.

When I reached a path that I knew was the shortest route to the village, I stopped as if rooted to the spot. The anger I felt made my whole body tremble. I drew the Krozair longsword.

In front of me an arrogant Kataki in full armor stretched his whip-like tail with its strapped-on dagger into the air, and dragged a screaming girl by the hair behind him. It was Pansy. She writhed and squirmed as her delicate figure was pulled along by the Kataki over the hard forest floor.

I must admit that I responded to this despicable sight with rage. I started toward the Kataki with my Krozair blade lowered.

"Hai, whiptail!" I said between clenched teeth. "Put the girl on the ground, gently."

He did not. He pushed Pansy aside. Then he threw himself forward with his two swords and daggered tail pointed directly towards me.

Four

How often have I thought about whether the Katakis have such a thing as humanity? Yes, there was Rukker, who had shown signs of compassion when I was in the Eye of the World. Nobody likes the Katakis. The fellow who stormed towards me, warped by irascible fury and pointed teeth in his mouth, was a typical representative of his race. Was I obliged to show mercy?

He wanted to get it over with quickly, and he wanted to finish me before Pansy came back to her senses and fled into the woods. He cut, stabbed, and cut almost simultaneously with his three weapons.

I relied on my skills as a swordsman and dodged, ducked and parried.

He literally drooled. I feinted with the Krozair blade in one direction. This completely wrong-footed him. I used the flat of the sword on the side of his skull. He was thrown to the side, nearly doing a cartwheel, and crashed to the ground. He lay still.

Pansy was silent. She stood tensely, pressing her hands to her chest, and stared at me. I forced a smile.

"He will not hurt you any more, Pansy."

"Is he... dead?"

"Oh, no. That was just a little tap. Come on! Help me collect a few creepers. We will tie him up properly and then..." I stopped abruptly. I felt I should shut my old black-fanged winespout. However, the words had had a calming effect on her.

We tied him up. I bound him tightly so that he could not escape, and I did not waste much thought on his comfort. Then I gave Pansy his two swords and the dagger which I had removed from his tail. I had not cut off his tail to remove the dagger, as so many men would have done.

On the way to the village Pansy told me they had been warned early enough this time. She had been captured when she returned later to the village, she told me quite easily. "It was my fault." The Fleures would never have opposed the Katakis to liberate Pansy, and the damned whiptails knew that.

The joy over her safe return encouraged me. Everyone believed she was lost. They all danced happily in a circle, these simple folk who lived in the clearings of this forest and were tyrannized by fear of visits from the devils.

No one else had been captured. The trail left by the slavers was clearly visible. An idea began to form in my mind. Whether poetic justice or not—I did not care what happened to them. It was a plan that appealed to me very much. I even smiled, by Krun!

I gave them the Remberee, this time for good, and followed the trail. The Katakis had followed the path leading out of the village, but where they had gone between the trees, they had hacked a path. I followed.

A long time later, I heard their voices and smelled the smoke of a campfire.

I crept up, pushed a few leaves aside and examined their camp.

Satisfied, I licked my lips. Their flying boat was a robust flier that at first sight looked to be quite fast. From it came a quiet wailing, a sound that could turn the stomach. So the Katakis had captured victims from another village in the neighborhood.

I prepared myself for the game and stepped out of the bushes large as life.

"Hai! Katakis! Whiptails! Cowardly scum! Blintzes! Rasts! Cramphs! Tapos! Shints! Vile, blasphemous abominations! Slimy beasts that have crawled out from under flat stones!" I jumped up and down and waved my arms. Then I made indecent gestures at them. "Bastards who carry out obscene practices!" Well, that was true, by Krun! "Vagots! Gaolers!" I gave them what they duly deserved, but cannot repeat here.

They sprang up from around the fire. They stormed out of the voller. They stopped and stared at me as if they could not believe their eyes and ears. Then they roared, and drew their weapons.

The time had come for the final insult.

I called it loud and clear. "Kleeshes!"

That was the trigger. That one little word can bring a Kregan to a frenzy! For me, a man of Earth, it had no meaning. But they reacted with such fury that they would have pursued me until their last breath.

After a final contemptuous gesture I spun around and sped off. Taking advantage of the trees as cover, I maintained a pace that did not allow them to catch up with me. Two crossbow bolts whizzed past me from behind—and missed. Since they had fired their bolts, they would either have to stop and reload or continue with useless crossbows.

It was a magnificent, exciting chase! We raced through the forest, and if hunting horns had sounded it would have completed the picture.

The Katakis had turned into a bellowing horde. Their screams echoed back from the trees. I maintained a careful distance and led them from their landing site to the other, very interesting, glade, which I had recently visited.

The noise had preceded us. When I shot from the cover of the bushes, I saw at once that the men in red were waiting with drawn swords for the cause of the disturbance. I swerved and leaped back into the undergrowth. The agitated Katakis ran on. They stormed into the clearing. Then the Dokerty cultists and the Kataki slavers were eye to eye. What happened next was no surprise.

And it was very entertaining and very satisfying.

Both groups just went at each other. Weapons clashed. Swords rose and fell, thrust into bodies and pulled out again. Cries of pain mingled with the noise. Oh yes, it was really very amusing, by Vox!

I did not watch the entertaining conflict for too long, but I waited long enough to assure myself that they were busy fighting each other. Blood flowed on both sides. Some wanted slaves, the others wanted victims for their devilish rites. Each side fought for their own objectives, and how!

With a soft click of my tongue, I turned away and ran into the woods.

By the ponderous thighs and mountainous hips of the Divine Madam of Belschutz! That was fun! If the fact that I rejoiced in the defeat of another person made me a villain, so be it. These particular people entirely deserved what they got. And I, Dray Prescot, would take pleasure in the part played by me!

It did not matter who emerged as the winner of this fight. If they all killed each other, that would be a good result, by Krun!

When I reached the Kataki voller, I was still happy and relaxed. No whiptails followed behind me. They had left a few guards who were quickly overwhelmed. I decided not to kill them, even though they deserved to have their evil lives ended.

The prisoners could not believe that they were saved. Some were from another village of the kind and gentle Fleures people, a little way upriver, and their spokesperson assured me that they would find their way back. They were all in a state of shock. I advised them to hurry up.

Before they disappeared into the forest, they began to sing. It gave me a tremendous boost. They were a great people, there was no doubt. They sang "The leaves of the trees will cover me." I liked them, I can tell you.

The voller rose gently into the air when I pushed the lever forward. It was packed with food and defensive armaments. The Fleures had rejected my offer to fly them home. They wanted nothing to do with flying boats. They were people of the green paths.

After a short flight, I circled over the fight. Dead bodies lay scattered across the clearing. The men in red and the Katakis still fought fiercely around the campfire. Weapons gleamed red in the flickering light. Each side had about the same number of men on their feet.

I brought the voller right over the Dokerty's flier on the ground and dropped two flaming fire pots.

They spun downwards and hit the fore and aft decks. Flames shot up. The voller was ablaze. I circled once more and rose into the air again.

And I laughed. I, Dray Prescot, Vovedeer, Lord of Strombor and Krozair of Zy, threw my head back into the wind and laughed and laughed.

Five

As it turned out, the city to the north was Lakensmot. The city wall was neither particularly wide nor tall, but it was in excellent condition. The vollerdrome—or the lifterdrome as it was called here in Balintol—lay directly below the southern wall. It was dusty or muddy depending on the weather, a place where you could park your flier for four pieces of silver a night.

The fellow who took my money and assigned me a place wrinkled up his face while considering the flier. He was a Brukaj with a chin like a bulldog, and a scowl, and he told me at once that he could not stand slavers.

I agreed with him. Then we began to haggle in a friendly, enjoyable way for a while. Finally, we agreed on a trade. I parted with the Kataki's prisoner lifter and got a nice little six-seater with brass fittings and a wooden steering cabin. The Brukaj said he would pull out the empty cages from the lifter and install seats. It would make a first-class business flier. To me it was only fair.

"That will be four pieces of silver, dom," he said.

"What for?"

"Four pieces of silver per night for the landing site."

"But I have just paid you."

"Oh, aye. That was for the slave lifter. The fee is for your new flier."

"Oh," I said. "I'm glad you remembered to tell me about it."

"All part of the service, dom."

After I paid him, I asked about a reasonable inn. He recommended the Vo'drin and Bucket, supposedly a comfortable, respectable inn. "I'll be found there later," he added.

There were a few airboats in the square. "If you are there you can buy a round; I know you can afford it."

His scowl did not alter. "Such are the times, now, dom."

He said his name was Bolgo the Rapacious. I made no comment. The Vo'drin and Bucket proved to be quite passable. Soldiers patrolled the streets instead of a city guard. They gave me no trouble, and I went in, paid for a room and ordered a meal.

Bolgo told me he hadn't seen Llanili's *Sparking Thunder*, and when I enquired about him in the taproom, no one had seen him for about a sennight, although Llanili was well known as a lifter captain.

I understood this news to mean that the flier had mastered the storm unscathed and flown on to its destination. At least, I hoped so. It could just as easily be a wreck amongst the trees, smashed into an unrecognizable heap of kindling. And the passengers? I knew nothing about them. They were no more than meaningless names, blank slates. As for their motives, they merely followed the lady Quensella, and her goal, by Vox, had only been to hasten northwards. But their fate concerned me.

Bolgo arrived some time later, looking as if he had lost a zorca and found a calsany. I handed him a jug of the local ale. When it was his turn, to my surprise he threw his copper pieces on the table without murmur. He began to hold forth with extremely sarcastic comments about the king and the regent, and it was obvious that he hated both. We sat in a corner alcove, along with a few of his friends. They shook their heads warningly.

"Come on, Rapacious. The king is too young..."

"He is young and a mischievous onker. A hulu. Someone should tell him about the state of his kingdom."

I said nothing, pricked up my ears, and drank the ale.

They continued their debate, and it painted an ugly picture. The father of the king had died at an early age—on that matter, there were a lot of rumors, by Krun!—and the lad was controlled with an iron scepter by his aunt, who had taken the reins of the regency in her capable and apparently merciless hands.

I was off to get the next round, and went to the bar. The door was pushed open and not only did the night air surge in, but also a group of soldiers. One of them, a huge hulking fellow in polished, prettily orna-mented armor, pulled a trembling, bald headed Gon on a chain behind him. The unfortunate man received a slap. "Well? Come on, you blintz." The Hikdar hit the Gon again. "What are you waiting for?"

Hardly able to raise his arm, the Gon stretched out his arm. He pointed at Bolgo the Rapacious.

"Seize him!"

In a moment Bolgo was grabbed and his arms secured behind his back. He looked at the Gon and his face held no reproach, only pity and regret. The Hikdar pulled at the chain. He leaned forward and glowered at Bolgo's friends. They sat stock still, and I could imagine that their innards had transformed into quivering jelly. "Well?"

The Gon shook his bald shiny head. The Hikdar straightened up, slapped his sword hilt and pulled the chain again. He was obviously disappointed. He was not sure if he should take the other poor devils in addition to his main suspect or not. Finally he pushed out his chest under his breastplate and left.

When I returned to the alcove with the ale, Bolgo's friends said: "You can't say we didn't warn him to keep his black-fanged wine-spout closed."

"What will they do with him?" I passed out the ale.

"Oh, they'll give him a good beating. They want to make us all afraid. I doubt that they'll throw him in the dungeon."

"No," said his companion. "That's right. They will try to beat him into silence."

"On whose orders?"

The local official was a certain Vad P'Pernorath, and the commands came from the capital which meant they came from the regent. He was powerless to resist these commands. So he did it—or risked losing his head.

I learned that a lot of seditious gossip was making the rounds. There was the inevitable resistance movement, which consisted mainly of guerrilla bands that lurked in the hills and wastelands. According to my informants, they had not been taken seriously until recently.

Of course, this meant that Prince Ortyg would not be talking with the young king, but with the regent. That would make life more interesting. This regent C'Chermina seemed to be a very powerful woman.

"And the Gon?"

He was a guy who had lost a wager to Bolgo over a racing lifter. So it had not taken much persuasion for him to denounce the winner to that cramph of a Hikdar.

Then the time came to climb the dark wooden staircase and go to sleep. In the bedroom there was a bench on the wall, which I transformed with the help of a ball of yarn, specially brought for this purpose from the lifter, into a pretty little trap by the door. I jammed a chair under the window latch so that the legs formed chevaux-de-frise. Then I had the same last thoughts as at the end of each and every day and closed my eyes.

A loud crash and a shout woke me.

At the door, a dark shadow wrestled with the bench.

Two steps brought me to him. I grabbed his collar in my fist and pulled him up. A quick look into the corridor showed me the shadow of a fellow who escaped from the circle of light at the other end. I let him go.

"Ow! Ow! My head!"

I looked at my prisoner. The Polsim boy had a rat-like face, and was dressed in grey. His dagger lay on the floor. I picked it up with my free hand and held it to the boy's nose. He narrowed his eyes.

"No doubt you are sorry, right?"

He nodded eagerly. A few questions and the corresponding answers convinced me that he was a simple thief. He had nothing to do with the seething state of affairs around us. He looked half-starved and said that his name was Nath the Quick. Whether this was true or not did not matter, because I was planning to travel the next day and could do without any trouble from the authorities.

Finally, I turned him around, pushed him through the door and sent him on his way with a swift kick in the backside.

There were no more alarms or distractions for the rest of the night, so I woke up rested in the morning. I ate a rich first breakfast, paid the bill and went to the lifterdrome.

A Brukaj who didn't look as grumpy as poor old Bolgo had assumed responsibility for the place. He introduced himself as the nephew of Bolgo the Rapacious. We exchanged a few words while I checked my new voller. "By Bruk-en-im!" said Balrey the Pretty. "My uncle has been betrayed in the worst way, and I'll deal with him myself."

By that he certainly meant the Gon. I nodded, limited myself to meaningless answers, and observing the fantamyrrh I climbed aboard. As I flew my new flier in a graceful curve through the sky, I was conscious again of the wonderful sweetness of the Kregen air. The different smells of the city remained behind me; I had hardly noticed them there, so quickly do you get used to your surroundings.

I needed to steer in a northeasterly direction. Prebaya, the capital of Caneldrin, was located on the banks of the river Largesse, about one hundred dwaburs from the east coast. The river originated in the north in a mountain range of considerable size. Although the capital was far away from the sea—in earthly terms about five hundred miles—it controlled the nation's maritime trade and did not need to rely solely on agriculture. The landscape that passed beneath was pleasant, and there were crops and livestock aplenty. The weather was nice and warm. I avoided the cities that I spied on the horizon, and all in all it was a quiet relaxing trip. Not that I needed any reason to relax, by Krun, but this self-deception was somewhat calming.

The old empire, which had many names, but was generally referred to as the Empire of Balintol, had left its mark on the country and its people. It was not so long ago that the invasion and subsequent retreat by Hamal had also left an indelible mark. Although there is on Kregen a marvelous abundance of different races, customs and architecture, many things avoid the need for change of any kind. A house has a roof and walls or pillars; the difference lies in the way the different elements are put together. The subcontinent of Balintol represents a colorful patchwork of all possible cultures, which are fascinating in their interconnectedness.

The longsword my clansmen of the Great Plains of Segesthes use from the back of their voves in a fight is a deadly weapon. Its shape has been copied and is widely used. This weapon, which of course should not be confused with the superior and larger Krozair longsword, is terrible in its effect. The further north you go, and the closer you get to the mountains that separate the great plains of Balintol, the more apparent is the use of the Balintol longsword. This does not mean that I would give the best Balintol longsword fighter a chance against one of my clansmen, oh no, of course not, as sure as Zim and Genodras rise every morning over Kregen!

Prebaya came into view on the horizon shrouded by a shimmering mist that in the slanting light of the Suns of Scorpio made its towers and pinnacles glitter like spear tips. A great number of lifters were arriving and leaving the city, and a considerable number of ovverers had set sail. In the soft, colorful, dazzling sunshine the city appeared calm and peaceful. But since we were on Kregen, of course, the opposite was more likely. Highly likely, by Krun!

My son Drak had sent ambassadors to our diplomatic missions in the major nations, among which several countries in Balintol had recently been ranked. He had hoped this step would eliminate at least one source of friction. Our ambassador in Caneldrin was Elten Naghan Vindo, who joined the diplomatic service from the Treasury. He was a thin, sober man with a sharp wit and he was useful for special operations. He had lost his whole family during the time of unrest in Vallia, and instead of starting over and marrying again he had begun a new career. I was hoping that the things I had asked Ling-Li to send me had arrived with Elten Naghan.

As I looked ahead, the reflections of the suns' light from Prebaya's towers and rooftops had gone. Darkness settled over the land. It started to rain.

When I landed the flier at a lifterdrome, it was still raining. A Polsim, drenched to the skin, pointed me to a berth and demanded eight pieces of silver. The prices in capital cities are usually considerably higher than elsewhere, so I paid without a murmur and hurried through the downpour to check for any messages from Vallia.

My code name was Varghan na Vernheim. As soon as I announced myself at the station, I was admitted. I shook the wetness from my shamlak and walked through the gate. The shamlak had been through a lot lately and looked decidedly scruffy.

Elten Naghan Vindo greeted me with a steaming pot of good Kregan tea. I was led into a small room where they had laid out fresh, dry clothes, but I went straight for the tea and food. Vindo did not wear the brown-yellow Vallian clothes, but a dull orange shamlak. His baggy trousers were inflated at the ankles. This was the fashion in the northern regions of Balintol.

He told me that Prince Ortyg had been received and welcomed by the lady Chermina with honor. "I have a few excellent sources of information. She has lofty plans for Tolindrin. And then..."

"Oh, aye," I interrupted him. "And then she wants to conquer the whole of Balintol. And then the whole world."

He tugged on his full goatee. "Something like that, Majister."

I asked him if he had ever heard of the ladies Froisier or Quensella.

"Froisier sounds like an invented name." He tugged at his beard again. "Quensella is not uncommon. The sister of the regent has that name."

"Oh, yes?" I sat up straight. Now, on Kregen this was not at all unusual. It could indeed be her. If she had been flying north to Prebaya to participate in the discussions with Prince Ortyg it might explain why she had been in such a hurry.

"And this young king? Yando?" That was the short version of a name that started with a double-initial, and was a few feet long.

The ambassador smiled in an almost conspiratorial manner. "He's a clever boy. But his education is inadequate for his role. Currently, he is passionate about the theater." Again with the cunning smile. "His greatest pleasure is to dress up as a great hero, to strut across the stage and defeat dragons and monsters."

"And?" I did not understand what he was getting at.

"Yes, Majister. He spends most of his time dressing up as Dray Prescot, the Emperor of Emperors, the Emperor of All Paz."

"When..." I continued to say, then stopped. "So the books and plays and all the other lies about me are known here?"

"Extremely popular, Majister, extremely popular." He was enjoying himself in his own dry way, and I couldn't blame him. Still...!

"I suspect this Chermina, the regent, is not thrilled by the idea that a person should rule all of Paz?"

"Not in the least."

"That does not surprise me."

"Majister. May I ask...?"

I nodded. Then I told him that a large part of Loh, and a good piece of Havilfar and Pandahem were already convinced. Segesthes was way ahead thanks to my clansmen. As for Turismond, little had been achieved there so far. "It is a task, Naghan, in which I find no pleasure, but for the sake of Paz and our future defense against the Shanks they must still be persuaded."

As a diplomat, he was diplomatic. "It is a task for all of the people whose heart is in the right place, to assist with all their strength, Majister."

"Aye. And I suspect this young king Yando knows nothing of the true story of Dray Prescot, doesn't read between the lines; for him there is only battle and bloodshed."

"He is too young and easily influenced."

Naghan gave me the things that Ling-Li had sent—a reasonable drexer and a golden pakzhan, which included a long pakai with far more gold than silver rings. I put it on after I had again donned my ragged red shamlak. I still wore the russet leather trousers. The ambassador insisted that I take an ordinary dark gray cloak. I thanked him with all my heart and stepped out into the downpour.

It was very, very wet. The rain was torrential. The gloom gave way to the darkness of the hour of dim when none of the moons of Kregen light up the streets and avenues.

The street was awash with water. Naghan had mentioned that it had been raining heavily for a while. Floods threatened. I went through the puddles and searched for the Quail and Cypher that Vindo had recommended to me. I had a plan, but it stood on shaky ground. I needed accommodation and the latest gossip before I could really get down to work.

The lights of the inn, which sparkled through the pouring rain, made a mighty inviting impression. I quickened my pace—and then stopped abruptly.

This was the place to find gossipy, fat, wine-guzzling drunkards. But not Dray Prescot.

Even though I was wet and uncomfortable and thirsty, I could not forget my duty. Not only did I have an obligation to the Star Lords, but also a duty to remain on Kregen, for Delia...

I pulled the dripping cloak tighter around me and directed my steps to the palace of the regent Chermina and King Yando.

Six

The path to the front entrance of the palace was a series of long wide steps. In the falling rain the marble shone and gleamed with all the colors of the rainbow in the light from the lamps, even though many of the lamps had been blown out by the wind. It was a stormy evening. I pulled my cloak tightly around me, climbed the steps and considered the interesting problem of which name to use.

Prince Ortyg would certainly remember Drajak the Sudden. In spite of the large number of names that I had used on Kregen, and from which I had gained a lot of pleasure, my own name had become much too familiar. Naghan the Arm? Kadar the Hammer? Jak the Sturr? Nath the Shot? Nath Deline? Or one of the many others?

The guards looked out from the protection of their guardhouse as the water dripped off the edge of the roof. They led me along a colonnade at the side away from the majestic hinged door which blocked the main entrance. The Deldar was a Rapa with green and yellow plumage, who was not at all pleased that he had been called. He looked at me impatiently over his beak. "And? This is not a night to be outside."

"I must see the lady Quensella."

"You're in luck. They are still in their meeting. What is it about?"

"It's private, Del."

He lifted his sharply defined head. "Deldar to you, tikshim."

I adjusted the neck of my cloak. In the light of a lantern the gold pakzhan flashed. The symbol of a hyrpaktun served its purpose.

"I understand. Well, you'll have to wait."

He wore the pakmort fastened with silver chains to his harness, and the silver mortilhead was clearly visible. These symbols that distinguish the most illustrious among paktuns are not easy to achieve. His pakai was not very old, so he had not fought many battles, and there was only one gold ring taken from a dead opponent. He made an effort to speak in a much more moderate tone of voice.

"The mercenary craft is a hard life, dom. I'll try to get a message to her. Your name?"

I shook my head. "That is unknown to the lady. Tell her that she saved me from a nasty fall from a lifter. Then she'll know who I am."

He looked somewhat taken aback, but nodded.

We went to the mess room where I was offered a cup of poor wine. I took off the cloak and discovered to my surprise that the red shamlak remained fairly dry. Then I took a place at the table. My plan was to gain access to the palace. Once in the maze of corridors and chambers that was found in almost every palace on Kregen, I could disappear into the shadows, find the secret passages and spy in peace. I had perfected this aspect of my more nefarious skills through frequent use. I knew that I was very good in matters of espionage. This is no superficial boast but a simple fact that over time has prevented my head and my shoulders from becoming separated from one another.

In the guardroom there was the usual mix of races, and the conversation turned to subjects that have fascinated soldiers for centuries. These were men of the palace guard who were paid by King Yando and who were apparently devoted to him, although they received their orders directly from the regent. The followers of the other participants in the noble meeting were housed deep in the palace. Many members of the old council, who had advised the late king, were dead. Chermina had called this new council into being to hear Prince Ortyg's proposals.

"Up until now she has ruled everything and everyone," said a scarred Rapa, who leaned on the table with a jug in his hand. He wore the insignia of a Delnik, a subordinate rank, similar to the Matoc of Hamal, and plainly had no hope of being raised to the rank of Deldar any time soon. "Why did she convene this council? Why?"

One or two crude responses were given in good spirits. I supposed that the rigorous Chermina was protecting her back. If the venture failed with Ortyg, she would not carry the blame herself, but the Council would. No wonder that Quensella—if the woman I had met and the sister of the regent were one and the same—had been in such a confounded hurry.

A young lad wearing a striking bronze chavonth-head at his throat—a sign that his comrades thought him worthy to be Chavpaktun—and was polishing his sword with water and brick dust, looked up from the work and stared at my pakzhan. I would have given a penny for his thoughts.

The dominant odors in the guardroom would certainly have offended the nose of a high-born young lady, but for an experienced mercenary they called up memories. Oiled steel and leather, sweat, the brick dust that the chavpaktun used still hanging in the air, food smells, the pungent perfume of a watchman, who was vainer than his comrades—all merged into a fragrance that evoked memories.

The boy, apim like me, smiled and pointed to the gold at my neck. "Sorry. Would you tell me how...?"

The Rapa Delnik's plumage bristled. "That's enough, Landi!" He wore a silver pakmort with a respectable pakai. "Show those who are above you more respect. See that you do not let your pakchav go to your head."

A Polsim laughed. "Otherwise you could lose it, by Smitoll!"

None of the men assumed that the Polsim referred to Landi's bronze chavonth head.

It was all quite nice, but I was becoming annoyed at being stuck here.

The guards continued their horseplay; these were rough fellows who enjoyed themselves whenever the opportunity arose. I heard from across the mess a few disparaging remarks about Quensella's guard.

One of the guard captains had not paid his men, but made off with the money chest. Another was so often drunk that he could not fulfill his duties properly. As for the new cadade that Quensella now had in her employ, "If you look at him wrong, you get warts!" And they all roared.

I asked a few questions, their significance immediately clear, shuffled my feet, looked around and then stood with a typical mercenary curse.

"To the left, then first on the right, dom."

I had to leave the cloak; it was hanging on a rack to dry.

In the rough comradeship of paktuns there are a few bad eggs. Many soldiers are just not nice people, but the reasons for being a mercenary on Kregen are quite different than on Earth. Most are honest and sincere and true to their oath. Many kill in the performance of their contract. It is not dishonorable to sell your military talents in the service of good men. At the end of the day—for example at the end of a battle when your own side has lost and it is pointless to keep fighting—you can agree on new terms in order to avoid bloodshed.

I was now fully accepted as a zhanpaktun for the time being. I had achieved my goal. I was able to sneak through the palace and find the secret passages. Good! Now for Prince Ortyg.

I nodded to the guard at the end of the passage and pushed open the door. Beyond it was an abandoned rain-soaked yard, and on the opposite archway a torch flickered. I went over.

A long, shimmering blue pillar of light appeared out of nowhere. Behind it the outlines of the wall could still be seen, but it thickened quickly, and the familiar facial features of Deb-Lu-Quienyin appeared. He did not smile. I instantly felt a renewed confidence.

"Jak! I do not have much time."

"Deb-Lu! I am honestly pleased to see you..."

"No time, no time. Listen."

His next words produced in me a feeling as though someone had poured a bucket of ice water over me. "Ling Li has mentioned to you about the Wizards of Balintol. Their true power is unknown to us, but we know that their kharrna is very strong. Exceptionally strong. They will have noticed by now that I am here in lupu. They will investigate. This means that our visits will have to be very brief." The ghostly apparition flickered. "We do not want them to discover..."

Deb-Lu's words were cut off and the blue radiance disappeared abruptly. I was left alone in the corridor. I took a deep breath. This was a serious matter. How serious could be judged by the fact that Deb-Lu had not spoken using Capital Letters.

There was more to it. If these Wizards of Balintol were indeed so powerful, they would, inevitably, be drawn into the terrible conflicts that threatened to set fire to the whole subcontinent—if I didn't manage to put an end to them.

Outside, the rain came down increasingly heavily. A flash of lightning tore through the darkness, and the rumbling thunder made the palace tremble.

By the black belly and putrescent eyes of Makki Grodno! Yes, it was bad news, deuced bad. I could not let them stop me from doing what I had to do. I was now standing at the end of a row of side chambers that were connected to the main part of the palace. The Deldar's runner would soon arrive back in the guardhouse. Maybe he had managed to give my message to Quensella. Maybe not. In any case, the Deldar would want to know where I was. I had to make myself invisible immediately.

Looking for the telltale signs of secret passages—they do not stand out, by Krun!—I wandered on through the corridors.

There were a few people going about their business; as in all the great palaces on Kregen, someone is always on the go. The architecture was immense, as was fitting. I came into a vast chamber with a pond in the center. In the water cavorted voryachin, which resemble the voryasen of previous bad experiences; they are an ugly fish, consisting only of jaws and teeth that can separate a person into two halves. Why those in power in this country would want such creatures in their homes, I have no idea.

The walls were covered with awe inspiring dark green curtains and the lighting was subdued. Voices and the patter of feet on the marble floor told me that it was not slaves who were coming closer. My presence would cause interest, if not arouse suspicion. I did not belong to the palace guard and was not a servant, so what in a Herrelldrin Hell was a blintz like me doing here?

I quickly pressed myself into the shadows of the green curtains.

The people who walked by gesticulating and furiously debating included some of those powerful people of whom I had just been thinking, together with their guards and henchmen. Servants went about their duties with bowed heads and serious faces. All were dressed in the latest, foppish, Caneldrin fashions. So these were the members of the council that the regent Chermina had convened.

I felt like a fly on a polished table, with the fly swatter hovering menacingly overhead.

They passed by discussing excitingly the topics that occupied them. Some of them were certainly smart enough to realize why Chermina had summoned them so suddenly.

Behind them a cheerful young lady wrapped in lace and silk followed, a young lady who was protected by a hard-nosed Chulik guard.

"I think the good Chermina is quite right," she announced in a breathless voice to her companion, a woman dressed all in blue with gaunt features. "And this terrible Quensella—well, a lady cannot say what should be done with her!"

A woman with a sharp-edged face answered something to appease her, and then they had passed the pond with the deadly fish and left the chamber. Relieved that everyone had passed by, I was emerging from my hiding place when someone else approached, and I had to quickly jump back again.

The twilight of the chamber emphasized her appearance. Tall and with her head held high, still in the grey-green dress, she strode by purposefully. Her hair—as black as a raven's wing—was cropped short and fitted here head like a helmet. Her cadade, an apim, walked at her side. He wore gold-plated armor and a pair of swords. His dark face showed no emotion as she spoke in her high, imperious voice.

"My servants, Nath. Where are those vulgar, lazy things?"

He paused before giving an answer. His thin mouth was crowned with a black mustache. "I'll go and find out, my lady."

"Good. And hurry up."

They stopped at the edge of the pond. She turned away from her cadade, clearly impatient at being without her. The captain of her guard, this Nath, took a step back to look for the missing servants. But only a single step!

I rushed out from the shadow of the curtains.

"Quensella!"

Nath moved towards her with arms outstretched. His hands were nearly at Quensella's back. He was going to push her into the pond of voryachins.

We three collided. I wanted to grab the fellow, but he evaded me and tried again to push Quensella into the water. She had wisely turned at my call, and that had saved her. Now we three wrestled together at the edge of the pond.

We gasped, swayed, slipped and found footing again, three people in a life and death struggle at the edge of eternity.

She did not scream. She called out with her controlled, hard voice: "Guards! Guards! Murderer!"

In the fray, she tried to hit me and struck me beneath the eye. I ducked and tried to separate her from the cadade. He wanted to draw his sword. I gave him a blow on his forearm, he yelped, and the sword landed with a clatter on the marble floor and bounced splashing into the water. We struggled on.

The marble of the pond edge was slippery. If we fell into the pond...

Nath tried to thrust his knee into my groin, but I blocked him, pushed Quensella to the side, and put an elbow in his face. He yelped again. Quensella was coughing and gasping for air, so I pulled at the arm which he had around her neck. We staggered and stumbled. Feet slipped on the wet marble. The strangling hands were pulled away. Nath cried out. He stumbled around with wildly flailing arms. He tried to find something to grab onto and caught Quensella's dress, while his other hand grasped nothing. I held on to Quensella to pull her from him. We were connected, a trinity of destruction.

And together we plunged into the water.

Seven

Some very unpleasant thoughts raced through my head. The damn voryachins! What fool abandoned of his senses thought they should be in a palace? We hit the surface of the water sending a fountain into the air, and sank to the bottom. Oh, yes, a nice little explanation occurred to me. Undoubtedly, the great kings here could get rid of unwanted persons in a clean and definitive way. A really nice idea.

With jaws like those they should call the damn fish voryachuns, not voryachins. They were cursed by their name, and I with them. The pool was not deep. In a jumble of bodies, arms and legs we touched the bottom. Of course, I had taken a deep breath before we were submerged in the water. A turn showed me a fish heading straight for us with jaws wide open. The grip I had on the cadade was a grip of death. A fierce shove sent him into the fish. I just hoped that the cursed voryachin had teeth hard enough to bite through the fellow's armor.

Quensella squirmed like a fish on a hook. She had to be got out of this mess immediately. A cloud of blood obscured the water—perhaps the armor had not been strong enough. I managed to get to my feet. The water came up to my neck. I took another deep breath, dove under, grabbed

Quensella in a pincer-like grip, turned, flexed all my muscles till they threatened to burst, and sent the lady literally flying through the air to the edge of the pool.

It is difficult to jump out of water onto the land, and I just hoped that her arms were strong enough to pull herself out the rest of the way. I went back into the depths, and my old sailor's knife slid smoothly out of its sheath. With the knife in hand I threw myself against the streamlined shape that rushed towards me. A roll to the side as it raced past me and the knife penetrated, was twisted and pulled out again—it all happened in only a few heartbeats.

A stroke with my arm lifted my head above the surface of the pool. Streaming water blurred my vision, but at least I could hear Quensella screaming like a banshee.

There was no time for dawdling here. The deadly sharp teeth down there wanted to tear me to pieces. I took another deep breath and plunged. Clouds of dark blood obscured my view. Nath's body turned slowly like a roast on a spit, and a voryachin slipped past him toward me.

It was fast and hungry. A second fish shot through the murky water behind it. I stepped aside and slit the first lengthwise, trod water, and passed the knife to my other hand, but the second killer fish swam right past me and shredded my shamlak.

With a last moment convulsive effort I drove the blade into the rear part of its body. There were more. The water roiled in a maelstrom of foam and blood. The others circled; dimly-outlined, threatening shadows in the gloom. Why weren't they pouncing on their bleeding companions?

A voryachin convulsed, twitching, a leather fletched crossbow bolt sticking out of its scaly skin.

For a moment I had a respite. It was now or never.

My feet hit the bottom of the pond like the hooves of a leaping vove on the parched soil of the dry season. My knees bent like two bows, then unleashed their power. I shot upwards.

The marble edge flew past my searching hands. I grabbed at it, pulled myself up, and blindly made a precautionary cut with the knife behind me. And, by Djan, the blade struck a solid body and was ripped out of my hand. A sharp pain shot through my heel, but I took no notice because I somehow dragged myself over the edge of the pool and then hands slid under my armpits and pulled me like a sack of flour up onto my feet.

As I wiped the water from my eyes and took a deep breath, I clearly saw the situation. A dandy hikdar brandished his rapier under my nose.

"At least we caught one of the blintzes!"

He had a smug face, his mouth distorted, the protruding teeth bared. He was keen to execute me on the spot.

Now, like any normal person I actually do not like to have swords waving around under my nose. Surely the matter would be resolved quickly if Quensella got involved. At least I hoped so. They would surely not suppose that I was involved in the plan to remove her by a push into a pond full of hungry jaws and teeth?

Putting that delicate question aside for a moment, there was still this dandy brandishing his damned rapier before my face. "When I'm done with his interrogation, he will..." he began.

A quick movement and his handsome rapier was in my gnarled fist, and pushed against his neck over the top of the knitted cloth which fell down in folds over his harness.

"He will what, dom?"

He swallowed. His red face was gray-green. Saliva ran down his chin. He wanted to say something, but could manage no sound.

It would not surprise me at all if in the next second they all pounced on me and I had to fight for my life. Since I had acted in the old, uncontrolled Dray Prescot way, I had to reckon with the consequences arising from that and accept the needle.

The Fristle that I could see out of the corner of my eye seemed better able to handle his unsheathed swords than the hikdar in front of me, so I would need to deal with him first. Oh yes, I was ready for a round of cut-and-thrust.

A hard, bright, haughty voice drowned out the uproar.

"Stop!"

I gave the hikdar a kick in the stomach—gently, because I did not want to have to deal with the consequences if things went bad. I threw him his rapier, and it landed clanking on the marble.

"This man saved my life!" she exclaimed. "Treat him properly."

She had not yet recognized me, did not realize who I was. All the toughness that comes from their origin, their blood, their ancestors, keeps these high-born strong in the moments after a terrible experience. Later—well, no doubt she would be overcome with a great trembling, as happens to the best of us.

The situation eased. The captain of the guard, this Nath, was fished out of the pond with a hook and dropped onto the edge, where blood and water poured out of him. I looked at him. The poor devil, bribed with money, strayed from the right path because of his greed, and now here he was dead and half eaten. His armor had been bitten clean through, but when I looked closer it became clear that the gold-plate was very thin and only for show.

"When he has dressed himself, bring him to me," barked Quensella.

"Quidang, my lady!"

An ancient old fellow came up to me, put his hands on his hips, thrust his head forward and peered at me. He was wearing a dark blue double-breasted robe that ended just below his knees and blue pants that resembled mine, which were now dripping wet and stuck to my legs. He approached the end of his life, was certainly over two hundred, and his face had the resigned expression of someone who had seen it all. His head was covered by a flat blue cap, the edge decorated with a wide band of gold lace. The golden belt studded with jewels at his waist held a slikker and a dagger. He wore blue silk gloves. His puffy eyes were aqueous blue above a powerful nose and a mouth so narrow it might as well be invisible. This man might be old, but he radiated power.

He turned to the overzealous hikdar. "Seems you've caught a clansman, Renko."

The hikdar picked up his rapier. An odd expression briefly flickered across his face as he looked at me, then he replied to his master. "That I have, notor, indeed. But when the life of our mistress Quensella..."

"Exactly."

The pool room was filling up with several people who were, no doubt, in the retinue of the old man. This hikdar Renko was obviously in his service, but I could not imagine that he was his cadade. The crossbowman who had helped me by shooting the fish was busy pulling it out of the water. That was for me the proof that the guard was composed of experienced paktuns; no matter how rich the employer, a crossbow bolt costs whatever a crossbow bolt costs.

"Your name?" His voice was quiet and friendly.

"Drajak."

"Notor!" exclaimed the hikdar. "You will address the Lord as notor!"

The old boy did not flinch. Given his age, I saw no reason to deny him the necessary courtesy. "Notor."

"Drajak. And is there more?"

I had already made up my mind. I almost chose Sturr, but this is a rather coarse name that designates a stubborn, introverted fellow who is rarely courteous. No. It should be something similar, but less coarse—a maverick. I said, "Drajak the Daxer, notor."

He did not forget the obvious. "Why are you here?"

The truth was safest. "I owe the lady Quensella a service."

He merely raised an eyebrow.

I told him the story. When I had come to the end—and the entire audience, with open mouths, could not believe their ears—he let out a sigh. "This is typical of Quensella," he said. "A headstrong girl. But I love her because of that." He dismissed me with a nod. "You will want to dry off and change your clothes. Then Renko will take you to Quensella."

Now, I know the great and powerful of Kregen well enough. And it is wise to be cautious and choose every step carefully. "I thank you for your timely intervention, notor. May I also know your name?"

He sucked in his cheeks and blew them out. Renko snapped to attention. "You have the honor of being in the presence of Kov L'Luminophrontesia!"

He might have gone on, but an indifferent gesture silenced him. "Kov Lumino," Kov Lumino said. "Lahal."

"Lahal, Kov."

I dared to ask a question. "May I ask the notor whether the deldar from the guardhouse has delivered my message to Lady Quensella?"

He shook his head. "As far as I know, she has not received a message."

Then he dismissed me with a graceful movement of his silk gloved hand. He walked from the pool room with his attendants, leaving only Hikdar Renko and I there alone, surrounded by silence.

I looked at him. He was apim and seemed like a tough fellow despite his mincing manners. A white scar ran down his cheek.

I stretched out my hand. "No offense?"

He did not hesitate. I had to hand it to him—and to Kov Lumino who obviously knew who he wanted in his employ and who not. We shook hands. "No offense."

We exchanged a few words as he ushered me deeper into the palace. The place was a maze of magnificent chambers and corridors.

"You were very lucky, by Nelacion, that the lady Quensella was flying the lifter."

Maybe someone else would have replied that it had been her good fortune to have flown so well. Had she not done so, no one would be able to thank her, and she would have had no one to rescue her from the vory-achin pool. There are no guarantees, by Vox! But it was not the kind of thing a notor from Vallia would say out loud.

We went to Renko's comfortable and generously provided apartments located in a part of the palace made available to Kov Lumino. I suspected that many of the nobles lived here instead of in their villas scattered around the city.

When I enquired about Quensella's bodyguard, Renko wrinkled his nose. He told me they had had considerable difficulty finding reliable people, aggravated by their habit of continually traveling around. Kov Lumino had been the best friend of her great-grandfather, and felt responsible for her, but her wayward travels prevented him from keeping her adequately safe, in his opinion. The king, who had recently died, had lost all his children except the young Yando. Chermina and Quensella had been the twins of the aunt of the king, who had married a vad. That explained why they were not princesses. Nevertheless, the line of succession was correct; Chermina was the rightful regent.

When I stripped off the torn shamlak, I discovered surprisingly long welts along the side of my ribs. The damned fish caught me after all. And the other had bitten me in the heel. Renko frowned.

"Best I immediately get a needleman. The bite of this fish is poisonous."

"Well, that's just perfect," I said, and left it at that.

The needleman, bald, nearsighted, awkward, nursed me. He told me the poison would work its way through the body, then he shook his head sadly. "If you're strong enough, you will survive it."

Meanwhile, I had had a pretty busy day, what with the flight and the fight, and although tiredness is a sin I could feel exhaustion spreading into my limbs.

How much was the fatigue honestly earned and how much the Opaz-cursed poison?

My wounds had not bled—apparently this was a normal side effect of the poison—so the needleman had opened them to allow them to bleed out and the inflammation subsided quickly. He shook his head. "That will help, but the poison is already in your body."

"Thank you, Master Illargo," Renko said and gave him a gold piece. I said nothing.

I dressed in a dark green evening robe and was ready to be received by Quensella. A servant brought the garment; it belonged to Renko. When I saw the color, I felt for a fleeting moment a feeling I had not felt for many years. I quickly suppressed the disgust and pulled it on. Then I set off to visit the noble lady. Renko remained at my side.

Her apartments were tastefully furnished in a simpler style than I had encountered in the palace until now. The decor was dominated by a gentle, soothing peach color, and the chair on which I was ordered to sit was extremely comfortable. It was an amazing moment when her eyelids dropped to regard me.

She was almost at the end of her nice thank you speech before she became aware that I was even there, and before she had looked at me properly. I was for them just any paktun. She wore a pretty, bright blue robe of striking simplicity, a sword and dagger hanging from their harness at her side. The black hair that looked so much like a cap was combed forward and formed two curved wings behind her earlobes.

Then she turned to me and looked at me more closely.

"Oh!"

"I have come to you once again to express my gratitude, my lady." I stood up and fell back heavily into the chair. The room swam before my eyes.

Renko said something about the voryachin poison. I swallowed, gripped the armrests and pulled myself together. It took a moment before I realized that she was still standing in front of me and not hovering near the ceiling, as I had imagined. Renko was no more than a vague noise. Next to the chair was a small, one-legged table, laden with delicious appetizers. Maybe a little bite of food would help. I grabbed the table and ended up on the carpet, along with the table and the food.

Then strange, seemingly disembodied hands lifted me up and put me back in the chair.

I tried to shake my head, and the famous old bells of Beng Kishi echoed through my vosk skull.

I heard someone say that I was looking for a blade to fit a sheath, which is a picturesque Kregish phrase for a quid pro quo. Then Quensella said a few words, and they came to me cold as ice. "When you are healthy again, Drajak the Daxer, I would like to employ you as my cadade."

The room was now clearly set in motion, jumping up and shooting into the depths like a swifter in a rashoon in the Eye of the World. I blinked. Spots of light danced before my eyes. Thunder rumbled in my ears. "Your captain of the guard?"

Confused, I came to the conclusion that it would put me in an excellent position to have access throughout the palace, which would greatly ease my spying mission. But it would also tie me down and restrict the freedom of my actions. I debated with myself in a rather idiotic way, and the advantages and disadvantages tumbled through my aching head.

Cadade or not cadade?

I remember with vivid clarity that my nose ended up on the outlines of a strigicaw that had been woven into the carpet at my feet. But I remember nothing more of that day.

Eight

The play that night was called 'The Great Jikai of Tacgide the Meek'. The actors were undoubtedly excellent, but I was not in the mood for it, even though I usually enjoy the dramatic arts. Somehow I had become Quensella's captain of the guard—and for the sweet sake of Mother Diocaster, do not ask me how. It just happened.

Being in the service of Quensella could have been so pleasant. But I was vexed. Of course I could not immediately resign from her service, but one day I would have to do it, and I reckoned that day would not be long in coming. For the time being I had to allow events to unfold naturally.

At least I had learned that the council was divided on Prince Ortyg's proposals. Those among them who were eager for the noise of battle wanted to gather the armies, set out immediately to the south and invade Tolindrin. Amongst themselves they did not mince their words about their future intentions—while we guards stood with immobile faces against the wall. After they had conquered the country, with Prince Ortyg's traitorous help, they wanted to get rid of him and divide the booty among themselves.

Other noble members of the council were of a different opinion. They could see the horrors that war may bring on the nation. This had often happened in the past. Tolindrin was a powerful enemy.

Although this information circulated around the palace, it did not leak out to the ears of the people on the street. Everything I learned I passed on to the Vallian ambassador. It was easy to imagine that in this situation far more than the destiny of two lands in Balintol was at stake. Vallia had a great interest in the outcome, and the stupid decisions taken here could result in all of Paz being in danger.

The play ended, and everyone hurried outside under the strict observance of the orders of social rank. We guards managed to make space for our masters.

No one tried to attack Lady Quensella. It was fairly obvious to me that her life was in danger. No cadade would try, without good reason, to push his mistress into a deadly pool. Probably there had been a lot of gold involved, and there could also have been threats, but it was most important to understand the motives behind the deed, which were currently unknown to me. Who wanted Quensella out of the way?

She had spoken out forcefully against the alliance with Ortyg. The lady Chermina would make her own decision, no matter what the council finally decided. If they rejected Ortyg's offer, Chermina would be vulnerable if the war was unsuccessful. This could be the reason. Chermina was widely detested, while Quensella was loved by all, and that was not unusual for sisters, one of them having the power and the other not.

So far I had met neither King Yando nor Chermina. Maybe, if there was time, I would explore some more of this puzzle.

About a sennight had passed since I collapsed during my interview with the lady who was now, amazingly, my mistress. The very next day I had looked over a couple of new recruits. We had both decided that her personal bodyguard had to be reinforced.

Elten Naghan Vindo had to draw on experiences that lay just outside his normal diplomatic duties to get me half a dozen Pachaks. They had just become tazll and were looking for work, so we were extremely lucky to get them. They gave their nikobi—the Pachak code of honor that was the reason we unconditionally trusted them and knew they would fight for us until death. I was very happy with them and wanted more first class paktuns of comparable abilities.

The interviews were held in an anteroom, and Kov Lumino had cleverly sent Hikdar Renko to keep an eye on everything. I had nothing against this obvious interference with my authority. Lumino just felt responsible for the great-granddaughter of his dead friend.

I sat at a simple wooden table. Drino, a hunchbacked Xaffer, sat to one side with a pen in his hand and a battered register before him. On the table was a strong lenken chest reinforced with iron bands. It was open, and the glitter of gold within was truly tempting.

"Next!"

A vulture-headed Rapa with mangy feathers blustered in wearing cheap clothes and three swords in his belt. It was obvious at first sight that he was not suitable, but I treated him kindly and sent him away with a gold piece that would soothe his wounded pride.

"Next!"

A limber youngster stood before the table; he had one of those open, rosy faces of the sort that arouses in every older woman the desire to give him a kiss. Aye, for a young girl it would be the same. He wore a red tunic and matching trousers, a sword and a dagger, and his mop of brown hair was covered by a wide-brimmed floppy hat with a red feather. He stood stock-still and looked at me. His brown eyes widened and his jaw dropped. I had to act quickly.

"Name?" I barked. "Come on, boy, your name?"

"Erwin, Maj—"

I interrupted him roughly. "So, Erwin! And where are you from, Erwin with the unbridled tongue?"

Drino, the Xaffer, gave a low, amused snort. No doubt he thought I was making fun of the boy's obvious discomfort. But I wanted at all costs to prevent the young Erwin from saying something stupid, and quickly, by Krun! Renko, whom I had befriended, would rush like an arrow to Lumino with such an important piece of news.

Erwin stuttered, and his wonderful, boyish face flushed.

"Vallia, I suppose. Well, Erwin, am I right? And you will call me Jiktar! Never forget that!"

"Not from Vallia, Maj— Jiktar. From Valka."

Well now, that was odd. My Valkans call me their Strom. The younger generations had likely lost this cheerful disrespect for their ruler. They had not fought by my side during the hard times of Valka and the Fetching of Drak na Valka. For the young people, the ruler—even a ruler who has abdicated—will be the Majister. Even the high-spirited bunch of men and women, all splendid fighters that make up my Stromnate of Valka, went along with it.

Erwin said that his hometown was Valkanium, and my thoughts went immediately to Esser Rarioch and the view of the bay. I took him on, and Drino wrote down his name neatly. But he looked up. "Erwin what?" Then he added, conscious of the freedom of his position and his race, whooping with laughter, "Erwin the Waggler!"

The poor boy! Whether he liked it or not, that was his nickname from now on.

Later I ordered Erwin to my private quarters and gave him strict commands. "It is Jiktar, or Jik!" Then I made sure that no one could overhear us, and we talked about Valkanium. He proved to be a reliable, likeable lad. Still, as nice as it was to converse with him, I knew that he was the weak link in the chain when it came to my disguise, which was essential for my spying activities.

Like many young boys who yearn for the exciting life of an adventurer, he had taken leave of his parents and had set out to be a mercenary. He was confident that he would soon ascend to chavpaktun, then to be mortpaktun and finally to wear the gold zhanpaktun with a long, dangling pakai. His father was an armorer, and I remembered his grandfather too, who had worked for Naghan the Gnat. Yes, as already mentioned, it is nice to chat over a glass of wine or three. Still, my duties could not be forgotten.

In addition to Erwin the Waggler and six first-class Pachaks I was fortunate to take four experienced Hytaks into service. Hytaks are very reliable in their own way, with a code of honor very different from that generally accepted among the fanatical Pachaks. I could well imagine myself able to transform these men into a force of bodyguards that would prevent even a hair on Quensella's head from being bent. At least I hoped so, by Krun.

When I had met her at the border, her own flying boat had just refused to work, and she eventually told me that it was at that exact time that an attempt was made on her life. She took just her two maids with her and booked passage with Captain Llanili which had cost her only the employment of her undisputed perseverance and a purse of one hundred gold pieces.

"You took a risk with me, my lady."

She laughed; a deep, contented, joyous sound, not a high pitched girlish giggle. "Oh, I realized immediately that you weren't the assassin type."

I kept my old black-fanged winespout closed.

She wanted me to wear pretty gilt armor over a purple uniform. I stubbornly refused. Purple is a nice color, and pastel colors are worn by both women and men nowadays. No, it was the lack of protection provided by such armor that I objected to. After some heated discussions, we agreed on simple leather armor reinforced with bronze plates. The helmet, also in bronze, was not too fancy or unwieldy. Like Tolindrin, Caneldrin appeared to have difficulties in producing high-quality iron and steel.

This is exactly why I insisted that the men of the guard use their own weapons, no matter what it was. This she vetoed. She wanted the boys to stand at attention in front of the doors and stairways holding damn great halberds and pikes that towered into the air. Now, it is an undoubted fact that a splendidly uniformed soldier armed with the halberd offers an impressive sight. If the crescent axe blade is decorated with beautiful patterns and colorful tassels dangle from it, the effect is even greater.

Since their value in a roguish sneak attack by black-masked stikitches was rather questionable, I resisted her commands to me. In the end we came to a compromise. The jurukkers would use their own weapons, but also carry halberds. That everyone would drop their long weapon after the first enemy contact was tacitly ignored; long weapons do have their benefits, and in the right circumstances they are indispensable. With regard to the name jurukker for a watchman, well yes, I know, guards are generally called jurukkers within an army. Nevertheless, the division that I put together developed into a truly effective juruk.

The oldest of the Pachaks, Molar Na-Fre, with the gold at his neck, and the oldest of the Hytaks, Nalan ti Perming, also wearing gold, were promoted to hikdars.

Nalan ti Perming carried his comrades' Balintol longsword. He described it as a clanscreetz for obvious reasons. The short form for this was clantzer. This clantzer, a longsword, must not, of course, be confused with the Vallian clanxer, a kind of cutlass. Such a mistake may well lead to one's head being separated from one's shoulders. Oh yes, by the Blade of Kurin!

Quensella lived in her own quarters within the cluster of buildings that made up the palace. We guarded the entrances and exits. The central parts of the cluster of buildings were reserved for the pompous affairs of state, and the nobles lived in the surrounding wings and annexes. The regent Chermina was quartered somewhere at the rear of the palace near the river. She held herself apart from the others, and kept King Yando on a tight rein.

I found all the routine extremely boring and annoying, but there was no getting around it. I had direct access to critical meetings of the council and to the far more important confrontations between the two sisters, which had so far not occurred.

Erwin proved to be a great consolation, for he told me enthusiastically about Valka, Valkanium and the bay. He had swum there all his life. "There is in the world no better spot!" he said.

I did not contradict him—I agreed with him—although there are, of course, many other places of unsurpassed beauty on Kregen. Erwin was very popular within the guard.

I took on a few more men: an apim, a few Brokelsh and, after some hesitation, a Khibil. The Khibil, fox faced and cunning, of course demanded a bonus, which he held to be justified simply because he was a Khibil. I considered that alone to be insufficient and quickly rejected him, so he agreed to serve for the same pay as the others. His name was Perempto the Shorn because he wore his reddish hair cut very short, and if it had been any shorter he would have looked like a Gon.

Erwin confided in me one day that his nickname was Erwin the Rose. "That is why it didn't bother me to be called the Waggler." On his face was a most excellent depiction of rosiness. With all the connotations that the word had acquired in my life, I was glad that his name had been changed.

While all the responsibility rests on the captains of the guard, they also receive benefits from its position. It provides them favors. So I was not in the least surprised when after the inspection of all positions on a beautiful day I felt a feather light touch on the shoulder. I turned around. The woman was young, had a pleasant appearance and was neatly dressed. She wore a half-veil, and her eyes.

"Lord. Here."

She gave me the envelope she held in her outstretched hand, then turned like a top and disappeared behind a lotus column.

Veil or not, I would have recognized her if she had been known to me. But she was not. I knew everyone from Quensella's household. Whether maids, nannies, servants, cooks, kitchen staff, bedchamber squires, wine masters or stablemen, they were all familiar to me, including the slaves. No one had been hired without my knowledge. These things must—or should—be known if a cadade is worth his pay, I might add.

I opened the envelope later in the seclusion of my quarters and read that I was expected at two bells past the hour of dim in The Pleasant Rest tavern, where Naghan ti Indrin would introduce himself. The message ended with the news that I would learn something to my advantage. I burned the neat handwritten message.

Shortly thereafter, Hikdar Molar Na-Fre came by and told me that a local group meeting of the Brotherhood of Paktuns would take place that evening. The Brotherhood of Paktuns, which had defined the various ranks such as gold, silver and bronze in solemn, withdrawn discussions, meets whenever there is an opportunity. They discuss levels of pay, working conditions, pensions, betrayal and many other things of relevance for everyone who follows the mercenary craft—whether male or female.

"Tonight there is a special item on the agenda, Jik. A new rank has long been spoken about. Now is the time to decide something, so that it is finally created."

"Right. But you can't all go. Our duties have priority."

"Of course."

"You and Nalan will go. I will command the guard tonight alone."

Although he resisted, as was proper, he did not want to miss the important meeting under any circumstances, so he agreed. I thought it an unlikely coincidence that someone wanted me to be away from Quensella's chambers at the same time.

My interest in snooping on the political goings-on aside, I took my duties as Quensella's bodyguard very seriously. Of all the characteristics and obligations a cadade should possess, the most important is knowledge of human nature. Imagine if I took a man into the team who was secretly working for those who wanted Quensella out of the way? I have to admit that this nightmarish notion troubled me.

Without proper monitoring a damned stikitche could sneak away from his assigned post and perform the evil deed. In the Pachaks I harbored no doubt at all. I had a strong feeling that I could trust the Hytaks. This was also true for the young Erwin. So I made sure that one of them was paired up with each of the rest of the guard. This was an elementary precaution taken by every good cadade. Then I went off post.

The news of the upcoming Shank attack immediately to the south had not yet reached Prebaya, that was certain. There were still Chuliks around, although I was not able to get any for Quensella's juruk. The young, haughty lady who had rushed past me in the pond room was the Kovneva P'Pinxi, as I learned later, and she woke up one morning to discover that her Chulik guard had abandoned her; it required only a message that their island was in danger from the Shanks.

If I have not mentioned that I had searched out the secret passages inside the palace, including those in the direct vicinity of Quensella's apartments, it is because I am convinced that you who follow my stories know something of my methods. I kept the spider-webbed passages between the walls of the public and private chambers always in mind.

The night was uneventful. Not because of my vigilance or the attention of the guards—it was just that nothing happened.

The next morning the two zhanpaktuns reported on the result of the meeting. The final decision had been passed on to the Brotherhood of Paktuns. There were still some uncertainties as to what the new honorary rank should look like. A gem should proclaim the glory; gold was no longer sufficient to symbolize the honor, we all agreed—but what gem should it be?

Sometime later in the day another messenger tapped me on the arm and handed me a sealed envelope. The message expressed concern that I had not appeared at the rendezvous, and once again emphasized that it would be to my benefit.

So I went that evening to The Pleasant Rest.

Because I never for a moment forgot that I was on Kregen I took with me my weapons and wore Quensella's coat of mail. I left the helmet behind.

The tavern turned out to be not what one would expect from its name. It was not quite a respectable inn; on a stage, performances were held that would have raised the hair of a plundering pirate. I ignored the antics that occurred in the glow of the lamps, and found an alcove in the back. I was expected. Someone slid onto the opposite bench and said, "Lahal. I am Naghan ti Indrin."

A little Fristle fifi conjured up glasses onto the table and put a jug of red wine within easy reach. When she had gone, Indrin leaned forward conspiratorially. He was an Advang; a dark cloak hid his porcine features and stocky frame. He kept his black, wide-brimmed hat on his head. "You're the lady Quensella's cadade," he said. He had a breathless voice, with a whiny tone. "You're lucky. A fortune awaits you."

From this point on, I listened without saying a word; I was already quite clear what this was all about. I decided not to reach out to take his thick neck and squeeze until his piggy eyes oozed out of his skull. I nodded, listening intently, and he babbled away way too much.

I felt a quiet sadness when I realized that Nath, the poor devil, had been bribed in the same way. His life had ended between the jaws of voryachins.

"Well, Drajak the Daxer? This is an excellent opportunity for you to earn a fortune. You'll never again have to suffer hardship."

I took a sip of wine, thinking.

"There is the honor of a Paktun that must be considered."

He brushed that aside.

"Your honor relates to your group and your comrades. Your honor concerns you and your future. Think of the gold! My Lord is very, very generous. Besides, you have no choice."

"Oh?" I took another swallow. "I'll have to think about it first."

He shook his pig-like head. "No. That will not be necessary."

Well, had I been naive I would have thought that it would have gone differently. They would have to kill me. That was clear. If I did not agree, they would have to cover their tracks.

The red wine was not very good. The stuffy air of the tavern depressed me. The performance reached its climax. In one of the alcoves opposite, six stocky men, all well-armed, sat at their table and drank and laughed and teased the barmaid. The ruffians were certainly with Naghan ti Indrin. At his signal, they would pounce on me.

I looked him straight in the eye. "It seems a reasonable offer. When should I arrange Quensella's fatal accident?"

Nine

Small beads of sweat shone at his temple, and the light of the lamps caught them as they welled beneath the brim of his hat. He shifted on the bench.

The situation was extremely delicate. There were plots and conspiracies, assassinations and simple murders, and the devil take the hindmost.

Lightning quick reflection convinced me that I should dig deeper. I simply had to take the risk. "I agree. I need the gold. But what will keep me from telling my lady?"

"Ah!" he sighed. His piggy eyes glanced furtively to the side. The ruffians pulled the Fristle fifi's tail, and I had to firmly remember that I was not allowed to intervene. So-called men who torment young women for pleasure are ripe for the garbage.

"You will be under observation."

Afterwards, I deciphered this as: "We have ways and means of knowing what you are doing." Instead, he said: "Your life is now in our hands. You will be notified of the time. The voryachin pond was an excellent plan which failed only because of your meddling. See to it that no one can interfere with you."

I kept my black-fanged winespout closed and listened. He looked up at me keenly from beneath his hat. "When you all fell into the water, we thought our plan had been successful. They told me it was an impressive sight when the lady was catapulted out of the pond and you stepped out of the water behind her. Impressive, by Dokerty."

This additional remark aroused a fierce sensation of extreme panic in me. It was far worse than mere concern. By the disgusting diseased liver and lights of Makki Grodno! Someone had been in the green draped chamber and had been secretly watching me! Someone in Quensella's household was a damned lying traitor! Whether a man or a woman, they were there, like pubic lice. I struggled for self-control. Whoever it was, they were controlled by this Indrin or his men but were not capable of committing the murder. They merely observed and reported back.

Right! I told myself. By the Black Chunkrah! Upon my return, I would check everyone, regardless of their position or how highly they regarded Quensella.

Indrin looked at me suspiciously. I took a sip of the tangy red wine, thinking. Quensella's maids had not been present at the crucial moment when Nath had attacked his lady. The girls were devoted to their mistress. They were always present. They were in the best position to carry out the monitoring that Indrin boasted of.

Oh yes, by Krun! I would ask the maids a few polite questions, with or without the permission of the lady Quensella.

So how could I agree to carry out this vile plot of the sleazy Advang and his men?

"Are you certain?" Indrin spoke so violently that spittle sprayed through the air. "You look... strange..."

"I am certain."

"Excellent. Remember, you belong to us, body and ib. Now go. I will follow later. I don't want to attract any attention." He picked up his wine glass. "We will let you know when it is time."

I stood up, turned my back on him and left the tavern.

Outside, the darkness was lessened by the fuzzy pinkish light of the

Maiden with the Many Smiles. I glanced up. This moon of Kregen, which is known as the first moon, only seemed bigger than the others because of its proximity. The many different appearances were apparently caused by its own atmosphere. I shrugged and gave a surreptitious glance back when I reached the next corner.

The quick glimpse told me that Indrin's group of thugs had left the establishment after me. Had I taken a direct path back to the palace, I would have allowed the men to follow on my heels. But I had no intention of returning directly to the palace. Oh no, by Krun!

I moved furtively in and out of the shadows, jinked a couple of times, doubled back, and they lost me. This happened entirely without problems. Then I picked a spot from where I could watch the guests leaving The Pleasant Rest without being seen.

He finally stepped into the street, not drunk, but pleased with himself.

Just as I was about to follow him to his hideout, two things happened. It started to rain and three of his henchmen came out of the shadows and talked to him. They waved their arms about, gesticulating. The rain would make my mission both easier and more difficult. I could not hear what they said. As is well known, in every intrigue there is a lot of discussion to plan everything carefully. I could imagine what was going on; it was clear to me that the three ruffians had gone to the palace but failed to see me arrive there.

They started off and I followed them, a scurrying shadow in the falling rain.

There was very little wind and the rain fell almost vertically, the hissing murmur covering all noise. The street lighting in Prebaya was not the best, and where the rain had extinguished the unprotected torches stuck to the walls of the houses it was darker than any honest man would have liked. Thank Djan I was not an honest man, because I pursued this bunch with sinister intentions.

The Largesse flows through Prebaya in a south easterly direction, and it is here that two tributaries join it from almost opposite directions. The royal palace is built on the V-shaped piece of land formed where the northern stream of the small river Radiant Light flows into the Largesse. On the V-shaped piece of land between the southern stream, the river of Green Rushes, and the Largesse, many of the temples of the city are located and some of the wealthy merchants have built beautiful villas there. The north-eastern part of the city is a maze of streets and alleys, and only Opaz knows what deviltries takes place there. In the south are workshops, market squares, and some of the more sophisticated entertainment venues. The city has a myriad of bridges. I followed my quarry across the river of Green Rushes into the temple area.

It rained unceasingly. Besides us, only a few people were on the glistening wet roads. I pursued my prey like a hunting leem.

At the end of a long alley they stopped under a canopy. They spent a moment or two with heads together, talking, then they entered a building. This must be the back of the building because above the covered door with the windows flanking it, the walls were unbroken to the roof. I crept along softly and stopped at the door.

I pushed down on the handle. Of course, the door was locked.

Just as I withdrew my hand, the scrape of a pushed-back bolt warned me. I stepped back as the door opened.

The three ruffians came out. They saw me, and did not hesitate.

They were probably no more than paid thugs. But they were not fools. In the moment they saw me, they understood why I was standing there and what my intentions were.

"You blintz!" exclaimed the nearest thug and tore his braxter from its scabbard. The other two moved to either side and also drew their swords.

The drexer came out from its leather scabbard. To be faced with three swords brandished in enemy fists was nothing new for Dray Prescot. Speed was the main necessity. Raging speed.

How good they were depended on the skill conferred on them by Kurin. Because of their profession they would have considerable experience in sword fighting. Two of them wore the glittering silver at their necks. Because they were what they were, they tried to attack me as a man. They did not come one after the other, as do many inexperienced fighters. A lantern hanging at an angle from the canopy gave their blades a deadly glare.

A wild leap from the side paired with a cutting blow to my neck was blocked by a clever upwards deflection of the fellow's braxter which broke at the hilt. The blade flew into the air. The speed surprised him, he fell back, and then a loud, bright, clanging sound echoed through the alley.

A really pleasing sound, I thought, as I whirled around, catching the sword of the next fighter on my own blade and kicking him from below. The braxter of my opponent broke in the middle, my drexer held.

My thrust was so low that my drexer easily slid under his armor and into his body. He did a jerky lurch to the left and backwards, freeing my blade to face the third man who tried to be overly clever and attack with a series of complex sword gyrations. He failed mightily in my opinion. There is no time for finesse in a wild cut and thrust of this kind. One must assess one's opponent, do whatever is necessary and turn quickly to the next one.

I jumped in one direction, while he leaped over his fallen comrades in the other direction, I jumped back and caught him with a tidy thrust through the neck.

The one who had lost his blade tore out his second braxter. His dark face was contorted with rage. Until now, he had shown no fear. His two comrades had died before his eyes, and the flickering lantern light made their greasy red blood look almost black. Judging by his reaction to my surprise attack, he was clearly an excellent swordsman. Maybe it was just the difference in the quality of the steel that had saved me. I am always—even in such trifling small fights as this—aware that I can meet a swordsman who is superior to me. As you know, I've never claimed to be the best swordsman of two worlds. That would only be inflated bravado.

You can be sure that I have never forgotten Mefto the Kazzur...

He came boldly up to me, I placed myself next to the dead bodies lying on the ground, and our blades clashed. As expected, he was very good.

I could not tell which school of the sword had trained him. He knew how to handle his braxter, knew the cut-and-thrust techniques inside and out.

The blades clashed together and I felt the blows right up my arm. My muscles responded and I sank into the sublime state of consciousness of a fencing sword fighter, all worldly things forgotten. My blade spoke for itself. He fought on, more and more desperately, and it was only when he attempted a risky lunge that the end came for him.

I stepped back, pulled my blade from his neck and thought about the fact that he had with his last lunge effectively impaled himself on my sword. So I raised my blade as a last salute; doing that was not embarrassing to me, by the Blade of Kurin, not at all. Even if he was little more than a thug, he had tried to earn his pay. I wished him an effortless passage through the Ice Floes of Sicce to the sunny uplands beyond.

The three dead men disappeared into the shadows where they could not be seen by the light of the lantern. I quickly cleaned my drexer on their clothing.

The door stood open invitingly. I entered.

The corridor was tiled and was poorly lit by a few scattered lanterns. The walls and ceiling were simply whitewashed. The doors were made of thin purtle wood with cheap fittings. But they were all closed—except for one standing wide-open at the end of the corridor. This was the back entrance to the building, and my man must have gone into one of the front rooms. I followed him.

The adjoining rooms and corridors were all deserted. They were fitted out with carpets, woven tapestries on the walls, and bright lighting.

The silence was oppressive. Where had Indrin gone?

Perhaps it would have been wiser to go back through the passage and round to the front of the building to get a better idea of the layout. Then I would know where Indrin might be.

I had decided to go back when the noise of approaching feet made me stop. An alcove to my right offered cover in the shadows. I slipped into it like a hunted paly and turned around in time to see a man and a woman pass by. The two didn't notice me, no, by Shansi, the Sprite of Love!

Both wore long red robes. They walked arm in arm, their heads touching. They walked past me so absorbed in one another that the whole wide world of Kregen had ceased to exist for them. I followed them because I thought they might lead me somewhere that would help me in my mission better than I could manage on my own.

After they had walked through a few corridors, they opened a narrow door and disappeared from view. The door opened soundlessly. The space behind it was long and narrow, and down one wall there were openings with metal gratings through which light could enter. The two lovebirds were more lying than sitting on the bench on the wall opposite the openings, and kissed each other passionately. Two gentle taps on each of their heads and they fell asleep, where they would no doubt continue their love-making in their colorful dreams.

It was no problem to bind them; I availed myself of their garments. In addition, I tied them together, covered their eyes and gagged them. They could not call for help, and they certainly could not describe my face. The red robes made me think. I held the man's robe in the air and looked at it thoughtfully. Yes. This would be useful if I was where I thought I was.

Beyond the wall with the spy-holes there was a brittle crackling sound, followed by a gong, and I whirled around.

I pressed an eye to an opening.

The chamber into which I peered was spacious and the walls were covered by red curtains. Evil-smelling smoke emerged from a tripod standing at the side. In the middle was a cage. Men and women in red robes were standing in obviously ritualistic formation in the chamber. They wore artifacts of gold and silver, which must be the symbols that embodied divine power for them. I took a hissing breath. Naghan ti Indrin was swathed in red with the others opposite the imposing figure standing in front of the cage.

The cage was interesting. The bars were thick, even very thick. By their blue shimmer I suspected that they were not forged from local steel. It was highly likely it had been imported from Hamal or Zenicce. The cage was at least twice the height of a man and constructed such that whatever was imprisoned was there forever; they would never get out—not at all, by Krun!

From a side door almost out of my field of vision came a little procession. The wall behind which I stood was solid stone, and the line of fretted peepholes undoubtedly made a pretty pattern when seen from the other side. If this procession led in a young woman who would be sacrificed in a blasphemous way, I had no way to break through to rescue her.

But there was no young woman—there came a young man.

They had wrapped him in a clean white robe. His face was relaxed and absent of any sign of worry, his walk upright, his shoulders straight. He looked happy. Well, in my experience, for many of the terrible cults and religions on Kregen it is a small matter to make sure that their victims are pleased to be chopped into small pieces.

The disgusting smell of incense came through the peepholes and irritated my nose. I did not sneeze. Music was played, then was drowned out by a long drawn-out chant, constantly repeated.

"Oltomek!" they sang. It could also be Altamek or Ultumak. The monotone cry rang out again and again as two symbols attached high up on their poles were carried in a ritual procession. First came a gilded beast that seemed to come from a nightmare; it was winged, taloned and fanged. The thing's ruby eyes glinted and sparkled. It was followed by the swaying symbol of a pair of upflung curving wings, joined at the tips to form an oval. The gilded poles swayed, the idols glittered golden and ruby red, and the incense stank. And the red clad crowd chanted continuously: "Oltomek! Oltomek!"

What was most interesting about the whole affair was the use of the name Oltomek. A horde of fanatics had sung this name as Dagert of Paylen—a charming scoundrel, gentleman and acquaintance of mine—the poor old Palfrey and I had secretly observed them and their procession in some ruins. Even at this moment, while I spied on this hocus-pocus, I remembered Dagert with the respect with which you appreciate wily opponents. What was that elegant conman up to at the moment?

At the end of the procession were a group of men and women whose hoods were not red but black. They carried trays covered by red cloths. They were menacing; I could feel the coldness emanating from their sinister disguise.

What happened next can only be described as diabolical.

On a sort of banking desk, which stood under the openings in the corridor wall through which I observed the infernal practices taking place in the chamber, was paper, quills and ink. The two lovebirds had had the task of watching the horrific scenes and writing it all down. The contrast between these two activities was so large that no normal person could comprehend it.

The young fellow in the white robe was subjected to terrible tortures. He was not maimed or injured, he just had pain inflicted on him. Impossibly, the whole time the expression on his face remained joyous; an inner force that welcomed the pain with fervor brought a glow to his face.

It reminded me of the expression on Duven's face when he believed he suffered a righteous martyr's death for Cymbaro the Just. Fanatics! According to some scholars on two worlds, the evil that they create nearly surpasses the good that they could do.

After some time, during which I had turned away from what was happening in the chamber of horrors, there was silence. The young lad had screamed when the pain was too bad, and staggered, until they supported him. As the eerie silence descended, I looked again curiously into the chamber.

The tortured man was dressed in his white garment again. He stood in a group with the high priest and priestesses, laughed and drank wine from a silver cup, gave the impression of cheerfulness and seemed very happy to be with them.

The red and black hoods made it difficult to identify the faces of these people. Indrin stood out from the crowd because I had seen him recently. But from the brief glimpse of a long or a big nose, a crooked chin, a bushy beard, beautifully curved, moist red lips and a narrow mouth that looked like a cut in a leather jerkin, I was able to create a tableau of these people in my mind. It was quite possible that I would recognize this slit mouth and those beautiful Cupid's bow shaped lips, should I meet them again.

The general murmur of conversation died abruptly when a trumpet sounded. The sound shrilled and echoed through the room. A woman in a red robe took the lad by the hand and led him into the cage. He turned around, as if he wanted to go, and I thought he wanted to kiss her on the cheek. But I was wrong. She left the cage, and he stretched his arms up into the air triumphantly as if to reach for the stars. He enjoyed the experience, this exultation of the spirit.

The woman stood by the side of a large, burly man. They both stared intently into the cage. The man raised his hand.

"May Oltomek grant us our wish! This test will prove that our ibs are truly holy!" He then held out both arms and was handed the pole with the golden replica of the wings that formed an oval.

The symbol swayed from side to side as the ecstasy took him under its spell. I could not see his face; probably his eyes were so twisted that only the whites showed—two half-moons of madness.

"Oltomek! Oltomek!"

The man waved the winged symbol around with a sudden and violent movement until it was in a horizontal position, and he pointed it directly at the young man in the cage.

An audible gasp went through the crowd of spectators.

Then absolute silence fell over the chamber, while the gold-plated pole with the wings at the end was directed at the young man. The red-gowned man roared a single word with a shrill voice.

"Dokomek!"

The lad in the cage flinched and stumbled back. He began to grow. His face swelled. The red glow of madness glared in his eyes. The white garment bulged out and tore apart as his chest swelled. The body changed to an unbelievable extent. The distorted features were no longer those of an ordinary young man; bloodthirsty madness was written on his face. The figure raised its arms, and its hands unleashed claws that slashed through the air in its desire to tear its enemies to pieces. I knew what had become of the young lad.

A diabolical spirit had taken possession of him. It was powered by a single thought: destruction. Ghastly and unnatural, it flung itself against the bars of the cage. Its insane rage was enough to freeze the soul.

Ibmanzy!

Ten

I had seen with my own eyes what one of these creatures from hell could do. It had torn people to pieces and thrown them around like confetti. Where a nice young lad had just been standing in his white robe, now a completely insane ibmanzy threw itself against the steel bars of its cage driven by the desire for destruction.

The gathering was speechless. What they had expected, only Opaz knows. What they got was a destructive, completely insane power from the depths of hell.

I wanted to get away, and fast. I knew what it would look like at the end of this experiment. It would not surprise me if the crazy monster had enough strength to break his cage, even if the steel came from Zenicce or Hamal.

If it should succeed, before it grew out of this body and the ribs burst through the skin and the eyeballs bulged from the skull, it would kill all of the priestesses and priests in the red robes.

But in any event this ibmanzy would end miserably as the ruined body of the young man who had volunteered himself so enthusiastically for this terrible experiment.

I had seen everything there was to see in this chamber of outrage. I picked up the red robe from the man on the ground, pulled it over my head and tore the material—it was too small for me. The couple were waking up; I cut through their bonds and hurried off.

The fresh, rain-soaked air on the street was a true blessing. The temple of Dokerty had been a cesspit! Before I could return to the palace, I had to perform a rite. The pakais of silver rings had to be removed from the two mortpaktuns, who lay lifeless in the shadows. This I did, but then hesitated. The lovers would report what had happened to them. They would find the three thugs. Now there was no way to hide my intrusion.

I could only hope that Indrin did not connect this incident with me.

The falling rain, the slanting pink light and the gloss of wet cobblestones created an appropriate, solemn backdrop for my return journey. The red robe had served its purpose, and I threw it away. Rather than using the normal palace entrance, I first explored the area where Indrin's three cut-throats would have had their lookout post.

So I strolled around the corner and used another entrance.

There were so many new developments that I had to reconsider my situation once I was alone. Quensella must continue to be protected. It was necessary to get to know Prince Ortyg's plans and to seek out the traitors within Quensella's retinue, and to bring the affair once and for all to a close. With these intentions in mind, I checked all the guards and then went to bed to sleep for a few burs.

The morning brought a bright and colorful light over Kregen. The twin suns burned in a cloudless sky. Zim and Genodras, the suns of Scorpio, sent their commingled jade green and ruby red beams to shed light into every corner and illuminate every roof. The city sparkled in the light of the suns.

And I, Dray Prescot, was on my feet and off to my work in this radiant light.

Yes, of course, there was no question at all of simply questioning Quensella's servants one after another and demanding answers. A hearing could not possibly stay secret. In my solemnly promised determination to find the guilty party, I had stumbled upon a leems-nest. How would the lady react if I told her? Would she panic and throw everyone into the dungeon, to the lowest scullion? There had been no opportunity to consider this earlier, although I was convinced that she was too stable to react in that way.

Tsleetha-tsleethi, as they say, softly-softly. I thought of my hasty conclusions from the previous day, then looked at the reality of the situation. I decided for now to simply reinforce the guard. Quensella would need to be told everything, but at the right time and in the right place.

Later that day she ordered her cadade to attend her. What she had to tell me was, to my ears, like rain in the desert.

"The Regent has asked me to accompany her to a meeting with Prince Ortyg of Tolindrin. Find four of your best men."

I uttered such a delighted "Quidang!" that she gave me a surprised look.

It was her nature to rarely refer to Chermina by her name or to call her sister; to her it was almost invariably "The Regent".

The four guards were: Hikdar Molar Na-Fre, Pachak; Deldar Como the Hump, Hytak; Jurukker Perempto the Shorn, Khibil; and Jurukker Erwin the Waggler, Apim.

She took one of her servants, the girl who was in charge of the others. She had brown hair, chiseled facial features, was plump and wore an inconspicuous blue dress. Quensella allowed her to wear decorations on the collar and hem, and Finzy the Oracular—that was her name—was wearing a necklace of semiprecious stones.

I admit, I examined her more closely than normal. Suppose she was the viper in our nest?

This serious problem had to wait until I had observed the noble young prince of Tolindrin. Our party marched off and took Quensella to her meeting. Finzy accompanied her into the inner sanctum; I did not. Quensella gave the command to wait outside until her return. At least she took seriously the threat of attack, even in the palace. Five capable lads should be sufficient to deal with assassins.

Should be sufficient... "Molar, I am going to get a few more men," I said to the Pachak Hikdar. "Watch out for these three."

He nodded, slightly amused. We stood before a door that was excessively decorated, but fitted in with the general picture. The guards of the Regent stood stiffly to attention on either side of the door. They wore foppish, foolish-looking uniforms, held long spears and were incredibly bored with their service. Nevertheless, they made a quite competent impression and undoubtedly had freshly sharpened swords.

I strutted about with the arrogance of a captain of the guard and examined this area of the palace very closely. I found two entrances to the secret passageways, and there were undoubtedly others that were better hidden. I arrived back in our guardhouse, ordered five other jurukkers to reinforce the other group, and after I had handed them into the care of the Pachak Hikdar, I came to the conclusion that I had both the inner and the outer floor plans clearly in my head.

I have to admit that it occurred to me that these admirably fitted out guards would be of little use if one of these hell demons, an insane ibmanzy, awoke here to life—this idea was an unpleasant reminder of the other, much more extensive deviltry that existed in addition to this secret meeting.

I chose to access the passageway between the walls through a door hidden in the recess between two pillars. After a long, searching look and two failed attempts, I found the movable base of the third chubby angel opened the narrow door. I slipped inside, and the door fell back into the wall behind me. As expected, the darkness was relieved by the usual slits and openwork reliefs. Cobwebs and dust were a clear indication that this narrow corridor was rarely used. I flitted quietly to the chamber where the secret meeting was taking place.

Now, as they say in Clishdrin, as a man wants, so Zair provides. I was quite close to my goal when a sneeze sounded so loud it was like a double charge of powder and grapeshot loaded into a twelve-pounder. I froze immediately.

I could see him only with difficulty. He was no more than a shadow standing motionless before a pretty ornamented spy hole and moved only his head. His sneeze had resounded along the secret passage; he would know from experience that it would not have been heard in the conference chamber.

The passageway that lay between us was full of debris, dust, and cobwebs that hung gracefully from the low ceiling. I had no chance to reach him without being spotted, no matter how quietly I moved. I would not know him—he probably belonged to Chermina's bodyguard—but he would recognize Lady Quensella's cadade, guaranteed.

I was furious. By the disgusting diseased liver and lights of Makki Grodno! I could not kill him. He was a comrade, a human being, a man who was only doing his duty. Killing him would have contradicted everything that makes Kregen so unlike Earth.

Chermina, the regent, took her security more seriously than the lady Quensella. That was certain. In the secret passageways between the walls of her apartments would be guard posts; by Krun, they could be teeming with them!

So much for my grandiose plans!

I examined his position again and came to the unfortunate conclusion that it would not be possible for me to overpower him and render him unconscious without him seeing his attacker.

By the mighty breasts and protruding buttocks of the Divine Lady of Belschutz! I was in a very ungracious mood. To hell with everything!

My nose itched. I blinked. Suddenly, my nose seemed to be on fire. No twelve-pounder would shake the dusty corridor—oh no, by Vox!—but a damned thirty-two pounder would detonate so loud that it would be heard in the kitchen area and the attic rooms of the servants.

By Krun, what an intolerable situation!

I, Dray Prescot, spun around soundlessly, pinched my irritated about to erupt nostrils together—and fled.

Eleven

"Hey! You, Drajak! Get your watch on parade. Immediately! Bratch!"

The fellow who stuck his head through the open door of our guardhouse the next morning and started shouting was Quensella's major-domo. His easy life had made him fat and soft. He wanted people to call him Tral the Strict. Behind his back they called him by a much more expressive name. He had not really bothered me—until now.

The boys sitting in the guardroom cleaning and polishing their equipment stopped work and looked on silently.

As you can probably imagine, owing to the bad luck that seemed to follow me lately and the problems that were like a millstone around my neck, I was still in the same ungracious mood as in the dusty, sneezy secret passage. This pompous, fat, sweaty little onker was the final straw. He wore a magnificent robe, rings on his fingers and a huge jeweled gold chain that reached from his shoulders to his chest. His eyes were small and hidden behind rolls of fat.

I went up to him and looked down at his red face peeking out from under the fancy many-feathered hat.

I spoke with a calm, quiet voice.

"If you talk to me in that tone again, I will turn your head around until you face backwards. So, what message did the lady Quensella ask you to bring to me?"

Indignant, he didn't at first say a word. Then:

"You cannot speak to me like that! I am..."

I placed my left hand around his neck, and I squeezed gently—well, not very forcefully, at least. I lifted him up until his face hovered above my head.

"I know exactly who and what you are. And I also do not make empty threats."

I dropped him on his feet so hard that his jeweled teeth banged together.

"Now spit it out!"

He gasped. I reduced the pressure of my grip enough for him to breathe. Spittle ran down his chin.

"There is to be an execution! The bodyguard of the lady must form part of the escort..."

"Like your execution, steward?"

He squirmed in my grip and dribbled. I let go of him, looked into his watery eyes and gave him a hard stare.

"Do not forget it! Now—schtump!"

He scurried away like a spider missing a couple of legs. This disgusting scene had not improved my mood—quite the opposite in fact. Such conduct is, I hope, alien to me, even if sometimes I unfortunately cannot avoid it. I felt humiliated.

I turned to the jurukkers. "Full equipment for roll call in five murs," I shouted.

They rushed off.

The rest of the morning was just as unpleasant.

Under the command of the regent's chuktars we took our seats at one side of a closed-off space in a spacious yard. A few spectators were back behind a cordon. In the middle was a platform. The executioner's block was stained by use and there was no doubt as to what would happen next. I let my eyes wander over the nobles and high dignitaries densely crowded together on a balcony; neither Lady Chermina nor Lady Quensella was there. I immediately wondered if their absence was for the same or for different reasons.

The poor devil they brought in staggered under the weight of his chains. He looked terrible; obviously they had beaten him. The crowd behind us was feverish with excitement. He mounted the scaffold and a pompous busybody who was as ridiculous as Tral the Strict read his crimes.

They had caught him spying; he admitted to being from Tolindrin and to have spied on the noble Prince Ortyg.

The axe went into the air and down again in the middle of a drum roll, and that was the end of the intelligence officer from Tolindrin.

I stood there in my foreign uniform, and the misfortunes of the poor devil shook me to the core.

As with all the other things that had happened to me lately, I was powerless here. Nothing was going the way it should.

As we disassociated ourselves from the event, and the body and the head were removed, I realized with greater clarity than before that something had to change. My existence here in Prebaya in Caneldrin had to change dramatically, and damn quickly, by Vox.

Of course, that fool of a major-domo had complained to Quensella. I simply replied that, as he did not have seemly manners, he had learned his lesson. She pushed a little of her lower lip between her white teeth, cocked her head and looked at me. I realized that she was more amused than anything. I was no longer worried. I had a last duty to perform, and I would do that now.

"He is tedious," she said, "but he is good at his job. Do not test my patience."

I nodded. Now? It was not the right time. So I bowed and left.

The following day was the Diamond Tribe day. The capital of Prebaya was located at the place where in ancient times the nine tribes had met in solemn assembly to decide their union, their separation from the kingdom of Tolindrin, and the establishment of Caneldrin. This was, at least, the official version. At this time of year there were nine days of celebrations—one day for each tribe; there were no real tribal affiliations any more. And once again my guards had to go on duty in their pretty uniforms.

The celebrations were meant to be joyful. There were many parades, wine flowed, flowers were scattered everywhere, music filled the air. In the afternoon it rained for only a bur, which bothered no one.

At some point someone touched my arm from behind, and I turned around. A seductive little Fifi placed the expected envelope in my hand and danced nimbly away. I almost grabbed her to squeeze out the name of her master from her. But I did not. She was just an innocent messenger, and there were other ways.

The letter instructed me not to arrange Quensella's fatal accident. Instead, they ordered me to another meeting.

That fitted excellently into my plans. Most bodyguards have their captain and their lieutenant, the shal-cadade. Hik Molar Na-Fre was obviously delighted when he was promoted to shal-cadade, though of course he had expected it. The Khibil, Perempto the Shorn, was promoted to hikdar. Then I gave Erwin and the Hytak Hik Nalan ti Perming certain commands. "Wear civilian clothes, and stay sober," I ended. They replied with a nod. They longed for a little variety.

The Tolindrin ambassador to Prebaya was closely watched. Just like me he could do nothing for the poor devil who had lost his head. And just like me, the ambassador would be seething, by Krun.

The revelers still crowded the streets when I went to The Pleasant Rest. There were drunks everywhere, with emptied purses and more than one lying dead in an alley with his throat cut.

Since the inn was at least halfway respectable, the bouncers were working overtime, and there existed at least something resembling orderliness. I went in and waited for Indrin. He walked towards me with a greasy smile on his sweat-soaked pig face, and his thugs, whose numbers were again raised to six, accompanied him.

"Lahal," he said jovially and sat down on the opposite bench. "The plan has been worked out precisely."

I nodded and stuck my nose in my tankard.

He went on to describe the details of an ingenious plan that would make the murder look like a sad and terrible accident. His six henchmen sat across the table from me and got drunk. I listened to his tribulations, nodded, and pretended to drink. In every army and every juruk that I have led, short shrift was given to drunkards.

When he reached the end, I nodded again—like a damned machine, by Vox—and left the tavern, waiting outside in the shade.

Eventually he came out swaying slightly. I went across the street and took his arm.

"We are going for a walk, Indrin."

He turned his flushed, puffy face to me. "What?" He tried to pull away. "You... my men are here... you're a dead man!"

Oh yes, he had immediately understood the situation. His misfortune was that he had not fully understood.

At the same moment he made his poisonous remark, a roaring, glorious tumult erupted in the tavern. Almost immediately a body flew through the window. People of a pusillanimous or a wise nature fled through the door to the outside. The noise echoed up to the stars. Oh yes, by Djan-kadjiryon, they were having a lot of fun in there. Beng Brorgal, the patron saint of tavern brawlers, was pretty busy, by Krun!

Indrin began to tremble.

I touched not one hair of him. I treated him politely. I invited him to accompany me to Lady Quensella's guardroom. There I pushed him effortlessly into a cell and closed the door. I did not say a word. He could stew in there until morning. Maybe it would wear him down.

In the morning, while my happy rogues told at epic length who exactly had done what and who had hit whom in the battle at the inn, I accompanied Indrin to an audience with my lady.

She looked attractive as well as serious this morning, dismissing her maids who had just finished brushing her hair. I did not let the girls out of my sight as the guard pushed Indrin forwards. As I watched, one of the maids flinched and put a trembling hand to her breast. Her pretty face went bright red and then immediately paled. She sank to the ground and burst into tears.

"Indrin, would you be so kind as to tell Lady Quensella what you said to me last evening?"

His Advang face lost all color, his whole body shook—did the hardhearted leem-hunter Dray Prescot not feel even slight pity for him?

"Please, my lady..." His voice sounded like the last desperate whimper of a poor devil who had fallen into a well.

Quensella was a great lady. She had grown up surrounded by luxury and privilege; in her instilled arrogance she expected obedience. Still, she was a generous woman. She looked down at her sobbing servant, and her face showed regret and compassion.

"Oh Sinkie, what have you done?" She looked up at me. "Report, cadade, before this man says anything. What has she done?"

I spread my hands. I was also sorry for her. "She was just spying, my lady. She must have been pressured, threatened; it's the same old story."

"Aye! Old and ugly!"

The great lady looked thoughtfully down at her servant. Had she ordered me to take Sinkie and make her a head shorter on the spot, my answer would be firm. Commands of this kind were her prerogative, and had to be expected. But I would have to make her understand that I was not her executioner.

Sinkie sobbed laboriously a few barely understandable words to explain that Indrin had threatened to torture and kill her parents if she refused to obey him. Quensella gasped. "Why did you not tell me, Sinkie? Why? Surely you know me by now?"

This concerned only the two of them. I had the feeling Quensella would resolve the problem in a way that could only befit a real lady.

Then Indrin came out with his story. Quensella was shocked by it all.

She sat the whole time, almost indifferent, and listened. "I've seen you before in the palace. Your name is not Naghan ti Indrin." She frowned, trying to remember. "That does not matter now. It will come back to me. Cadade, beat him but do not take his head. Wait until he comes to me again. Then I'll take care of him. Lock him up until then."

"I could ask him who his master is."

"Maybe later, but not before I remember. Now take him away." She spoke as if telling a slave to scrape off street dirt from the sole of her shoe.

With that unpleasantness out of the way I felt I had fulfilled my obligations towards the lady Quensella. I would not leave without the appropriate Remberee. She would have to promote Molar to cadade. I had built up an excellent juruk for her. She was now as safe as any noble could be on this beautiful yet terrifying world of Kregen.

Twelve

The stone-bow was small, light and well-made. It was no more than a forearm in length. Nevertheless, it had enough pulling force for a decent shot. The projectiles were not stones, but cleanly cast lead balls. I weighed it in my hand and looked into the little Och's eyes. His shop was crammed with weapons and armor, everything was properly oiled and gave off that very special fragrance that belonged in any armory.

He wiped his middle left and upper right hand on his leather apron. Then he told me his price. I grimaced and offered half.

In the end we settled on three-quarters of the original price, and I paid for the little crossbow to our mutual satisfaction.

I wore a rust-brown shamlak with a narrow gap down the front and black embroidery, and trousers of the same color that reached to my ankles. These garments were brand new. The air smelled sweet, the slanting mingled rays of Zim and Genodras flooded the city, and I felt a new impetus. Events rushed on.

The cloak that Elten Naghan Vindo had lent me was long gone in the way of all things transitory. Its successor was a nondescript gray and had a deep hood with black trim. It hid my arms in a satisfactory manner.

The parting from Quensella was confoundedly difficult, more so than I could have dreamed. She sent her servants—Sinkie was no longer among them—from the small room, which was comfortably furnished with feminine taste. When the girls had gone, she rose. She wore a long, flowing robe of a mid-blue color. Silver slippers peeked from under the lace hem.

Her black, tightly arranged hair had a blue shimmer in the light of the lamps. Her smooth, unadorned face was strikingly pale. She looked at me for a long time—at least it seemed so to me—silently. Her chest rose and fell with each breath.

"Why?" she whispered. "Why must you leave me, Drajak?"

"You now have a good bodyguard. Other—tasks—are waiting for me."

"Are they more important than being close to me?"

That was unbearable. I moved the Pakzhan on my neck because I had nothing better to do. "It's just... I cannot explain it, my lady. Believe me..."

"Not at all!" she roared. Her pale cheeks flushed. "There is a woman. But of course there is. Well, Drajak the ungrateful...?"

"That's not true, my lady."

She bit her lip. I had only one wish: to be able to get out of there as quickly as possible. An image of Makki Grodno haunted my thoughts briefly. She took a step toward me. We stood close together. I could feel her sweet breath on my cheek.

"If you have to leave me, then you must do so." She raised her arms and let them fall helplessly. "All right. Go—I wish you all the best." Then she shook me to my core. "One more thing before you go, Drajak—wherever that may be."

"Yes, my lady?"

She took one final step. Our bodies touched. "Kiss me, Drajak, before you leave me forever."

I knew pretty much what Delia would have said in this embarrassing situation. Kindness is second nature to Delia, but which was kinder here: to kiss Quensella and leave her with a turmoil of feelings that had taken an inevitable course, or not kiss her and put her feelings into another troubled state that could only cause pain? I did not know. She took the decision out of my hands.

Her lips were soft, warm and demanding. So I returned the kiss in an appropriate manner, stepped back and tried to smile. If she felt sorry for me in this moment, is that not understandable?

"Go!" she said hoarsely, and with tears in her eyes. "Go!"

I went, and felt an emptiness that I did not like.

Saying Rembceree to the juruk that I had put together in so short a time created problems of a different nature. The changes to the duties and ranks was done in due form. So many people who have no idea have only ridicule and contempt for military protocol, and as it is written in the truths of old Kapt Nath the Lame, many ridiculous ceremonies, common among the uniformed dandies, are greeted with sneers and laughter. In the dark moments when a ball whistles past the head on Earth or blades aim for the heart on Kregen, oh yes, then discipline, camaraderie and immediate knowledge strengthen the fighting spirit and toughen the muscles. The bodyguard was composed of reliable fighters—and they knew that, by the Blade of Kurin!

The formal parade marched. The young Erwin wore the standard, a colorful representation of Quensella's schturval. Flanko the Fish, a Fristle with a strange history to explain his nickname, blew the trumpet. We made the prescribed about-face, marched on and were dismissed.

Then the guards were assigned for the night, and the rest of us retired to our quarters where a huge celebration quickly turned into a boisterous shindig. In the temperate zones of Kregen the many different cultures use both barrels and amphorae to hold liquids. We did our best to empty all the vessels—and since all knew my attitude, no one got drunk. We were all happy. We sang from the gut, as befits a true Kregan.

We sang "The Maiden with the Single Veil" and "Slinky Sylvies of Comfort" and belted out heartily the refrain from the famous song that goes "No idea at all, at all, no idea at all" heartily. We brought the rafters to tremble, as they say in Clishdrin. Erwin sang a Vallian song, 'The Daisies of Delphond,' and I thought not to allow the fact that it made me upset or even maudlin.

Naghan the Flabby, an Och that I had taken on as a water carrier, offered "The Cup Song of the Och Kings". When he had come to the end he allowed himself, as prescribed in ritual and tradition, to pitch headlong, flat on his face.

It was a rollicking good time. Shortly after the hour of dim I got up, told the assembled gloomy squad Rembereе, and left. A few burs sleep, and I would be as good as new again.

Then the important part of the nocturnal activities could begin—which was damn dangerous, by Vox!

Everyone had wanted to try out the new stone-bow. They had shot at anything that would skip into the air when hit. I must confess that the fun ended when an empty amphora unfortunately ended up lying on the ground in a heap of shards. When I set off on my mission the cloak hid the crossbow, and in addition to all my usual gear a bag of lead shot hung from my belt.

It was no problem to leave the outer corridors of the palace behind. As always, the urgent steps of those who maintained the operation of the fortress-like palace echoed through the corridors even at this late hour. I waited until no one was in sight, and slipped through the secret door. Dust and cobwebs greeted me. Then I slipped noiselessly along the way I had gone before. I was confident that the maze of hidden passages between the walls of the conference room would take me to the chambers of the Regent located near the river.

This time the dusty passage was not blocked by any guard, so the path before me was clear. I peered through a peephole, saw the conference room was empty, and went on.

It was only a matter of time. Bread, cheese and a canteen full of water would quench my hunger until I found the right spy hole.

There were many wondrous things to see in the lavishly equipped chambers.

Finally, as was to be expected, a soldier stood at his lonely post in front of an observation slit. The crossbow was loaded. I took careful aim and squeezed the trigger. The lead ball hit the target with great force. The noise of the guard as he fell was much too loud for my taste, and I hurried out of cover to see what he had been guarding.

The chamber on the other side of the wall was empty. It was permeated with luxurious decadence: the upholstered furniture, the statues, tables overloaded with wine and fruit, the soft carpet and the melodramatic images on the tapestries were all testimony to a carefree life. Lamps were everywhere. The chamber was silent, waiting for residents who were used to a life of abundance.

The guard was breathing shallowly. He was a hard-nosed, tanned apim, no ordinary hired mercenary but a mortpaktun with silver at his neck. It did not take long to drag him down the passage a little way and to tie him up and gag him. I returned to the spyhole at the same moment that the door of the chamber opened.

An impressive entourage entered, composed of guards, slaves and servants, including a half-dozen beautiful dancers clothed in transparent garments and bangles who were of all kinds of diff races. The center of all the attention then strutted in, spinning a longsword over his head. He was young, arrogant and had a rosy face. His smooth features reminded me strongly of his aunt, Lady Quensella. He was wearing only a red loincloth.

A dark-bearded man with a low forehead and piercing eyes who ensured he always remained beyond the reach of the sword—obviously a silver-painted wooden rudis—drew my attention. He wore a pale white evening gown, with a silver belt holding a sword. His dark hair was combed back on his head. A great aura of power came from him that was almost tangible.

"How did you like my performance tonight Granumin?" chirped the young king Yando.

It was good that the actor king, unlike me, could not see Granumin's face when he replied. Contempt froze the dark face into a grimace of bitter mockery. "Excellent, Majister. A tribute to your genius. The applause..."

"Well"—a casual whirl of the sword—"they clap just so that I will be generous towards them. Only your opinion is really important Granumin."

"You honor me, Majister." He coughed. "Your aunt, the Regent, has asked me to invite you today to her rooms."

"So?"

He strutted around for a while, no doubt in the belief that the importance of his person rose the longer he kept his aunt waiting. He put on a

scarlet cloak and threw the rudis onto a sofa. After a time with his retinue buzzing around him according to protocol, he was escorted out of the
room with his bodyguard, leaving Granumin and the dancers behind.

What place this Granumin occupied in the intrigues that are woven into
this palace, I could not say. Quensella had once casually mentioned him as
an adviser to her sister. At that time, I heard that she did not treat the fellow with much affection. But it had yet to be confirmed.

I realized that I eavesdropped the wrong room, and decided to move.
The secret passage was lit by the light invading from the room beyond it. I
carried on further, and I had the tiresome task of searching high and low
for my target.

There was no secret door to the royal chambers, at least none that was
easy to find. I was about to finally move away when a side door swung
open. What I saw enter the chamber kept me rooted to the spot.

Schrepims!

There were two of them, their lizard-like bodies driven by an exuberant
strength, and they rushed silently and with brutal reptilian speed on the
scattered standing guards.

Thirteen

Most people give a wide berth to schrepims, who rarely leave their homes.
Three important things characterize them: their speed, the effort you have
to expend to kill them, and their reputation.

Except for one, all Granumin's paktuns earned their pay. The wretch in
question acted in a manner which admittedly represented the instinctive
reaction of any normal person in an attack by schrepims. He spun around
and fled, screaming loudly. The others tried to protect their masters, and
were killed.

The skin of schrepims consists of gray-green scales bordered by a rich
blue color. As usual, they wore coats of mail. They had no shields and their
swords were braxters. They balanced and whirled around with incredible
speed on their thick tails, which differed in every respect from the whip-
like tails of the Katakis.

Reptilian, lightning fast and unscrupulous, they utterly destroyed the
guard.

The dancers rushed screaming to the door in their billowing robes, in
blind flight, powered only by the single thought of escaping these monsters.

However, schrepims are rational beings who are intelligent and calculating, with a lizard-like manner. They bleed, even if it is a greenish liquid, and have a place on Kregen.

I stood frozen, not in a position to do anything. Granumin, senior adviser to the Regent, could not escape.

A blade severed his head from his shoulders and it rolled into a corner. A sudden silence returned to the blood-spattered room in which death reigned.

The schrepims—they have something against the name Slacamen—looked around for other victims. This is their great weakness. Once they have started with the killing, they tend to lose control and become veritable berserkers. Although they would make excellent assassins, they are rarely hired for that reason. They have too much in common with those infamous, crazed warriors. Their unpredictability makes them just as likely to fall upon their client as on their kitchew, the target of an assassination order.

Together with my Och companion Unmok the Nets we had faced schrepims in distant Huringa in Hyrklana. The memory of the experience still gives me the shivers. The Slacamen in Huringa had been arena fighters. Maybe that was why they were here. The Balintol arenas had not had any big events lately, yet they still tried to arouse public interest for such decadence.

Of course it is one thing to escape from the Jikhorkdun. To find their way to the royal palace and assassinate the chief adviser of the regent is quite another.

The schrepims scurried through the room with jerky reptilian movements, making sure each body lying on the ground was actually dead.

Then they turned their lizard-like heads to the door and rushed out, predatory, killing machines on two legs.

I exhaled.

There must be a way to enter the luxury apartments from the secret passage, so I continued to look for an entrance.

The terrible events I had just witnessed had to be considered in context.

If the reptilian killers were hired as Stikitches, the intriguing question was who was the client? For me, it was quite obvious who the individual was. I admit that as I stealthily crept through the dusty corridors, I decided not to call that person by name. Anyway, it was quite possible that I was mistaken, by Krun!

The intrigue and mystery that seethed around here indicated to me that it was unwise to make unproven accusations or assign blame.

The alarm had spread like a forest fire through the palace. The two schrepims had made short work of Granumin's bodyguard, and as far as I could tell they had not suffered any injury themselves. They were a fearsome threat, which would require considerable military force to overcome. Anyone who had any sense would gather bowmen with plenty of arrows—assuming they were alerted before the frantic lizard men fell upon them and took them down.

The passageway went on quite a bit further. Finally, I came to a dead end. As I stared at the bare stones I noticed that the cobwebs were damaged. Further examination of the right angle where the walls met revealed to me a vertical column that was free of dust. I had to fall back on all the skills that I had acquired over time to discover the hidden button or lever.

The lever turned out to be a vertical piece of stone, which was marked with horizontal grooves. I pulled. The dead end split apart down the middle, and the two halves of the wall swung back to the left and right.

The edges of the door were jagged. When I pushed back the lever in its camouflaged position on the outside, the door closed and the irregularities fused together, taking on the shape of the masonry.

In the corridor beyond the secret door there was not a speck of dust. No cobwebs adorned ceiling or walls. Rays of light penetrated through peepholes. This area was so different from the previous one, and differences of this kind required caution—extreme caution, by Krun!

It looked like the passage surrounded a hexagonal shaped suite of apartments; I rounded the second corner then paused before the next turn. I heard dull, strangely distorted voices.

A furtive glance around the corner showed me two men in full armor leaning against the wall, eating and chatting.

The lead ball shot from the stone-bow hit the first man on the temple, and before his companion could react, he too was on the ground, struck down by a bullet on his chin. Both were still alive.

They were tied up and gagged with their own clothes. I had to pull myself together and harden my heart to knocking down the two soldiers, who were doing nothing other than making their pay. On the other hand, if you hire out as a paktun, it is quite likely that at some point you will be wearing a few nasty bumps.

Their easygoing attitude was a clear sign that the schrepim alarm had not yet reached them. Both were kitted-out in first-class clothes and armor. That told me that I was approaching my destination. I crept on, and the spy holes gave unobstructed views of magnificent chamber after magnificent chamber. Altogether, I had three more guards to deal with. As I already said, a clear indication that I was in an important part of the palace. The soldiers kept an eye on the apartments and on a door hidden in the plain wall, which blocked access to further secret passages.

The corridor forked. One fork led to a heavy door; there was noise beyond. For an old mercenary it sounded suspiciously like men in a guardroom. I quietly took the other fork.

After the next bend—which now no longer followed the hexagonal shape as the walls here were at right angles to each other—I saw through a spyhole into a room that was obviously an anteroom. Guards lined the walls, a couple of men and women sat on couches. I looked closer, puzzled. This was totally unnatural! Did no one know that two deadly schrepims were scouring the palace? It occurred to me that the lizard men had managed to escape and were on their way back to the client to report their success. But honestly, I could not believe this. No, by Vox!

I listened. The muffled conversations brought light into the darkness. A gesticulating, red-faced man said that the stikitches should be executed, immediately and on the spot. I took the words to mean that the guards had done the only sensible thing and had shot down the schrepims. They had been slightly wounded, caught with nets and then beaten unconscious.

That calmed the courtiers. Not me.

An unimaginably dressed servant danced into the hall, asked for silence and announced that there would be no further audiences this evening. The courtiers stood up and left the room with angry and disappointed mutterings.

I hurried around the next corner, because from there I would be able to peer into the private rooms located behind the wall. The feeling that I was getting closer to my goal inspired me.

Only two guards blocked my way to the spyhole, and the reliable little stone-bow shot its lead bullets, and the two men sank into dreamland.

The first overwhelming impression of sheer power emanating from the chamber was confirmed and even intensified by my second look. Everything was designed to impress. Dusky red columns supported a stormy blue sky, on which silver stars sparkled. The arras and tapestries showed scenes from the mythology of the kings. Lamps were mounted cleverly to emphasize the power that emanated from the person on the elevated throne. She sat stock still; her scarlet skirt billowed below the narrow belt and surged over her hidden feet and the narrow steps that led up to her throne.

Her golden bodice was covered with diamond shards, which shone like flames. Her close-cropped black hair shone like her sister's but was not cut quite as short. Her features resembled Quensella's but their regularity was replaced by a beauty that took your breath away. Everything and everyone in her radius was subject to her will. Her bare arms decorated with bracelets rested easily on the sides of the throne. Her fingernails were painted blood red. She smiled.

King Yando marched up and down impatiently in front of her and was interrupted in his jabbering. There were other people in attendance, but I watched C'Chermina.

"Yes, Yando, yes. Granumin is a great loss. But you have always trusted me before now. You know that everything I do is for your own good. One day you will be king." Her smile would have launched ten thousand ships. "Whoever sent the Slacamen will be found and punished."

The cynical Dray Prescot, who knew exactly how it went in the world and could be surprised by nothing anymore, allowed himself the thought that the boy would likely never get to be king because it was very unlikely that this intimidating woman would ever give up her power.

She leaned forward a bit. "It will not change our important diplomatic objectives. Vallian insolence must be curbed. The problems with Winlan remain."

Yando looked up. "We cannot conquer their walls either on foot or by air!"

"That's right. Their magicians have tremendous kharrna. I shall devise ways to resolve that problem."

"Aunt, you said yourself that the problem of Winlan's illusionists must wait until we have defeated Tolindrin." He stopped, and his fist closed around the handle of the small jeweled dagger stuck in his belt. "When do we invade?"

"We currently gather our armies. We will invade when we are ready." She nodded graciously to the side. "When Prince Ortyg has completed his preparations. Once everything is in place."

I looked closer. There he stood. By Krun! There he stood.

He looked different. His experience had curbed his youthful impetuosity. His weasel face was resolute, his lips narrow. He wore a black shamlak with double lacing, apparently his favorite clothing style, and he had three swords on his belt. Only now he piped up and reported that unexpected obstacles stood in his way. "Within a week of the Maiden with the Many Smiles, everything should be ready, my lady," he concluded.

"Good."

That told me how much time I had; it was almost too late. This small-fry Ortyg was a prince, he could gather his loyal followers around him and bribe or buy the rest. He was to be the infiltrator, that was obvious. He would betray his own country Tolindrin to Caneldrin to achieve his goal: the crown of Tolindrin. And yet I could understand him up to a certain point. His ambition and the feeling of being despised by the other nobles devoured him. It had never been possible for him to spread his wings. The last Tolindrin king had appointed Tom by decree as successor to the throne. The intrigue that had triggered this action would soon lead to war, bloodshed and death—if Dray Prescot failed.

Then the Star Lords would intervene and send me back to earth, they would banish me from Kregen and Delia; it was the equal of being buried alive.

I scowled and listened to them—and a wild rage crept into my dark mood. A Khibil stood by conceitedly, as do most Khibils if given the chance. He was called San M'Marmor. He wore white just like Granumin, and was armed with swords. His foxlike face showed a rigid expression that differed significantly from the haughtiness and arrogance normally written on the faces of Khibils. I've actually always felt that this superior posturing of Khibils is amusing; I found it hard not to laugh at this man's self-consciousness. He had been appointed as Granumin's successor.

The meeting went on. My impatience made my skin itch as if I had chi-kas of the Great Plains, those small annoying ticks that dig themselves under the skin of the pasture animals. When would they finally end this momentous evening? Didn't they have beds to go to?

I had long since discovered the secret door through which I would enter this forbidden room. I knew exactly which projection I had to press to open the latch. Now if only these powerful people would leave so that I could finally put my plan into action.

Finally, Opaz be praised, a soldier rushed into the room. His armor hung in shreds from his body. He was covered in blood—it was red and green blood.

"The Slacamen! Escaped..." He could barely get the words out. "The lizard men—escaped—they murder and kill..."

In the luxurious but oppressive chamber, there was uproar.

Fourteen

The bodyguards took C'Chermina and Yando into their midst and led them out in a hurry. Some of those assembled fled. M'Marmor took Ortyg's arm. Both men were in a state of high excitement and fear.

"Not that way Prince. Here come the Slacamen."

Ortyg tore out one of his swords. "So?"

"This way!" The newly appointed supreme advisor rushed directly to the secret door—and so to me.

That was convenient, very obliging of him, by Krun!

I opened the door and stepped through. The three of us were alone in the room. They remained rooted to the spot, staring at me.

I decided not to draw a weapon.

"M'Marmor, you may go!" I said calmly and rationally. "Ortyg, you're coming with me!"

That provoked a laugh from him. The sound was more like a cackle. In this tense atmosphere, the most insignificant movement was Grand Guignolesque.

"You stupid blintz!" he yelled. "Out of the way!"

He had not recognized me. The shadows were favorable. M'Marmor stormed off. His whole Khibil self-confidence had deserted him. He left Ortyg and literally threw himself through the open door into the secret passage. I let him go.

The weasel-faced prince stared at me darkly. As it had become second nature to feel like an important person able to command ordinary people like me, this suppressed some of his anxiety. He threatened me with his sword.

"I am a prince, tikshim! Get out of the way!" Then he screamed without stopping, "Watch! Guard! To me!"

I knew exactly what would put an end to his shrill cries for help, but was immediately taught a lesson. The ordinary guards would be wandering around somewhere, the bodyguard of the regent and the king would only be concerned about their charges; the whole palace was like a troubled ant nest filled with tumultuous panic. But one of Ortyg's men obeyed the order and came rushing into the chamber with a drawn rapier.

Even in this moment in which I had to admit to having made a mistake, I heard the faint scraping of a sole on the marble floor at my back. I jumped aside like a leem.

The Khibil's treacherous attack was inspired by passionate hatred and the awareness of his own superiority, his dagger cutting through the air at the exact spot where moments before my unprotected back had seemed to give him a perfect target. Undoubtedly his Khibil hyper-confidence had suppressed his fear long enough to attack me. After that he would have fled immediately.

I still did not pull out any weapons. I spun around, knocking his arm aside, grabbed him and went along with the movement of his attack, jerking him around and aiming him at the open door. Then I pushed with all my strength. He vanished screaming into the dark rectangle.

"Really pretty," said a familiar, easygoing voice with a clearly amused undertone that recalled dark currents under a motionless surface. "But now you are facing a new opponent."

At the same moment as he spoke, Ortyg took his chance to attack me with his sword. He struck wildly. I ducked and the blade shattered a hanging lamp. Glass tinkled, brass jangled, and burning oil splashed onto the marble floor.

A shadow passed over me.

And the newcomer stepped smoothly into the light.

He had not changed much since our last meeting and was still the swashbuckling dandy personified. Slim, muscular, always on guard. Under the cloak shone good armor and he displayed the footloose, free, adventurous image of a dashing cavalier. His clear dark eyes looked searchingly into the shadows behind Ortyg. And of course he ran his gloved fingers over the black, pencil-thin mustache above his narrow mouth.

"If the prince would be good enough to step aside? I'll take care of this fellow, but then we have to go."

The rapier with its jeweled handle described a graceful arc, and he stood before Ortyg. "Flee or fight, nulsh. But decide for yourself, quickly!"

I drew my rapier and quietly stepped into the light. He looked at me. The quietly amused laugh, almost a giggle, came again. He raised his sword in an ironic salute.

"By Hanitcha the Harrower! You! Only you could be..."

"At your service," I replied.

"Come on, Dagert!" hissed the prince angrily. "Take him down! For that is why I ultimately pay you!"

"Ah... my prince..." Dagert did not move. "If only it were that simple."

"How is friend Palfrey?" I asked politely.

Dagert of Paylen looked genuinely surprised. Palfrey was his personal servant, errand boy and general lightning rod. "Palfrey? How's he doing? Why in the name of Havil the Green should I know? By Krun, as far as I know he's alive."

As if on cue, Palfrey's unkempt mop of hair appeared in the doorway. His clothes were patched but clean. The shiny short sword in his hand was immaculate; there was no trace of green blood to be seen. The round face with the snub nose twisted in disbelief as he entered. He had recognized me immediately. He swallowed. "Notor!" he exclaimed. "We have to hurry—the schrepims are coming!"

"Kill him!" shrieked Ortyg. "Immediately!"

Dagert ignored him. He looked at me. "You want to kill the prince?"

I assured him that was not my intention, I just wanted to take him into custody. Then I added that I would not recommend anyone to try to stop me.

He ran his finger over his mustache. "If that is so..." He turned his head slightly towards Ortyg. "Herewith, I dissolve my contract with you, my prince," he said over his shoulder. Then he became vigorous. "Come on, Palfrey, you fambly. We should be far away from here."

Ortyg started yelling and brandishing his sword.

Palfrey began walking, and Dagert followed him. They disappeared side by side into the shadows of the chamber. You could always count on good old Palfrey to find a suitable bolt-hole in good time!

I turned to Ortyg. "Come on, boy! Put the damn sword away. Just come with me, and no fuss."

He gasped. His eyes almost bulged out of their sockets. He spluttered. It was incomprehensible to him that his situation had fundamentally changed so quickly.

A few steps forward, the grasp of a leem-hunter, and I held his sword in my left fist. I decided to forgo any drama and did not slide it back into its scabbard. This kind of overblown gesture can be found in theatrical romantic fiction; in this upstanding specimen of a princely hothead it would probably bring you death. His remaining weapons were to be kept in mind, but for now we had to run for our lives. But it was already too late!

A schrepim with a crossbow bolt sticking out of his left shoulder burst in. Green liquid ran down his scaly armor in dark rivulets. His blade was stained with blood, and it glowed red in the light of the lamps.

He saw us and immediately attacked.

I dropped Ortyg's braxter. Now was not the time for niceties. I pushed the rapier back in its scabbard and drew the Krozair blade. The longsword moved in that cunning two-handed grip of its own accord, parried the first attack, described a deadly arc—and found empty air. The schrepim was no longer there. His speed was inconceivable despite his injury. He jumped at me, I turned swiftly, parried his blade aside and tried to hit him in passing—and rebounded off his neck.

The large flat tail braced against the marble floor and gave him support. He went to his knees. Then he was on me like a rashoon of the inner sea.

This time, I dodged left and right, calculated his movement again, and made a lunge to the left. His blade missed its target. Mine landed a heavy hit on his side. Pieces of scale armor flew through the air.

He hissed in anger. Naked bloodlust had transformed him into a frenzied berserker, yet he remained an excellent fighter.

We met each other again. The sheer ferocity of his attack was within a whisker of finishing me. Our feet slid across the floor as we circled around. He attacked and stabbed and cut continuously, driven by his furious bloodlust.

Ortyg hopped around, trying to duck behind me as we circled, and keeping out of the reach of the crazed killing machine.

I no longer consciously noticed his continuous shouting and blabbering. For me there was only the bloody blade of the lizard man. The swords clashed. I turned and struck his sword down, he retreated with incredible speed so that my subsequent surge fell short. By the Blade of Kurin! This monster had to be finished quickly, because soon the whole palace guard would burst in, shoot a hail of arrows and bolts in their fear of the lizard man, and all of us—Prince Ortyg included—would be dead.

Every fight is different. Oh yes, there is the rage and fear, bitter steel, wild exertion, the smell of spilled blood. How often I have expressed my loathing of pointless killing! How often I have longed to hang sword and bow at the Great Hall of Esser Rarioch and spend my days in the palace overlooking Valkanium filled with happiness! To spend my life at the side of Delia, Delia of the Blue Mountains, Delia of Delphond! But fate, circumstances and the orders of the Star Lords have determined otherwise. That is my lot.

I circled him, stabbed him, ducked and dodged back, parried his blade, forced it aside, stabbed and missed. It was like fighting a shadow. And yet—he was tired. Blood seeped from him in a thick greasy trickle down the scale armor. His reptilian eyes lost their luster. He reacted more slowly.

This fight could end only one way.

But had I any right to kill him?

Just because the blood in his veins was a different color than mine? Was that enough reason and justification to slay him? No, it was not. Schrepims are very hard to kill. They cling with a reptilian tenacity to life, which demands admiration despite the revulsion the red-blooded diffs have for them.

Now he was on the defensive, on the retreat. I did not let him rest. He was still fighting wisely and drawing on his great experience. He sustained another injury.

He turned in a circle, trying to escape the final, fatal blow. He jumped back, dropped his muscular tail to the ground fast and used it as a support on which he rotated one hundred and eighty degrees. Then he ran up the steps to C'Chermina's throne.

He stood up, balancing on toes and tail, and lifting the sword he offered the perfect image of desperate resistance.

The lead bullets of my little crossbow would simply bounce off him like dried peas from a child's peashooter. We both paused, staring at each other.

The schrepim hissed. From the wide, vicious mouth came shrill words. "You will be caught up in the coils of Ratishling the Sinuous and crushed until your bowels smoke, apim." He lowered his sword, half fell, half sat down on the throne. The lizard's head fell to his chest, but then jerked back defiantly. "And yet, you know how to fight. I would pay you the Jikai, but I cannot."

I raised my sword in salute. The schrepim was no more a threat to me or my plans. I took a few deep breaths. I barely noticed the stench. Then I looked around for young weasel-face, the high-born and powerful prince Ortyg.

He was no longer in the oppressive room.

The unkind cuts of fate drove me to distraction. A quick look at C'Chermina's throne told me that the lizard man still sat there upright, his tail wrapped around the chair leg to prevent him from falling, his whole body covered with green, slimy blood. He was surrounded by a pitiful aura of greatness. His reptilian eyes that had lost their luster were still open. He had already begun the last, long journey that would take him to the Ice Floes of Sicce—or wherever the lizards may end up.

Where had the young princeling gone? By the black putrescent entrails nd pendulous posterior of Makki Grodno! All the trouble, the pain and .he blood—and the cramph had simply fled.

As for me, I could not stay here any longer. At any moment the guards would burst in. And so I gave the dying schrepim, sitting alone on the royal throne and offering a bizarre sight, one last parting glance and went on my way.

I did not use the secret door. I walked past the red columns and went in the direction that Palfrey had led his master Dagert of Paylen.

As I knew, friend Palfrey's first act at each new place was to search for an escape route. It was possible that Ortyg had also used Dagert's way out. The massive architecture and excess of rococo-like furnishings that prevailed in the corridor outside the stifling chamber clearly betrayed the wealth that the kings of Caneldrin presumed. I crept on, without meeting anyone. Except for the guards, where a stiff drink and the promise of a reward in gold had instilled new courage, everyone else had disappeared into their hiding places. The guards would come into the chamber through the entrance that I had avoided using. Would they fill the poor devil of a schrepim with arrows...?

Lamp-holding gold statues lined the walls. The carpet was probably not of Walfarg weave, but was still extremely valuable. The tapestries glorified the deeds of various long dead heroes of Caneldrin. At the next junction I came to a wider corridor that offered good prospects of leading away from the turmoil. A movement at the other end immediately caught my attention.

The furtive movement was repeated. There was something gray green, then steel flashed; it was immediately clear that there lurked the second schrepim who was just waiting to kill anyone who stood in his way as he searched for a way out.

With extreme caution, I slipped into the narrow shadow cast by a column. A statue with a lighted lamp stood behind me in an alcove. The warm, stuffy air was stale. I stood very still.

Maybe the recent fight had slowed my reflexes. Maybe I had allowed fatigue to betray me. A very sharp steel tip scratched the skin of my neck above the shamlak. A low, hard voice said: "Do not move, or else..."

I do not know what else that person wanted to say and I did not care. I slid to the side and moved my head faster than the dagger could follow. My left hand went upwards, my tanned fist closing like a vice on the hand that held the dagger. The hand was then mercilessly twisted inward so that the dagger tip floated under the nose of its owner.

"Quiet, please!" came a faint whisper from the floor.

Dagert's face showed surprise—mixed with the usual mocking arrogance—as his own dagger threatened to cut off his nose.

"You truly are an amazing man..."

"Shut your black-fanged winespout, tikshim!"

"Notor!" whispered the mouse-like squeaky voice from the floor. "You will address the lord as Notor!"

Dagert's thin lips were compressed. His bright eyes betrayed nothing of his thoughts. He jerked his head to the side.

My whisper reached only his ears and Palfrey's. "Perhaps the schrepim has now lost his bloodlust. He seeks an escape route."

"If that is so," said Dagert wickedly, "why do you not go to him and tell him to hurry up a bit?"

"You were creeping around here the whole time."

He did not deign to acknowledge my criticism with a reply. Instead, he asked me to let go of his hand, which, he claimed, was slowly losing all feeling. That was so typical of Dagert of Paylen that my good mood immediately took the upper hand. He had been in the service of Khon the Mak, failed there and fought on Prince Ortyg's side. That position had also brought him no luck. The thought gave me a bold idea.

The whole time I had divided my attention between Dagert and the schrepim. "I will let your dagger hand go on one condition, sunshine, which will amaze you."

Palfrey gave a few squeaking sounds from the place where he sat huddled on the floor.

"Condition?" asked Dagert. "I am a lord, an Amak..."

"The lowest rung on the ladder of the higher nobility. I would venture the suspicion that your possessions are run down in Paylen, probably as a result of your lavish lifestyle." This provoked an angry reaction; he tried in vain to squirm out of my grasp. "You left your worthless lands and are looking for your fortune as an adventurer in the wider world. You were not very successful."

His voice was icy in its self-control. "You are insolent..."

"Oh, aye." The movements of the schrepim were difficult to make out. What in a Herrelldrin Hell had he been doing down there while we chatted here? I stared at Dagert and the old Dray Prescot Devil Look flashed briefly. "I offer you a position, Dagert. I'll take you and Palfrey into my service. You will be paid handsomely. Well?"

The icy arrogance on his face turned to amazement. "You're joking! Who are you? A simple paktun, by Krun! The one who is hired!"

"Until recently I had the honor to be in the service of the lady Quensella. I was a paktun, I am currently tazll. Coincidentally..."

"You wear the pakzhan at the neck!"

Our voices were louder, we were not whispering any longer.

Palfrey gave a pained whimper. "Notors! Notors! Please be quiet, I beg you!"

"All right, Palfrey," I said. "That poor hulu of a lizard man is no longer a threat. If we go on boldly, everything will be to the good."

"Master!" he groaned.

Dagert moved his dagger hand. I squeezed a little harder until he winced. "I can pay you and Palfrey but I want an answer right away. I want your solemn oath that you will serve me faithfully and wherever possible."

Now Dagert of Paylen was a very honorable rogue, a villain who plumbed the depths of infamy and dishonor, while at least still preserving the fragments of his self-respect. He understood perfectly how to balance on the tightrope. Work was work, and work meant gold.

"Since it is likely that you would otherwise break my fingers, I agree."

"I assume Havil the Green means nothing to you. And whatever religion you once practiced, you will certainly have long forgotten. Swear to Krun that you will faithfully serve me."

He nodded. On his pale face barely a drop of sweat was visible. "All right. By Krun, I swear it."

"Good."

"What do you want...?"

"The most important task at the moment is," I interrupted brusquely, "to find the young prince. He followed you. I have not seen him. Where did the onker go?"

These two had not seen Ortyg either. He had disappeared somewhere along the way between the chamber and the corridor, and you didn't need to be a genius to come to the conclusion that he had literally crawled into the wall. I said that we would not go after the lizard man. This news made Palfrey breathe a sigh of relief. Then I strictly ordered the two to quickly find Ortyg. Dagert did not ask why I wanted the prince. If I had judged him correctly, he executed the plots of his employer without racking his handsome head about their motives.

I could have sworn that Palfrey's teeth chattered. "Schrepims are evil—evil," he squeaked. "And, sir, you stink of them!"

That was true, by Vox! The green blood exuded a strong, unpleasant odor. "If we have time, I will take a bath!" I said. Then I grabbed Palfrey by the collar and pulled him to his feet. He was trembling all over. "And now, friend Palfrey, use your wits. Where has that damn Ortyg disappeared to?"

It did not matter to Palfrey how one called other princes and nobles, as long as one addressed his lord as Notor. He shook himself and announced that he would scan the path as we walked along. Somewhere there must be a secret door. The prospect gave him new courage. Dear old Palfrey rallied!

"Get moving, fambly!" Dagert snapped. "Our new and oh so generous employer will not appreciate it if you make him wait," he added with his typical quietly amused laugh.

Obediently, Palfrey walked back the way we had come. Until now we had not been disturbed by guards—how long this desirable situation would last we could only guess.

A bulge in a carving that ringed a large column caught my attention. Palfrey's triumphant squeak and his outstretched fingers confirmed my suspicions. "There, notor, there!"

Apparently, there was no way into the thick column but there might be access through a trap door in the floor. Palfrey cocked his head, studied the ornaments and pressed a bulbous fruit. A door swung open.

Prince Ortyg crouched like a hunted wild animal in the narrow recess. Obviously this was a hollow column in which a guard could store items. The weasel's face twisted, pale and bathed in sweat. His eyes had a haunted look.

"Come out of there, my lad." I spoke quietly.

He began to furiously brandish his weapons, stumbled out and almost fell. Dagert would not help him. He screamed incoherently—he was a prince, we would all end up with severed heads. I nodded to Dagert and he pulled out a handkerchief and gagged the mouth that was uttering nothing but nonsense. I felt a certain satisfaction. After all, this strange new relationship with Dagert and Palfrey, his servant, had started with a small success. Of the future, only Opaz knew.

Now we just had to find a way out of this place and leave Prebaya as soon as possible.

Fifteen

"Come on, Palfrey, you fambly! Hurry up with that junk!"

The poor Palfrey moved the heavy bag on his shoulder, gasped "Yes, Notor!" and tried with all his strength not to let it slip. Dagert went on with his chin held high and his left hand on the rapier grip, the familiar poise of the nobleman personified. I walked a step behind him, as befitted a cadade. We found an empty bedchamber, and I tried as best I could to clean the green lizard blood from my clothes. Now we were a nobleman and a captain of the guard, both known to the palace staff, and accompanied by a servant who carried some of their possessions.

Of course the bag with our possessions contained the bound and gagged Prince Ortyg of Tolindrin.

And so we marched unmolested through the royal palace of Prebaya. Which was most satisfying.

My main concern was that the new First Advisor M'Marmor could have spread the word around that there was a boorish bully creeping through the corridors, who had offended his sensitive Khibil feelings to the extreme. We learned that the second schrepim had been tracked down and peppered with crossbow bolts. This incident and the panic that it had triggered almost turned the palace into a madhouse, and apparently made sure that every word from M'Marmor was forgotten. In any case, we left the palace without anyone getting in our way.

The morning suns sent forth a misty, apple green and palely pink light. The rain that fell during the night had cleared the atmosphere, and the sweet Kregen air with its lavish scent was pervasive. Not even the smoke from the cooking fires for the first breakfast could pollute the air—at least not this morning. Throughout the city, thin columns of smoke rose up. There was a dead calm. We walked with our heads held high and our swords swung with our long strides. Oh yes, everything was in perfect order—admittedly, the poor Palfrey limped along carrying Prince Ortyg in the sack over his shoulder.

"Give it to me, dom," I finally said. Palfrey handed me the sack gratefully. He straightened up, groaned and held onto his staff. "Ouch! I'm crippled. My spine is bent!"

"Stop whining, you big fambly!" Dagert snapped, without looking back. "Or I will bend your spine into a circle!"

Palfrey reminded me of our previous meetings with a grimace that meant something like: listen to the Notor, of course he does not seriously mean it. That is, probably not.

The early birds had already prepared the markets for the day in the dark murs before sunrise; soon the servants would make their purchases. In the short time between there were few people on the streets.

A guard division marched past at a crossroads, and we waited patiently until they were gone. They consisted entirely of mercenaries. When I had once asked why the local nobles hired only paktuns as bodyguards, they gave no good reasons, only half-hearted explanations. Apparently the nobles did not trust their people enough to protect them. This is a common, historical phenomenon. The army did take men from Caneldrin into the paktun regiments. Quensella, for example, paid for her protection and tried to take good men into service. Well, I had already seen one result of this practice, by Krun! She would not have dreamed of taking on one of those strong young lads who were born in Caneldrin, not to mention Prebaya. When I compared this with my efforts in Vallia, I became aware of the tragedy that lay therein.

The few organized revolutionary movements hid in the mountains. As far as their effectiveness was concerned, that had to be judged by what they had achieved during my stay in Prebaya. Namely, nothing.

All this speculation over the political and military situation in Caneldrin had not managed to divert my attention from my stomach. The morning fires sent their smoke into the sky, the smell of breakfast penetrated my nostrils, and I got very weak in the knees. By Vox! I was on the verge of starvation!

Still, I was determined to leave Prebaya immediately. Quensella's pay-master had paid me, so a few gold coins jingled in my pocket.

"When will we finally stop for breakfast, Notor?" Palfrey asked sullenly and in a plaintive voice, but I went on resolutely with Ortyg over my shoulder, Dagert of Paylen a step ahead of me. Poor Palfrey, constantly grumbling, followed behind.

I gave Dagert a direction with a few words, and soon the lifterdrome came into view.

A boy came towards us on the road. A brown apron concealed bare legs, and on his tousled mop of hair he wore a large tray covered with a yellow cloth. Dagert stopped him. He lifted a corner of the cloth and sniffed. "By the potbelly and generous ladle of the master chef Ramdiz of the Recipes! I'm starving. Here, boy." Dagert threw a copper coin into the air, the limber boy caught it. The noble gentleman took a spiky bread roll containing a mixture of various still steaming meats, and let the cloth fall again. Then he immediately began to eat with great gusto.

Palfrey said nothing, but he rolled his eyes heartbreakingly.

"Here, boy." I gave him four copper pieces and took enough breakfast for me and Palfrey. By Mother Rushi of the Puddings and Cakes! The meat-stuffed buns tasted divine!

Then I remembered something. I held on to the boy, who was pleased to go home so early after an effortless sale, and bought yet another bread roll. The bag at my feet did not move. Ortyg could eat his breakfast later.

The bag was back in its place on my shoulder, and I held it with my left hand, pushed the bread and meat into my mouth with the right, and we were back to walking. Mind you, the magnificent diffs of Kregen who are equipped with more than the two arms of mere apims could buy breakfast, pay for it and eat it without having to put down the bag, by Krun!

At this early hour the lifterdrome was barely operating. We paid the exorbitant fees, checked out the flier and flew into the brightness of the Kregen morning.

I handed Dagert control and ordered Palfrey to free Ortyg from the bag. We took the gag off, and before the expected flood of words could come out of his mouth I stuffed the piece of bread between his teeth. He was forced to chew and swallow. We did not remove the shackles on his hands and feet. "Feed him bite by bite with breakfast, friend Palfrey, and then gag him again."

"What course?" Dagert wanted to know.

"Oxonium."

"Ah!" Dagert bent his head over the controls, then raised it again and looked at me. "Er—I do not think it particularly wise. Some people there will not be very pleased when they see me. You understand that, my dear fellow?" He made a gracious gesture, but refrained from stroking his black mustache. "At present, Oxonium is damned unhealthy for me. Damned unhealthy, by Krun!"

I had anticipated this. "Here." I poured out the gold coins that Quensella's paymaster had given me.

"Oh no. Oh no! The pay of a simple cadade is an insult to a gentleman of my rank. You understand that as well, right?"

"I will go to the capital. You will find a comfortable refuge for you and Palfrey. There you can wait for me until I have completed my affairs in Oxonium." Then I added sharply: "When I return, there will be a lot of gold!"

"To Hanitcha the Harrower with it! What shall I do with you?" He looked forward, pulled the lever back slightly and slowed our climb. "You always have an answer for everything in advance. You are a simple paktun, but you know how to behave." He shook his head and pushed the speed lever forward. We shot through the air.

What should I do with him and Palfrey? At the time, the bold idea to take him into my service had some merit. But now I saw all the dangers that were associated with it. This man knew no loyalty. He would make a hasty retreat when the danger to him from whoever stood in our way did not agree with him. Well, by Vox, he showed only common sense.

The problem was, I knew I could not rely on him. Oh yes, he was charming, morally depraved and courageous. And an out and out villain. If I put them in an inn in the country with the cadade gold and then did what I had to do, the problem might solve itself. If they were still there when I returned, well and good. If they had made off, the matter was likewise settled.

A pressing problem demanded immediate remedy. The couple of burs sleep that I had allowed myself before all the excitement had kept me upright until now, but the inevitable weariness was close.

"Will you wait in Caneldrin or Tolindrin?"

Without hesitation, Dagert chose Caneldrin. I nodded. That fit into my plans, by Krun!

I pondered on what might happen if I lay down and slept to the full, and came to the sobering conclusion that I'd prefer to do without it. Dagert of Paylen might get the idea that a prince would give him a greater reward than a rabid mercenary, whether a zhanpaktun or not. A dagger would slit my throat, my body would quickly go overboard and the last thing I would hear would be a fawning statement from Ortyg as his bonds were loosed. Oh yes, by Djan, a really pretty scenario that would take its course just because I had dozed off.

During the flight to Umrigg, an isolated village with an inn of satisfactory quality, which was mainly used for trysts and was known to Dagert, Palfrey and I carried on a sporadic conversation. He told me that his father had been a witness to how Donggi, the old Amak of Paylen, had beaten his young son Dagert to unconsciousness on the many evenings when he was dead drunk. Dagert's mother had long before given up and then had the decency to die without fuss. Dagert's childhood had been the whetstone that he had to thank for his sharpness as an adult.

Umrigg turned out to be one of those villages that would have adorned a postcard if it was on Earth. Very pretty. The picturesque houses and taverns and the famous inn had no surrounding wall. During times of war everyone would pack up his things and go to the nearest fortified town. I set Dagert down, took a meal myself, drank a gulp and left him behind with the patiently suffering Palfrey. If they were still there when I returned, well, then I would be obliged to consider my options.

As we raced towards Oxonium, Prince Ortyg became very subdued. I could sympathize with him. That's what happens when one day you have tremendous power and the next you are tied up in a bag!

I took off the gag and counted on a flood of abuse. I was not disappointed. Anyway, as I freed him from the gag, it turned out that I had unwittingly done something rather fortuitous.

He spoke. He expressed himself eloquently. He threatened. He informed me that my days were numbered, that Tolindrin was doomed, and listed all those who were loyal to him. When I finally got to speak again, I told him that I did not intend to harm him. In his response, he described in detail everything that he wanted to do to me. When I gently pointed out to him that he was not in a position to make threats, he swallowed hard, turned bright red and his shoulders slumped.

"You'll see, you blintz! C'Chermina was about to destroy the foolish Illusionist of Winlan. And at my urging she will release her terrible weapon on Tolindrin." His knowledge made him giggle. I hoped that he did not lose his mind. "You'll see! Wait until everything is destroyed!"

Trying to make him understand the impact of his plan by explaining to him what he was doing, turned out to be pointless. He had only one goal: Tolindrin's throne and crown. When I mentioned that Caneldrin would take the power itself, he just laughed hysterically. Such an idea had no place in his head, his arrogance would not allow it. I sighed and left him in his bag and got everything ready to fly over the border at high altitude and at high speed.

We floated through the windless sky of Kregen. High and fast, a passing shadow between pale clouds, we crossed the border between Caneldrin and Tolindrin and then flew further into safety.

Shortly thereafter, I landed the lifter on a deserted plain next to a grove of trees where I could hide it. I made sure that the prince was securely bound and gagged in his sack, then I rolled myself in a blanket and fell asleep after I had thought my usual last, sweet thoughts.

As we flew on, rested, Prince Ortyg chose another tactic to try to scare me. He boasted of the huge armies that C'Chermina had in position. They would sweep through Tolindrin like a fire through a bone-dry forest. He complained bitterly about the lack of Chuliks. These excellent yellow-skinned fighters were all going south to their home islands. Let the devil take them.

I patiently explained to him the reason for the return of the Chuliks. "The Shanks!" I said, and I must admit that my voice sounded vicious even to my ears. "Those predators are tough, cunning and brave. They want to deprive us of Paz. And in order to achieve that goal, to kill and pillage. So we must stop them."

He was none too impressed, but my fierceness made him flinch. "I do not believe they will attack the Chulik islands. They have suffered a defeat there before. They will pounce on Balintol—and that means Tolindrin. So do you understand now...?"

"When I am king, I will settle this matter."

Well, I did not hit him. I tried to bring him to his senses, but the words bounced off the armor of his haughtiness, which had become even more impenetrable since his trip to Prebaya. To say nothing of his greed for Tolindrin's throne. So I put him in the bag and I concentrated on getting the flier to Oxonium by the fastest route.

It had not even occurred to this hot-tempered, weasel faced prince that I could have killed him. What? A pitiful mercenary who had the audacity to murder a real prince? He had completely internalized the superiority which the scum of the world concedes to the kings and the noble houses—and of course I, Dray Prescot, was also scum. That he had not lost courage while in the sack was understandable in the circumstances; he had not had time to become aware of what was actually happening to him.

As might be expected, he had offered to pay me, to bribe me, and he even made the offer to take me into his service. This proposal did not even deserve a response.

You can probably imagine how relieved I was when Oxonium came into view under the cloud cover. The hills surrounded by the trenches suddenly awakened in me the feeling of coming home—now that was a truly ridiculous thought, by Zair!

Down in the narrow channels, gangs were certainly busy trying to earn money dishonestly, and to fight for territory in villainous ways. On the hills the powerful would be taken care of by slaves and servants, living their comfortable lives and accumulating riches, in many cases also dishonestly. As we got closer, the traces of the earthquake were visible: fallen towers, broken down walls, collapsed domes. The noise of a big city penetrated upward, and shortly afterwards the stench.

It was not difficult to decide who to contact first. King Tom did not know all the details. Hyr Kov Brannomar was the man of the hour.

The fact is, I had a plan. Well, I have so often told of the great plans that I have worked out on Kregen, and you listening to these tapes know how often these fine plans have failed, and disastrously, by Krun! This time Five-handed Eos-Bakchi, the unpredictable Vallian spirit of luck and good fortune smiled down on me. Everything went like clockwork.

Well—almost everything, as you will hear.

The lifterdrome fees had risen in my absence. I paid and left. Ortyg stayed behind; he could stew in his bag, tucked out of sight. I had fed him and given him something to drink, and the bag was beginning to smell. The young prince would just have to endure it. His situation was not bad, certainly better than that of many pathetic slaves.

By a whisker I could have been denied entry into The Crystal Griffon. The tavern was distinguished, and even though I had cleaned myself and my clothes as well as possible it was with great difficulty that I passed the examination of the doorman. Eos-Bakchi smiled on me because the red eyepatch immediately caught my eye. Its owner was sitting alone at a table and eating. I went to him.

Nalgre ti Poventer looked up. Since our first meeting, he had learned much about the art of espionage. He said: "Lahal, Drajak."

I sat down, ordered a meal—Nalgre would pay—and told him what I wanted. He nodded. When we had eaten, we rented a vehicle and went to the lifterdrome. I took the bag and saw to it that Ortyg could not make any sound or even move a limb. Near the Vallian embassy we paid off the porter and carried the bag the rest of the way ourselves. They let us in immediately.

I told the ambassador the bare essentials, urging him to hide the young prince under close guard out of sight, then put on something more elegant, thanked them and left. Now it was the turn of Brannomar.

Just as expected, I was immediately admitted after the guard had reported my name to his Hikdar. Escorted by guards I entered Brannomar's palace. This was not my first visit; previously the circumstances had been quite unpleasant, and it had ended when the Hyr Kov had found out to his dismay and his astonishment that this Drajak the Sudden was, in reality, none other than Dray Prescot, possibly the future ruler of all Paz. Afterwards he had gladly agreed to work with me. As I had been told, he was incorruptible.

He received me in his private quarters, and we talked in private.

His ruby-red garment, devoid of unnecessary decoration, and the simple sword at his belt, fitted well with his tanned face, silver beard and his close cropped silver hair. He said: "Lahal—Drajak, right?"

"Aye, Kov. I am glad to see you." I told him bluntly that I had hidden the young Prince Ortyg in a safe place. "Now he cannot help Caneldrin any more or plot against you."

He sat down, poured two glasses of sazz which sparkled in the orange light penetrating through the window, and shook his head. "What they say about you is understated, by Tolaar; the truth is even more outlandish!"

He quickly recovered from his surprise. The crazy leem Dray Prescot had the Ortyg problem solved simply by stuffing him into a sack and hiding him. Ortyg had been removed from the game.

"The young Prince is unharmed?"

"He smells somewhat and his pride is badly shaken, but he has suffered no physical harm. My people will keep him locked up until this whole affair is done. That is, of course, only with your consent, Kov."

He waved his hand, took his glass, but only held it and did not drink. He had to have realized that my words were no more than mere courtesy; the complicated situation dictated that I had to hold Ortyg, whether he agreed or not.

The long scar on his left cheek stood out clearly from the surrounding skin and jerked involuntarily as he processed what was happening and began to ponder how it was likely to proceed. But he was now forced to incorporate what he knew about Dray Prescot—or thought he knew.

"Men and women call you a wild leem-hunter. The books, the plays, not to mention the puppet shows." He took a sip of the sazz. "And I can't help but think of the knot of the Kovneva Sinkie."

I nodded. This famous legend is common to the whole of Paz, and although its topic—the solution of a difficult task—resembles the Earthly story of the Gordian knot, it is quite different. When Alexander cut through the knot, he laid claim to the whole of Asia. On Kregen, the everlasting knot held closed the night robe of the Kovneva Sinkie. And who was the legendary figure who solved this delicate task? Well, of course, none other than Kyr Nath, well known from many stories and songs.

I drank the Sazz and suggested to Brannomar that the problem of Khon the Mak could possibly be solved in the same way.

Brannomar's pursed lips protruded between mustache and beard. He told me that the Hyr Kov Mak had not until now been able to recruit Chuliks, which did not surprise me.

"My agents have told me," he went on gravely, "that this man has other plans still. But up to now we have not been able to discover the details."

Suddenly, loud cries were heard in the antechamber. Brannomar jumped up and grabbed the hilt of his sword. I reached the door and opened it with my sword drawn, too. Brannomar breathed heavily at my side. The noise echoed through the antechamber like a rashoon.

The focus of attention was one of the Kov's guards. He was an Yvonnim;

he had no tail and only two arms. His hair, which was usually worn projecting vertically from his head, had been cut and was flattened by the prescribed uniform helmet. The Yvonnim are considered fairly good infantry soldiers, who have particularly sharp hearing through their floppy ears. Their noses are broad and flat, reaching from cheek to cheek, and their eyes are deep under a wide, protruding forehead.

This fellow was in the uniform and armor of the Kov. The armor had already been torn apart by the gigantic forces raging inside his body. The uniform tore. He was bigger and wider. He ballooned. The other guards screamed and backed away from him. In the elegantly furnished antechamber naked fear and chaos erupted.

We had only one chance: we had to kill the poor devil before he reached the full size of an ibmanzy. Once the demon had taken over, nothing could stop the destruction that it would unleash.

Brannomar let out a curse. The antechamber emptied rapidly as the guards fled. I could not blame them, by Krun!

There was nothing I could do with the thraxter. I put it away and pulled the Krozair blade. In that brief moment, that split second, something totally unexpected happened with the growing ibmanzy. He raised his hands, and from his fingers the first talons were already emerging. His face contorted. But he did not grow any more in height! His head sank into his body. His feet... From the tattered leather strips of his soldier boots, black slime spilled!

This unexpected change made me pause, and I watched as if frozen.

More and more black slime gushed. Now it came through the rents in his uniform, it sprayed from every part of his body. A glistening black jet of slime shot from the distorted mouth. The man shrank and became less and less until in the end there was only a smelly black puddle of slime spreading over the whole carpet.

Sixteen

"Often, miracles performed in a religion are called magic..."

"And many religions certainly originate in magic, so..."

"But religion and magic are clearly two different things."

The arguments positively flew around Brannomar's chamber, with no conclusion. Sana Besti, his twin sister, had joined us. She still presented a macabre figure; her sparkling eyes and pointed nose were surrounded by a towering, untamed mass of hair, and her dress gave the impression of a bundle of rags. She grabbed her morntarch and the three skulls protruding from the dangling threads clattered together. Her small mouth and thin lips, that so resembled her brother's, were normally pressed together firmly and opened only when she had something meaningful to say. As a sorceress she was tolerated, and she had a clear-cut opinion on everything concerning the ibmanzy.

"They are onkers who summon demons to do their dirty work for them. The human body is not made for this demonic energy."

We came to the conclusion that the ibmanzy, which had transformed back leaving a pitiful mangled human corpse, had fulfilled its task. The monster, which had dissolved in that terrible way into black slime, had failed. And for that you could only thank Opaz!

The two now knew everything I had learned about the ibmanzies through experience. They promised to find out more. "Whoever is doing these terrible things does not possess a good heart," said Besti. She gave off the sweet scent of lavender.

What was left of the black slime had been mopped up and taken to her private quarters. She would examine it, but she had no great hope of finding out more from the gunge than we already knew.

New information arose when Lord Jazipur, the right hand of the Kov, arrived with the cadade. They reported that the Yvonnim, a fellow named Lycon the Standard, had been recently hired. A friend of the cadade had highly recommended him. The captain of the guard was stiff and reserved, he was extremely uncomfortable. "Lorgan ti Mindlo it was who highly recommended him, Notor. I did not hesitate to hire him. Tolaar knows that the Yvonnim are reliable people." He sweated and squirmed in his armor. "By the Holy Golden Sash of Tolaar, I swear that no gold changed hands. Not one coin!"

Brannomar looked at his man. Loyal cadades are worth their weight in gold. He nodded. "I trust you."

Jazipur, who only knew me as Drajak the Sudden but knew I had played a role in the dispute over the succession to the throne and what I had accomplished, snapped, "I know that Lorgan ti Mindlo. He was seen in the company of Khon the Mak before he fled."

So that's what lay behind it. They had tried directly to assassinate Hyr Kov Brannomar in his own palace. The ibmanzy had been a stikitche—undoubtedly sent by Khon the Mak.

Had the attack been successful, there would have been nothing more to fear from the dead Kov Brannomar. Even so... "I'll take care of the matter," said Lord Jazipur. He spoke with an ice-cold rage that left no doubt about his intentions.

When I describe these people in the aftermath of the terrible event as calm and reasonable, you must not misunderstand me. They had calmed down slowly. But by the dangling inflamed eyeball and festering hairy nostril of Makki Grodno, they were clearly very distressed. They had suffered a massive shock, by Krun, which had shaken them to their toes!

Then I had an interesting—and I think, sobering—thought. The Dray Prescot who had originally been brought to Kregen would be furiously storming off to prune this Mindlo tidily—and boshli, as they say on Kregen. Today, I just stood there and was much more controlled than all the others put together. And yet the blood that pulsed through my arteries and veins was as young as ever. After the dip in the sacred Pool of Baptism in far Aphrasöe that had assured me a full thousand years of life, my aging process had slowed down. Perhaps Delia's yearning hope had been realized, and I had acquired some common sense.

Over the next few burs everything gradually returned to business as usual, and Jazipur learned the news concerning Prince Ortyg. He responded with shocked surprise, mingled with reluctant consent. "At least the young pup will be out of the game for a while."

Jazipur's men returned and reported that Mindlo was not to be found. It had been impossible to keep the event quiet or to prevent the rumors spreading like wildfire throughout Oxonium. Everyone knew about it. Mindlo, unnerved by his failure, had fled.

We sat down to a meal, and despite the early hour a sip of wine was served—diluted with water, naturally. I did not know what the Kov had told Jazipur about me. In any case, Jazipur looked at me, the simple Paktun, thoughtfully.

"And you will proceed with Khon the Mak in the same manner?" he asked almost gently.

This was a question that had kept me very busy of late, as you can imagine.

I shook my head and pointed out that Khon was still not in a position to recruit an army, and the greater threat was in the north. The loss of her puppet prince Ortyg would not prevent C'Chermina from pursuing her fantasies of conquest.

Brannomar mentioned our earlier conversation in which I had reflected on whether I would be able to stop Khon the Mak in a similar way to Prince Ortyg. He agreed with my opinion that the greater risk was from the north at the moment.

Sana Besti was silent the whole time, as if she were immersed in her own magical world. Once or twice she shook her morntarch briefly. The ribbons, bells and skulls dangling from the top of the bar gave a sinister, menacing sound that echoed through the room.

"What is it, sister?"

She did not reply, but stood up. She paced up and down restlessly.

Her behavior resembled her manner when she had discovered that the wizard of Khon the Mak spied on us in lupu.

Brannomar wanted to say something and I had the impression he was irritated, but Besti suddenly shook the morntarch crazily. She sat in a corner of the chamber, under a window. We all watched.

A hazy round object peeled out of nowhere and slowly began to take shape. Jazipur gasped. The cadade's fist closed around his sword hilt. Brannomar closed his mouth. The object hovered in the air between the floor and the windowsill.

It was an eye.

It was the size of an orange, pupil and iris clearly recognizable. From its underside, arm-length tentacles grew like the roots of a tree and stretched and coiled around each other again and again slowly and deliberately.

A turquoise haze enveloped the ghostly apparition.

It was not necessary for one of us to blurt out: "We are being spied on!"

Again there came the eerie rustle of a morntarch. The eye blinked. The purple eyelid fell, lifted up and fell again. The morntarch trembled, sending strange sounds through the room.

The old wildness took me. My hand shot with a smooth and instinctive movement over my right shoulder, seized a terchick—and the throwing knife darted through the air like silver lightning.

The blade hit the eye exactly in the center. Nothing stopped its flight. It flew on and crashed clattering against the wall.

At the moment I had intemperately thrown the knife, the eye opened again. It opened wide and stared at me with such vicious intensity—all while the knife whizzed through the air—that ice cold ran down my back. I instinctively lifted my head to meet the challenge. And we stared at each other. For a tiny moment we were isolated from the others, inextricably linked in a personal showdown.

Abruptly, I was aware of the eeriness of what was happening to me. It took only a heartbeat, a heartbeat in which the rest of Kregen ceased to exist.

The bells and skulls of Besti's staff jingled and clashed against each other. In one of the adjoining corridors a dog let out a piercing howl. The eye rose slowly into the air, and the tentacles uncoiled. The spiritual struggle held me captive in its spell. I stared at the eye.

For maybe half a dozen heartbeats, nothing changed in the tableau.

Then the eye disappeared silently.

No one said a word.

Only after another mouthful of wine—this time with less water—did a stormy Sana Besti demand an explanation.

Her whole demeanor betrayed the struggle between two opposing feelings. There was the pride and satisfaction that it was she who had discovered the occult manifestation first and then banished it. But this gratification was wrestling with the knowledge of what had actually just happened. It was a bad omen for the future of Tolindrin—and this was no mere conjecture, but a simple realization.

In the many disciplines and secrets of the wizards of Kregen there were huge differences when it came to ability and performance. As far as I knew and had seen the Wizards of Loh were by far the most powerful among them. But lately my comrades had been blocked in Balintol. They had indicated that the mysterious Wizard of Balintol could monitor the activities of the Wizards of Loh. I had even been forced to the supposition—by the words that my friends had not said—that their work was hampered or even negated.

Not a pleasant notion.

The late king had banished all sorcerers from Tolindrin—Sana Besti was tolerated. The minor practitioners of the magical arts were tolerated. In my opinion Sana Besti was anything but insignificant, by Krun! Her position as twin sister of the Hyr Kov contributed substantially to her survival—that and her thaumaturgical skill.

Since my arrival in Balintol the reputation of the subcontinent as a place of secrets had vexed me. I had gotten to see very little of this, or at least so I thought. But now that demons transferred across to our plane of existence and the bodies of young people were torn to pieces, I was forced to change this opinion.

During an awkward conversation Besti told us her belief that the eye was not sent by Khon the Mak's new Wizard of Loh. He was just another bungler, with much to learn. I agreed. When the Wizards of Loh want to watch something from afar, they put themselves into Lupu—which is done in various ways—and snoop around. Sometimes they use a signomant, a device that was placed at the target of the observation. I had never seen a disembodied eye—at least as far as I could remember.

Besti said—and she emphasized her uncertainty—that in her opinion there had been a manifestation of the illusionist who ruled Winlan, San W'Watchun, in the eye.

The Divine Lady of Belschutz came immediately to mind when I saw how the audience reacted to Besti's opinion. They were horrified. The emergence of the ibmanzies had driven fear deep into their bones, and this had increased with the materialization of the eye; this third shock gave them the balance.

At these events, there had not been a fight with gleaming blades and spurting blood; nonetheless it had been a struggle, and indeed a clever and diabolical struggle. A struggle that could cost us our lives.

Brannomar's First Pallan Lord Jazipur said: "It could well be that the wizard's attention was drawn to the manifestation of the ibmanzy." His dark face, clearly of Xuntalese blood, took on a determined expression. "W'Watchun wants to learn as much as possible about the demons. He..."

"That means," broke in Brannomar angrily, "he was here earlier, with certainty. How long has he been watching us?"

"We'll probably never know, brother."

"Aye, by Tolaar! To Sicce with the criminal!"

I, Dray Prescot, determined to abstain from comment.

As I had realized, this W'Watchun had gained power and eliminated many other magicians of Balintol. His Kharrna was now of a downright grotesque size.

Winlan had segregated itself. It was ruled by a powerful warrior caste that held the existing slaves from the other half of the population under a knout of iron. A few foreign merchants were permitted into the country but their activities were strictly monitored. Farms, factories and roads were in the hands of slaves who possessed the necessary knowledge. But if a slave overseer failed to bring in the prescribed harvest the warriors just gave the order to make him a head shorter and installed a new overseer. Those overseers would try very hard to avoid this fate.

A wizard must have a very powerful kharrna to ascend to such a high position in a warrior society. The warriors lived according to a very complicated and precise code. They were a proud and choleric bunch who despised foreigners. That was, as has been suggested, one of the reasons they had surrounded their country with the famous wall.

A cynic would have suspected that the wall served to prevent people from escaping from such a disagreeable nation.

Of course, it was entirely possible that the damned insubstantial spy eye was not sent by the sorcerer W'Watchun, by Krun!

Maybe my Opaz-cursed Dokerty friends from Prebaya were on my trail. Maybe their demonology gave them power to send a spy eye after me. But how would they know I was here? Could they follow me around through a terrible plane of existence from another dimension? In the religions of Balintol there were many strange ideas, which elsewhere on Kregen would have been called magic.

Well, by the loathsome liver and dwindling eyesight of Makki Grodno! I had a job to do in Caneldrin, and that is exactly where I would go as soon as I had worked out what needed to be done in Oxonium. By Djan, yes!

Some time later, after our conversation was exhausted under the peaceful moons hovering over our heads and two excellent meals had found their way into our stomachs, we went to bed. Brannomar showed me to an available chamber. In the early hours of the morning I awoke to a sound at the door. With sword in hand, I looked out.

In the light of the samphron-oil lamps I was greeted by a sight that forced an involuntary groan from my lips. Four black-skinned men from Xuntal tried to overpower a light-skinned man who pranced around vigorously, and how the soldier cursed as he tried to avoid being cut with their swords. All five men were in uniform and armor and were obviously in the guard of the Hyr Kov—presumably they had been reassigned to guard me.

My muscles tensed as I prepared myself to go between them fast and deadly and save this poor devil from these thugs.

I paused. I took a deep breath. From what I already knew, I attempted to identify friend from foe. Maybe... At that moment a blow with the broad side of a braxter sent the cursing man to the floor. The black-skinned assailant stepped back and shouted, "Do not hurt him! The Hikdar will take care of the blintz!"

A curtain gaped open and a small Fristle fifi staggered out and collapsed into the arms of the Xuntalese men. Her face swelled in an ugly way already. Her threadbare dress was torn, her body covered in blood. Her tail with its bright red tassel dragged across the floor.

So it came about. The cursing guard had tried to violate the Fristle girl and the Xuntalese had intervened to stop him. I sighed. All my experiences of the Xuntalese had shown that these black-skinned folk were a decent people, and to be honest—Opaz is my witness—this is probably why I had not intervened immediately.

The Hikdar arrived. He was a Ranstak and had the hooded eyes and compressed facial features of his race. He was very forceful, and had his sword tail sticking up. The villain was hurried away at a run. The Fifi was carried away gently in strong black arms. So it was not necessary that I intervene. Thankfully, I went back to bed.

And yet, by the Mother Diocaster, all things considered I could draw a lesson, an important lesson, by Zair!

Originally I had intended to limit my time in Oxonium, but one thing led to another, and so I was held up almost a whole sennight. I learned very little about my friends.

Tiri remained in Farinsee, where she was putting the finishing touches to her magical powers. Fweygo, my Kregoinye comrade, had probably fallen into an adventure somewhere on the orders of the Star Lords. Princess Nandisha and her entourage were holed up in a country estate.

One thought was sobering: When would C'Chermina attack Tolindrin?

We had long discussions, looking for the best way to ward off the demonic ibmanzies. Sana Besti checked the area continuously for the presence of spying eyes. No more were found. Throughout this entire time, I could almost feel the hot breath of the Everoinye on my neck.

As much as I would have enjoyed going down into the runnels between the hills, there was just not enough time for it. I wondered how it likely went for my friends, the gang members of Nagzalla's Nasty Neemus. You could wager a gold rhok that they were still going about their business. Whatever that villainy might be, by Krun! When I finally boarded my lifter—after observing the fantamyrrh—and headed north, I felt relief in my heart.

I had relieved the Vallian embassy of a considerable sum in gold and jewels and was quite confident that we could bring Dagert on my side with it. When I reached The Zorca's Heart, the famous inn in Umrigg that basked in the glow of the sun, a single message was all that was waiting for me, of course.

Dagert of Paylen had written only that he had savored to the last drop the loan of the pay of a simple cadade and had resigned from my service. He and Palfrey were gone. I was not surprised. Also, I knew—by Djan Kadjiryon, I knew it!—that I would meet this charming villain and his evilly exploited servant Palfrey again. That was as sure as Zim and Genodras rising every morning over Kregen. The only question was: in what villainy would he be involved?

I took a quick meal, drank at a gulp and flew on to Prebaya.

I put the flier in the lifterdrome, grumbled about the exorbitant fees and made my way to pay Lady Quensella a visit. She received me immediately. When she greeted me, her face had more color than usual. Her appearance gained from it and she had lost some of her aloofness.

"Well, Drajak. I am... pleased... to see you. Have you returned to command my Juruk again?"

I controlled myself, because I had decided not to take a chance on a Prescot smile, and told her that was impossible. She looked at me, speechless. "In the apartments of the regent there has been an incident," I continued. "Granumin, the first Pallan, was murdered."

She looked at me calmly and now completely under control.

"And?"

I must admit that I was just trying to satisfy my own curiosity. The whole affair was finished. If I was right in my assumption, would she admit it? To a simple cadade?

"Schrepims do not make good stikitches, my lady. Presumably, only someone in a desperate position would rely on them."

"I think so too."

Her chest rose and fell, making the blue sensil move and adopt all the colors of the rainbow. We were alone. I just hoped she would not do something stupid, something she would later regret.

There was absolutely no doubt that there was a tension between us. That this tension only emanated from her filled me with compassion. Her lips were moist. Onker that I am, I made a daring foray.

"Now the deed is done, my lady, you will be safe from further attacks?"

She raised her head. "Does that mean, do you think I...?" she began, then paused, licked her moist lips and shook her head. "No, Drajak. You are right. Why should I deny it? The blintz deserved what he got. Poor Sinkie! Naghan ti Indrin also got what he so much deserved. The matter is settled."

"Queyd-arn-tung!" No more need be said on the subject.

She smiled. The topic of conversation changed. She offered wine, palines and miscils because it would be a few burs until the next meal. I inquired about the new pallan, M'Marmor.

"The Khibil believes he can now decide everything." She pushed a yellow paline between her red lips, chewed and swallowed. "If T'Tolaar thinks his time has come, he will very likely meet an unpleasant end."

The double initial did not escape me but I said nothing.

Everything here was rather nice; I had satisfied my curiosity and would have to say goodbye in a dignified manner. But there was still something that rankled me. And since Dray Prescot is a get-onker, I heard myself say: "Be that as it may, my lady, that business with the schrepims was excessive. I think of the guards who were killed, the servants, the..."

This put her in a rage, her arrogance was revealed. Now she was quite the noble lady, to the painted toenails. "You dare to question my actions? You, who I made the captain of my guard and who let me down so?"

"I have not let you down," I snapped, "as you know perfectly well!"

No sooner had I said this than I had the uncomfortable vision of summoned guards taking off my head, but something else entirely occurred—she broke down. She slumped in her chair. With one hand she clutched at her throat, with the other she reached out to me a rosy invitation.

"Oh, Drajak, Drajak! How little you understand!"

I stood there like a fool. I understood, by Krun, I understood only too well. I tried to find the right words to extricate myself from a situation that could only have an ugly end. I was too slow by dwaburs. She jumped up and literally threw herself on me. She clung tightly to me, covered my face with kisses, sobbed.

Her blue sensil robe slid from her shoulders. Her hair came loose. She wrapped her arms around my waist and fell groaning to the ground, where she clung to my legs.

By the pustule covered and fearsomely extensive anatomy of the Divine Lady of Belschutz! By all the disease-ridden disfigurements of Makki Grodno! She did not let go. She clung on firmly for a long bur, wept, wailed and uttered barely intelligible words to herself, which resulted in a sobbed declaration of mortal passion and everlasting love. This embarrassing spectacle had to stop.

Even in that moment I could not bring myself to slap her face to bring her to her senses. She clung so desperately that I almost fell. I took her in my arms, gently broke her grip on my legs and placed her on the chair. I drew her dress up to cover her and caught hold of her clutching hands, forcing them to her sides. Then I took a quick step back.

"Drajak! Please! Please!"

I must confess I felt like the most villainous rogue on all of Kregen, who had escaped the gallows until now.

"My lady, I have to go now. I'll let your servants know. Best you calm yourself again. There can be nothing between us."

"Nothing! Nothing! Oh, Drajak..."

My Val! And then, thank Opaz, the magnificent image of Delia rose before my mind's eye, to give me courage and to guide me.

"You have my respect and loyalty. Please do not make me go back on that. You..."

"Respect! Loyalty!" She was trembling, her eyes looking wildly through the strands of hair that hung over her forehead. Her robe slid down again. "I don't care about that! I want your love, your passion—I want you!"

"Then, my lady, we must part. But I will remember you for all time with a feeling that comes very close to affection." I was clever enough not to say to her that I was sorry for her or that she had my sympathy. I managed a few words of consolation and realized that at that moment it was impossible for her to see reason. She would get over it. At least I hoped so.

She panted, as if she had run a dwabur with a full water jar on her head without stopping. She brushed back her hair. She talked wildly: Didn't I consider her pretty? Or did I find her ugly—compared with her twin sister, the regent C'Chermina? That shocked me.

If the little lady had it in her noble head that I had fallen for her sister, I was really in a bind!

I said, "I do not know the Regent. If you'll excuse me, I must go."

If she did not believe me, if her jealousy of her sister took on such proportions, she was quite capable of giving the command to give me an unpleasant time before she decapitated me, by Krun!

Someone banged loudly on the door.

Quensella looked around wildly, as if waking from a dream. She gave me a last piercing look, jumped up from the chair and ran to a hidden alcove behind a curtain. "I'm not done with you yet, Drajak. You will not be able to reject me forever!" she called back over her shoulder.

The knock was repeated, the door opened, and Tral the Strict waddled into the chamber. He knew that I had visited Quensella. "Where is my lady?" he demanded.

I pushed past him, stepped through the open door and told him that she had retired and was asking for her servants.

By all the saints and demons on Kregen! That was a bad experience. I would not like to have to go through it before breakfast again, no, by the purple eyes and cherry red lips of the Princess Luciliah Debliah of the mystical woods!

Seventeen

Why, in the name of the glorious and radiant Opaz, can I, Dray Prescot, not keep my big nose out of other people's affairs?

The ugly sight that presented itself to me in the mingled streaming light of the Suns of Scorpio had nothing to do with me.

Nothing at all.

So why did I stop in the shade of an arcade? Why did I not continue on? Why did my hand drop to my sword hilt?

I want to remind you of the devastating mistake that I almost committed when the four Xuntalese did not beat the white-skinned apim, but merely tried to arrest him. Had I gone in between them with a wild battle cry on my lips—my Val! What a mess I would have made there! Without a doubt such an error would have caused a setback in my plans.

People going about their daily business made a wide berth around the affair, as do most sensible citizens after all. Their tense faces and frightened eyes peered around corners, out of alcoves and from behind columns and colonnades. The kyro, saturated by the light of the suns, lay deserted except for the leading protagonists in the drama taking place there.

During my uneasy career on Kregen in the service of the Star Lords I had developed the experience to determine from the most meager evidence the rights and wrongs of a situation. At first glance, everything seemed to be clear here, but taking the duties and interests of all parties into account there could be all sorts of reasons for the incident. It was a hard to grasp, nasty mess, by Krun!

An audo—that is a detachment of soldiers, in this case there were ten men—stood warily and with drawn weapons in battle formation facing a man unblinking and full of scorn in the center of the square.

I had encountered his kind before. He wore black lacquered armor that covered his entire body and sparkled gold and green in places. The tools of his trade hung from his belt, a bag full of death stars, a long chain with at one end a three-blade knife and at the other a tripartite grappling hook, just like a Japanese Kyoketsu-shoge, and a chunkscreetz, an iron swordbreaker. He wore two braxters and a number of daggers. He had no shield—his kind detested shields as the mark of a coward.

He stood there like a weathered oak in the forest, every muscle of his body under firm control. His face, with colorless tusks, penetrating eyes and a stern and bitter mouth framed by a spiky drooping mustache, told of a lifetime of bloodshed on behalf of his masters. Some of the best fighters on Kregen claimed that his style of combat began with skills and training where the Chuliks' left off.

Oh yes, I knew what he was. He was commissioned by his master to go on a mission that he would pursue as long as there was one breath in his lungs and a drop of blood remaining in his body.

He stood there tough and invincible; in his heart there was no spark of humanity any more—at least that was commonly said.

The Deldar of the swods licked his lips.

"You're coming with us. The Prefect wants to ask you..."

"I am a Kanzai warrior brother." The words echoed bitterly about the place. A flock of little matfuls, fat gray and white birds very similar to pigeons, fluttered startled into the air. "I am on a mission for my master. I have simply entered your town to buy supplies." His tone was dark and threatening. "Stand aside!"

His four hands were empty, but he threw back his proud scarlet cloak and two hands hovered over the various weapons.

The soldiers were ordinary swods of various diff breeds. Their armor was more or less uniform. Their swords were mass produced braxters, which would probably break during a normal fight, but would with absolute certainty shatter into useless metal splinters in contact with the weapons of a Kanzai warrior brother.

The swods knew it.

It was also clear to them that their ten were outmatched.

The Deldar seemed to be a typical experienced old soldier, a stocky, coarse fellow with a powerful voice who had worked his way up as far in the military hierarchy as it was possible for him to go. Vikatu the Old Soldier had seen to it that he had been well trained. Nevertheless, he was one of that kind of soldier who follow the orders of others, because that is all they can do. To follow orders was the focal point of his life. That he was liable to die did not matter—orders were orders.

The participants in this impasse stared at each other.

Maybe the example of San Yo the Prophet could provide a solution. He could summon bright, colorful, moving images. I, however, stood still and contemplated San Yo while ten human beings were on the verge of committing suicide.

It was not easy to decide who was right in this situation. The Kanzai warrior brother followed the orders of his master just as blindly as the Deldar followed his. Clearly there was nothing wrong with a fellow walking into a city—even if it was around the capital—to buy supplies, as long as he behaved. Certainly the Prefect had the right to watch anyone who entered his district and might cause trouble. Well, by Vox, the issue was none of my business.

So I turned away.

The suns continued on their way. The birds flew. A light breeze was blowing. It was not the end of Kregen. The air, the sweet air of Kregen, suddenly no longer smelled so sweet and fresh. I paused.

What significance did a Kanzai have for me? Or ten soldiers?

I turned back around. Suddenly the mad thought settled in my old vosk skull that this urgent matter concerned me very much if I claimed to be the Emperor of Emperors, Emperor of all Paz.

I stepped out into the radiant brightness of the sun, crossed the kyro and set myself exactly between the Kanzai and the soldiers. The swods gasped in surprise. The grim face of the Kanzai betrayed no emotion.

The Deldar took on a menacing attitude.

"What is this? Get out of here! Schtump!"

"Del, you're dead, all of you, if you do not listen," I said.

"Who the hell are you to come crawling out of the crowd..."

You do not think that I was going to tell him? I simply turned my back on him and gave the Kanzai a hard look.

"I have nothing against you," he said. "It is better you step aside."

Now the Star Lords had absurdly chosen me as ruler of Paz because I command the yrium. A power that far exceeds normal charisma, the yrium is both a curse and a blessing, as I knew only too well. I gave to the iron-hard Kanzai warrior brother the dark look which some call the Dray Prescot Devil Look. He did not flinch; he blinked. "Likely you could kill these ten men, but that would seal your fate. Your mission would have failed. Your master would not be pleased." I did not stop watching him as I spoke.

He replied only: "Do you want to compete against me?"

His upper right hand closed around the hilt of a braxter. It was definitely not mass produced, but was made of first-class steel. It was completely open, who would win in a battle between us. As you know, I hate people who boast about being the best swordsman in the world. I never forget Mefto the Kazzur.

I put even more power into my unbearable, intimidating, insuperable look of authority.

"No, you fambly, I do not want to kill you."

He blinked again.

I told him that if he was not guilty of any crime, it would be wisest to pay a visit to the Prefect. Once he had finished with the petty bureaucracy, he could fill his knapsack and move on. Finally, I added that his master would certainly agree to such conduct.

He plucked at his long mustache with the left upper hand. There was a faint hope that, unlike words, an action would get through to him. I had tried before to thrash out something with a Kanzai warrior brother.

"I will go to this worm of a Prefect... if you accompany me."

By the abscess covered and veined legs of the Lady Dulshini! I had no time to wander around here. I had to take care of the ibmanzies. I had to prevent wars. Balintol was the dress rehearsal for the whole of Paz. I said, "I'll come with you."

"Good. I see you are a real man."

Kanzai warrior brothers move in their own incomparable way when they face a threat or need to take action. They move—for the briefest time—lightning fast. Between these bursts of movement, they remain perfectly still, calm, self-possessed. In this they have something in common with the schrepim. When this representative of the mysterious Kanzai brotherhood moved to my side, he did it like every other fighter, with head held high. By the Blade of Kurin, he made a magnificent picture.

The Deldar and his audo marched behind us. There goes a bunch of relieved swods, I thought, amused—admittedly, there are people who think my humor is malicious.

If I have presented this incident in a completely matter of fact manner that might convey a false impression... in truth, the air had crackled with tension.

My Val, yes! A whirlwind of destruction could have seized the peaceful little kyro and in the circle of vaol-paol who could say how things would have turned out? Oh yes, as we walked through the street I sent a heartfelt thank you to the various gods. At this point I still was not convinced that the flare up of my famous—or infamous—yrium had overwhelmed the will of one of the most egocentric and strongest-willed beings on Kregen, but things were looking up, by Vox!

Most onlookers walked on, but one fellow followed us. He was a Gildrim with a long baboon-like nose, close-set eyes and an unruly mop of hair. He wore eye-catching half-armor, which was gilded and fitted with an abundance of feathers. Of course, he had strapped on two or three swords in the best Kregen tradition. I did not like the way he gave me significant glances.

With all Gildrims it is important to keep their tail in mind. Although they have only two arms like an apim, that damn tail is a more than fiendish compensation. Unlike other movable Kregen tails, that of a Gildrim is relatively thick but flexible in an almost miraculous way. The average Gildrim does not strap a six-inch blade firmly to the tip of his tail like a Kataki. Oh no, by Djan! He secures a damn great club to it, a skull crusher, with six triangular blades protruding from it. When confronting that you have to be on guard because he can flail it over his shoulder or smash an opponent with a running horizontal blow to the ribs. With their sad baboon-like faces Gildrims are a grumpy bunch, but it's good if they are on your side.

This specimen certainly belonged to the other side.

Eventually he quickened his pace and disappeared ahead of us on the road.

The Prefect and his soldiers resided in a beautiful building with a roof crowned with many turrets—a notable feature that caught the eye involuntarily. Most people instinctively crossed the street and walked by on the opposite side to the Prefecture. Strange—and important.

When we reached the arched entrance, I was already expecting problems with the Prefect, and I was very angry about the unwanted interruption to my plans—but I was resolved to seeing through the typically stormy Kregen course of events. Considering the situations a Kregan must sometimes confront, the expected obstacles put before us by the Prefect and his men faded as a more immediate situation presented itself.

Two uniformed groups were arguing loudly and threatening each other with their fists. Faces were bright red. A lot of wrongness spilled from the archway into the street. Our Deldar overtook us and left his unit at rest. He looked surprised.

Quite unlike me.

One of the quarrelling groups wore the uniform of C'Chermina's followers, the others belonged to Quensella. The Prefect had probably summoned the jurukkers that I had recruited to interrogate them about two issues. One was the disappearance of Naghan ti Indrin. The more important one was the brutal murder of Pallan Granumin by the schrepims. The Prefect would regard the two events as connected with security rather than with each other.

Presumably that was what the noisy argument with insults and threatening fists was about. But no, by Krun, of course this could not be, not as long as the twin Suns of Scorpio float in the sky, for San M'Marmor strode out of the entrance.

The Khibil opened his mouth to shout energetic commands at the guards. He looked at me. There was not the slightest chance to escape the intolerant, foxy look. He saw me and recognized me immediately.

Well, yes, it could not be otherwise, by Vox!

He immediately turned into an angry imitation of Kov Largos the Irritated, who in the old legends of Kregen drove the heavenly host in his bronze vessels over the horizon. He exploded. With gesticulating arms and quivering red whiskers he gave shrill, almost unintelligible cries.

"Seize him! Seize that man! Bratch!"

My lads from Quensella's personal bodyguard turned around and saw me. The bureaucracy had annoyed them quite a lot and their blood was almost reaching boiling point. M'Marmor's men hastened to obey the shrieked command. They pulled their swords out of their sheaths and came towards me. My men saw it. They did not pause to think. Weapons flashed in the sunlight.

In the next few tumultuous seconds fighting broke out in the street.

Eighteen

The deadly six-bladed club at the end of the Gildrim's tail swished close. Just in time I moved my head to one side, but the suddenness of the movement pulled me over. I rolled and came up onto my feet with rapier and main gauche in my fists.

The baboon-faced fellow wanted to go at me again. But in the turmoil the broad side of a sword blade slammed him in the temple. He fell headlong to the ground. Perempto the Shorn allowed himself a satisfied grin that spread over the whole of his foxy Khibil face. Then he spun around and stood in the way of a Fristle who wanted to take down Nalan ti Perming from the side.

Oh yes, the bad blood between the twins, the Regent C'Chermina and Lady Quensella, extended also to their guards, and some of that bad blood would be spilled in the next bur.

M'Marmor hopped around on the spot and screamed for help.

Obviously the Gildrim was in the employ of the First Pallan. He had needed just enough time to see me as I was traveling with the Kanzai and deldars of the audo. A few moments longer and M'Marmor would have been informed about my arrival in time and had his reception committee ready to capture me effortlessly.

The battle spread out across the street. Erwin the Waggler hit a pretty gilded helmet, ducked and threw himself in the other direction to catch a Rapa whose beak was bent significantly from the blow.

Quensella's juruk was successful in giving C'Chermina's bodyguard an efficient beating. They, of course, continued to defend themselves. Up until now no one had been killed. But that would change if the fight went on much longer.

The Deldar and his audo kept out of it. They did not understand what was going on. There was no sign of the prefect and the Deldar obviously hesitated to take action on his own initiative.

As for the Kanzai warrior brother, he stood motionless with a grim face, still like a gnarled oak, and looked disdainfully down at the crowd.

As I emerged from under a stroke and replied with a blow that hit the attacker on his ear, it occurred to me that the contempt of the Kanzai was probably due to the fact that a considerable number of corpses would have been scattered on the ground had he been involved in the fight.

One of Quensella's men, a Hytak I didn't know, fell down with an ugly dent in his armored side; blood shone on the greasy iron. Until now, it had only been a hard fight. Now it was suddenly serious.

I circled a man with a long two-handed sword who wanted to make me a head shorter, feinted to the side and pricked him in the neck with the rapier, just above the edge of his armor. The blade tip severed strained muscles. He cried out and fled.

When I withdrew, someone hit me with a hard blow to the back of the head. My old vosk skull exploded stars, and I stumbled forward. The Bells of Beng Kishi resounded in my skull, and I spun around. The fellow who had struck me was a medium sized Trinkim with a thick bald head and bulging eyes. While he fought, saliva flowed down his stubby fangs. He had used the bottom end of a short shafted axe to hit me, obeying the command to capture me alive. Had he used the blade, the world of Kregen would have swirled around me as my head rolled across the cobblestones.

I turned towards him. There was just one problem—I saw two of him. I blinked. My vision was blurred, which made me mad. I shook my head. The axe rose again.

That is—two axes rose, damn it.

I used an old, desperate trick of the bravo fighter, and threw myself flat on the floor with my body propped on my left hand which still held the main gauche. The rapier went under the deadly swing of the axe and cleanly pierced his lower leg.

The Trinkim let out a surprised cry of pain. I withdrew the blade and rolled away instinctively. A sword struck a loud clatter on the pavement where my head had just been and broke into several pieces. The Rapa who had tried to eliminate me didn't react to the destruction of his blade; he just pulled out his second braxter lightning quick and came after me.

My forward roll ended with me raised up on one knee with the rapier and main gauche held outstretched defensively. The Rapa scratched himself as he lunged at me, yelped and stumbled back. I jumped to my feet and used my dagger's pommel to send him into the land of dreams.

This was all well and good. M'Marmor had screamed instructions at the guard to take me alive. My boys from Quensella's juruk were not protected by such a command. If this went on for much longer, they could all die.

A Polsim, with sneaky determination on his narrow weasel face, stood behind Nath the Chanter, a decent Torana and chavpaktun who would soon achieve the mortpaktun. The Polsim's sword rose for the kill. Nath the Chanter had eyes only for the Fristle in front of him. It seemed very unlikely that he would have his promotion.

I saw it, and at the very moment that I dashed off to help, a broad-shouldered, greasy Advang emerged out of nowhere to slit me.

"Chanter! Behind you!" I yelled. I parried the thrust of the Advang and showed him my blade tip.

In that fleeting moment, I saw from the corner of my eye another Polsim, wearing Quensella's colors, rush with a gleaming sword into his fellow diff. The braxter hit skillfully; the slash of the first Polsim missed. A second, precisely targeted strike switched it away. Nath the Chanter got his

Fristle with one of those down below backhand strokes, which the Torana are famous for.

The Advang in front of me impaled himself obligingly on my rapier, and I withdrew the blade with a jerk.

The pungent stench of spilled blood filled the air. Gurgling cries became soft moans. The fight had become serious. I looked around.

In the encounter between the two Polsims two things were notable. First of all, of course, was the fact that after my departure they had taken Polsims into Quensella's bodyguard.

And second, this fight was a clear example of the thought processes of Kregish mercenaries. Polsims do not have much time for other diff races, but this man had not hesitated for a moment to kill one of his own race to protect a member of another race. A paktun took his pay in gold and did his duty; he was faithful to the colors of his masters. As for tomorrow—well, dom, maybe then we fight on the same side.

The battle raged wildly. It is in the nature of unlawful brawls that there are no strict formations. It was mostly mano-a-mano, with a supportive comrade intervening as needed—as when the Polsim assisted Nath the Chanter.

Despite the lack of a battle line, from time to time it came down to maneuvers where we stood facing C'Chermina's damned blighters in close formation. A front would form, which then broke up into duels, and the fight spread all over the street again.

During one of these maneuvers, I knocked down two swods who had been pushed forward by their comrades. When the two went to the ground, the men who swarmed behind them saw me. The thought that here was a fat chicken in front of them, just waiting to be plucked and end up in the cooking pot, was clearly written on their faces, by Inglos Brandmal! They attacked.

Meanwhile, battle and the stench of blood had pushed all thoughts of M'Marmor's commands from their minds.

Now they just wanted my death!

I jumped backwards, mindful of a headless corpse, took another step back to give myself enough space—and came up against a wall.

A shadowy movement in the corner of my eye caused me to leap sideways. I managed to parry the first blow of the leader of the forward raging group, I gave way to the side and glanced at the spot where I had just been standing.

There was the Kanzai. He stood there quite still, did not flinch and gave the turmoil around him no attention.

After I dealt with the deadly blade thrusts of the first three attackers with fierce contortions, the rest pulled back panting.

Their faces were flushed and each showed his anger in the way that was typical of his race. They growled and threatened with their weapons. In their eyes, hatred flashed. They hopped from one foot to the other like savage jungle animals. It would not be long before they were on me, the lone fighter, rushing in to kill me once and for all.

And in this tiny break in the midst of the uproar of noisy battle, a trumpet sounded from the tower over the gate.

The bright tones echoed through the terrible tumult of the street battle.

A rider on a magnificent zorca came out of the gate.

His armor glittered in the bright flowing light of the suns. Colorful feathers waved on his helmet. His face bore the impassive, strict expression of an official who intimidates his subordinates and the public.

For the sake of sweet Opaz, I swear by the Blade of Kurin that it was not possible to suppress a particular, immediately arising thought.

He sat astride his zorca, yes. But in the flickering image in my mind I saw him standing there with fists on hips jumping up and down on the spot angrily while he asked: "What is the meaning of this?"

It was the Prefect of Prebaya.

He would perform without hesitation or inquiry any command of the regent C'Chermina, no matter how vile it might be.

Meanwhile, this street fighting disgusted me. Must my brave boys from the juruk I had created for Quensella lose their lives, and completely in vain—not to mention the price being paid by the hated enemy?

And so I called out fiercely: "Look, Kanzai brother, there is the blintz of a prefect who wants to see you."

Before the warrior brother could answer—always assuming that he would have deigned to—the Prefect spoke a few words in a painfully shrill voice. At the sound of the trumpet the fighters had paused; the Prefect's words were for the most part discernable.

"Wretched creatures of Quensella! Lay down your weapons immediately!" The purplish eyes in the doughy face turned to the Deldar and his audo who had led us here. They were still standing by the roadside watching, fascinated by the bloodshed. "You there! Deldar Nalgre the Planks! What are you waiting for?"

The Kanzai shifted his weight from one foot to the other and then once again took up his motionless stance.

The Prefect took a wheezing breath. All eyes were on him.

"You loyal men! Support the Prefecture! Arrest Quensella's blintzes! Take them—at once!"

His shrill voice died away. It was followed by a moment of frozen time in which nothing moved. It was a strange, waiting, breathless, ominous moment.

"If not for you, Kanzai brother," I said, "there would not be all this nonsense here..."

He surprised me. Because he talked to me.

"You fight well, apim," he said.

Now that was not as incongruous a remark as one might think, given the circumstances, maybe. A Kanzai's life is determined by his weapons and combat—and, of course, death.

For him, the rights and wrongs of the struggle resulted from his knowledge of the people involved. In our previous short conversation he must have formed a pretty good opinion of me. I suspect everyone will be able to imagine what he thought of the Prefect.

He expressed with his remark about my skill in battle his support—even if it consisted only of words.

He was on a mission, which was very important to him and his master. I harbored no illusions that he would use his incredibly violent martial arts to help my boys against the Prefect.

In this eerie moment of silence an absurd idea came to me. Blood throbbed in my veins, I was upset, the stench of death polluted the air, and I had the crazy idea of taking the Kanzai brother into my service, as I did Dagert of Paylen—well, I had bribed him with gold—and to pay him to fight for my boys.

The idea was ridiculous, and I rejected it in the same instant.

But, by Krun, I think that casts a revealing light on the state in which I found myself. In just a few moments this oasis of deceptive peace would cease to exist, and the jurukkers of this excellent bodyguard that I had created for Quensella would be in a dungeon facing death.

As for M'Marmor, he had made off at lightning speed from the dust and tumult of battle and bloodshed. I had not finished thinking this when he popped up behind the Prefect again. Behind him stood rested soldiers who would flow out from the archway and overwhelm us.

The whole incident was so stupid and narrow-minded that its futility made my blood boil again. I felt it had not once occurred to any of my fighters, facing all-powerful adversaries though they were, to retreat. The thought didn't even come to me that this altercation was my last big fight and I would end up with a Hai Jikai!

The whole nonsense would not even earn a small Jikai.

And so I made a decision. I, Dray Prescot, Vovedeer, Lord of Strombor and Krozair of Zy, raised my old foretop hailing voice.

My hail would need to wake the sleeping zombies in the Outer Pannoilia beyond the lake of fire. I did not hail, by Krun, I yelled!

"Quensella! Quensella! There is nothing more for us to do! Come to the retreat! Disappear! Get out! Go—Bratch!"

Would these hard, stubborn fighters flee?

If not, then...

After my call a few long heartbeats of deafening silence prevailed! I could see all my men in a single glance. They stood there, wild-eyed, panting, with disheveled hair and smeared with blood—and stared at me. A few heartbeats only, then I raised my rapier in a commanding gesture.

The spell was broken.

My tough, proud juruk, my boys, took flight.

I let out a small, quiet, sigh of relief.

Long before our enemies understood what was going on, my swods were gone. They jumped like the palies in the forest, moved with breathtaking speed and disappeared into the branching streets.

Of course, C'Chermina's guards and the Prefect's men immediately took up the pursuit. But I knew they would not catch any of my men.

Their days in the service of Lady Quensella were over—that was clear. They were mercenaries and would find other employers. With this last order I had released them from their oath. But do not think I was forgetting the unpleasant fact that Quensella no longer possessed a single bodyguard.

The Kanzai threw me a stern look.

Was it foolhardiness? I do not think so, as you know. But I caught myself blurting out, "Yes, Kanzai brother. My code differs from yours. I will not die for nothing, or sacrifice my comrades because of arrogance. Opaz be with you."

Then I ran.

Nineteen

At the street corner, I quickly glanced over my shoulder. The Kanzai still stood there, motionless as a pillar of iron. He made no move to hinder the guards rushing past him.

Well, why should he? He was on a mission, and that was all that interested him. The iron determination of the Kanzai is comparable in many ways to the steely resolve of the Krozair.

I threw all thoughts of the Kanzai, honor and conduct to the wind, and ran on, ducked into the first side street, raced to the end, turned left, went up the next street and took the next turn, which led back to the main road. At the end of the shadowy street I stopped and looked cautiously around the corner.

The Prefecture was not far away from me. The light of the suns reflected off the beautiful armor of the Prefect, he was in the same place and had not joined in the chase. San M'Marmor had obviously found enough courage, judging by his presence next to the zorca, to come back out onto the street.

Well, bad cess to both of them, by Krun!

As the dust settled, life on the street once again fell into familiar ways. The people went about their business.

I shrugged my shoulders, lowered my head and left the sidewalk. That was completely normal. As I already said, the citizens crossed the street when they had to pass the Prefecture. I honestly felt relief when I stepped into the shadow of the houses.

There was only one problem, and that a weighty one: in my current attire someone would recognize me sooner or later. A change of clothes was needed. But I could not possibly beat an innocent passerby over the head and steal his clothes. That only happened in the puppet shows and heroic legends of Kregen; for Dray Prescot, Krozair of Zy, such behavior was out of the question.

I still carried a lot of the gold I had been given by the Vallian Ambassador in Oxonium. If I acted quickly enough, I would be able to buy new clothes. I needed something completely inconspicuous, since the tailor would be interrogated by the Prefect's people without a doubt, or he would voluntarily give them information on such a dangerous criminal.

But I did not have much choice about what the shopkeeper would do, by Vox! I headed to the first clothes shop at the entrance to the market—and forced myself to stop. Onker! I could not enter the very first one—I had to enter the market quite unsuspiciously and select the store that caught my attention. I did, and after I had shown my gold, the tailor, whose tape measure hung around his neck like an atra, rubbed his hands together obligingly.

In the end, I stepped out onto the street wearing dark blue trousers with tight-fitting cuffs at the ankles and a tight-fitting tunic. I had rejected the idea of a new shamlak; I did not want to look fashionable.

Over the whole, I wore a new dark blue cloak. My weapons were reasonably well hidden—but easily accessible.

My next step was obvious.

Do not think that I had forgotten Quensella. But the immediate danger to her was averted with Granumin's death, and I knew my Pachaks would provide the lady with some halfway reasonable protection before they withdrew their nikobi.

I took as much consolation from the thought as possible and put myself in motion.

The demands of my stomach were best met at an open booth, where tasty, meat-filled pastry rolls and salad were sold. A cup of parclear quenched my thirst.

I wiped my mouth with the back of my hand and was quite of the opinion after the recent excitement that By Mother Zinzu the Blessed! I needed that!

The way to the back entrance of the temple was still clear in my memory. I stood frowning outside the door. It was pointless to wait for someone to come out. As pointless as trying to break in. All right. I would skirt the wall until I eventually reached the front door. That's what I did.

Like all Dokerty temples it was an elaborately designed building with lavish ornaments and embellishments, decadent in a way inappropriate for an upright religion.

As I watched people streaming through the entrance and up the stairs, I thought my luck was in.

They seemed to be perfectly normal citizens. Some were dressed better than others. Most were quite young; this was quite apparent, even if one considered the only slight exterior changes to which a Kregan is subjected in the course of their long life. As usual, the men carried weapons. Most of the women were appealing, if not pretty. I mingled effortlessly with them and climbed the stairs.

With the help of the techniques taught to me by San Deb-Lu-Quienyin, the famous magician from Loh who was a good friend and whose ghostly visits I missed, I changed my appearance. A slight change in the shape of the cheeks, a few other small adjustments, and I was confident that no one would recognize me immediately. The pain that this technique brings with it is less each time it is used. This does not mean that it did not sting and tingle, by Krun!

The interior of the temple was huge and ugly, with ruby-red wall hangings and tapestries everywhere and many strange statues and lamps. The corridors and chambers were filled with light. The happy chatter of people around me told me that they were overjoyed to be part of the cult of Dokerty.

"It is so wonderful!" crooned a smooth Fristle fifi to her companions. "Finally I feel that I am doing something meaningful with my life!"

"Dokerty is the only true religion," agreed her friend, all the while clutching the hilt of his scimitar. "Finally we escape the intolerance of Tolaar. Dokerty be praised!"

Their words made me breathe a satisfied sigh. By Vox, I was lucky! These were acolytes who were joining the cult. I would be exactly in its center, and could strike at the heart of this religion! Excellent!

I swore to myself that there would be no better acolyte than me in the whole temple!

To prepare for the ritual we were led into a room that served as a dressing room. Beyond the marble columns was a large pool of steaming scented water. The bathroom was surrounded by greenery and looked very inviting. Honestly, I felt the urgent desire for a long session in the baths of nine. However, this was just a simple basin, which, after we had tucked our clothing and weapons neatly into the boxes provided, we simply walked through and exited on the opposite side. We followed the instructions and warm water splashed onto the marble tiles.

The red robed priest led us, naked as we were, down a corridor into a rectangular room with a high ceiling. We were told to wait.

Eventually, one of the female acolytes was fetched and the door in the opposite wall closed behind her. After a short time the next Dokerty-follower left us. Everyone waited, eager to be next. I sat down on a bench in the corner and waited.

In any organization, whether it is of a religious character or not, you can do much more harm if you work against them from the inside. I felt honored.

When only two girls and myself were left, the door swung open. Two men dressed in red came through the door and pushed a naked young woman in front of them. Her long flaxen hair swirled about her face. She was apim with extremely pale, beautiful skin dotted with nasty abrasions, bruises and cuts. She turned to face her guards in a defensive stance. Blood flowed down her body from a cut over her left breast. I stood up.

She tried to scratch out the eyes of one of the men and he struck her in the mouth with the back of his hand. She fell to her knees. "You'd better behave, Veda," the other guard snarled. "You cannot refuse the gods, and you know it."

"Wait, doms," I said. "That's no way to treat a lady."

They looked at me like I was something that had just crawled out from under a flat stone.

"What did you say?"

"The little one needs the services of a needleman. There is no need to push her around."

They stared at me with open mouths.

"A suggestion," I said. "I'll take her to the bathroom where she can clean herself. That would be a start."

As if my words had triggered a hidden mechanism, they both pulled their swords from beneath their robes. They directed their blades at me.

"Just stay out of it. It does not concern you."

Well, given the mission that I had to fulfill for the Star Lords, this matter really should not be any of my concern.

On the other hand—as you who follow my stories know only too well—it is impossible for the old intemperate vosk skull of an onker called Dray Prescot to stay out of things which do not concern him.

You will not have failed to notice that I had not immediately launched an attack on the two repulsive fellows over their mistreatment of the girl. I was trying to behave in a mannerly way, by talking with them first. As far as I knew, it might be that the girl had been caught in an attempt to poison the High Priest. Of course, she would then have immediately become my ally, by Krun!

I had addressed the matter in a way appropriate for the new Dray Prescot, and I had bungled it.

One of the men growled: "Sit down and wait until you are called."

The other hit the girl behind her ear, which sent her sprawling face down onto the ground. Her flaxen hair spread out like a veil on the tiles.

I leapt forward.

The other two girls had taken refuge in the corner, from where they watched the events with wide, fear-filled eyes. I had enough room to maneuver.

One of San Blarnoi's more amusing sayings is: See to it that it is you who strikes the first blow!

The two swords looked sharp and dangerous. Opposing weapons empty-handed is not an advisable pastime if you do not know what you are doing. Turko the Shield would have broken both the swords in half and thrown the pieces behind him over his shoulder before the men had the opportunity to open their ugly mouths to scream.

Turko's Khamorro disciplines had often been put to the test by the Krozair disciplines when we had wrestled on the mat. Neither of us could claim superiority after a few falls, and the question remained in abeyance.

"By Beng Drudoj Grip and Fall!" Involuntarily I thought of these words as I leaped.

The left hand sword hissed past my side without touching me. My right elbow brushed the broad side of the other blade and thrust it aside. A blow against the trachea of that man and a kick in the groin of his companion, and they both tumbled back. The necessary distribution of force had halved the power of the blows, but they were enough that I could pick up a sword and stand firm, prepared to deal with the rasts, as was proper, if they wanted to pursue the matter further.

Perhaps the force of the blows had not been as great as they could have been; but the guy whose guts were squashed together in so evil a way doubled over and spat out his last meal. The other wanted to say something, but got out only a gurgle.

I looked around. This was all well and good, but by the disgusting inflamed left eyeball and clogged right nostril of Makki Grodno! What now?

The two girls in the corner held each other and whimpered, only to fall silent in horror under my gaze.

Veda, the girl who had caused all the trouble, pushed herself to her feet. Her figure was stunning, and her breath came in panting gasps. For a moment I thought it was a reaction to the harsh treatment she had suffered. That was a mistake.

This quickly became apparent, oh yes, by Krun, very fast!

She threw herself on the choking Dokerty follower and went at him with nails and teeth, her hair billowing like a golden halo around her head, her panting breaths rhythmically accompanying her punches and kicks.

Well—what else would you expect?

Judging by her condition, she would blindly go for me if I made any attempt to tear her away from him.

The voice behind me was low and controlled, almost expressionless, and revealed the indifference of a man who was accustomed to instant obedience.

"Drop the sword. Do not move." Then, with a touch of sharpness: "Seize Veda and bring her to her senses before she hurts him."

I did not drop the sword. I also did not keep still.

I turned around.

Granumin stood in the open door, dressed in a red robe. He had guards with him. I was not seeing right. Granumin was dead. The schrepims had torn him to pieces. There was only one logical explanation: this arrogant fellow with the presumptuous nature had to be Granumin's twin brother!

The similarity was remarkable. As you know, on Kregen twins are nothing special, but they usually differ significantly from each other. For a moment I stared at Granumin's brother like a fool, then I was forced to turn my attention to his bodyguard.

A few of them moved to pull Veda away from the vomiting man, who she still kicked and struck furiously. The rest stood motionless in their black armor of iron strips stitched together with bright brass rivets. Six of them held crossbows aimed at me. Their helmets were small and round. Behind their helmets they held their armored daggered whiptails craned in the air, stuck stiffly upwards, and yet trembling in the pent-up desire to rip into something.

Katakis!

Damned Katakis!

Slavers and subjugators of men and women. They were standing much too close to me to hope that the six crossbow bolts would fall short; too close for me to dodge the missiles or knock them from the air. And they were too far away for me to reach with a sudden and desperate attack before they shot me down.

As I said, damned Katakis.

I stared at the Opaz-cursed whiptails grimly. Probably Veda's screams had attracted them. At the last she had made enough noise to wake the dead marching from the infamous Mount Cookdav.

Veda's fair-skinned, blood-smeared, still fighting form almost tempted me to risk my life in a game that I could not possibly win.

The Katakis stood in a half circle with me at its focus. With my sword

I would be able to fend off the projectiles from one side but the others would pierce me as sure as Zim and Genodras rise every day on Kregen. The cold, impersonal voice sounded again.

"I will not hurt you. Throw the sword to the ground or you're a dead man."

By the dangling belly and bloated upper limbs of the Divine Lady of Belschutz! What a stupid mess! I threw the sword to the ground. Almost—but only almost—I threw it at Granumin's inflated twin brother. But I controlled myself. I must not allow myself to be killed by a couple of silly crossbow bolts.

"You do not treat women the way they should be treated," I said in a voice like shifting gravel. "You..."

He interrupted me.

"What I do is none of your concern, blintz." His tone had become sharper and now had a misleadingly amused undertone. "Because you love the shishi so dearly, you may accompany her."

He made a barely visible, yet unmistakable gesture with his left hand and pointed a stiff finger at the door. The Kataki Hikdar, who stood at one end of the semicircle of crossbows, obeyed.

"Immediately, Notor!"

Veda's now limp and unresisting body was half-dragged and half carried to the door. Since I could do nothing else, I joined her.

You can imagine that I was conscious of the ugly crossbow bolts trained on my spine, by Krun!

The door opened. The corridor, with ceiling lamps that transformed the walls and floor into a bright magical land, led to a door of grand proportions. The timber was decorated with gold-covered carvings and colorful inlays. The motifs set in ruby-red mainly represented mythological animals. A musky scent hung in the stifling air, creating an oppressive atmosphere. We walked on.

Granumin's twin brother again uttered a command in his ice-cold, indifferent way. The splendid doors swung open. A blaze of glaring light flooded over us and reduced the light from the corridor lamps to that of mere tallow candles. The musky scent was overpowering. Veda reared up one last, futile time in the grip of the Katakis.

Granumin's twin saw my instinctive reaction.

His face betrayed understandable amusement. "Very chivalrous! You can watch what happens to the shishi; it will be a learning experience for you. Then it will be your turn."

We entered the chamber with the lights, the stinking air and the closely packed multitude of red-robed believers.

I had thought it so clever to penetrate into the inner sanctum of the Dokerty-lovers. I had relied so much on my conceited ingenuity.

Now I recognized immediately and with a terrible clarity what I had brought on myself. I knew where I was. I knew what would happen.

Oh, the ever-so-clever Dray Prescot, onker of all onkers!

Twenty

As I stood there and denounced myself as the greatest get-onker on two worlds, someone gave me a violent push in the back. I stumbled and had almost regained my balance when a strong Kataki tail between my ankles tripped me and I landed face down on the floor.

This performance in front of the red robed assembly brought forth great merriment. Bad cess to 'em, by Krun!

The chamber smelled of incense and bitter musky scent. Tall gold and silver candlesticks were everywhere. Their light merged with the light of the exaggeratedly magnificent candelabra hanging from the ceiling. I took my time getting up.

Veda was in a state of shock. Or perhaps it was numbness in the face of what was going to happen to us. I wondered if she knew and had given up hope. I was wrong. Suddenly she threw herself with the ferocity of a zhantilla defending its young at the imposing figure standing before us.

Could a Krzy stand idly by and watch such an example of desperate courage? By Zair! Of course not!

Our pitiful efforts bought us shackles on our hands and feet, and we were dragged along like pieces of wood. A quick glance told me that these were not lesten-hide ropes; evidently these unfortunate people were not aware that I was Dray Prescot. So this was not a major hindrance.

The imposing figure had the narrow lips and pointed nose that I had seen before. I looked the man directly in the eye, believe me, by Vox!

I was deposited in a chair while Veda was placed onto the altar-like platform on which I had last seen a young boy in a white robe, triumphant at the secret rites. Dokerty was called upon and welcomed.

A group dressed in black entered with their trays full of devilish instruments. The overwhelming stench of the place, the suffocating feeling of being buried alive, knowing what was about to happen to Veda—all caused my head to blaze with anger. These rites were secret. The Dokerty worshipers were watching. A brief command from Granumin's twin and the Katakis, who had done their duty, marched edgily out of the room.

The fellow with the pointy nose and thin lips, who was apparently in command here, did not carry the rod with the stylized pair of wings this time. It was held along with other symbols by the proud believers who stood around the edge. The steel cage was nowhere to be seen.

I wondered if the two lovebirds sat behind the bronze-edged spy-holes in the wall with paper, pens and colored ink ready to hand. The spectacle that they were about to see would be vastly different from the events of that other time!

The smoke-red wall hangings, which retained the smells and the stench of this terrible place, seemed to suck me in. The followers in their ruby-red robes feasted greedily on the nascent suffering, delighted in the inflicted pain. This insight was of huge importance; I realized how much the Dokerty-lovers enjoyed the process.

There was a short delay. Veda resisted despite her fetters, and would not keep still. The delay was caused by believers bringing in a wooden triangle. It was positioned on the platform. Once Veda's naked body was tied to it, she would not be able to move. Moreover, it would make the already complicated situation even more difficult.

There was no time to waste.

As noted earlier, the bonds were not lesten-hide.

A savage jerk shredded the rope around my wrists. I bent down. An equally savage effort broke the shackles around my ankles. Then I stood up.

Of course I did not get up as if I were in an elegant lounge and a lady had just entered. Oh no, by Djan! I shot up out of the chair like an arrow shot from Seg's most powerful Lohvian longbow and threw myself at the group of Dokerty-lovers in the immediate vicinity. They toppled like skittles. I did not stop. I jumped over them and reached the platform in a single bound. A few selective, extremely hard and cruel blows that broke noses, smashed teeth and crushed guts swept away the men who held onto Veda.

Now, this Veda with the flaxen hair, blue eyes and stunning figure was no constantly screeching blonde who always fell into a swoon. Oh no, by Krun! She threw me a look which, I must confess, strengthened the backbone.

When I broke her bonds—and I was a little more cautious than with my own—she said: "Thank you, Jikai. I'll show a few of them before the end."

Meanwhile, everything was in turmoil. Everyone was on the move, some brandishing weapons. But still no one was ready to storm the platform to restore order.

"If you mean death at the end, that cannot be. I have too much to do to be killed here. Come on!" I had time to snarl before I jumped off the platform.

I grabbed at her hand to help her, but she would have none of it. Her long lissom legs, which the candlelight showed off advantageously, were the first off the platform.

And then she showed them, and how, by Krun!

It was clear that these distinguished believers did not intend to soil their sensitive hands on scum like us. They waited for the arrival of their paid mercenaries, the damned Kataki swods. I was not going to be here then. That in turn meant pushing some of the Dokerty-lovers out of the way, and since it was mainly armed men with swords, they did not like that. They were forced to stand against me.

As it turned out, the candlestick that I seized was made not of gold, but of brass. About three feet long, it proved to be somewhat cumbersome. Nevertheless, it was admirably suited to smashing the skull of the first fellow I met. The fat candle was extinguished, spraying sparks into the crowd.

And so I made my way through the altar chamber armed with a brass candlestick.

The noise increased somewhat.

The men and women who held the sacred symbols no longer sang "Oltomek! Oltomek!" They screamed in panic, fleeing headlong from the chamber. Veda shouted: "Come on, Jikai! This way!"

She sank her toes into the thick belly of a man who did not dodge in time and then ran to the opposite wall. Since I assumed that she knew a way to escape from this labyrinth, I followed her. The brass candlestick whirled and struck a few skulls.

The quicker the spirited young lady found a way into the secret passages between the walls the better. I had only one thing in mind—to leave this hellhole behind me as soon as possible. There were many urgent tasks awaiting me in Balintol.

I took a sword from a fellow I sent to the ground with a blow from the candlestick to his ear, but it broke with the first stroke. I threw the useless hilt at a red hood and ran on.

The pale skin of Veda's legs flashed in the light as we rushed through a narrow door into a dark corridor that smelled of food. She took the lead.

How long would it take for the disgusting Katakis to show up with their vicious whips, chains, nets and daggered tails?

I gradually realized which direction we were moving in. Veda took us through side passages to the front part of the temple. We walked through a wider corridor and came upon slaves going about their eternal slave labor. We slowed our run to a fast walk. Even a slave's drab gray was clothing. "There is no time now, Jikai! Come on! Hurry up!" exclaimed Veda, as I stopped a slave to take his loincloth.

I quickly caught up to her.

Then we encountered a group of temple guards standing in our way. There were no Katakis.

I rushed at them with candlestick swinging. They went down. I suffered a fiery stinging scratch on my side. Veda grabbed a sword that had fallen to the ground and stabbed furiously at a half unconscious man who wanted to get back on his feet. This time he stayed down.

At the end of the corridor it branched to the right and to the left.

Veda stopped and hesitated.

"Get us outside," I said with a rumbling voice. "The fastest way that leads out of this temple of evil."

She turned to the left. Soon the air was warmer and interspersed with scents. One last door brought us into the room with the basin of scented water, the water I had splashed through in ignorance of the events to come.

Located beyond the pillars was the locker room. My mood improved dramatically. There lay my clothes, and we would be able to find a garment to cover Veda's beauty. But it was not the thought of clothes that cheered me, oh no, by Vox!

The room lay in complete stillness. The warm perfumed air, the pretty plants, the peace—all offered a stark contrast to the horrors we had just experienced.

There was no one to be seen. Veda ran along the pool's edge, and I followed her. At the other end, beyond the columns, a door opened and a young fellow entered. Veda stopped, rooted to the spot. I bumped into her and we almost fell into the water.

I held onto Veda and watched as a second person came through the door from the shadows, wearing the red robe of the Dokerty-lovers. The young man was dressed in white. When the red robed man raised both arms, I caught a glimpse of his face. Pointed nose, thin lips—oh yes, I knew who it was! He lifted the rod with the winged symbol at the top. He pointed it directly at the young man, his thin lips curled.

"Dokomek!"

I leaned forward. "Run past both of them," I whispered breathlessly into Veda's ear. "Search the changing room. Leave the clothes." I described to her where she could find what I needed. "And hurry up, you hear, Veda?"

She nodded slightly. Then she said, "Jikai!" and ran off like lightning, a lissom, very feminine young lady. Wherever she came from, they knew how to make women, by Krun!

She passed the boy at the exact moment that his white robe ripped from collar to hem. He expanded. I briefly glimpsed Veda dash past the high priest. Then the demon took total possession of the unfortunate lad. The ibmanzy grew in height, claws pushed through skin. His face contorted into a horrible grimace of insane rage. With the strength of an obsessed madman the ibmanzy lashed out wildly and jumped up and down on thick curved legs, while from the fang-filled mouth saliva dripped. He screamed and roared—and charged.

The demon had only one goal: Dray Prescot, Vovedeer, Lord of Strombor and Krozair of Zy—armed only with a brass candlestick.

I had one tactic open to me. If the insane monstrosity got to grips with me it would tear my head from my shoulders with its clawed hands. So—I backed away. I fled. I crouched down and threw myself to the side. I kept out of his reach. Twice he almost caught me, and only the candlestick, which beat his hands aside, saved me. Oh yes, how I dodged!

The high priest was long gone. He had obviously planned everything, cleared the area, brought this poor misguided lad into the room, pointed his bloody winged symbol at him, called "Dokomek!" and then quickly retreated.

The claws of the monster raked down my side, and I flinched back, cursing my slowness. It was very fast for its size.

I circled the ibmanzy in order to be closer to the door. Then I backed away, step by step, further and further back. He stormed forwards, arms outstretched to grab me and crush all my ribs. He almost caught me. At the last moment I was able to duck under the reaching arms and escape. By Krun! That gave me quite a sweat!

I immediately discarded the seemingly obvious solution of jumping into the pool. His height would have been a huge advantage to the deadly ibmanzy. It would have no trouble wading behind me while I would have to swim.

I didn't know how long this could go on. How long would it be before the demonic monster exhausted and destroyed the borrowed body?

I was horrified by the terrible anger that animated this terrifying creature, the evil power inherent in its brutal wrath. It had only one goal—destruction!

I pushed away the unwelcome thoughts that came with startling frequency. I just would not believe that Veda had not made it. Although our acquaintance was short, I could not imagine that she had fled, that she had let me down. If she did not return, then certainly it was because the high priest had alerted his Katakis and she had been captured. I refused to believe otherwise.

The demon showed no signs of fatigue. I had a hard day behind me, I could not afford the sin of exhaustion. This fight would continue until...

The soft clapping of bare feet on hard marble could be heard in spite of the roar unleashed by the ibmanzy behind me that told me to dodge to the side immediately. I took a quick look back.

Veda came running with blond hair flying, her bloodied body as naked as the day she was born, her face full of determination—she was a dazzling vision to behold. The Krozair longsword glittered in her fist.

"Jikai!"

With the ferocity of a leem I stepped back, spun around and flung the candlestick at the ibmanzy's slavering mouth. I stretched out my hand. "Throw, Veda!"

The Krozair sword described a graceful arc, descended, and landed in my hand. I spun around.

The Opaz-cursed murderous ibmanzy had almost reached me. The feeling of the Krozair blade in my fists—ah! The blade cut deep. I put force into the stroke, using my momentum for balance. The jolt as the sword hit made my backbone tremble and continued up into my head.

One of the demon's arms flew in a fountain of blood through the air.

The next moment I had to leap wildly to the side. The demon struck out with his remaining arm and lunged at me, unfettered, thirsting for blood.

Well, I did not want to have to fight against ibmanzies. Until now, I had avoided fighting with one of these monsters, conscious of their ways. But needs must when it comes to the fluttrell's vane, as they say in Clishdrin. The demon had taken root in a body, so I had to deal with him as with other large wild animals on Kregen. It was not fun, it even causes me something like shame; but with a damned demon, who has only one goal in mind, it is different. Oh yes, by the Blade of Kurin!

I dismembered him. It was a messy affair, and he did not die. In the end he did, but not before his form broke apart and turned back into the unfortunate young man he had once been.

Veda's white body seemed darker than her face. When I went back to her, blood-stained sword in hand, she stumbled. I put my left arm around her waist. "You deserve the Jikai, Veda. Now we must..."

"Oh yes," she whispered.

The blood still trickled down from the cut over her left breast, and I did not like it. I hurried into the changing room, half-supporting her. Undergarments torn into strips was used to stem the bleeding. She had to see a needlewoman in the very near future. What is more, the aftermath of the terrible struggle had to be washed away. I did not think to feel responsible for the death of the poor boy.

I searched through the many garments looking for something suitable and finally put an exquisite blue cloak around her shoulders. Then I quickly slipped into my clothes. Torn undergarments served to wipe the blood away; we both required the services of a needleman.

Veda gathered her strength. The discovery of a small bottle of wine in the pocket of a fashionable shamlak helped. She told me that she knew of a door to the outside which would be guarded by only two temple guards. "A mere two men will be powerless against you, Jikai."

"They call me Drajak the Sudden."

She frowned, her flaxen hair hidden in the shade of the blue hood. "How appropriate."

In the corridors she led me through, there was no more trouble. The two guards obediently sank into dreamland. I did not kill them. I had already shed enough blood.

We went outside cautiously, walked down the steep steps and found ourselves in a side street. Veda swayed, so I steadied her again. The ibmanzy blood had been wiped off the Krozair longsword and it was back in its sheath. What would the person who had given me this sheath think of Veda? Of course, I knew the answer to that question already. A little smile, a cheeky tilt of the head, and Delia would make a suitable, witty remark.

Longing for Delia suddenly hit me like a punch in the stomach. She meant more to me than Earth and Kregen together! She meant everything to me, everything!

Before me lay the problem of Balintol. The Star Lords had commanded. Balintol must unite to stand against the Shanks.

But these damn Dokerty-lovers could turn dozens, hundreds, maybe even thousands of ordinary people into ibmanzies. They could go anywhere on Kregen, into every country, and once there transform and destroy everyone in their vicinity so C'Chermina's armies could march in unopposed.

The Star Lords had given their command. I, the simple sailor Dray Prescot, had to stop the scourge of the ibmanzy.

Or else...

By Vox, I can tell you! Life on Kregen is anything but easy, by Krun!

About the author

Alan Burt Akers was a pen name of the prolific British author Kenneth Bulmer, who died in December 2005 aged eighty-four.

H K Bulmer wrote over 160 novels and countless short stories, predominantly science fiction, both under his real name and numerous pseudonyms, including Alan Burt Akers, Frank Brandon, Rupert Clinton, Ernest Corley, Peter Green, Adam Hardy, Philip Kent, Bruno Krauss, Karl Maras, Manning Norvil, Chesman Scot, Nelson Sherwood, Richard Silver, H. Philip Stratford, and Tully Zetford. Kenneth Johns was a collective pseudonym used for a collaboration with author John Newman. Some of Bulmer's works were published along with the works of other authors under "house names" (collective pseudonyms) such as Ken Blake (for a series of tie-ins with the 1970s television programme The Professionals), Arthur Frazier, Neil Langholm, Charles R. Pike, and Andrew Quiller.

Bulmer was also active in science fiction fandom, and in the 1970s he edited nine issues of the New Writings in Science Fiction anthology series in succession to John Carnell, who originated the series.